Fur Coat Big Knickers

PART 2 OF THE FUR COAT SERIES

C.B. MARTIN

POOLBEG

Published 2018
by Poolbeg Press Ltd.
123 Grange Hill, Baldoyle,
Dublin 13, Ireland
Email: poolbeg@poolbeg.com

1

A catalogue record for this book is available from the British Library.

ISBN 978178199-318-7

www.poolbeg.com

About the Author

C. B. Martin was born in London in 1967 to Irish parents. Caroline worked in the hair and beauty industry for over 30 years before finally pursuing her ambition of becoming an author.

Caroline currently resides in Northamptonshire, England. She has three adult children (who are the lights of her life) and a wonderful long-term partner who have all helped her realise her dreams of becoming a full-time writer.

Other books in the series

Fur Coat No Knickers

Fur Coat Holey Knickers

Acknowledgements

Thank you to the many talented people who helped me put this book together:

Developmental Editors: Teena Lyons, Domenico Marsala.

Copy Editors: Teena Lyons, Domenico Marsala, Sandra

Martin, Ellie Baldwin, Francesca Marsala, Martin Ouvry.

Proofreading: Marie Quinn, Stewart Imber, Christiano Marsala, Sandra Martin.

Consultants: James Murphy, Lenore Mayon, Charlotte Clarke, Louise Martin.

Note from the author

I'm sorry, I'm sorry, and again, I'm so sorry for the delay in getting Fur Coat Big Knickers out. But just wait till you hear my reason ...

Something strange began to happen to me in 2009, and gradually over the years, (guess-timately) 75% of my brain cells began packing up and fecking off on holiday—without me. (How very rude.) Until the end of 2015, it seemed no one could explain my laughably long list of symptoms:

- My skin aged twenty-something years overnight.
- My hair started falling out (apart from where I needed it to). Then my eyebrows also disappeared—*oh, how I miss them so.*
- Relentless migraines.
- Brain fog ensured I couldn't think straight; from driving on the wrong side of the road, to not being able to spell my own name (let alone string a sentence together). My memory rivalled that of a goldfish.
- Stuttering speech. Then my voice disappeared altogether due something called 'dysphonia', which sounds nicer than it is.

- Hourly mood swings; from nail-biting anxiety, to despairing depression. I became a recluse – not wanting to see or speak to anyone.
- Bouts of insomnia, despite being constantly exhausted.
- Being unable walk or climb the stairs—it felt like I was constantly wading through treacle.
- Loss of hope. In fact, I nearly lost my mind altogether (well, to be fair, there wasn't much left by the end of all this, anyway) ...

In a nutshell: I was pretty fecked, to say the least. But after years of searching for an answer, and being misdiagnosed with this-that-and-the-other, a postcard arrived from something called **Hashimoto's disease**:

Dear Caroline,

I'm an autoimmune disease, and I'm the one who's been holding your brain cells hostage! I've had so much fun causing chaos and destroying your thyroid gland (AKA the body's second brain).

This means you don't have an overactive thyroid OR an underactive thyroid; you have either/or, depending on what mood I'm in!

Just to add to the fun, your body can't actually absorb the vital hormones your doctors have been prescribing you—no wonder you've been getting worse! In fact, you'll have to go on a wild goose chase to get the hormonal balance right. (Dodgy medication from Mexico, anyone?)

Ciao!

After reading Stop the Thyroid Madness (www.stopthethyroidmadness.com), and a visit to some of the UK's top thyroid specialists, we finally started to understand just what the bloody hell was going on.

I'm glad to say, I'm slowly—very slowly—getting back on my feet. I still wobble, and my brain still often gets confused, but on the whole I am making progress.

This incurable disease has made me appreciate my life and the people in it more than ever. I wholeheartedly owe my life to my family and consultants as they tirelessly held my hand and mopped up the buckets of tears. I wouldn't be here today without you – thank you, thank you, thank you!

Finally, though writing this book was often the bane of my life, it was also what kept me going in my darkest hours. I've laughed, cried and learnt a great deal, and I hope you will too.

Thanks for waiting,

C. B. Martin

P.S. — If I don't make it as a successful author *(ahem)*, I'll be starting my own luxury sun-lounger company.

#BoobsForBetterSunLoungers

I dedicate this work to my fellow thyroid sufferers.

Don't give up hope.

Chapter 1

There are just three golden rules that apply to first dates:

1. Thou shall not get so pissed that thou cannot think straight.
2. Thou shall not participate in rumpy-pumpy of *any* kind.
3. Thou shall not confess one's love to the other.

I mean, breaking just the first two out of three rules isn't bad going, is it?

It wasn't my fault that Lewis went and broke the third.

Oh, but it was so romantic. Lewis and I had just had *the* craziest, mind-blowing sexy-times in a poppy field overlooking his vast plot of land. (*Land*, for Christ's sake. With big trees and a barn and everything. Talk about punching above my weight!) And for the cherry on top: that's when Lewis—the gorgeous, most-definitely single landowner and veterinary surgeon—confessed his love to me! And while our first date was probably way too soon for him to be dropping the big L-bomb, let alone for us to have sexed already, I knew in my heart I would feel the same way about him eventually. (Probably.)

It all started when Lewis popped the cork on that damned champagne. Annoyingly, he then insisted that he wouldn't drink a drop and drive, especially with such 'precious cargo'. As flattering as this was, it also put me in a precarious dilemma. See, as a child, I would have got a clip around the ear if I ever left anything on my dinner plate. 'Waste not, want not,' Mum would always say, before stuffing the remains of my unwanted cabbage down my throat. So, obviously, I had little choice but to consume the whole bottle of champagne to myself; hence, I fully intend to blame my mum for turning me into a greedy little piggy, and for the monumental disaster that was about to occur.

By all accounts, it had quite possibly been one of the happiest days of my life ... right up until the moment we were packing our picnic away and I saw that godforsaken message on my phone:

[Text from (unrecognised)]
Hi Tara, hope you're good.
Turns out the baby isn't mine.
I still think about you every day. I need to make things up to you.
Please will you meet me?
Travis x

At first, the words spilled over me, not fazing my tipsy little brain in the slightest. But I guess that's what kind of happens when you've had a gallon of fizz all to yourself.

I looked over to Lewis, packing up the remnants of our picnic into the saddlebags of his motorbike. He gave me his cheeky, signature smile and I flittered a clamped-mouthed one back before returning to my phone.

Then another message came through from my ex and I nearly dropped the phone altogether.

[Text from (unrecognised)]
I know I hurt you ... and I'm probably the last person you want to hear from.
Tara, I can't even begin to say how sorry I am.
I just know you would understand if you knew the whole story of what happened last year.
Please ... let me explain in person and hear me out.
Everyone deserves a second chance ...
Travis x

And that was the moment that the ticking, unexploded bomb finally detonated: Travis—*the* Travis Coleman, Ireland's Head Rugby Coach and Bastard Extraordinaire—wanted me back?

Holy Mary Mother of God!

My eyes winced involuntarily, as if they were trying to block me from reading his messages again. I actually couldn't believe this was happening. This was a man I never thought I'd ever hear from again.

I've only had one bottle of champers, right? Or have I passed out and I'm now having a nightmare? I'd had countless dreams about Travis in the six months since he'd brutally dumped me, so this could well be a another one. But by now, I had a pretty good system for distinguishing between dreams and reality. It might be a cliché, but the classic pinch-yourself reality-check technique has come to my rescue on many occasions; so to be sure, I gave my bicep a fairly hard pinch—*Wake up Tara, you stupid mare!*

I felt nothing, but then remembered that I was in fact more than just spannered, so, just to be sure, I checked Lewis wasn't looking and went to the next stage of reality checking, with what I would consider a firm but fair slap to my face.

Oww. Bit too hard, that!

No … this can only mean one thing: I am awake and … oh-my-God-oh-my-God. THIS IS REALLY HAPPENING.

Pop! went my blissful bubble of romance, sending my drunken mind into free-fall, as a severe case of *the spins* ensued. My legs wobbled and I frantically looked around for something to steady myself on. In sickening fast-forward, everything around me began to tumble, as the all-too-familiar feelings of pain and regret rose from the grave, reopening the wounds I'd spent months trying to heal. Travis's words darted across my mind, spinning the wheel faster, causing my brain to aquaplane around inside my skull. Through the distortion, I could just about make out Lewis striding towards me.

'Tara? Are you okay?'

Stumbling forward, I reached out to grab hold of him, but I missed by several metres, with my face breaking the fall—or to be more precise, my nose.

Oww. Owwww. Owwwwwwww. Wincing in pain, my body slumped as the cocktail of shock, anger and hurt swept over me.

'Tara!' Suddenly Lewis pulled me up into a sitting position and supported my back.

'Are you okay?! What's wrong?'

'Huh? Oh ... umm, I'm fine, I just feel a bit ... unwell,' I mumbled, drooping back into his arms like a lump of jelly.

'It's okay,' he said, positioning my head between my knees. 'I've got you. It's all okay.'

I hung the weight of my spinning head in between my knees and stared at the ground, wanting to throw up.

'Deep breaths, Tara, just take deep breaths,' said Lewis, brushing the soil from my hair and holding my chin up while scanning my face, 'I don't understand – you were fine a couple of minutes ago ... what's happened to make you like this so suddenly?'

I opened my mouth to explain, but somehow, miraculously I managed to slam on my tongue brakes just in time. How could I tell him that Travis – the most addictive and destructive force I'd ever encountered – had just crawled back into my life? There's no way could I tell him – I couldn't even *look* at him. Mortified, I just stared back at the ground, silently praying to God that Lewis wouldn't ask any more questions about my sudden turn.

'I guess you didn't really eat much of the picnic this

afternoon,' he said, thankfully not detecting the truth. 'I knew I shouldn't have let you drink the whole bottle of plonk, but I didn't want you to think I was, well ... trying to control you.'

God, he's such a nice, decent man. Now I feel even worse! How was he to know that my whole world had just dropped away from beneath me?

Moments later, I felt him twitching and I looked up to see him stifling a laugh—and failing miserably.

'Umm, what's so funny?' I asked, all weak-limbed and slack-jawed.

'Sorry ... It's just ... Please don't hate me, but a minute ago you looked like a tree falling in the forest. All I could hear in my head was *TIMBEEERRRR*,' he said, breaking into a snorting laughter.

Not finding this in the least bit funny, I pulled a face that said as much.

You've just lost sooo many brownie points there, Sunshine!

I instinctively reached up, felt my nose, and gently massaged it, praying it was at least central. I was sure I could feel it beginning to swell.

Another nose job—on top of all of this feckin' shite? I let out a sob against my will.

'It's okay,' he said. 'I've got you. It's all okay.'

I just nodded my head as beads of sweat trickled down the back of my neck.

'You're worrying me. Look at you, you're trembling all over,' he said, smoothing the sweat away from my forehead. 'How many fingers am I holding up?'

'*Err* ... two,' I answered in a whimpering whisper and a frown.

He looked perplexed. 'Oh dear. I'm actually holding up three.'

'I wasn't counting your thumb. It ... was, *err* ...' I mumbled, flashing back to when my older sister used to play this trick on me.

My voice wavered as I tried to think up an excuse. 'I just lost my balance. Too much champagne, that's all; and like you said, not enough food.'

'Look, my place isn't far from here. Maybe we should get you back to mine so you can lie down? And don't worry, this isn't me trying to get lucky again.'

Brownie points restored.

Now, if he had asked me that five minutes before, what with Lewis being a vet (which officially makes him a doctor), we could have played *Doctors and Patients*. I'd have gone back to his place, tongue dangling, knickers dropped, legs akimbo – no problem at all. But not now – not after this disaster. The idea of having to keep my shite together after receiving those messages actually made me feel sick. In fact, how could I ever look Lewis straight in the eye again, having received this earth-shattering news from Travis? I'd probably turn into an emotional wreck, reveal all and break down crying; then he'd chuck me out and never speak to me again. The whole date up until this point had been God damn wonderful so far—I just needed to call it a day while things were still on a high (in his mind, at least).

'I think I just want to go back to my place. On my own, that is ... sorry. I haven't been feeling right for a few days now,' I lied, avoiding eye contact. I loathed myself for lying—or rather, withholding the truth—

Lord knows he deserved better than that. But what else could I do?

'It's okay, no pressure,' he said, looking deep into my eyes. 'I'm sorry you're feeling unwell.'

Then a terrifying thought crossed my mind: *where's my phone? What if Lewis sees the messages? Where the feck is my phone?!* In a blind panic, I frantically scrambled around for the missing device.

'Looking for this?' Lewis asked innocently, handing it back while tenderly supporting my elbow.

My heart sank, feeling like it landed in my stomach, causing another wave of nausea. Quickly snatching the phone from his hand, I slipped it deep into the back pocket of my biker leathers. I could feel it there, boring a hole of deceit into my arse. In a hope to distract him from my odd behaviour, I beamed him an overly thankful toothy grin, to which he returned a puzzled smirk. Still trembling, I continued to battle against the sick feeling while fanning my face.

'You still look quite pale, are you sure you're okay to go on the bike? I can call a cab if you're not up to it. And just this one time I'll even resist calling you a chicken,' he said with a smile.

At that particular moment, Lewis owning a motorbike had totally lost its appeal. A nice, warm ambulance would have been far more appropriate, with a crash team and an intravenous drip of Valium awaiting my arrival—not forgetting the essential ice pack for my hooter.

'I'll be fine, honestly,' I said, ignoring his joke. 'I just need to get home and get to bed.'

'Okay, well, only if you're sure.'

I wasn't sure, but I figured the fear of death would be a welcome distraction.

'I'm good. Let's go,' I said, trying to sound confident. I somehow managed to stand on my Bambi-like legs, dust myself down and flick as much grass off me as possible in an attempt to look a little more respectable.

'Okay, so when we're on the bike, remember to keep your arms tight around me, and if you need to stop at any point, just give me a nudge and I'll pull over. Okay?'

I nodded.

Lewis pulled on his helmet, mounted the classic Ducati and kick-started the engine. The spluttering engine startled me, causing me to break out into another shaky sweat. Donning a brave face, I pulled on my helmet and reluctantly threw a trembling leg over the saddle to board the old beast. As instructed, I hugged Lewis tight, gripping him between my thighs, trying to feel his warmth.

Lewis gave me a pat on the leg and within moments, we'd whizzed away from the cut-in, and were gliding along the country roads as the sun began to set. The twilight air whipped through my body and the vibrations from the roaring bike intensified as we picked up speed.

I could just about see over Lewis's shoulder, trying to focus on the road ahead in an effort to keep the nausea at bay.

Lewis squeezed the brakes as we approached a sharp bend, dropping his knee and leaning the bike down. Between the stomach churning G-forces and organ rattling B-road bumps, I felt twelve again, at the fairground, deeply regretting my decision to brave the teacup ride.

I sent a silent prayer to the Big Man Upstairs: 'Please, please, your ... Holiness, I know we've not spoken in a while (again) but, I plead you—in fact, I'm begging you—don't let me be sick. I really, *really* like this guy and I'm sorry for drinking myself into oblivion and having rampant sexy-times with him on the first date ...

Alas, my prayer must've been stuck at the back of a queue because here it was, the unsubtle reminder of gluttony and heartache in the form of impending vomit climbing up the back of my throat, desperate to expel itself.

Unable to take anymore, I signalled Lewis to pull over. But just as I raised my hand, I was forced to hold on for dear life as we approached a sharp corner. He shifted down a gear, leaned the bike down forty-five degrees and powered out of the corner, snapping up one–two–three gears in quick succession.

Oh God, I can't hold it in any longer ... [panting] it's okay—just swallow [constrained swallowing]—pretend it's something nice, like hummus or guacamole ... Oh God [gagging] no, no, this is nothing like hummus or guac—[retching]. Battling with the chinstrap, I managed to prise the full-face helmet off just enough so that, when the moment was right, I could gracefully spew over the side of the bike, hopefully with Lewis being none the wiser.

But just then, out of the corner of my eye, I saw a van overtaking a car ahead of us. Lewis jerked to the left to avoid a collision, but the counter-momentum jolted my helmet back down over my face, just as the vom gates burst. Champagne and a half-digested cucumber sandwich exploded into the enclosed helmet, and everything went black.

Am I dead?

Sadly, I was reassured of my survival by my heaving and retching, drowning out the sound of the bike's engine. Half-blinded and spitting frantically, I opened the visor, but the incoming wind simply spread the offending sewage up my already-swollen nose and into my hair. Fair play to me, I didn't move my hands once. I just took it, even though the dribbling was beginning to wheedle its way inside my ears. *Plenty of time in the future for your boyfriend to see you puke, I thought,* as a pathetic sob squeaked out of my throat.

Lewis raised his right arm and gave me the thumbs up, to which I returned the gesture. He then reached back and lovingly patted my knee, clearly oblivious to the catastrophe merely centimetres behind him.

*How will I ever get out of this with even an ounce of dignity? This is not, Tara Ryan, I repeat—**not** okay—on a first date!* This could easily have made the list of the Top 5 Low Points in My Sorry Life So Far. Stinging tears of misery and shame streamed down my cheeks, adding themselves to the gruesome cauldron inside the helmet. I prayed for it all to be over, or for me to fall off the bike and disintegrate so I wouldn't have to face the inevitable humiliation at the end of the journey.

There was no way I would get him to pull over, even if I was now potentially blind. Torture I could handle;

Lewis seeing me like this, I could not. So, I squeezed my eyes shut and battled on.

It's all that custard launcher Travis's fault. Texting me that bullshit out of the blue – how dare he?! And now look at the state of me! I'm going to look like I've done a dodgy DIY chemical peel with all this acid eroding my face!

After what seemed like hours of cursing Travis and woe-is-me-ing, Lewis and I came to an abrupt stop, jolting me back into the here and now.

Thank the Lord. We must be back at my place. Instantly I pulled the visor shut and attempted to survey my surroundings. *Okay … I don't think I can actually open my eyes.* They were cemented together. With uncharacteristic quick thinking I lifted the visor, frantically poked and prodded at my eyelids and managed a minor (and I mean a minor) clearing, till I could just about see through my left eye, thus enabling me to make out the streetlights illuminating the rows of terraced houses on my street.

Under no circumstances was Lewis allowed to see or smell me up close, so I wasted no more time and took my chance. Holding my breath, I slammed the visor back down and vaulted off the back of the bike, gymnastic style. Obviously, it would be rude to just leg it, so I leaned in towards the fuzzy shape of what I hoped was Lewis' helmet and … butted it.

'Thanks for a nice day—speak soon!' I mumbled through my helmet as I bolted towards my front door. By some divine stroke of luck, I found my house keys in my bag without having to take the helmet off. I plunged the key into the lock, but it wouldn't open.

Argh—wrong key …

'Tara, are you okay?' Lewis called. 'What are you doing?'

Ignoring him, I tried my actual front door key, but the feckin' door still wouldn't budge.

Further panic ensued as I felt Lewis's bewildered eyes burning into my back. Out of desperation, I tried forcing the key and shouldered the door—suddenly it swung open and I blundered in, colliding into *someone*. Whoever it was screamed, so I screamed louder.

'Get out, you thieving swine!' screeched the female voice as she whacked me on my helmet with a blunt object.

'*Oww! Stop!*' I yelped. '… Mrs Cohen?'

My neighbour … what the feckin' hell is she doing in my house? …

Ohhh, shit. This isn't my house.

The pensioner continued her violent assault with a rolled up newspaper.

'Mrs Cohen! It's me, Tara—your neighbour!'

'GET OUT, NOW! I'm calling the police!'

Then I remembered that the old bat was partially deaf. With no other option, I pulled the helmet off to identify myself.

'… *Tara?* Tara—you silly, *stupid* girl. You nearly gave me a bloody heart attack!' she said, clutching her chest. 'Ohh … my goodness, you've got cucumber stuck to your face … have you just had a facial? That cream doesn't smell very nice, I must say.'

Recoiling in embarrassment, I lifted the helmet to hide my face.

'*Ohh*, I *err*, sorry, Mrs Cohen—I got our front doors confused.'

'Oh well, that's quite all right, dear,' she said, immediately poking her head out the door. 'And who is that gorgeous man out there? I do hope you haven't been riding around with him on that motorbike—they're very dangerous you know; what with all these foreigners going around not knowing which side of the road to drive on.'

Now wasn't the time for one of Mrs Cohen's misinformed anecdotes, as entertaining as they could be. Resuming crisis-management mode, I decided I had no choice but to put the sickly helmet back on if I wanted to escape without Lewis seeing the state of me.

'Sorry for scaring you. Got to go now, but I'll see you next Wednesday for your hair appointment. Bye!'

Front door key at the ready, I held my breath and grudgingly squelched the helmet back on. The stench was worse than before. I imagined myself doing a task on *I'm a Celebrity... Get Me Out of Here!* before counting down: *three, two, one ... a half ... a quarter ... an—ahh, feck it—GO!*

Without once looking at Lewis, I deftly hopped over the short brick wall around to my *actual* front door and managed to open it first time before slamming it behind me.

I can't believe it—it's finally over! I breathlessly wrenched off the helmet and vowed to never, ever take fresh air for granted again. Tears of relief sprang from my encrusted eyes as I collapsed onto the stairs.

But, someone began insistently knocking on the door.

'Tara!?' Lewis called. 'What's up with you? Are you okay? Why did you just run out of your neighbour's house?'

Christ. He must think I'm a complete and utter lunatic.

Ignoring him like an unwanted door-to-door salesman, I dropped my possessions onto the side table and made for the stairs, pounding up them two at a time.

'Tara, can you please come to the door and talk to me?' asked Lewis through the letterbox.

'Sorry, I'll be down in a minute!' I shouted from the top of the stairs, not knowing if I would be down in a minute, a month, or ever.

Having escaped to the sanctuary of my bathroom, I instantly locked the door behind me.

'Shit-shit-shit! Not good, not good …' I raided the bathroom cabinet like a crazy blind lady, scavenging for something to fix my face. Upon obliterating my neatly arranged line-up of Clarins bottles, my hands seized upon what felt like a packet of baby wipes. Fumbling with the packet, I managed to produce a daisy chain of wipes, like some kind of desperate magician. *If they can clean up the mess that comes out of a baby's arse, then surely they can do something about the shite on my face!*

With some frantic rubbing and pulling, I managed to prise open my eyes fully for the first time, revealing the repulsive banshee staring back at me in full HD.

'Feckin' Christ Almighty, look at the state of you!' Two black eyes looming back at me, and my nose was approaching the size and consistency of a bouncy castle. I couldn't believe what had just happened—I just wanted to put my head in a carrier bag and give it a good kicking. Everything was soiled: my hair, my face, my breath; even the biker leathers. As I peeled the vomit-encrusted strands of hair from my cheeks, it dawned on me that there was far too much to be done for me to even consider speaking to Lewis face to face, so I legged it downstairs to the front door and peered through the spy-hole. Miraculously, Lewis still stood there, looking confused as hell.

'Hang on a minute! I shouted, bolting towards the kitchen. Rummaging in the freezer drawers, I pulled out a bag of frozen peas and held them to my poor inflated nose, before sprinting back to the front door, praying he was still there.

'Hi, Lewis, I'm so sorry! I'm here now.'

... Why isn't he saying anything? ...

'... Oookay, so am I coming inside, or are you coming out?'

'*Ohh,* right. *Umm*, neither, actually. Sorry ... I'm, *umm* ... naked. So, I can't open the door. Can't we just talk like this?'

I felt awful, but what other option did I have? Give him a goodnight kiss? Invite him in? No chance!

'Uhh ... okay, I guess. I don't really understand what's going on here—am I about to get lucky again,' he said with a chuckle, 'or is this the end of our date?'

The cheeky bugger! I'm glad one of us is finding this funny—wait till you see the present I left inside your helmet!

'Umm ... I'm sorry but I'm gonna have to leave it here,' I said to the door. 'I'm just feeling quite confused—*umm*, I mean, *unwell.*'

Shit! 'Confused', Tara? Get your excuses straight, you imbecile!

The silhouette of his head rested against the frosted glass pane beside the door, listening intently. You could almost physically feel the awkwardness, even through the solid oak door.

'Hmm ... *okay*. Well, I hope you feel better. And as for being confused ... that makes two of us.'

Oh, feck. I've really, **really** ballsed this up.

'No, Lewis, please don't get me wrong; I'm not confused—I mean, I *am* confused, but—I do like you, it's just ...'

Cue another long, awkward silence. What was I meant to say? That I'm having some kind of allergic reaction to my ex contacting me out of the blue, and that I'm evidently not over him yet? ...

He doesn't deserve this. I'm an awful human being. An awful, unattractive human being.

With a long sigh, he said, 'Okay, I think I get the point. Call me if you ever stop feeling *confused*. Goodnight, Tara.'

And with that, his silhouette vanished from behind the glass.

Shit. This is exactly what I didn't want to happen. So much for ending things on a high!

I crouched down and shouted through the letterbox, 'Thanks for today! I'll call you ...' But the roaring of the bike engine drowned out my words as he sped away.

'Feckin' bollocks. Bollocks.' I stomped around, cursing myself. 'BOLLOCKS!'

Nice one, Tara. No wonder you're pushing forty and can't keep a decent man held down. Or any man at all!

Chapter 2

Shell-shocked, I sat on the stairs in the dark hallway, surrounded by thawing soggy peas. I was so convinced that my recovery had been going well. In my (non-professional) opinion, I was at least 78% over Travis—but then again, maths never was my strong point. Things between us were supposed to be dead and buried, yet after just two messages from him, my reformed life had flipped over, landing me quite literally face first in a muddy poppy field. And to top it off, because of all of this, I'd now blown it with Lewis, my Probably Mr Right (I was 82% sure about that).

'*Argh!* Why did this shite have to happen on our first feckin' date?' I yelled to the Big Man Upstairs. 'The third, or even the *second* date, but not the first poxy one!'

I must've done something really bad in a past life to deserve this crock of shite—suddenly my heart stopped as my phone vibrated and illuminated the hallway.

Please let that be Lewis …

[WhatsApp from (unrecognised)]
Hey Tara, it's Travis.
FYI, I know you're getting these messages. WhatsApp tells you when someone has read them ;-) I really need to talk to you … Can we meet up? Xx

Oh … Jesus, I thought, breaking out into another shaky sweat. Whichever eejit figured that creating this 'read receipt' function was a good idea ought to have their feckin' head examined.

'Yes! I have been reading your messages—and what of it, you date-spoiling, good for nothing, cheating bastard!' I shook from head to toe, stropping around like a demonic toddler. But before I could dwell or hyperventilate on it any further, another message came through.

[WhatsApp message from (unrecognised)]
I miss you so much.
I know that deep down you must still have feelings for me too.
[…]

The presumptuous tool!

[…]
Just wish you would give me a chance to explain in person.
I'm begging you xxx

Whoa! Now he was begging me? My heart rushed. Finally, it was *me* in the driving seat. I knew it was wrong, but I couldn't help feeling a twisted sense of satisfaction and empowerment from his grovelling. But, this wasn't just about power; *oh no* ... the idea of finally tasting revenge would be rather delicious too.

Oh, how the tables have turned. Justice at last! Your balls are in my court now. Let's see how you like the silent treatment and being left in limbo for eternity!

I would dedicate my award to my female comrades who had fallen in the Battle of the Booty Call.

So, despite having a million or two things that I wanted to scream at the philandering bastard, there was absolutely no way I would cave in and give him the satisfaction of responding. No way!

Basking in the glory of my victory for a few moments, I then caught a whiff of my vomit-laden hair and gagged. Huffing and puffing, I clambered up the stairs. Holding my nostrils, I peeled off the soiled leather biker wear and stripped down for a well-needed shower. But first things first – I needed to brush my teeth and get the stomach acid off my beautiful, expensive porcelain veneers before any more damage was done. I nearly swallowed my second round of mouthwash mid-gargle when another message came through.

[WhatsApp from (unrecognised)]
I keep thinking about all the good times we had.
The Christmas party, where we first met ...
Playing Kings and Queens at Castle Contarf ...
That time together at your salon after hours ...

I really miss those times. xxx
[Photo attached]

I'd never seen this photo before. With trembling fingers, I pinched the screen to zoom in on all the details.

The photo was from the night Travis and I first met, at a Christmas party over in Dublin. Someone must've taken the photo without me knowing during the drunken, pretend wedding we had outside the bar. Travis, the groom, had scooped me, the blushing bride, up in his arms and carried me through a human archway, supposed to be the threshold. Everyone in the photo was laughing and cheering, but I was the one who had the biggest smile on my face. Of course, we all knew it was a silly game, but for me it had planted seeds. Travis and I looked like the perfect couple.

Looking back at that moment suddenly brought tears to my eyes. Zooming in on Travis's chiselled face, my heart began to melt at the idea of what could've been.

[WhatsApp from (unrecognised)]
I'm so sorry for leaving things the way I did. It was all such a mess ... she meant nothing to me. I wanted to tell you the truth but I didn't think you'd understand. I didn't even know the truth myself until recently.
Please, just give me a chance to explain?
Travis x

For the second time now he had mentioned this 'truth' that clearly I wasn't privy to. I couldn't help but recall a memory of Mum telling me as a child, 'Tara, there are two sides to every story. And your side *I do not* believe. Now get to your room.'

> *"I wanted to tell you the truth but I didn't think you'd understand. I didn't even know the truth myself until recently."*

What the feck does that even mean? What kind of possible excuse could there be? He fell over and his toad just happened to fall into her hole? But then, he did say the baby wasn't his, so there had to be more to it than that. In my head, up until now, the story had been very simple:

Things had been going well and we were deeply in love (well, I was anyway). He told me there was no one else and he wanted to spend the rest of his life with me. But, inexplicably, he stopped returning my messages and calls, and for a whole month it was like he'd fallen off the face of the earth. Then, without warning or explanation, he brutally dumped me by text message. I couldn't accept that things were over. So, in one last-ditch effort to win him back, I sold my dignity to the devil and flew to Dublin, wearing nothing but a fur coat and no knickers. To my utter surprise, he was actually waiting there at the airport—but not for me. I saw him and his very young, very pregnant girlfriend together, leaving the airport hand in hand.

To top it off, I then received a call from a nurse informing me that actually I wasn't pregnant at all, but was in fact experiencing an early-onset menopause and wouldn't be able to have children.

Despite the seemingly obvious answer to why Travis had gone silent, deep down part of me knew that something about the situation didn't quite add up. I couldn't explain why; I had very little information on what happened. Thousands of possibilities had crossed my mind as to how there might've been more to it.

Not getting that concrete closure had pushed me over the tipping point, eventually sending me spiralling into a mental breakdown. I began living in the land of limbo, drowning in an ocean of unanswered, unending questions. I ended up overdosing on sleeping pills and was saved by one of my best friends, Siobhan. In the last six months since my breakdown, I'd undergone a ton of therapy at the hands of my sister, Laura, to rebuild my life from scratch. That was now six months ago, and I was convinced that I'd gotten through the worst of it all, finally having achieved closure – in my own mind anyway ... or so I thought.

Now, after seeing Travis's messages, I realised I'd never really left the land of limbo, I'd just learned how to survive there. They say 'time is a healer', but when you live in the land of limbo, there is no time. The idea that I may have achieved closure on that chapter of my life had now been categorically destroyed, like a house of cards in a hurricane. I must've unknowingly duped both Laura and myself into thinking that I was fixed. The reality was that I had merely buried the truth—it had been bubbling under the surface the whole time.

Now the unsolved case had been cracked wide open again, reigniting my burning need for answers. With my mind entering another spin, I pushed through and ran to the shower. Impatiently waiting for the water to warm up, I nearly jumped out of my skin as another message came through.

[WhatsApp from Unrecognised]
This silence is killing me … L
Tara, I'm going on a tour Down Under for a few months with work. I NEED to see you before I go.
The team is being badly affected – we're losing matches because I can't function without you. Ireland needs you … I need you!
Xxxxxxxxxxxxxxxxxxxxxx

Each message felt like a blow from a battering ram, breaking down the defences I'd worked so hard to put up.

Maybe he is serious this time? Only last night I saw on the news that Ireland had been doing poorly in the World Cup qualifiers; my family certainly wouldn't be happy if they knew I was responsible. I could see it now: I'd be barred from every pub in Dublin, with my face plastered on every Pubwatch poster—*WARNING! Tara Ryan: Single-handedly ruined Ireland's chances of winning the World Cup*.

Just before stepping into the shower, I placed my phone on a towel beside the cubicle door, with the screen in full view.

Then I checked to see if I had enough battery and put it back down.

Then I checked if I had enough signal.

I could've sworn I heard a vibration, so I checked it again.

If he calls, should I answer? What would I say? I suppose I could make him beg for forgiveness ... The thought exhilarated me. But my phone stayed mute, so I hopped in the shower, confident it wouldn't be long before he'd contact me again.

Standing under the hot water and lost in my head, one particular thought echoed over and over:

'There are two sides to every story.'

I knew it was true. The need to hear his version of events grew inside me like a balloon, the pressure building with every laboured breath I took. I knew deep down that I'd regret not finding out what he had to say for himself. I could finally get out of limbo, once and for all. And after all I'd been through, the truth was the least I deserved. I mean, it's not like I'd be signing any kind of contract by hearing him out in person. Clearly, I hadn't made any real progress getting over him anyway, so I didn't have much to lose by meeting up with him, but there was a hell of a lot of potential for gain.

Maybe, just maybe he had a valid excuse – for months, the endless possibilities invaded my dreams both in the day and night. The most plausible theory I'd come up with was that he could be a spy leading a double life, and due to some kind of complication he had to break things off with me because I was in immediate danger. Another theory was that he had a split personality disorder. Or maybe the pregnant girl had gotten hold of his phone and sent me that fateful message.

I just didn't know, and there was only one way to find out. I decided at that moment that I had no other choice but to meet him and hear him out. And if he did still turn out to be a liar, I would use the opportunity to have my revenge at last!

I heard the vibration of another text coming through. Rubbing away the condensation from the shower, I saw the dormant phone had no new messages.

… Must be hearing things.

Oops—I knocked over a bottle of conditioner. But the sound of the bottle clattering into the shower tray sparked a déjà vu flashback, mirroring a scene just like this one. It was the night Travis had ended our 'relationship', when my obsessive need to love and be loved by him was at its peak. In my longing for his affection, I had been accepting scraps of virtual affection instead of a loving, human connection. The déjà vu could've been from any one of what felt like thousands of lonely nights, just hoping for him to contact me. To want me. I couldn't see the damage I was causing myself by holding on to the hope that things would get better.

Completely at his whim, once again I could feel the need to check my phone becoming the all-consuming object of my mind. I realised that, actually, I was an addict, and I was on the edge of relapse.

How is it possible that he still has this kind of power over me? How could I allow this to happen again, after all I've been through?

The shame made me feel dirty. I turned up the temperature as hot as I could bear in an attempt to wash it all away. The burning sensation on my skin was a welcome distraction, as was the bitter shampoo I let trickle into my mouth. But no matter how much I scrubbed, I still felt wrong.

'For feck's sake ... I was finally doing okay! I hate you for doing this to me—I hate you, Travis Coleman!' I stamped my feet in temper, so hard I thought the shower cubicle was going to crash through the ceiling downstairs.

I kicked out at the shower door in frustration, and then sank slowly down to the soapy shower tray. I sat in the foetal position, drowning in my homemade tsunami of confused emotions for a moment, and then suddenly I had a small window of clarity over what the hell I was actually doing.

Falling apart, yet again!

Sobbing in a cloud of misery, I dragged myself out of the bathroom, threw on my dressing gown and then read each message again.

My finger was trembling, poised and ready to respond.

Don't do it, Tara! Do not respond! Just let it go. You know this will come to no good. Just ignore it and he'll go away. You don't want to go through this all over again ... you know where this will lead!

I needed advice. Time to bring in the cavalry, pronto.

With my hair still sending great drops of water down my back, I tried to coordinate my trembling fingers to call Laura, my older, know-it-all sister; who also happens to double as a professional psychotherapist (which is both handy and really annoying at the same time, because she kind of does know it all). In recent times, Laura had become my go-to girl for guidance and life advice. She'd got me through this once before with Travis. She'd know what to say.

But the call went straight to voicemail. *Balls.*

'... Please leave your name, number and a brief reason for the call and I will get back to you as soon as possible. [BEEP]'

'Laura, it's Tara. We need to talk A-S-A-P. But, while you're listening ... I puked in his helmet and ran off without really explaining what'd happened— Lewis's helmet, that is. And that was a real helmet, not his ... you know, down there, helmet. Sorry, I'm rambling. Before then, I— *we* had been out on a date and it was all going so well and, well, please-don't-think-bad-of-me but after the romantic picnic, we had ... sexy-times. In a poppy field. I know it was only the first date and probably a bit too soon, but it felt right at the time. I mean, it was so wonderful and lovely and I was so loved up and drunk on champagne ... but then *he* ruined everything – that basta—'

As the words were about to splutter out of my blabbering mouth, I realised that if Laura found out about Travis making contact, she'd kick up a massive fuss and get a restraining order on him or something. Not to mention the murdering that would happen. Back on the leash I would go, not being allowed out to play whilst the wolf was in town. If I wanted any freedom in my life for the foreseeable future, I'd have to keep this a secret and deal with Casanova myself.

I continued the voice message: 'Okay, thanks for listening, I feel better already! You're such a good counsellor, you know that? I'm just a little drunk and tired – I'm sure things with Lewis will be fine once I apologise. Okay, got to go now. Thanks. Bye!'

Finding my emergency cigarette packet, I flew down the stairs and nearly pulled the front door off its hinges, and that's when I saw it: a beautiful, bright red poppy, eerily lying outside on the porch. It took a moment to register that Lewis must've left it there after our ordeal through the letterbox. The little red flower reminded me of his tenderness, and how he'd confessed his love to me only earlier today.

Camilla, Lewis's sister, had told him all about what I had been through. She told him the heart-breaking facts about how ill my dad had become and how the neglect and abuse in my last relationship had triggered my breakdown, and how I'd managed to get through it all. He told me that he respected how strong I was after everything, and how I could still run a successful business. He told me that he too had been betrayed by his ex-fiancée, who had an affair with his best friend.

All that time, Lewis had been admiring me from afar and I didn't even know it. And so, when we finally did meet, the chemistry was perfect. He knew how to treat me. He told me he loved me, but he didn't need me to say it back; he was just saying how he felt. I admired his honesty and his bravery, especially for someone who had been hurt so badly in the past. It couldn't have been easy for someone like him to let himself be vulnerable again. I knew in my heart that this man would never deceive me like Travis had.

I felt an instant stab of guilt. It should've been Lewis I was waiting to hear from—*he* was the one that had treated me like a princess—Travis had done nothing but lie and neglect me. So why was it only Travis I could think about? The man clearly never gave a shite about me. He hadn't showed the amount of love in six months that Lewis had showed me in one day. I know they say that women love a bastard, but that's not me ... is it?

I am a fool and a complete bitch for feeling anything for Travis when someone like Lewis is in my midst. I am better than this—I can fight this! The guilt rose up inside me, pressing me into action. Right then I decided to give both Lewis and Travis what they truly deserved.

I deeply inhaled a few puffs of my ciggy, and then chucked it. It was time for a cleansing: no more bad cigarettes. And no more bad men!

I picked up the poppy from the porch and vaulted back inside, slamming the door behind me, and carefully placed the poppy in a glass of water and positioned it on my kitchen windowsill.

Laura used to bang on at me that meaningless messages on a screen were no way to address matters of the heart, especially broken ones. 'Love is an *action* word,' Laura would always say. Judging by his texts, clearly, Travis hadn't changed; he still didn't know what it meant to have a real connection.

With grim determination, I picked up my phone and immediately sent him a message:

[Text to (unrecognised)]
Travis, it's over.
I don't care whether the baby was yours or whatever else you think happened to you.
You had your chance and you blew it!
Don't ever contact me again.

Then I deleted the message thread entirely *and* blocked his number.

My heart, once broken, was in fact still working. I couldn't yet stop the mental barrage of texts that played over and over in my head in a constant loop; but I'd get there. I knew I would. Meanwhile, I would keep the whole 'Travis resurrection thing' a secret. No one needed to know. I was sure I could handle this alone. I was stronger now, and there was no way I could allow myself to get sucked back into Travis's orbit. Besides, I had put my family and friends through hell with my breakdown, and there was no way I was going back down that slippery path, dragging everyone with me again.

He was the past and that was final. Even if I did still wonder what really happened, I would make myself forget about him in time.

I was briefly startled as the phone came to life, the ringtone sounding louder than ever in the quiet of the night. It was okay. It was Laura.

'Tara, sorry I missed your call, everything okay?'

I sighed heavily with relief. Just hearing her voice confirmed that I had made the right decision.

'I had a maj … er … minor wobble earlier, 'but …' I continued resolutely, before she launched into one of her speeches, '… I'm fine now. I had my first date with Lewis. It didn't go quite as well as I'd hoped, nerves I guess.'

'That's only to be expected,' she said thoughtfully. 'He's a great guy. Just relax and have fun, and if you wobble again just remember that 'Emotional Freedom Technique' I taught you …'

Chapter 3

ONE YEAR LATER ...

'Do you, Tara Ryan, take Travis Coleman to be your husband, to have and to hold from this day forward, for better or for worse, for richer, for poorer, in sickness and in health, to love and to cherish, from this day forward until death do you part?'

'... I do.'

'Then I, Father Patel, in the name of the Lord, now pronounce you husband and wife. Go now in peace and love, and may your days be long on this earth. You may kiss the bride.'

Beaming from ear to ear, I leaned in for the most important kiss of my life.

Holy Mary Mother of God.

Jolting upright, I woke with a start to the buzzing radio alarm. In a panic, I drew back the covers to reveal Lewis's face, gently snoring away in blissful ignorance.

'It's okay, just another dream,' I told myself, sweating profusely. This was the second one I'd had about Travis that week.

Once my heart rhythm had stabilised, and after taking a few moments to assert reality, I twiddled my engagement ring, watching the solitaire diamond twinkle in the early morning light. This had become a little ritual of mine, a daily reminder to myself of how lucky I was to be marrying Mr Right. Did I mention that he was the absolute head off of Bradley Cooper? – I think I may have – but I will mention it again and again because, my female comrades, how lucky am I? Smiling, I heaved myself out of bed and shuffled over to the en suite bathroom to retrieve my dressing gown.

Coming back into the bedroom, I watched Lewis lie there. His messy, dark blond hair waved across his forehead, and when he woke, he would look at the world with those mesmerising emerald eyes of his. Stubble covered his strong chin but only a few hairs sat on his beautiful chest. His physique was lean but toned. His quarter sleeve tattoo went from the top of his shoulder to the bottom of his bicep, featuring an image of an owl, an elephant and a deer, all done in a seamless, animated design. I never thought I'd be into tattoos, but damn, every time I caught a glimpse of it I had to bite my lip.

Lewis had slept straight through the alarm, probably due to exhaustion; he was leaving this morning for his stag-do for five days, so we'd been up till the early hours doing extremely naughty things to each other.

His plan was to ride from London to Wales on his motorbike, meet the rest of the stags, camp out somewhere in the arse-end of Snowdonia before getting utterly spannered down in Cardiff and (please God) returning safely home by Sunday.

I'd only met two out of the five other stags. They seemed like decent enough chaps, but we all know what men can be like once they start egging each other on, even if they were all approaching forty. Lewis knew most of them from his university days, so inevitably they would be keen to relive their wild histories together in a show of mid-life macho-ism, AKA 'lad banter'. Like most brides-to-be, the prospect of these activities terrified me; but of particular concern was that he and his friends would be climbing one of the highest mountains in Britain, completely shite-faced and without a St. Bernard rescue dog in sight.

I could just see it now: six stags passing around a bottle of Jack Daniels while battling gale-force winds and horizontal rain, carrying their own body weight in ugly backpacks and wearing horrific Thinsulate fleeces (is it mandatory to wear clashing, luminous nylon outfits for such endeavours?). Not to mention they'd be sleeping in said shitty weather in—get this—a *tent*, which is no more than a glorified extra-large carrier bag, if you ask me. And after all that, there's the high probability of being attacked by a bear every time someone needs to do a number two.

Now, I know I'm not the sharpest tool in the shed—Lord knows I've been told often enough—but even I could tell you that this was a dumb idea. I mean, why would anyone in their right mind voluntarily do such a thing? This isn't Lord of the Bloody Rings. I'd checked – there was no hidden treasure to be found at the summit; only a puddle of leftover testosterone from the last stag party, having realised that it all wasn't worth it in the end.

I'd begged Lewis to do something less life-threatening for his stag-do. Even if he wanted to go to a lap-dancing club, I would've given him the green light (or at least a begrudging amber one). I mean, what if he breaks a leg? What if there's an avalanche? For the love of God, had he not seen *Vertical Limit?*

But Lewis insisted I was overreacting and that climbing Mount Snowdon was a 'walk in park'. *Try telling me that when you have to fight off a bear.*

Leaving him to sleep a little more, I went downstairs for my morning caffeine fix.

The house was undergoing a huge renovation, converting the place from being a rundown barn into the house of our dreams. Lewis had floated the idea of converting the barn on our very first date. Even then, he seemed to somehow know we'd end up living together.

Lewis earned a good living from being a veterinary surgeon; however, he'd also inherited this large plot of land from his grandmother's Surrey estate a few years before, along with a healthy lump sum, which he put towards converting the barn. The original barn made up the entrance segment and main bulk of the house, which now had two new wings running parallel up the sides, creating a kind of squared horseshoe shape with an open courtyard in the middle.

It was, in all, a striking sandstone building, and once we'd added a gravel driveway and a minuscule (and I mean minuscule) version of the Trevi fountain (true!) at the front, plus wrought iron electric gates, I couldn't have been more proud of what we had achieved so far.

There was still work going on in the West Wing, but the East Wing had recently been finished and was finally habitable, so a couple of months ago I let my house to a nice young family and moved in with Lewis.

All the housey magazines were shouting 'bring the inside outside', so I pleaded with Lewis to have a terraced area at the base of the courtyard for al fresco dinner parties in the summer. Agreeing, we'd added a long, teak table and matching chairs; while terracotta pots filled with neatly trimmed evergreens surrounded the edge of the decking, like something you'd see on an Italian terrazzo. The inside space had an open-plan feel, with double-height windows and lofty ceilings. We wanted things to be a harmonious mix of old and new, so opted for stripped wooden flooring with a scattering of contemporary rugs, two white leather Chesterfield sofas, a log fireplace in the living room and an obligatory big-screen TV for the man-boy.

We'd recently had a Shaker-style kitchen fitted, with white hand-painted cupboards, curved end cabinets and a central breakfast counter with a dedicated wine fridge built into the side.

Together our love had flourished under this roof, but suddenly I realised that tonight would be my first night in the house on my own.

Finishing my coffee, I went to get ready for the day and tried to distract myself from the worry. Tottering up the stairs, I headed back to the bedroom and whilst waiting for my shower to warm up, I took a quick peek in the mirror and immediately wished I hadn't.

Up until a few years ago, I had always been told I was too thin; nowadays those same people tell me I look much 'healthier'. On the one hand, I put the extra weight down to being more content with my life. But on the other hand, recently, things had gotten out of control since being diagnosed the year previous with having early onset menopause (about fourteen years too young. I was still in my late thirties, for Christ's sake!) As a result, I had no choice but to be put on rather unsightly HRT patches to prevent me from turning into a dried up old prune and becoming a raging Antichrist. Among the wonderful side effects, three stood out: migraines, nausea and—most cruelly—insatiable hunger.

After furiously complaining to my doctor, she said, 'HRT itself doesn't directly make you gain weight, it only makes you feel more hungry.'

'That's the same thing!' I wailed. 'This menopause has taken me hostage and is literally forcing me to eat food. I don't even want it most of the time—I'm just eating for the sake of it and grazing like a feckin' Friesian cow. It won't go away. It's always there. I'm a bottomless pit – please, please … help me?'

'Without coming off the HRT, all you can do is exercise more and eat healthier when you feel the cravings come,' said my twenty-something-year-old doctor, with her willowy frame, who wouldn't understand menopause if it slapped her in the chops.

She knew full well that neither of the above suggestions were a possibility; she just wanted to get rid of me!

Ha! Well, I wasn't going anywhere just yet. Where

there's a will, there's a way.

'Would I qualify for a gastric band at all?' I begged. 'Or what about that thingy where they staple your lips together?'

She shook her head, 'You are *not* clinically obese, Tara.'

Self-consciously I peered behind, at my arse, which seemed to be expanding before my very eyes, and not in a sexy, Kardashian sort of way.

Well, I'm certainly heading that way, I thought, deciding to give it one last shot.

'I don't suppose the NHS do a dog muzzle … for like … humans?'

She didn't have to say a word; her youthful face said it all.

The extra baggage had at least given me an excuse to renew my wardrobe. My style had changed a lot over the last year: less menopausal Barbie, more sophisticated Sindy. In an attempt to go for the edgy, Vogue-esque city-girl look, my hair was now ash blonde, cut very short and tapered tight into the nape of my neck, rock chick style. I'd side-part my long, angled, weighty fringe, which would flop in a sultry manner over my cheekbones, or wear it dramatically side-parted and waxed back to within an inch of its life. Choosing to go for the latter, I enhanced the look by adding dramatic, heavily pencilled eyebrows and fire-engine-red lipstick.

Today I would be pulling out all the stops, making myself look suitably hot for Lewis so he wouldn't forget me for a second whilst away on his trip. I'd already planned to wear my slick, city-girl ensemble for his departure. He'd seen me in it for a whole eight seconds before nearly tearing the bloody thing off in a rampant frenzy the night before, so it was pretty much guaranteed to have the desired effect. Plus, I wanted to show the outfit off to everyone in the salon. Especially as we were all going out after work for drinks to celebrate our new staff member Leonardo's birthday.

A shadow of guilt dimmed the feel-good glow once I'd put the outfit on; I really had been spending way too much on Net-a-Porter recently.

But it wasn't my fault ... not completely, anyway.

In the beginning, it all started out with just a small flutter, casually browsing Net-a-Porter and other high-fashion retailers, filling my basket with designer treasures usually totalling in the thousands upon thousands of pounds. But no matter what, after basking in the basket's glory for a few hours or so, right at the last moment—*Poof!* —I would delete the entire basket and my credit card would remain virginal for the month. I *resisted*, and would never go any further than that—not with a wedding to pay for and a house to renovate.

I called this delightful activity *faux-shopping*, and it was exhilarating. You get the highs like with real shopping, but not the comedown that's inevitable with having such an unaffordable habit. A bit like drinking Diet Coke—it tastes similar to the real thing, but without those guilt-tripping little feckers otherwise known as *calories*. Win-win, I like to call it.

So there I was, mid-*faux-shop*, minding my own business, building up one of the juiciest baskets I'd ever dared put together, when suddenly the doorbell rings. In swans James—unannounced, as usual—and before I know it, he unceremoniously commandeers my iPad and presses *CHECKOUT* on the whole basket. I was powerless to resist (I swear!)

'No ... *nooo-ho-ho*. What have you done? I'll be ruined!' I whined in a pathetic attempt to protest.

'Tara, darling, whoever says money can't buy happiness obviously doesn't know where to shop,' said James, waving away my gasping horror with a flick of his perfectly manicured hand. '*And*, let's not forget that with every purchase you get the Net-a-Porter measuring tape, which is just amaze-balls!'

Like somehow adding another promotional measuring tape to the three I already had would justify the atomic bomb he'd just dropped on my credit card.

'But James, you haven't even seen what I ordered,' I said weakly, as the enormity of what we'd just done began to sink in. My poor credit card; and there was still a wedding to pay for.

'Anything that Net-a-Porter stocks will be fabulous,' James prattled on, flicking through the website and beginning to fill my basket once again.

And *that* was the day my discipline, along with my bank balance, crumbled into oblivion.

However, later that week, I absolutely savoured the moment I signed for the fridge-sized brown box that contained 'The Black Box'.

This is it.

Placed neatly inside, like a perfect little family, were my black wax-coated J Brand super-skinny jeans, a crisp white Jil Sander shirt, and, oh yes, the fitted black Yves Saint Laurent jacket. Oh, and not forgetting my black Gucci ankle boots.

My present to myself.

Everything was so incredibly on-trend, but I really couldn't justify buying it all, could I? I mean, I could buy something Lewis and I could both enjoy with that astronomical amount of money, like a new piece of artwork for the home—

The internal battle began ...

—Owh, but the outfit wouldn't be right without everything together, I thought, clutching the garments tightly – and not only that, it would be a criminal offence to send any of it back – and anyway I really don't want to offend Marcella the style consultant, who spent hours on the web chat advising me how to put this lethal combination together.

I raised the gorgeous Gucci boots and hugged them close, smelling the new leather.

Feck it, I'm having the lot!

Snapping back to the here and now, I checked myself in the mirror. I knew I'd perfectly achieved that smoking-hot androgynous look, like something out of a Helmut Newton photo. There's no way Lewis would be able to take his mind off me.

As the early morning progressed and Lewis packed his gear into the motorbike's luggage boxes, I just casually and coolly as you like leaned in the doorway, smiling at him as though him going away was no big deal at all. (Which was complete horse-shite, obviously, as I was out of my mind with worry!) I even tried to come across a little bored, with a look that said, hurry-up-and-go-already, as I deliberately fiddled with one of my blood-red acrylic nails.

Midway through slipping his arms into his biker

jacket, Lewis walked over to the front door and leaned in to kiss me goodbye. With quick wit, I teasingly shook my head, pointing at my newly applied red lipstick, offering him my cheek instead. (*Good job, Tara, act as nonchalant as possible*). Alas, he quickly countered, and started butterfly kissing me down the side my neck … the sly fecker.

Cue shivers, goose bumps and a very rampant Tara. I launched myself at Lewis, wrapping my legs around his waist and latching onto him vampire-stylee, nearly eating my poor, helpless fiancé alive. I made sure our snog involved plenty of wandering hands and extra loud groans from my side. At one point I got a little carried away and sucked so hard on his neck that I gave him a hickey – my parting gift to him. Now he's got his very own tramp-stamp—not that I'm a tramp of course, just marking my territory. And rightly so. Anyway, just at the point where I was sure he'd carry me back upstairs for one last romping, he pulled his face away, peeled my legs from around his hips and put me down, tapped his watch and gave me a knowing look.

What the feck happened there? I was sure I was on to a winner!

'Tara, come on now, I've got to go or I'll be late for the lads.'

'Okay, okay. I'm just afraid that something might happen to you while you're away … I know you're a grown man with thick skin, but please, *please* be safe out there on that mountain. And don't give in to any peer pressure from the boys, like try to fight a bear or something—'

'Tara. Babe. Don't worry. There are no bears anywhere near where we're going. And the only time I'd fight a bear on purpose is if you were there and I could use you as a human shield. I hear they like the taste of silicone—*oww!*'

I jabbed the cheeky git in the arm and pointed my finger in his face, 'Lewis Copeland, if you hurt yourself—*at all*—you'll wish you were—'

Lewis pulled me towards him, cutting me off.

'*Na'ww*, baby. It's so nice that you care,' he said, ignoring my threats and embracing me tighter. The smell of his leather jacket was a comfort, if only for a moment. 'We're gonna be absolutely fine. It's only a little mountain—children climb it all the time without any horror stories. The only real danger is of us getting attacked by rabid, diseased sheep.'

I let out a muffled laugh against his jacket, as the fear subsided slightly and was replaced by the idea of being without him. Even though he would only be gone five days, the soppy sod in me knew I'd miss him so much. I had to fight off the tears to protect my masterpiece that had taken an hour to apply earlier (I certainly didn't spend forty feckin' quid on my Anastasia Beverly Hills contour palette for my cheekbones to melt off before he'd even gone!)

'Tara, my darling fiancée, love of my life, I promise I'll be careful,' he said. The man knew how to disarm me; every time he said *fiancée* I would fantasise about our magnificent wedding and drift off.

'I'll be back Sunday. Our stag and hen-do's are probably some of the last times we'll have apart from each other for the rest of our lives, so try to make the most of it,' he said with a smile. 'I'll call you when I get there. I love you.'

He kissed me on the lips one last time.

'Okay… I love you too,' I said, feeling uneasy again. 'Have lots of fun.' *But not too much, I whispered under my breath.*

Watching Lewis take off out of the driveway, I closed the door behind me. Despite the feeling of loss that he was gone, I knew I'd achieved my goal of stirring his desire for me.

That is, of course, until I conducted a routine, quick glance in the hallway mirror and stopped dead in my tracks.

Ooh, shit.

The smooching with Lewis had caused total chaos on my face. My pencilled eyebrows had smudged and skidded over my forehead and wandered down towards my cheeks. (I'm thinking Adam Ant here, but not in a good way.)

Cursing myself all the way, I stropped up to the bathroom to rearrange my face into something more respectable.

So much for looking hot and irresistible!

Parking up, my platinum white Fiat 500 glimmered in the May morning sunshine. (I had generously donated the car to myself after having such an abysmal previous year.) I heaved my oversized black leather Mulberry bag, which was weighed down by half a dozen bride-to-be magazines, and made my way towards my hair and beauty salon, Glamma-Puss, under a towering London skyline.

I turned the key and the salon's automatic shutters ground open, welcoming in the first rays of sunlight after being closed for the bank holiday weekend. I pushed open the glass door and breathed in the cool, empty room, the familiar scent preparing me for what would no doubt be a busy day. Six days per week, from 8.30 a.m. till 6.30 p.m., the now peaceful room would transform into an auditorium for loud gossiping, life-story narrations, and brazen banter. Every morning I tried to soak up these precious few moments of silence before the somewhat-organised chaos ensued.

Glamma-Puss had been regularly reaching its capacity and we'd been taking a very healthy profit; and coupled with the two British Hairdressing Awards we'd won, it made good business sense to move to bigger premises. So, after a long-winded process, we relocated Glamma-Puss to a unit a few rows away from Regent Street, then added new staff and new services to bolster our offerings.

Along with the new man, a new look, new car and the new house, the new and improved Glamma-Puss completed the new *me*.

The new salon had a warehouse-conversion vibe, with high ceilings, an industrial air duct system and exposed brick walls illuminated by spotlights in the floor. Wrapped in buttoned black leather, the surface of the reception desk perfectly matched the proud black Chesterfield sofa sitting in the waiting area. A tall, ornate glass chandelier hung down over the reception area, drawing the eyes of passers-by. We kept the huge boudoir-style mirrors from the last premises, which sat opposite a white feature wall, from which hung a huge ultraviolet painting of the silhouette of a woman in a bathtub. This was created by a local artist and was the salon's centrepiece, often provoking *oohs* and *ahhs* from clients.

Every day I would bring the salon to life with a satisfying ritual. *Click* on the stereo, injecting a lively atmosphere into the space. *Click* on the coffee machine, energising the mood. *Click Clack,* the sound of my heels on the weathered oak flooring to the reception desk, where, like a teacher, I would wait for the pupils to arrive before school.

Jackie, our beauty therapist and north Londoner, strolled through the door at 08:15. Clients knew that she gave an unmatched level of service and the very latest treatments: silk lash extensions, HD brows, contour body wraps, laser hair removal, massages—even Oxygen facials that had just broken out from Hollywood. You name it, she did it. She had an innate ability to keep customers coming back time and time again.

I admired Jackie's strength and resolve, seeing as she'd recently been through a messy divorce, following the discovery of her husband's infidelity. But not only that, the scandal goes deeper, as the *other woman* turned out to be one of our very own staff members: *Jayde.* Thereafter swiftly resigning from the salon, Jayde's name was promptly banned from the Glamma-Puss collective vocabulary (instead, she was referred to as 'The Infidel', 'The Home Wrecker' or 'that filthy trollop who used to work here'). Of course, Jayde wasn't the only one to blame; Jackie's philandering ex-husband was as much the culprit and target of our collective detest.

Courtesy of her generous divorce settlement, Jackie

had become rather well acquainted with her surgeon's scalpel. Despite now approaching her mid-fifties, she looked more early-forties. Jackie was short, as was her copper-red hairstyle, and her calm blue eyes matched her loving, tranquil personality.

'Good morning, Jackie. How're you?' I asked.

'Morning. Good thanks—had a lovely relaxing weekend with Graham,' she said, referring to her recently acquired toy-boy. 'I love the jacket, is it new?'

'*Aww*, thanks. Yep, freshly delivered,' I said, twirling around to show the rest of it off.

'Wow, very fetching,' said Jackie eyeing me up and down. 'Sorry, I've gotta get the wax pot heated up for the back, sack and crack I've got in at quarter to,' she added, throwing the words over her shoulder as she scurried into the beauty room at the back.

Camilla, the general manager and senior stylist, rolled in at 08:20. Camilla also happened to be Lewis's younger sister, which is how Lewis and I met. She had the same green eyes as her brother, with long, wavy blonde hair and a tall physique. Camilla was the girl next door with a big sense of humour and wit.

She held the place together in a fun yet professional manner and ensured we turned a healthy profit. We'd become good friends since I hired her to replace The Infidel.

Camilla greeted me with a kiss on the cheek. 'Morning, babe. Oh my – loving the outfit, where did you get those *boots*?'

'Well, a true lady never kisses and tells; all I can say is, James victimised me into splurging online last week—'

'Helloooo, Glamma Pussies,' said a magnanimous James right on cue. 'And how *are* we all today?' he asked rhetorically, checking himself out in the mirror by the door.

'*Ahhh*, Master James. I was just talking about you,' I said, deliberately stepping into his line of sight.

'*Ooowwhhh,*' he squealed in a pitch way too inappropriate for that time in the morning, 'well, aren't you a sight for sore eyes? Absolutely gorgeous.'

James minced over, stroking and groping as if the outfit was worn by a mannequin and not an actual human being. 'Oh yes. Yes. Yes. *See,* I told you I wouldn't let you down. It's even slicker than I thought. Especially those boots—I was afraid you might send them back. Worth every penny, darling.'

The compliments dulled the pain of the outfit's price tag, if only slightly.

In short, James was my nail technician, my joint best friend and the self-proclaimed 'other Queen of England'. In *long*, he was a cartoonish exaggeration of a man-boy straight out of a fashion magazine. Melodramatic and flappier than a bird with clipped wings, James defined the term 'flaming homosexual', providing an endless source of entertainment for anyone within earshot. That said, he could also turn a situation toxic with his infamous barbed tongue.

'Well, you'll never guess whom Siobhan and I saw last night at the swingers' bar,' he said, quickly moving the limelight back on himself.

'*Ooh,* do tell, oh majestic Gossip Queen of the West End,' said Jackie, striding back across the room so as not to miss the event.

'Wait ...' James whispered, looking around conspiratorially like a paranoid pigeon, 'is anyone else here yet?'

We shook our heads.

'Good,' he continued, now in a louder whisper, hands strategically placed on hips. 'So, as I was saying, dearest Siobhan and I were out in Soho last night after downing a couple of vinos, and we ended up visiting *The Manhole*. And lo and behold, whom did we see there? None other than our very own in-house married couple: Leonardo and Suyin.'

James waited for our pantomimic gasping to finish before rambling on. 'There they were, both of them dressed to the nines, flirting with anyone and everyone. How they didn't expect to see someone they knew in such a notorious swingers' bar, I do not know. I always told you lot that their marriage was as open as a hooker's legs, but you never believed me; not until now, at least.'

Jackie, Camilla and I looked at each other with sceptical expressions.

James continued, 'Of course, I couldn't walk away without giving our dearest Leo the old wink and nod. He tried to plead ignorance, but he should not underestimate the nose I have for such debauchery. Now the cat was out of the proverbial bag, I wouldn't have minded being Leo's pussycat for the night,' he said, scratching the air and purring, setting Camilla and Jackie off with the giggles.

Tantalising as the story was, everyone knew that any gossip, rumour or myth coming from James's mouth ought to first be seasoned with a fair few pinches of salt. Whether *he* actually believed this stuff was anyone's guess. But, to his credit, he did occasionally unearth stories that would make your eyes pop out.

James rattled on, 'Of course, if one was to bring Leonardo over to the *dark side,* it would make for quite the awkward love triangle here at work; never would I stoop to the level of *she who shall not be named*. But *Siobhan* on the other hand doesn't technically work here, so she was fair game, drooling all over our poor Italian stallion like a diabetic on a Mars bar. Meanwhile, Suyin seemed too busy in the corner with a *much* younger man to notice her hubby being waylaid by such a predator.'

'*Nooo …*' said Camilla, gasping, 'was Suyin actually kissing this younger guy?'

'Well … I couldn't see exactly, but I'm sure they were actively recruiting for a threesome, a foursome, or moresome, or worse yet—'

'*Shhh,* here they come,' whispered Jackie, pulling out of the circle in an attempt to look less conspiring.

'James,' I said quickly, pulling him to one side, 'don't be spreading unfounded rumours about our staff. What they do in their playtime is their business *only.*'

Leonardo pushed open the glass door for Suyin, both of them wearing conspicuously bright smiles.

'I rest my case,' whispered James before an over-friendly chorus of *good morning* and *happy birthday* came from the circle of gossips, including myself.

Leonardo and Suyin (or *Lee-Su* as they're referred to as a couple) were the two latest recruits to the salon. Born to a Japanese mother and French father, stylist extraordinaire Suyin had high cheekbones and a perfect little button nose, oriental slanted eyes in a contradictory blue colour. She wore a graduated, choppy black bob with licks of bright red that seemed to spark from her head. With the body of a teenager, you would never have put Suyin at 32. Despite being a vegan and an avid lover of animals, Suyin had a feisty temperament that perfectly matched her East London accent. She had the most incredible tattoo body art I'd ever seen, depicting a tasteful array of lilies, butterflies, caterpillars and bees, which spread from her outer thigh all the way across to her opposite shoulder. Needless to say, both men and women would double take when she entered the room.

Leonardo, thirty-five today, had trained in Milan and moved to London five years ago where he met Suyin. With a head completely devoid of hair and a strong nose upon which rested thick black Armani glasses, he sported a precise-cut goatee along with sharply angled sideburns. He could usually be seen with a tuft of chest hair peeking out at the top of his unbuttoned shirt, wearing trendy silver jewellery, a fitted waistcoat, leather loafers and tight-fitting jeans. He also had the kind of cliché Italian charm that our clients and indeed many other women couldn't resist. Despite speaking with a slight lisp, Leonardo was masculine and assertive, which created a nice balance to an otherwise oestrogenic atmosphere (James being the biggest contributor to this).

Until recently, both Leonardo and Suyin had been working in a competing salon nearby, until their landlord decided to double the rent, forcing the owner to shut down. Naturally, I sympathised with the owner and staff (we certainly wouldn't have survived if that had happened to us), but still, it had a positive effect on us, as we took on a surplus of new high-end clients and two of their best staff. To help with the increased demand, we also took on a part-time student Rosie to be our hair-sweeper, tea-maker and general skivvy. (Jackie would affectionately refer to her as the *tea monkey*, which she found hilarious.)

From nine o'clock onwards the day began like most others: clients were calling, hair was falling, dryers were blowing, tints were mixing, gossip was flowing, magazines were flicking; and always of comic value, the occasional yelp from a waxing victim. I busied myself counting stock and advertising a job vacancy for a new colour technician to meet the demand from the clients we'd taken on from the closure of the rival salon.

During a rare, quiet moment, I browsed on my iPad for some much needed wedding inspiration. Excitement fizzed through my veins as I flicked from one 'plan your dream wedding' website to another. Everything else just had to match the standard of my 'custom-made' wedding dress that was already on order. (I hadn't told a single soul about my choice, it was Top Secret!)

But what really got the pulse racing was my daily ritual of looking at the latest Agent Provocateur lingerie. *Sweet Mother of God,* I thought, looking at the chained diamante ensemble as I zoomed in to the maximum. *I'd probably hang myself just trying to get into that!*

So, I moved on, scanning through to the white scanty crotchless knickers section. The models looked so hot with their perfect just-about-everything on show.

Maybe, just maybe I could get away with what those women were wearing if I trimmed down my booty a bit—I could pop to B&Q, pick up some gaffer tape and fashion a DIY muzzle to stop my incessant eating.

I am brilliant!

I pulled my tummy in, taking a huge breath before letting it out in the form of a huge sigh.

Perhaps I should just settle for something more traditional? I wanted naughty but tasteful, in a soft palette of creams or whites, for my groom. Though I may not have been the age of a young, blushing bride, I wanted to be damn sure I looked and felt like one.

I also wanted a lavish food spread ... but, then again, they do say to keep it simple at weddings. *People can be so picky.*

How many would we invite? I wanted a formal, traditional event ... but the trend these days was to have it intimate and casual.

As for the venue, I'd gone from castles, cathedrals to manor houses and dainty churches. But ultimately I wanted (correction, *we* wanted) a home wedding, like I'd (*we'd*) seen in the *HELLO* magazines. Our house wasn't finished yet but the grounds would make for a dazzling venue once complete.

Looking through the websites, I began to get very confused: my brain had far too many tabs open, rapidly switching between hen-do mode, venue mode, bridal-underwear mode, honeymoon mode, then wedding cake mode. Even my iPad seemed perplexed after freezing for the twentieth time.

Between running the salon, organising a wedding

and planning my happily ever after, my head spun. So much to do, so little time!

Apart from my wedding dress and the venue, one of the only things I actually did have sorted was the wedding date: Saturday 20th September. *The Big Man Upstairs had better have perfect weather planned for then, or there'll be trouble.*

Chapter 4

Before I knew it, lunchtime arrived. I'd arranged to meet Siobhan for a quick bite in our local café, Zorro's, so I could inform my chickies about the chosen Spa location for my hen-do.

I hadn't officially asked anyone to be my maid-of-honour yet. But choosing between my sisters would've kick-started World War Three and James wasn't technically allowed to be a maid (despite his child-like protests), so I guessed the most sensible candidate would have to be Siobhan.

When describing Siobhan, the appropriate box to put her in would be one with white padded walls and a securely locked door; anything could and would happen with her. She started out as a client of mine, but that escalated quickly into a close, sisterly friendship. Well, actually, if I'm being entirely honest she was more like a naughty little brother that needed constant monitoring. But one thing's for sure: her unpredictable and upbeat personality always endeared her to me.

Born and bred in Dublin, Siobhan was the only girl of six children; she was undeniably, tough, boisterous and brave. She was as Irish as a leprechaun watching Gaelic football and drinking a pint of Guinness, but somehow she had olive-skin and hazel eyes.

Siobhan had tried many different professions including bricklayer, film extra, landscape gardener, receptionist (lasting a whole morning before being escorted from the premises for causing a riot in the canteen, a food fight no less), mystery shopper, and perhaps strangest of all, a shepherd. What she actually did *these* days was anyone's guess. 'A bit o' dis an' dat' would be her usual response to such a question. To be honest she could turn her hand to anything—that girl had special powers.

I spotted Siobhan sitting at the back of the café as she waved me down.

'Wowzers—lookin' smokin' hot there, girl!' she said as we exchanged kisses on the cheek.

'Aww, thank you, I didn't think anyone would notice,' I beamed, banking one more compliment for the ego. Always feeling compelled to return a compliment; I fired one straight back. 'I love your ... err ... *shirt*,' I mumbled, pointing out her multi-coloured floral blouse.

'*Ahh*, you're lovely, babe. But I hate this bloody thing, it's made of that nylon shite—every time I lights a fag I'm terrified it's goin' to go up in feckin' flames. I'd rather not have Tesco's Finest melted on me skin permanently,' she said, howling with laughter. 'I've enough shite tattoos as it is!'

She wasn't wrong about the tattoos; one on her calf depicted Lionel Richie dressed in *Where's Wally* clothes and captioned '*Hello ... is it me you're looking for?*' Another recent tattoo on her back was simply her ex's name: *DANNY*. But he was so creeped out by this that he broke things off with her, so she promptly had the tattoo amended to read '~~DANNY~~ *(... shit happens!)*'

'You're not goin' to feckin' believe this, right,' Siobhan said (she almost always started conversations like that), 'so I was there at the *The Manhole* with—wait, hang on ... JEZZA!?' she shouted to the startled man behind the till, raising her hand up, 'Yeah, *err,* me and Tara will be havin' our usual there now, plus two lattés and two o' those raspberry doughnuts, alroysh?'

'—Please, Siobhan,' he said, 'you'll have to get in line behind the rest of the customers, we don't do table service here—'

'—*Err*, what? Are you kiddin' me? *I'm* not gettin' in the feckin' queue ... you seem to be forgettin' our little agreement, Jez, ye li'l gobshite,' she said with a deadpan expression, drawing more stares from customers.

'Okay, *err* ... sorry' said Jez, breaking out in a sudden sweat; 'I'll bring it over to you in a few minutes.'

'Good. And make it choppy!' She turned back to me with her madwoman's laugh, but by then I'd already ducked behind my menu, half hiding away from the commotion, half in a fit of hysterical mortification.

Siobhan then leaned across the table and whispered, 'Here, listen. That fecker owes me one, I tell you. So, basically, I rode Jez a couple o' weeks ago, after goin' back to his place—'

'*No* … you're joking me … *him?*' I asked, my eyes darting back and forth between the pair of them.

'Yeah, him … I know, I'm just gettin' to that. So, anyway, I wakes up in the mornin' with a stinkin' hangover and turn over to realise that Jez—let's face it—has a face like a dog's arsehole. Anyways, there I am, pullin' me jeans on fast like, to make a sharp exit, and then didn't I go and see a picture on his bedside table of him and some woman, smoochin' away. So, I wakes him up like, err, "Who the feck is that?" and he's like, "*Oh, err, that's my girlfriend.*" Like he'd just neglected to tell me that small fact before we got a cab home together the night before; for feck's sake, like. So now I'm kinda—what's that word? … *Blackmail*—I'm blackmailin' him. But only a small bit now, nothing major. All I wanted was some bloody free food and to not have to queue up when I come to this shitehole. I'll be havin' words with the little git if he tries to pull another fast one like that, let me tell you—'

Siobhan broke off with a smile and watched me keel over in laughter.

They say some people are like a breath of fresh air, whereas Siobhan was more like a hit of laughing gas. Something about her just seemed to set me off; sometimes she didn't even have to say anything and I'd be creasing up.

'Anyways, Tara, lets stop tomfoolin' around, we've some very important business to be takin' care of, like your *hen-dooo*,' she said, drumming her palms on the table.

Now we're talking. I couldn't wait to tell everyone about the spa weekend options I'd been looking at. I had mentioned my idea to Laura a while ago but she hadn't come back to me about it. As for the other girls (including James), somehow I'd managed to keep my lips sealed.

I'd spent weeks researching the best spas in the country – the only thing left was to choose from my shortlist of three. In fact, I'd been rehearsing the pitch for a couple of days now: 'A long weekend of twice-daily massages, yoga, meditation, holistic therapies and deliciously detoxing food – all in premium accommodation to ensure we experience the most relaxing, pampered and transformative experience imaginable ...'

Retrieving the bridal magazine from my bag, I opened the spa packages page and placed it in front of Siobhan for her eyes to feast on.

Clearing my throat, I began. 'So, I've whittled the spas down to three options. Now, picture this: A long weekend of twice-daily massages, yoga—'

'Yeah, let me stop you there, babe,' said Siobhan, sliding the magazine to the other side of the table. 'Now lookit, Laura tol' me all about your plan to have us a crappy, borin' frolic in a fookin' water tub all weekend, and it does sound interestin', but the thing is, like ... it is actually a shite idea altogether.'

My eyes widened and mouth gaped open.

'I'm sorry like, but the chick committee has democratically decided that a spa weekend would be a terrible sin for all parties involved. It would just be, like, plain wrong. *No*,' she ranted, somehow managing to make *me* feel bad for my choice. 'It's just not right and it's not fair!'

'But ... but, they have the most *amazing* organic, free-range menu—they've got microbiotic salads, walnut soufflé, Brussel sprout soup—'

'Ahh, me point exactly ... Brussel-fookin-sprout-soup, Tara. Are you okay in the head, woman?'

Siobhan then mimed a gag, complete with flopping tongue and sound effects. I just shrugged and looked at the floor.

'Brussel sprouts are the grapes of the devil. They're shite; as are spas, rabbit food and fookin' yoga. Us, your hens, won't allow you to do this to yourself. And us. We are not havin' any of it.'

Jez brought our sandwiches, coffees and doughnuts over to the table.

'Oh, thanks, Jez. Pleasure doin' business with you,' said an angelic Siobhan, as Jez stalked away as quickly as he came.

I slouched back on the chair and sighed deeply, giving into the fact that I'd never win this battle. My dream of losing a couple of inches (or six) off my waist had been monumentally crushed._

'But don't you be worryin', we've got you covered—we've all agreed on somethin' much more suitable for everyone involved.'

I braced myself for impact ...

Out of nowhere, Siobhan produced a glossy brochure, the cover image showing a pure white sandy beach, blue skies and a beautiful, skinny woman sipping a cocktail in her scanty bikini. And that's when I saw the heading:

IBIZA – Your ultimate guide to heaven on the White Isle.

'What? *Ibiza!* You do realise this isn't my 21st birthday?' I huffed, trying to sound outraged, although secretly the cover had me curious.

'Err, yeah, *Ibiza*. Like where the hell else?'

I immediately grabbed my phone and decided to Facetime my sister Laura. Out of everyone, surely she'd be sensible enough to derail this ridiculous Ibiza train?

'I've been expecting this,' said Laura answering the call. She must've been at Mum's house, judging by the out-dated curtains in the background. 'Now listen, Tara, it's been well over a year since you've properly let your hair down and partied with the girls. It's going to be the last chance you'll get to do something like this as a single woman, so you'd better make the most of it. As your therapist and wiser, more travelled older sister, I am strongly recommending—*insisting*—that you just give it up and go with the flow.'

The conspiracy ran deep, it would seem.

'Well, thanks for nothing, some sister you are,' I sulked. 'I guess I'll just have to go along with whatever you conspirators want to do!'

'Now, calm down, Tara. Don't throw a wobbly on us,' said Laura. 'You can melt yourself slim under those glorious rays.'

Great! I thought, even my sister thinks I need to lose weight, and I haven't even seen her in months!

'Yeah, all that sun, swimmin' and dancin' will help you lose that spare tyre you've been bangin' on about,' piped up Siobhan. 'It's win-win.'

'Pristine white sand, warm, turquoise waters,' said Laura in a soothing, hypnotic voice, 'topless men walking around in budgie smugglers; gorgeous fruity cocktails ...'

'Yeah, and not to mention the all-night raves and endless supply of marchin' powder,' I heard a voice in the background say.

Ahh, yes, I might have known. My younger sister Katie—twenty-four going on fourteen—also appeared to be plotting against me.

'Katie, who else is there with you? Have you got me on speaker at a feckin' conspirers conference?' I asked. 'And exactly how much have you lot actually planned behind my back?'

'Ahh, look, don't be such a spoilsport,' said Katie, 'it's rare that any of us get together, and we don't want to waste that time sharin' a sauna with some fat businessmen staring at our diddies. Cop onto yourself, Tara, everyone just wants to get pissed and have a good time, you know—and we think you'd be better off for it. I mean, once you get hitched you'll be even more of a bore than you are now, so you may as well have one last blowout before you sell out.'

I didn't know where to start with her abrasive and offensive reasoning, but somewhere in there, I could kind of see her point. Plus, I didn't have the willpower to fight back, knowing full well it'd be a losing battle from the get-go. Nonetheless, it didn't stop me throwing out some obligatory questions:

'But what are we actually going to do when we get there? Isn't Ibiza just full of teenagers?'

'No!' said everyone in unison.

'Look, we've arranged a surprise for the Saturday night.' Laura said, now sitting beside Katie on mum's floral sofa. 'You can get all the massages you want before *and* after the surprise, plus the apartment we're booking has these amazing luuuxxury padded suuun-lounnngers you love ...'

... Shut the front door.

They knew my weaknesses well: luxury sun-loungers are my Achilles' heel. No, it's not some weird fetish—there's logic as to why having luxury sun-loungers is an absolute must ...

— SIDE NOTE —

(Brace yourself, I'm going off on a tangent here ...)

Each year, we only get a few precious days to go on holiday. And the twenty-four hours in each of those days can be evenly split into three categories:

i) Sleeping / dozing / humping a significant other if you're lucky) — 8 hours
ii) Eating / drinking / all-inclusive buffeting / getting ready to go out — 8 hours
iii) Leisure time — 8 hours

The first two categories are the mundane stuff you could do at home (and for free). It's the *leisure time* we're really interested in; it's why we pay big bucks year in year out, so we'd bloody well get our money's worth out of that time.

But what should we actually *do* in that small, leisurely eight-hour window?

The only logical answer: *sunbathe. Why,* I hear you ask? Well, us northern Europeans are vitamin D deficient through being deprived of sunshine approximately 364 days of the year. So, therefore:

Enjoyment of holiday = Number of sunbathing hours x Quality of sun-lounger

From this, it's obvious the sun-lounger is the pièce de résistance of the entire holiday.

But of course, there's a problem—not all sun-loungers are equal. I'm talking of course about shitty, sub-standard sun-loungers. There are sun-loungers that give you a serious exfoliation, the rough hessian type that put Shredded Wheat to shame. You can feel the harshness even through your fluffy John Lewis towel. I mean, why do we look forward to our holiday all year, to then spend most of our precious leisure time lying on what is effectively a plastic cheese grater? It's wrong. It has to stop.

Not only this, but when it comes to flipping the meat in order to tan your back, these flimsy excuses for furniture rarely if ever recline all the way down. This leaves us with two options. The first is to *become a gymnast* so you can arch your back in order to lie comfortably (or just spend a fortune at the chiropractor's when you get home). The second solution is to lie *the other way around* on the lounger altogether. This might be okay if you're a man, but as a woman, lying on our fronts on these plastic monstrosities is awkward and uncomfortable at best.

Somehow the 'designers' have managed to overlook the one critical factor that affects 50% of the entire population of their users ... *Boobs.*

Dear sun-lounger designers (who must somehow

***all* be 'male' for this epidemic to have gone unnoticed),**

How have you not considered boobs in the design of your sun-loungers? We know breasts seem like mystical, divine objects sent from the heavens, but they have feelings too. We can't just slide them under our armpits, the way you men can just tuck your junk into your undercarriage. No, boob physics simply doesn't work that way.

(Come on guys, seriously. It's not like you lot don't think about boobs all day already. And if this is received by a woman ... well, shame on you!)
Only you can put an end to this insane and unnecessary struggle.

Yours faithfully,
Women of the World

So, until the sun-lounger design revolution takes place, we should boycott any loungers that don't perform the following recliner settings at minimum:

LEVEL 1: Upright. Optimal straw-to-mouth position with minimal effort. Allows for best peripheral vision; however, this position maximises exposure of tummy creases.
LEVEL 2: Optimal book reading posture, also ideal for phones or tablets. Also known as *Perv Position* (fake snoozing with sunglasses on,

secretly spying man-candy and/or comparing oneself to the infuriatingly beautiful women in the vicinity).

LEVEL 3: Nearly horizontal, but just upright enough to keep a loose eye on AWOL children or to dismiss looky-looky sellers, et cetera. At this angle, gravity finally becomes our friend as the faux flat tummy appears, emphasising one's loveliness for the eyes of passers by.

LEVEL 4: Fully horizontal. Optimal snoozing position; however, beware of dribbling. Also, be sure to smother oneself in lotion in order to prevent lobster-fication. Also ideal for *flipping the meat*, whereby one can lie on the tummy and let one's boobs comfortably sink into the padded gloriousness.

Thanks for reading. #BoobsForBetterSunloungers

— END SIDE NOTE —

'Earth callin' Tara!' shouted Siobhan, clicking her fingers inches from my eyes.

Back to the here and now, I practically snatched the travel brochure from her. 'Show me the bit about the luxury sun-loungers?'

'Here ... you nutter.' She pointed out a section at the bottom of the page, bookmarked by a Post-It note with the section already circled in red. They'd planned their ambush well; they knew exactly what they were doing.

'You could cop yourself a shag on one of those after clubbin' all night and then stay there for sunbathin' for the mornin', nodded Siobhan. 'Easier than leavin' a towel on them.'

I read and reread the sentence about the sun-loungers; which was, as usual, only in the small print. Clearly, the marketing bods at this company needed to elaborate on the description for this potentially deal-breaking feature.

'*Hmmmm*. I guess these loungers do sound pretty good,' I agreed, nodding. In all honesty, it did sound like a lot more fun than the spa weekend. I just wouldn't let them know that.

A tense silence hung in the air from Siobhan and my sisters on the phone.

I let out a big sigh. 'Fine ...'

Resounding applause and whooping ensued, turning more nosey heads inside the café.

'It seems I don't really have a choice in the matter anyways. And besides, I was going to suggest this kind of a thing as plan B,' I lied, trying to hush the commotion. 'But please check that everyone else is happy with the idea before booking—'

'Already have!' whopped Siobhan. 'Everyone agreed last week, so I'll just go ahead and book it now!'

'But don't you need everyone's passport details, get people to book time off work, et cetera? I know that all of Lewis's stags had an absolute nightmare trying to get the same time off, which is why they ended up going away so early.'

'Don't you be worryin' about that – everyone's already signed up. We just needed you to give the okay before pressin' the button and we're home free!'

Grinning like a Cheshire cat, Siobhan proudly

slapped my passport on the table like an ace of spades she'd been holding on to. 'James swiped it from your place last week,' she beamed proudly like it's not an offence to steal someone's passport out of their house or anything. I snatched it back and checked the contents, shocked-but-not-really-shocked that he'd somehow managed to find and swipe my passport without my knowledge.

Returning from Zorro's Café, I opened the salon door to the sound of (Whoa!) 'We're Going To Ibiza!' by the Vengaboys blaring on the speakers. James was prancing around, hairdryer in hand, leading a parade of both staff and clients in a sing-along. Clearly, word had got out fast about the destination of my hen-do.

James proceeded to drag me over to the conga chain now snaking around the salon. I couldn't help but smile and follow Laura's advice to just 'go with the flow'.

'Right, you scallywags,' I said once the song had ended, trying to bring some kind of order back, 'stop having so much fun and get back to work!'

Just as everyone resumed their stations, the salon phone rang. Catching my breath, I walked around the reception desk to answer.

'Good afternoon, Glamma-Puss hair and beauty, how may I help you?'

'I don't think I've ever seen a more stunning vision,' said a man with a deep, husky voice and distinct northern accent.

My blood turned to ice and my cheeks flamed like beacons of fire.

No, no, no. It can't be ...

Eyes wide, I whipped around to the window.

There he was, just metres away. His shadow darkened the storefront, like storm clouds blocking out the sun. I could see his dark eyes staring through the glass directly at me.

He needed no introduction.

Chapter 5

Panic-stricken, I clamped my hand over my open mouth and grabbed the edge of the reception desk to steady myself.

There he was; large as life. Nothing but a pane of glass separated me and the infamous Bastard, Travis Coleman.

Shit, shit, shit, SHIT!!!

Convinced that I was going into cardiac arrest, I waited for that shooting pain in your arm they talk about in *Holby City*. Maybe then I would just wake up in a hospital and the fecker would be gone already?

Nothing. *No heart attack? Shite!*

Fight or flight?

Flight. I'm a feckin' coward and I don't care who knows it!

Dropping to my knees like a bomb, I scrambled under the reception desk. I didn't know what I was trying to achieve here; he'd obviously seen me.

Drawing my legs up to my chest, I tried to make myself as small as possible.

'... Tara? What are you doing?' I heard him ask.

With a start, I realised I was still holding the phone to my ear – so immediately hung up on him.

With hammering palpitations, I shuffled around on all fours, a few inches to the left, and then a few inches to the right. Forward, back, forward, back – getting nowhere, like a trapped animal.

Suddenly, I spotted a smallish gap between the desk and bins—*aha! My escape route. Now, if I can just get my planet-sized arse through that gap ...*

Plucking up the courage, I reversed around to the left side of the desk, furthest away from the window. *All I need to do now is bum-shuffle my way to the staffroom, and I'll be home free.*

Three ... two ... one ... Out of nowhere, Suyin's skinny-jean-clothed legs suddenly blocked my path, before chucking a dustpan of hair into the bin, missing entirely. She was completely oblivious, while my new jacket and I endured a greasy blizzard of brunette wisps ...

SUYIN! Spitting and cursing under my breath, I dusted myself down and prepared for my Great Escape. I was ready for take-off, but once again, my flight was cancelled as the phone began to ring in my hand like an air-raid siren, freezing me to the spot.

It was him. I could feel it.

No Tara, do not answer!

Nope. I'm not. Feckin'. Answering.

'Where's Tara?' I heard Jackie's voice ask from across the salon.

'Dunno, I'll get it,' Camilla said, as the *clip-clop* of

her heels stalked over to my hiding place.

Feck it! I had to pick up, or face Camilla answering the phone – she was the last person I wanted speaking to Travis.

With trembling fingers, I clicked the answer button, cowering under Camilla's shadow as she hovered over the reception desk.

After what seemed like an eternity, she walked away and I finally spoke into the receiver. 'Hello ... Glamma-Puss salon, how can I—'

'Tara, why are you hiding? I know you're there ... I just want to talk.'

'Uhhh ... sowwy da'ling you must haf wong numba,' I said, conjuring the first accent that came to mind.

'Well, that's strange because I just saw a smoking-hot woman just duck behind her reception desk who looks *exactly* like Tara Ryan.'

'Ooh, Tawa! Yeah, she no wok hee no maw – she sole up an lef country abou siss manph agow!'

Like a meerkat, I slowly poked my head above the trench line.

'Ahh, there you are,' he said with a smirk as I ducked back under.

'I told you to never contact me again!' I whispered aggressively. 'Please, just go away!'

'No, I can't. I'm sorry. I've been losing my mind ever since I broke things off with you. Don't tell me you don't think about what we could've been? Didn't you ever wonder why I ended things like that? Why I asked you never to contact me again?'

Of course I bloody did – despite all my efforts to

move on. Just last night I'd dreamt about marrying the swine, and not for the first time either!

'Please, please don't do this to me.'

'Do what?'

'*This!*' I spat. 'Please, just go away. I'm happy now!'

'Well, I'm not! I've never felt so God-damn unhappy in my whole life ... I was stupid to let you slip away,' he continued. 'No matter what I do, I just can't get over you—and I've tried, believe me. Tara, I was being blackmailed, so just trust me when I say that I had no choice but to break it off with you. You deserve to know the whole truth ... but I can't tell you anything more until you agree to meet me somewhere more suitable.'

The shock of it all intensified my confusion, almost causing a physical pain in my head. I just didn't know what to say or believe.

'I'm not going out of my way so you can feed me more of your bullshit!' I said, poking my head around the reception desk to make sure no one was witnessing the scene.

'There's so much to talk about, and I don't want to do it while you're playing a game of hide and seek,' he said. 'You told me to never contact you again, and for the last year I've been trying to do just that. But I just couldn't get over you. Look, Tara, all I want is a chance to talk face to face, so I can at least explain myself. I'm begging you ...'

My mouth went bone dry.

'I—I can't. I just can't do this ... things have changed now,' I said, 'I've moved on. Look, I need to get back to work, or people will get suspicious.'

'Okay fine, I'm coming inside ...'

'No, wait–wait–wait! I pleaded, bolting up to my feet in horror at the very thought.

'If anyone knew that we were even in the same postcode, they'd kill you. Just *go*, before you cause a scene ... or I'll—I'll set James on you!'

'Tara, I'll leave for now but until you hear me out I'm just going to keep turning up here unannounced.'

Shit! I knew from experience he would stop at nothing to get his way. I couldn't risk him coming into the salon; people wanted his head, and frankly, I didn't want my new salon being turned into a murder scene. Travis was hated even more than Jayde—and that's saying something.

'Tara, please, just look at me ...'

I opened my eyes a crack and saw him stepping closer and pressing his forehead against the glass.

'... I still love you.'

Boom. Direct hit.

I struggled to breathe, and the salon began to spin. Each syllable was a bullet slamming into my chest, sending me off balance. Eyes squeezed tight, I shivered in undiluted shock at his declaration. I panicked and instinctively began my Emotional Freedom Techniques, tapping on my wrist and face, frantically attempting to send calming waves to my brain. It had worked well in the past, under Laura's able guidance, but I hadn't felt the need to tap in so long that I couldn't remember which points to hit. I desperately began tapping all over my face and arms at a crazy pace, while working the catastrophic situation through in my head.

[Tap-tap-tap]

The man I allowed to smash, mangle, and break my heart has just told me he still loves me!

[Tap-tap-tap]

'Tara?'

I jumped as I heard Travis speak from the phone that was still clutched in my hand.

'What?' I whimpered as I brought the phone back up to my ear.

'Why are you hitting yourself around the head?'

'… None of your business!'

'Did you hear me? I'm telling you, I still love you.'

Woman down …

'… Tara, just say you'll meet with me?'

'I–I can't … Just tell me why you dumped me, and let me go,' I pleaded, nervously looking back into the salon, checking our encounter was still undetected.

'I wish it was that simple,' he said. 'Look, I'm leaving for Ireland tomorrow, so if you want to talk you can find me at the Langham Hotel at Portland Place. I'll be there in Palm Court from nine o'clock, and *then* if you don't like what you hear, I promise I'll leave you alone.'

I knew deep down that if I didn't agree to meet him I would never truly get over what happened.

'O … kaaay,' I said, caving in and gulping hard.

He let out a sigh. 'Great. See you then.'

And with that, he was gone.

It took a couple of attempts to replace the phone in its cradle, and I managed to knock over the stationery pot in the process. My coordination was shot to pieces; I simply couldn't make sense of what had just happened.

Warily, I glanced over to Camilla. To my relief she had her back to me, and appeared to be in deep conversation with a client, holding a colour shade chart. In fact, no one had seemed to notice my unexpected visitor. Taking my chance with a bowed head, I flew across to the staffroom.

Once out of view, I held onto the staffroom wall and lowered myself onto a stool, still consumed in total and utter disbelief. I felt like I was in a stupor after a vivid dream.

Did that really just happen?

Thank God no one saw him at the window—especially James. Travis would've been tied to a chair while James got to work on his nails (pulling them out, that is, not manicuring them). Though the thought was somewhat pleasing, I don't think the landlord would've appreciated the bloodstains. And oh my God, if Camilla had seen him and reported back to Lewis ... don't even get me started!

Suddenly, my heart plummeted even further as Camilla waltzed into the staffroom.

'Ahh, she's a great laugh, Mrs Warren,' said Camilla, flicking on the coffee machine and picking out a Nespresso pod from the dispenser. I couldn't help but see a glimpse of Lewis in her right at that very moment; she looked and acted so similar to him, it was spooky.

'She just told me ...' Camilla's voice trailed off when she saw my face.

'Tara, are you okay?' she asked, cocking her head. 'You look like you've seen a ghost.'

'Err, *yep*. Good. Thanks. Fine.'

'Hmm ... are you sure?' she asked, adjusting her

leather scissor pouch and pulling up a stool. 'Err ... I don't think *this* belongs to you.' She smiled and pulled a clump of brown hair from my jacket. 'And is that some kind of new fashion accessory?' she asked, pointing towards my arm.

I looked down and saw a used wax strip, covered in short, curly hairs, stuck there for all to see. Flinching in disgust, I ripped it off and threw it in the bin. *My new bloody jacket as well. I'd murder Suyin if I wasn't trying to keep things quiet.*

Camilla tried to stifle a laugh, but seeing that I didn't find it in the least bit funny, she just squeezed my hand in a sisterly way.

Since hiring Camilla eighteen months before, we'd become close friends, both in and out of work. We talked about everything (except sexy-times with Lewis – the line had to be drawn somewhere). And just like her brother, she was very intuitive, hence why I found this situation so uncomfortable. Usually I would've told her about something of this magnitude, but there's no way I could tell her about Travis's sudden appearance, and especially that I was considering meeting him later that night.

Just then, Leonardo strutted in to the staffroom, John Travolta style, inadvertently taking the heat off me.

'Tara, you no lookeh so goodeh,' he said in his thick Italian accent.

'Got a migraine starting,' I said, rubbing my brow.

'Bella, I get deseh, eh—*migraine*—all o de time. Here, takeh dese,' he said, handing me a strip of foiled tablets from his mini bum bag. 'Deseh from America, you know how they like a de strongeh prescriptioneh. I takeh dese for my back—they de only thing that work, believe me. Very good, very strong—'

Just then, Leonardo's phone rang. He waved off our conversation and began jabbering away in Italian, leaving Camilla and me alone again. Wanting to avoid her, I got up and fixed myself a glass of water to take one of the painkillers. I hoped to God it would numb the feelings leftover from Travis's wake.

Regaining eye contact, Camilla rubbed my shoulder tenderly. 'I think you might be taking on too much. You've got all your wedding plans, the renovation on the house, and the salon's been so busy recently … you're probably burnt out.'

'Hmm. I think you're probably right,' I said with a sniffle and a nod. 'It's just these stupid crazy menopausal hormones; a migraine can just spark out of nowhere.'

'Yeah, it doesn't sound like much fun. But remember, you've got so much to look forward to—we'll be going on your hen-do before too long. Just imagine yourself relaxing with James and us girls, sipping cocktails without a worry in the world …'

But her voice washed over me. My mind was a million miles away.

This wasn't meant to happen. Everything was going so well …

I mean, one minute I'm minding my own business, deciding on scanty bridal underwear, and the next I've agreed to meet up with my ex who I thought I'd never hear from again! Worse still, I was *actually* considering going to a posh London hotel with said ex, while my fiancé was roughing it up some poxy bloody mountain!

I hoped for some kind of divine intervention, some kind of escape. My mobile should ring and I'd have to fly out to Dublin for some kind of family emergency. Or Lewis would burst into the salon saying, 'I came back early from my stag-do and saw your ex outside, so I knocked seven shades of shit out of him.' Or, even easier, the Big Man Upstairs could telepathically fill me in on what really happened with Travis, so I could avoid having to meet up with him altogether.

I felt suffocated just thinking about it all.

'Sorry,' I said, abruptly rising to my feet and looking at my watch, 'just remembered I've completely forgotten to pick up Leonardo's birthday present! I need to pop out and get it before the shops close. Camilla, can you cover my clients this afternoon? I'll meet you guys at Bar21 later on.' I hoped my white lie would throw her off the scent – the present was, in fact, nestling in the bottom of my handbag.

Before Camilla had a chance to protest, I snatched my handbag off the shelf and paced my way out through the salon onto the busy street. The fresh air was a relief, even if it was the polluted London variety.

In a trance, I waved down a black cab on the other side of the road, fixing an icy stare at the elderly couple competing for the ride. Luckily, the driver ignored the couple, pulled a U-turn and came onto my side of the road. (My new androgynous look must have won him over. Thank you, Net-a-Porter.)

I clambered into the cab and clipped my seat belt in place, then sat there for a moment, wondering why the driver hadn't taken off.

'... Where ya going then, luv?'

Thinking ahead, the 'Glamma Pussies' weren't due to arrive for Leonardo's shindig for another couple of hours yet, but I figured I could get there first and settle my screaming nerves with a drink before they arrived.

'... Bar21 in Covent Garden, please.'

As the taxi pulled away and nosed through the late afternoon traffic, I replayed the scene from the salon window on a loop.

After what seemed like an eternity, the sound of the cab's handbrake abruptly woke me from my daydream. We had stopped on Henrietta Street, on a corner of the iconic Covent Garden market. In a trance, I paid the driver and crossed the square towards Bar21.

Inside the bar, being pre-five o'clock, it was predictably quiet. I headed downstairs to find somewhere private, and found a booth set deep into a bare brick wall.

As soon as I sat down, a waiter appeared from nowhere.

'Good afternoon, Madame,' he said in an accent I couldn't quite work out.

I hate being called *Madame*. It makes me feel old, like old enough to have been on the feckin' *Titanic*.

'What can I get for jew?'

(Must be Spanish.)

People always seem to drink brandy in a dire situation like mine – well, in the movies, anyway. But then I remembered that I actually couldn't stand the stuff.

'I'll have a Prosecco, please.'

'Is that a bottle or a glass, Madame?'

'Just a—'

'The bottle is on special offer: £25 reduced from £35.'

Hmmmm. The bottle would be good for sharing, and the others will be here before too long. Plus, I won't be staying that long, so I'll essentially be buying a round ahead of time.

'You're a good salesman, no need to twist my arm … Go on then, I'll take the bottle. Thanks.'

'Of course, an 'ow many glasses would jew like? And would jew like anything from de food menu?'

The thought of eating made me want to puke.

'No. No food, thanks. Erm … like, five glasses? I'm waiting for some friends to join me shortly.'

'Okay, no prollem. I come right back.'

Slumped in my booth, the millions of buried unanswered questions broke through the surface. The *what ifs*, *if onlys* and *why nows* whirled the mental merry-go-round faster with each pass. It felt like my head had suddenly been invaded by a swarm of loud angry bees.

What if Travis really had changed? He said he *still* loved me, theoretically meaning he had to have loved me in the first place, and had never stopped. Maybe Laura was wrong about him all along? I mean, what about this other side of the story he kept referring to? He did tell me his life was 'complicated' when we first met, but I was far too worried about playing it cool to ask him about it.

All I had to go by was that he *said* he was being blackmailed, but that didn't tell me anything. I just couldn't seem to shift him from my subconscious, even if I was happy with Lewis now. Could I still be in love with him and somehow not realise? And if I did still love him, could I ever forgive him for cheating? And then, could I ever trust him not to do it again? Theoretically, if the answers to these questions were the right ones, going back to him would make a very attractive package indeed. I wish he wasn't so good in the sack, hand-bitingly gorgeous and a famous rugby coach.

God, why is this so hard? Then I couldn't stop thinking about his masterpiece … Jesus. He was always so … big, so ready …

The waiter returned with the Prosecco, interrupting the torrent of thoughts. Mesmerised, I watched him pour the pale fizz into the elegant flute. Unable to wait for the froth to subside, I took a huge swig of the chilled, bubbly wonderfulness, shivering as the warm, tingly sensation spread throughout. But then, as if by some kind of allergic reaction, my migraine instantly returned. Leonardo's painkillers clearly weren't as strong as he'd said, so I popped two more capsules into my mouth and chased them down with another mouthful of Prosecco.

I put my glass down and saw that it was already empty. Well, that obviously didn't count as the *one* drink I'd allowed for myself. Plus, the froth always makes it seem like there's more in the glass then there actually is, so I poured myself another, asserting that the flute was particularly small, and took another swig. *That's better*, I thought, loosening up a bit.

Then, from nowhere, I started to well up.

Then I started to wail.

'Madame?!' I heard the waiter say, rushing over to me with a look of concern. 'Your Prosecco is not satisfactory?'

'*Nooo*. No. It's not the wiiine, [sniffling] the wine's fine. It's men. *Men* are the problem … not you, I mean. Just one man.'

I gratefully accepted the napkin he passed me and blew my snotty nose into it.

'I—I'm sorry for your tears, Madame. If there is anything I can 'elp with, plis let me know. Otherwise I will leave you in piss,' he said, half-bowing away.

I took a stabilising breath and managed to pull myself together. Sighing deeply, I twirled the flute by its stem, looking intently into the bubbles, hoping my answers would somehow be inside.

Why did this this stuff always have to happen to ***me****? Katie and Laura never have half the amount of shite I have on my plate.*

I would've usually called Laura for counsel on such matters, but there was no way I could tell her; she'd have had my head on a spike if she knew I was even remotely thinking about meeting up with Travis. I tried to think of someone else I could confide in, but realised that Siobhan, James, Katie … in fact pretty much everyone I knew would've also lost their shit if they knew what I was planning. Camilla and Lewis were out of the question, obviously.

Taking a deep sigh, I tried to think about how Laura *would* approach my situation if she were in my shoes. She was so logical and rigid at times, it was like talking to a bloody robot. I could just imagine her now:

ERROR:

Cannot connect to the server, 'HAPPILY EVER AFTER' due to unresolved issues.

The application 'TRAVIS COLEMAN' is still open.

ACTION REQUIRED:

To fix unresolved issues, choose from one of the following options.

(WARNING: This process is permanent and cannot be reversed.)

To keep
LEWIS COPELAND:

- Read the user manual:
  Travis_Excuse.pdf
- Insert disc: CLOSURE
- Uninstall TRAVIS COLEMAN.app
- Reinstall LEWIS COPELAND.app

OK

To keep
TRAVIS COLEMAN:

- Read the user manual:
  Travis_Excuse.pdf

- Insert disc: FORGIVENESS
- Uninstall LEWIS COPELAND.app
- Reinstall new version TRAVIS COLEMAN-V2.app

OK

Having translated the machine's output into English, my options were to either forgive Travis or get full closure and move on—living in denial for the rest of my days was an unthinkable alternative. In either scenario, I'd have to meet with Travis to find out what he had to say for himself. But then I'd be reaching a fork in the road; left with a decision that would no doubt affect the rest of my miserable little life.

Surely, this is a simple decision to make?

Obviously not. My frazzled brain simply couldn't take any more, and by force of habit, I caught myself twiddling my engagement ring, flashing back to when Lewis proposed ...

Chapter 6

Knee-deep in mud, I shuffled from one cold-footed wellington to the other as Lewis inspected the heavily pregnant cow next to us, who I'd named Daisy.

I just loved going with Lewis on *the rounds*, watching him help the animals. Well, maybe not so much at this precise eye-watering moment, seeing as he was currently up to his elbow in poor Daisy's arse.

I had gotten used to doing this with Lewis on my days off, even if it was sometimes not so romantic to say the least (lambing season is not as cute and wonderful as it's made out to be, let me tell you).

You lucky cow, I thought, stroking her. I'd go through having a hand up my jacksie if it meant being able to have children.

Daisy mooed and shuddered as Lewis delved deeper to check the calf's position inside.

'It'll all be over soon,' I whispered in her ear, stroking her on her side as she shifted awkwardly.

Finally, Lewis removed his gloved arm and patted Daisy on the behind before releasing her from the cattle restraint. The poor thing, she must've been delighted it was over.

I just prayed she wouldn't end up in a Big Mac.

'The calf's getting on fine in there; she's in the correct position,' said Lewis to the farmer, who was hovering anxiously nearby. 'Should be a nice trouble-free birth.'

'Great,' said Ted, nodding before escorting us back over to the farmhouse. 'Thanks for coming over on such short notice. Put it on my tab, will you?'

'It's on the house, Ted,' smiled Lewis, scrubbing his hands in the sink by the back door and sanitizing them. As he did so, he smiled over at me, his gorgeous face, strong and open, suggested he had something else on his mind.

We headed back to Lewis's old, battered Land Rover Defender and climbed inside.

'Tara, can I ask you something?' he asked with a peculiar look on his face.

This sounds ominous …

'Umm, sure,' I shrugged. 'I don't see why not.'

'You know that my whole life was turned upside down when my ex cheated on me with my so-called best friend: I was badly hurt, and found it difficult to trust again. But, I … I knew from the moment I met you that there was something there. You're different from anyone else I've ever met.'

I wasn't totally sure where he was going with this.

'I guess what I'm trying to ask—and please don't be offended by this—but what I need to know is … can I trust you?'

I was taken aback. It was a strange question indeed; but I understood why he asked. We'd only ever had one major argument before – the time I caught him going through my phone behind my back. I'd been planning a surprise birthday bash for him, so had been acting shiftily for the week leading up to the party. One day I came out of the bathroom and caught him scrolling through my messages. Things quickly escalated into a full-blown row, but he managed to talk me around, explaining why he'd acted like that. My shifty behaviour had triggered a spate of paranoia on his behalf, caused by memories of his ex's aloof behaviour during the time she'd been having an affair.

All of this meant I couldn't really blame him for asking me whether he could trust me—I certainly had major trust issues of my own after Travis had thrown a hand grenade into my life and scarpered. But even though I was wary at the beginning of our relationship, I never for a moment questioned my own trust in Lewis. I just needed to convince him that I would never betray him like she had.

'Yes, of course you can, Lewis,' I said, looking at him with my most trustworthy eyes.

Right then we both made a promise to each other that we would be honest, open and communicate as much as possible about our feelings.

'So anyway,' he said, giving me his warm smile, 'I've been thinking about a little impromptu getaway. How would you feel about coming to Paris with me next week?'

I had no idea what impromptu meant, but it must be a good thing.

How could any girl refuse Paris?

* * *

The following week we arrived at the enchanting Hôtel de Vendôme in Paris. The art deco hotel sat right in the centre of the French capital, in the vibrant theatre district.

From the moment we walked through the revolving doors, I felt like a character out of *The Great Gatsby*. Shining, patterned marble lined the floors and walls of the atrium, with floor-to-ceiling ionic columns standing alongside a French-polished wooden reception desk that you could see your reflection in. Moulded frames adorned every surface, giving it that grand, iconic 1920s feel.

'Bonjour, j'ai une réservation sous le nom de Lewis Copeland,' Lewis said to the receptionist, casually leaning against the counter.

Sweet Jesus … I knew he could speak a little French, but I'd never heard him actually use it. If I could speak another language, I'd make damn sure everybody knew about it!

I leaned in and tried to figure out what the hell they were saying to each other. All I could focus on was the way the receptionist *umm*ed, and the way she exaggerated her R's, making the language sound even sexier than it already was. There was just no need for it. I didn't need to speak a word of the lingo to know that she was flirting with my man. *Back off, lady, he's mine!*

I comforted myself with the thought that, while I

couldn't impress Lewis with my command of the French language, I had at least made myself look the part. I wore a black and white striped blouse and black culottes, topped off with a long, grey, fitted military coat with brass buttons. Of course, I accessorised with a rouge beret – how could I not? I also considered accessorising with my pretty convincing English-with-a-French-accent (Franglais), but thought better of it.

As Lewis and the overly flirty receptionist finished their exchange, a bellboy in pristine uniform came to collect our bags.

'I've asked for champagne to be sent to the room,' said Lewis, smoothly reverting to English. 'Is that okay?'

I could only nod, stunned by his suaveness. *God, he's so clever, so cultured, and so friggin' sexy! I couldn't wait to rip those clothes off of him. And then he's going to teach me the basics of French so I can compete with these flirtatious, gorgeous women who seem to be everywhere.*

The bellboy escorted us to the grand, oval-shaped elevator. Lewis and I exchanged excited glances as we ascended to the top floor. Even the corridors were extravagant, with those varnished wooden doors that could've been seen on the *Titanic*.

The bellboy finally stopped outside our room. The butterflies in my tummy had gone full speed as he held open the door.

Blown away is an understatement. I'd never seen a hotel room like it—not even on TV.

A display of black and gold gave the room an exquisite Art Deco feel. The plush cream carpet reflected the sunlight from the floor-to-ceiling windows at the end of the room, surrounded by luxurious black and gold curtains. White sculpted geometric architraves surrounded every window and doorframe. Back-lit patterned coving was subtly illuminated with golden light. The queen-size bed was draped in gold satin throws and crisp white sheets. Ornate ceramic lamps with nude female figures produced spheres of soft translucent pink light. Plump black and gold cushions perfectly complemented the black velvet club armchairs.

I didn't feel like a princess; I felt like a queen!

Lewis handed the bellboy a twenty-euro note as I busied myself running around the expansive suite, chasing my own tail in excitement, inspecting every detail between squeals and gasps.

Arms folded and smiling proudly, Lewis observed me prancing around in my child-like excitement.

I bobbed into the marble-adorned bathroom, gasping at its beauty and decadence. Enthralled, I rushed to the large, ornate mirror, gawping at the various lotions and potions lined up on the shelf below. My fingers ran seamlessly onto the golden mixer taps, then onto the glorious his-and-hers bathrobes. I lifted one of the white, fluffy towels and smelled the subtle scent of jasmine.

Exiting the bathroom, I saw Lewis opening the balcony doors and stepping outside. I followed him up the three steps to the double French windows leading to the balcony. Ornate iron railings ringed the balcony, with the roof of the building slanting down on the near side. The balcony was furnished with modern, simple outdoor furniture and choice evergreen plants in cubed pots around the perimeter. I stood next to Lewis as we looked down onto the street below, admiring the beautiful pre-war buildings that housed the infamous cafés, restaurants and shops.

I'd dreamt about this scene since I was a little girl. My breath had been well and truly taken away. Finally, I was in Paris. Finally, I was in the city of love.

'I love it!' I squealed, turning back inside and bounding down the steps.

I tore off my coat and beret and threw them onto one of the leather club chairs before performing a Charleston dance around the room.

Lewis took off his shoes and sprawled out into the middle of the bed. I swiftly joined him, kicking off my boots and playfully wrapping myself up in the satin throw.

'Everything is so, so ...' I didn't quite have the words. He could speak French, and I couldn't even find the words in English. '... sumptuous!' I said, squealing again and thumping my legs in excitement on the bed.

'Wow, look at the detail,' he said, gazing at the elaborate cornice mouldings running around the ceiling.

I, however, had suddenly become distracted by the shiny brass ceiling directly above our bed—a mirror, in other words. I could see a perfect reflection of myself and Lewis, both of us staring up in wonder and curiosity.

'Wait here,' said Lewis, sliding off the bed and opening his holdall. Moments later he returned, holding a delicate white feather. He didn't say anything;

we just sat on the edge of the bed, gazing into each other's eyes. I became aware of the sound of his heavy breathing, and saw intention in his eyes.

A tiny, inaudible squeak escaped my throat as I watched him toying with the feather, slowly rolling the nib back and forth between his thumb and forefinger.

I narrowed my eyes at him. My heart beat hard against the inside of my chest and I could feel my pulse beating through my fingertips.

'Feathers have always had symbolic meanings, for example in ancient tribes,' Lewis said as he laid the feather on the bed between us like an invisible barrier, increasing the tension. 'Some tribes see them as gifts from the sky. Feathers speak to us of freedom, of hope and transcending boundaries.'

Boundaries ... I thought, oh God—please don't tell me he's gonna try that tie-me-up, tie-me-down nonsense! I like the *Fifty Shades* phenomenon as much as the next woman, but nobody actually wants it done to them, do they? Not all that pleasure and pain shite. Fair play to anyone who does, but Christ, no, not for me.

Sitting bolt upright, I nervously glanced around the room at the corners of the bed and the curtain rails.

Nope, nothing there that would even come close to taking my weight.

I couldn't quite work out whether I was excited by this unexpected turn of events, or scared.

May as well get it over and done with, but I will so be putting my foot down if he thinks I've got the energy to shag five times a day.

Screwing up my face and sighing heavily, I held out

my wrists, ready to be handcuffed, gagged and bound, or whatever.

To my surprise, Lewis gently turned my wrists back over and slowly glided the feather down my hands and to my forearms and chest.

Eh? No tied-up wrists? …

Oh no, not bum slapping, please! He wants to leave welts on my arse – I just know it! And I certainly didn't think about packing any Sudocrem.

He moved closer to me, then slowly, agonisingly slowly, he began running the feather up and down my arm, brushing my chiffon blouse lightly and giving me goose bumps. Then he moved down to my ankle and began gliding up the length of my body. I could feel its progress, inch by inch, sending electric shivers down my spine.

I gasped in surprise and pleasure.

Right now he could do anything he damn well wanted. (Apart from blindfold me; I was scared of the dark at the best of times.)

'Can I ask you something?'

'Umm, yes, you may,' I said with a nervous smile, unsure of his intentions.

'You do trust me, don't you?'

I nodded, yet felt an overwhelming shyness flooding through me. Then, with the gentlest of touches, he undid each button of my blouse, still breathing heavily but keeping controlled, performing every movement with slow precision.

His eyes feasted on the black lacy bra he had revealed. Then, in one sudden but soft manoeuvre, he laid me back down and pulled himself on top of me, lifting himself on his muscular arms, so that his face was just inches from mine.

'Tu es belle,' he whispered, inching still closer, 'très, très belle.'

I had no idea what he was saying. It didn't matter. Right then he could have whispered his Tesco shopping list in my ear and I would have fainted with desire.

With one arm keeping him up, he used the other to bring the tantalising feather into action, making its way to my cleavage, tracing a figure of eight around my breasts. My nipples were rock hard underneath the bra that I'd bought especially for the trip.

Then Lewis raised himself to his haunches and peeled off his T-shirt. One look at his defined muscles and toned abs and I just wanted to rip everything off and immediately get him inside me.

We didn't need to say anything. We were communicating by some non-verbal means. We both understood that we were to take our time and savour the experience we were about to share.

I just knew I was about to experience something different, something spiritual.

Smiling, I gently pushed him onto his back and pointed upwards, indicating that he should watch. Sitting beside him on my knees, I began unbuttoning his jeans and slowly unzipped them. Glancing up at the mirror again, I saw him looking back at my reflection with a broad smile.

'C'est incroyable,' he groaned, as I began to pull off his jeans and boxers (awkwardly, which is the only way possible), freeing his love-muscle.

Once he'd been de-clothed and I'd thrown the

restrictive garments aside, we exchanged a knowing smile. Then, pointing my toes, I lifted my leg up over him into straddle position.

'Permettez moi,' he said, sitting up with those strong abs, reaching behind and (masterfully) undoing my bra with a click of his fingers.

He drank me in with his eyes as I slipped off my bra and tossed it on the floor. I gripped his torso, looking straight back at him, fighting off the desire to increase the pace.

Then, in one deft movement, he lifted me up and gently laid me down so he was on top, my legs spread either side of him. He pointed up at the mirror, indicating that it was my turn to watch.

I obliged, watching our reflection as he slowly crawled down my body, his shoulder and back muscles rippling as he went. He took the feather with him, tracing it down my stomach and stopping with his face just above my waist. He leant on both arms to unfasten the clasp of my culottes with his teeth. His subtle facial hair tickled the base of my tummy as he pulled down my zip. Again, he paused for a moment, admiring my matching little black lace knickers.

The desire for him to tear them off and let him have his way with me mounted. I could see in his eyes he felt the same, wanting to rip off my panties. But he stayed strong, willing to prolong the moment for as long as possible. His discipline both impressed me and at the same time drove me wild. I'd heard of this style of lovemaking before, tantric sex, the kind where you achieve authentic love; a deep and passionate connection and some sort of spiritual enlightenment.

Lewis was about to take me on a journey I'd never travelled before.

He pulled my culottes down over my legs and threw them across the room before returning to his favourite spot.

With superhuman patience, he leaned his head in close so I could feel his warm breath on my already soaking-wet lady-garden. I felt like I might bubble over at any moment. With each breath I trembled as prickles of adrenaline flowed through my body.

Just enter me now! I implored with my eyes. *Please.*

Using the feather, Lewis traced along the lines of the lace on my panties, first across my pubic bone, then down between my thighs. I groaned at every touch, unsure how much longer I could carry on without him inside me.

Very slowly, he hooked his fingers over the top of my knickers and began sliding them down. I lifted myself up to help him, watching him watching me, taking in every moment.

As he pulled them off over my feet, a rush of cold air stimulated my lady-garden and I drew my legs together in a moment of shyness. He responded by gently shaking his head and stroking my outer thigh to settle me. Upon meeting each other's gaze, I gave him a look that said 'I am yours' as he prised my legs open and lowered his torso in between. I was giving myself to him utterly and completely; I was opening like a flower and Lewis was the bee, coming to collect the nectar.

But still he didn't enter me.

Using the feather, he caressed my inner thigh and then travelled all the way up, tantalisingly brushing from the bottom of my lady-garden up to my sweet spot. I could feel each and every fibre caressing and stimulating my begging nerve endings, causing me to jolt and spasm in ecstasy. My consciousness travelled up and down my spine, between my heart and my lady-garden, where Lewis loved to play so much. I could feel every sensation in my body; everything was heightened and I felt intoxicated with pleasure.

He wasn't wrong about the feather. No wonder the tribes used them.

With each moment, I grew wilder, gripping his shoulders, urging him on. He dropped the feather, reached up and squeezed my breasts, so I put my hand on his and squeezed them harder—almost to the point where it hurt. The pressure felt amazing and I gasped. I'd gone into autopilot, possessed by the need to feel him inside me. Amid the ecstasy, my eyes involuntarily closed for a moment and I had to force them back open—I had to keep watching the mirror image of us locked in this erotic embrace.

I couldn't hang on any longer for fear of breaking.

'Lewis, I need you,' I begged, as I pulled him up to eye level with demonic strength. He smiled but resisted, crawling down below again.

I groaned gratefully as his warm, nimble fingers began gliding gently up and down my downstairs lips, working me before rising and gyrating on my sweet spot. Wailing loudly at this point, my fingers tangled with his hair, and at times Lewis had to pause so I could stop myself from juddering. Opening my eyes, I noticed that in the reflection I was biting my lip as he brought me close to orgasm with just his fingertip.

The need to come rose within me suddenly, and I was about to pull him upwards to slow him down, when, on cue, he came to a halt, climbed up my body and looked down into my eyes.

We stared at each other in this moment as I felt his shaft slowly enter me. I breathed and panted at the bliss I had been dying for. It was at this moment I felt we were both equally vulnerable and open to each other, and I began to feel a connection with him I had never imagined possible. We were offering ourselves to each other, wholly. It felt amazing as the tension continued to build, now in a different way, fulfilling me from inside.

Watching him in the mirror, I enjoyed the show as his lithe, toned body thrust up and down. Sweat glistened on his shoulders and back as we wrapped around each other.

Our once shattered hearts were coming together to make one.

God knows where the feather ended up. But I didn't care—I was in heaven.

I just hoped our room had soundproof walls.

* * *

'Morning gorgeous. It's time to get up now.' Lewis, already fully dressed in a white V-neck and jeans, gently woke me by stroking my arm. I could smell his enticing aftershave, which made me feel strangely hungry ... for *him*.

My eyes adjusted to see a tray of food lying next to me: strawberries, raspberries, blueberries, banana and mango. And, of course, several obligatory croissants with exquisite-looking fruit preserves (which, let's face it, is just posh *jam*).

I never was a morning person; especially that day, considering we'd stayed up making love into the early hours, so I snuggled back down inside the crisp, gold satin throw.

'But it's too nice in this snuggly bed to go outside.'

Lewis clearly wasn't buying my whimpering excuse. He walked over and opened the curtains to reveal the bright Parisian morning, causing me to squint.

I knew full well there were thousands of sights to see, but the only sight I was really interested in was this man being in bed with me in our hotel room. I just couldn't get enough of his ruffled dark blond hair, tanned skin and the beautifully tattooed body art on his shoulder and arm. And that's before we even get to that wonderful, delicious butt on top of those long, muscular legs, contained in his low-waisted jeans that highlighted the peachiness so perfectly.

Ooof. Despite having seen all this hundreds of times, after last night I felt like he was a new man to me; he gave himself to me completely and I could now see him in all his glory. And, dear lord, he was magnificent.

'*Ooooohhh* ...' I half-yawned, half-moaned, and stretched. 'Come on, just come back to bed—just for a *little* bit. What's the hurry? Don't you want *this*?' I asked, pouting and drawing back the covers slightly to reveal my naked flesh.

'*Hmmm*. You know I do. But ... there's so much we have to do and see.' He gestured to the window, deliberately directing his attention away from me. 'We're only here for a few days. Aren't you all sexed-out after last night?'

I accentuated my pout and shook my head. 'If we're going to perfect the ancient Eastern spiritual practice of Tantra –' *thank you, Google* '– then we must get back to practicing. I hope you don't think last night was a one-off ...' I drew back the covers some more and could see Lewis scanning me out of the corner of his glimmering green eyes.

'Oh, you're such a minx,' he said as he rushed over and dived on top of me, nuzzling his soft stubble into my neck. I held him in place and giggled at the ticklish sensation, raking my hands through his hair. (One good thing about men is that it's obvious when your seduction has succeeded, and judging by the large bulge sticking into me, I was definitely onto a winner).

Ideally, I would have wanted a repeat of last night's tantric performance, but I couldn't find the white feather anywhere.

Taking a strawberry from the breakfast plate, Lewis began playfully teasing the fruit around my lips. Like a hungry newborn chick, I gobbled it up and bit his fingertip seductively. He responded by kissing me passionately, and I suddenly found myself attempting to snog and chew the strawberry simultaneously. Just as I thought I'd got hang of it, the strawberry ended up going down the wrong bloody hole.

Gagging, spluttering and eyes leaking, I subtly regurgitated the offending strawberry into my hand before reaching up and dropping it over the top of the headboard, never to be seen again – all the while trying to snort back up the strawberry-flavoured snot leaking from my nose.

'Now, where were we?' I asked, trying to resume some kind of remotely sexy composure.

Well, if the feather was out of the question then maybe I could be more inventive ... *ahh*.

'Lewis, pass me that honey, *honey* ... I've got an idea,' I said mischievously.

'*Nope*. I know exactly what you're planning! Let's save that for later, I really wanna go out and experience the real Paris—'

'But this *is* the real Paris—'

'From *outside* the bedroom, you devil,' he said, grinning.

With that, he kissed me on the forehead, pulled himself up and tossed me a white robe.

I pulled my well-practiced sad face and jutted out my bottom lip in protest.

'No. I'm not falling for that!' He crossed his arms. 'Up. Now. And I won't take no for an answer.'

'Okay, okay,' I said, sighing, 'I give in—I'll *go!* But at least come and join me in the shower first? I promise I'll be good ...'

'No way, José; I've already had a shower. It's much safer out here – I don't trust you for a minute.'

Tutting playfully, I eased myself onto the edge of the bed. '*Fine*. But you have no idea what you're missing ...'

With that I stood up, dismissing the white robe, and, trailing the gold satin throw over my shoulder provocatively, I glided across the room to my iPhone. *What music to put on? ... Ahh, perfect! This should plant some subliminal seeds so I can get another practice session out of him.* I played Kings of Leon – 'Sex On Fire' – and turned it right up before releasing the throw and, not taking my eyes off of him for a second, dropped it to the carpet and walked naked towards the bathroom, all blasé.

Damn, I can be sexy when I want!

'*Hmmm*,' I heard Lewis mumble as I locked eyes with him, trying to lure him into my lair.

'Where are you going?' he asked.

Kings of Leon are right: I'm so on fire!

'It's too late—you missed your chance, big boy!' I said, quickly closing the door behind me, trying to lock him out. But there wasn't a lock, only a ... *key-card slot.*

... This isn't the bathroom. This is the hallway.

I'm locked in the hallway ...

I'M LOCKED IN THE HALLWAY!

Immediately covering my lady-parts, I thumped on the door with my elbow, the only tool in my arsenal.

'LEWIS! *Lewis!?* ... Open the door!' I knocked hastily, praying no one would walk past or come out of their room at the commotion. In fact, I couldn't even look around due to fear and shame.

'*Ahh* ... room service,' said his muffled and highly amused voice, 'I didn't order any room service—'

'LEWIS! Open the door! *Right now!*'

One hand covering my bum, I pushed myself flat against the door to free up my boob-covering hand so I could thump the door some more.

'*Ohhh!*' said Lewis with an evil little chuckle, 'I remember being in a similar situation myself once; I seem to recall being locked out on our *very first* date and having to wait outside for ten minutes ...'

The absolute asshole ... he had me there. But this was clearly very different.

'LEWIS! You *know* that was different! I WILL KILL YOU—'

'Well, I'm not going to let a potential murderer into the room now, am I?' he said, still laughing. I had to change my strategy if I was going to get back inside so I could wring his neck.

'*Please.* Pleeeease open up—I promise I won't kill you ... Oh *shit*—someone's coming!' (A lie.)

The door swung open, revealing a cowering man shielding himself behind a pillow. He had the biggest grin I'd ever seen. *Time to wipe it off.*

I whipped the door closed behind me and turned slowly towards the culprit, cocking my head, my eyes wide, like an unhinged lunatic.

'No! We're even, now ...' He began backing away, holding the pillow at arm's length. '*Even Stevens*—you're not allowed to get me back!'

'I lied, you idiot!'

'*Ooh* ... I've never seen you this angry before ... It's really ... cute.'

'*Cute?!*' I asked, nodding erratically.

'Umm—I mean—*hot?* ... Really, really hot?'

That was it. I ran at him and pounced, tackling him to the floor, with me landing on top, mounting him and pinning him down. I bit him on the neck as hard as I could, trying to draw blood. *This'll teach you to mess with an Irishwoman!*

He screamed like a little girl, wriggling vigorously to

try and shake me off. But it was no use—I'd latched on like a leach.

Dribbling like a rabid hound, I let go to come up for air. 'Say you're sorry or I'll bleed you dry!'

'Never! More—*more!*' he wailed, to my utter disgust. He certainly didn't look like he was enjoying it. There was already a huge welt on his neck.

This strategy clearly wouldn't work—the masochistic *bastard*. But I knew his weaknesses too well to give up now. See, though Lewis appeared to be a strong, rugged man who apparently enjoyed the pain of being bitten, he was also in fact extremely ticklish.

I went to town on his armpits and around his ribs.

'Okay—okay! Stop—I'm sorry ... *sorry!*'

'And why are you sorry?!'

'Because ... because I should have opened the dooorrr!'

'Say: "I'm a horrible bastard and I will be Tara's slave for the rest of the day." ... Say it!'

Gasping, he muttered, 'I'm ... a horrible, *horrible* bastard. And I will be your slave for the rest of the day. I promise!'

'*Good.* Now take your clothes off and get in the shower with me or I will do some real damage.'

* * *

Only two hours behind schedule, we finally left the hotel and joined the thousands of gawping tourists at Paris's magnificent attractions.

Lewis led the way with an itinerary of the best places to go and which order to go in so we maximised our time. He'd researched the current exhibitions to see, which museums and galleries were best at this time of year, where the architecture and landmarks were most breathtaking—the works. He was a bit of a nerd when it came to this kind of thing.

I, on the other hand, was more interested in the fashion, boutiques, shops, cafés, the lifestyle and the romance. But what really caught my eye were the stunning European women that seemed to overflow from every crack in the pavement. I couldn't help but compare myself; I envied everything about them: their natural beauty, their fashion, their nonchalance, their grace.

Since the dark days, I was in the process of making a new start on life, so I had to take a seriously hard look in the mirror (metaphorically speaking, which was a first for me). I learned that the fake tan, hair extensions, excessive makeup and Botox was perhaps a little excessive and that I didn't really *need* all of it. As a result, I'd dialled all the excessiveness back. Not 100%, of course, perhaps 2%. The hair, for example, is always an exception. And I was still very much partial to a designer handbag. And the nails; no one likes shoddy nails. Some sneaky Botox every now and again, but other than that – almost nothing.

I'd been told to embrace the 'real me': my pale Irish skin; dressing for my age, not my shoe size; not checking my reflection every five minutes, et cetera. These days, when I thought about how I wanted to look, I did it for me, not for some hypothetical Mr Right. I was just lucky that my man, who turned out to be Mr Right anyway, loved the way I looked when I was being real. (Ahem).

My goal was to like myself for who I was, not who I could be. And having Lewis love me for who I was made that difficult journey a little bit easier.

All that said, I still envied the celestial-looking beauties on the streets of Paris. *How could I not?* I couldn't help but try to emulate them.

Lewis wasn't the only one who'd done his homework before coming to Paris. I had YouTubed models walking on a catwalk and had developed a sure-fire method to compete with them.

How to strut like a catwalk model

1. **Attitude:** Stern. Never, ever say your please's or thank you's. Assume everyone is jealous of you and wants to be you.
2. **Face:** Subtle pout, maintaining Resting-Bitch-Face at all times. Don't look at anyone directly (if you must, then look through them, not at them).
3. **Posture:** Hold head high (not in a snotty 'look at me, I've got it all' way—more of a 'I don't hate every single inch of myself' [providing I stick to long-distance mirrors] kind of way). If you need to practice, place several books on your head. (If they slide off, cling-film them and tie under chin like an Easter bonnet.)
4. **Chin:** Lower chin by facing down slightly. If turkey neck is prominent, raise and jut jaw forward (if you need to have a conversation, wear a neck scarf. Otherwise, just don't talk.)
5. **Shoulders:** Shoulders back to the point of nearly being out of their sockets (allows arms to dangle like loose ropes).

6. **Hips:** Hips must be thrust forwards, just about to the point of dislocation (you can't pull your arse in or try and dislocate it to make it smaller, as this pushes your hips out. See 'Feet').
7. **Legs:** At least two feet ahead of your body (the aim is not to allow your upper body to catch up with them). Keep your strides long and controlled by raising and then extending the leg. Think: *exaggerated horsey prance*.
8. **Feet:** Zig-zag feet over and across each other. Toes should be facing inwards slightly. When done quickly, this gives the body that characteristic swing. To prevent walking around in circles, focus on an object at eye level; this will keep you going straight ahead.

Several times Lewis asked me if I was okay when I was attempting to catwalk, but after a while I managed to nail it and got far less looks from people on the street.

Hand in hand, we walked from Place Vendôme, with its picturesque hotels and up-market fashion boutiques (Lewis had to physically drag me out of Dior), down towards the Louvre Museum. The crowds were way too manic for our liking, so we walked on towards the river Seine.

A short walk later we reached Pont des Arts, known as Lovelock Bridge, overlooked by Notre Dame Cathedral. The bridge had gained its colloquial name from couples that, in a symbolic gesture of their unbreakable love, had attached padlocks to the railings and thrown the keys into the river. I'd been dying to see it, possibly more than any other landmark.

As we approached the bridge, I gasped at the sheer number of multi-coloured locks, each one inscribed in tiny letters with a unique, intimate, loving message. I'd read there were close to a million locks attached to this bridge alone — so many that people had started 'love-locking' on other bridges and sites around the city.

One particular lovelock caught my eye. Adorned with a worn red ribbon, the minuscule inscription read, 'My love, my life, my medicine. TC <3 PF 2009'. Another read, 'R. Taylor, my soul mate – RIP'. Many of the other locks were in different languages—French, Spanish and some that I couldn't make out.

I felt like I was absorbing the love from each and every message. It was even more romantic than I'd imagined.

Lewis and I exchanged looks. The late-afternoon sun lit up his smile, and I think he could see I was getting mushier by the second. Strangely quiet, he embraced me from behind, and then together, truly absorbed in the beautiful moment, we watched the sun begin to descend in silence.

'*Ohh* ... it's so romantic. Can we go and get a padlock, *please?*' I asked, spinning around to face him.

'Yes, we can. In fact, I've got a padlock right here,' he said, patting his jacket pocket.

My face lit up like a child being told she's going to the toy store.

'*Really?* Can we put it on now? What should we write? *Gimme, gimme, gimme!*'

'*Wait* ... wait. Not so fast. We can only put it on once I've asked you something,' he said, taking me by the hands and staring deep into my eyes.

'Tara,' he lowered himself down onto one knee.

My heart did a flip. *I* nearly did a flip. *This had better not be a prank!*

OH. MY. GOD. OH. MY. GOD ... OH. MY. GOD!

I automatically dropped down to meet him.

'No, wait—you stand up there for a sec,' he said, smiling and raising me up with his shaky hands.

He took a small red velvet box from his pocket and opened it up to reveal an exquisite, at least two-carat solitaire diamond ring.

'Tara Ryan,' he said clearing his throat, 'would you make me the happiest man in the world and marry me?'

I'm not dreaming, right? He did actually just propose, and meant it?

'Ye-yes, I will!' I beamed, nodding uncontrollably, and then promptly burst into tears.

A smile exploded across his face that could've been the length of the bridge. He took my hand, slipped the ring on my trembling finger, and then kissed it.

Lewis jumped up and embraced me, squeezing me like he'd never let go. Our lips collided, as tears spilled from our eyes.

Applause, cheering and camera flashes erupted around us.

'Thank you for loving me,' he whispered. Lewis uncurled one arm and reached into his pocket, took out his iPod and placed one headphone in each of our ears. He clicked play and the gentle melody of 'Je T'aime Moi Non Plus' by Jane Birkin & Serge Gainsbourg—quite possibly the most romantic song ever created—filled my head. This man was faultless; he'd even remembered my favourite song!

Locked together, we began to sway to the dulcet tones, dancing nose to nose. I didn't even realise I was still crying until Lewis reached up and wiped away my tears with his thumb. Feeling completely safe in his arms, I closed my eyes; everything felt just as it should be, for the very first time in my entire life.

Although there were thousands of people staring in our direction, for us it felt like the most intimate scene of our lives. There was just us and it was perfect. If I had died at that moment (although perhaps not before I'd showed off my rock-of-engagement ring), I would truly know I was the happiest woman in the whole wide world.

Eventually, the song ended and Lewis whispered in my ear, 'So, according to tradition, we need to put a lock on the railings and throw the keys into the river.' He produced the padlock from his jacket pocket along with a marker pen.

There wouldn't have been enough space in a notebook to write what I wanted to say, let alone enough space on a padlock. Instead, we spliced our names; simply writing, 'Lewara 4ever' (the name we would later give to our home).

We somehow managed to find a gap at the bottom of the railing, and together we secured our padlock to remain forevermore.

'Okay, make a wish!' he said, holding the keys in both our hands.

I just want to spend the rest of my time on this earth with this man. Nothing more.

Then, jointly holding out the keys, we dropped them

into the water, completing the ritual of a million lovers.

'So, what did you wish for?' he asked, holding me close.

'If I tell you, it won't come true—will it, *fiancé*?'

'Well, I'll tell you what I wished for ...' said Lewis. 'A nice burger. I'm starving.'

Chapter 7

Crowds of people began to enter the bar downstairs, snapping me out of my Parisian daydream.

Now the shock of seeing Travis had begun to wear off, I knew what I truly wanted—and it was Lewis. He was my Mr Right, and that was that.

But if I wanted my fairy-tale life with Lewis to go according to plan, it meant ridding my life of Travis once and for all. The only problem left was figuring out how exactly I would achieve that.

Of course, I could've just flaked out and not showed up to the hotel to meet Travis; but then he did say he would keep turning up at the salon until I agreed to meet with him privately. I couldn't have a repeat of today's episode, not for a lifetime ... the fecker was forcing my hand and he knew it!

I'd tried just about everything else to try and shake him. I'd tried talking about it. I'd tried not talking about it. I'd tried to *just give it time*, and, well, they say time is a healer, but I think that only applies to people who can stop picking at their scabs. I'd tried praying—my prayer was obviously lost in the post or something. I'd tried numbing the memories with sleeping pills, but even overdosing didn't solve my problem. I'd tried to 'just get over it' (whatever that means), but I just ended up burying my head in the sand. I'd tried therapy. I'd tried getting over him by getting on top of someone else—in fact I'd taken it so far as to get engaged to the guy I'd got on top of—and it *still* hadn't worked.

None of it worked. And I couldn't go on with my life always seeking out new solutions to get over him. Without hearing Travis's side of the story, without closure, I'd never be able to give my all to Lewis. The only way to get the cure I needed so badly was to open up Pandora's box and face the demons inside. I owed it to Lewis, myself, and our future together.

But I couldn't just stroll into the dragon's lair unarmed; I needed a plan, a military-style operation, clinical and brutal. There was no room for failure—if I ballsed this up, it could end in a disaster.

Pulling out my diary from my handbag, I decided to jot down my mission:

OPERATION: CLOSURE

OBJECTIVE 1: GET ANSWERS

Be sure to threaten him before asking anything: 'If I don't get the whole truth and nothing but the truth—so help me—I will give Siobhan your home address,' etc.

- What is this other side of the story you keep banging on about?! Why did you dump me so brutally? (It had better be a seriously good excuse—I'm talking Hollywood movie script good.)
- Why her? Wasn't I good enough? Was it because she was younger? More beautiful? Funnier? Better in bed? I thought men were supposed to love blondes!?
- Why didn't you just TALK to me and explain? I could be over things by now!

OBJECTIVE 2: GET REVENGE

Make sure I look irresistibly hot to inflict raging jealousy, then do the following:

- Turn on the waterworks to make him feel terrible about his bastard-like ways.
- Mention the addiction I developed because of his actions ... I nearly died from an overdose! Then I nearly lost my salon! And I nearly lost my friends! And my family! (Not really the last one, but say it anyway.)
- +5 points: Rub my happiness with Lewis in his face. (Dramatically reveal engagement ring?)
- +10 points: Make a big scene. Pour a drink over his head and/or scream at him—men can't handle public embarrassment.
- +50 points: Make him cry.
- +100 bonus points: Make him beg for forgiveness in front of everyone.

- Finally, when he's begging for mercy, forgive him, but tell him you never want to hear from him ever again.

OBJECTIVE 3: GET OUT

Escape without being captured by the enemy.

Ensure to bring pepper spray in case he tries to kiss/touch me inappropriately.

~~Have James and Siobhan waiting in a van outside, just in case. Travis is unpredictable and not to be trusted, after all.~~

I crossed out the last point; Siobhan and James would probably kill me first if they knew I was meeting him. Plus, I had to stand on my own two feet now—even if those feet were currently shaking in their boots.

I can do this!

It won't be that hard – I just have to stick to my plan. The prospect of putting an end to my situation actually made me feel excited and relieved—triumphant, even—even if it was perhaps a bit premature.

Unfortunately, I realised my mission would have to remain top secret, to the extent that even my closest allies wouldn't be allowed to know about it … probably ever. The reason being: I instinctively knew that by trying to protect me, my friends and family would actually be a hindrance to my cause. If they had their way, there'd be no chance I'd be meeting Travis whatsoever, indirectly sentencing me to a lifetime in the land of limbo. They just wouldn't understand that I had no other option. They weren't the ones being bombarded with messages, or having their subconscious invaded by him in their dreams, or experiencing his sudden appearances at their Hair & Beauty salon.

This was the third time he'd entered my life. The first time, I'd fallen for him. The second, a year ago, I managed to ignore him. And now, third time lucky, I would put this all to bed and move on. Hopefully.

My phone rang in my bag—I could tell instantly by the ringtone it was Lewis.

About bloody time!

'Well, hello, stranger,' I said, adjusting my tone in the hope of sounding a little less conspicuous.

'Hi, baby, just wanted to let you know that I've arrived safe and I'm with the boys now—and we haven't even been attacked by bears yet.'

'*Haha*. You're hilarious,' I said, swallowing down the lump in my throat. 'I've been worried out of my mind.'

'Sorry, it's been a long day's ride. Plus, I've had to sneak away from the boys to make this call. If they knew I was speaking to you I'd have to drink a pint out of Darren's shoe; and as much as I love you, baby, it's just not worth it. Darren's feet are ming—'

'Lewis, I really need to speak with you about ... about ...' I squeezed my eyes tight, desperate for him to pick up that something was wrong. (He didn't.) '... About whether you remembered to pack your thermal socks?'

What a shitey excuse!

'Yes, baby, I have. I'm fine, honestly.'

'Erm … I'm just worried about you, that's all.'

'You've got nothing to worry about. I'm safe and my tootsies are perfectly warm. Look – I really don't want suffer the consequences of getting caught calling you, so I'm afraid I'm gonna have to love you and leave you—'

'No—please don't go. Stay on the phone a bit longer, I need to hear your voice.'

'Tara … what's up?'

'Oh, erm …' *I've arranged to meet up with my ex and I'm shitting my pants. Got any advice?* '… Nothing.'

'O … kay, well like I said, babe, I won't be able to call you again so just remember to enjoy yourself while I'm away. Enjoy Leonardo's birthday – make sure you let your hair down. You deserve it.'

Oh God, if only he knew.

'I will. Enjoy your stag-do, and please be safe.'

'Bye, gorgeous.'

'Bye.' As I hung up, feeling uncomfortable, a noisy commotion began to filter downstairs, bringing in a new, excited atmosphere into the room. Within moments, Siobhan had trotted down the stairs and shrieked like a banshee, flying into the booth and tackling me into the leather. The Glamma Pussies followed, practically mobbing me at my once peaceful table. Within moments, I found myself covered in party popper debris and confetti. I forced a smile at seeing a half-cut Leonardo wearing an oversized 'BIRTHDAY BOY' badge.

Let the madness commence.

James minced over with a tray of tequila shots,

accompanied with a saltshaker and an array of lemon wedges.

'Aww, thanks, James, you shouldn't have,' I said, impressed by his generosity.

'Don't worry, darling, it's on the Glamma-Puss account.'

'But … there isn't a Glamma-Puss account?'

'Well, there is now!' he said, throwing his head back with a hearty laugh.

I sighed. *Tomorrow will be a slow day in the salon, no doubt.*

'Oh, help yourselves, guys,' I said, pointing out the bottle of Prosecco I'd bought earlier.

'Ahh, you're the best.' Siobhan leaned over and poured herself a glass. '*Ahh*, there's only a li'l dribble left,' she moaned, slamming the bottle down. 'We'll be gettin' ourselves another few of those bottles ordered, won't we, Tara?'

How can that be? She's only poured herself a quarter glass … I haven't drunk that much, have I?

If I have, *it didn't even touch the sides—no wonder it's on sale!*

Out of embarrassment, I immediately got up and waved at Marco.

'Another bottle of Prosecco, please,' I asked, hoping no one would consider where the contents of the first bottle had gone. 'This one seems to have evaporated.'

'Yes, it is very 'ot in here isn't it, Madame?' he said with a cheeky wink. If I wasn't so pleasantly merry, or so charmed, I'm sure I would've been offended.

James herded everyone around the table for more tequila slammers. Once everyone had an appropriate salt and lemon wedge on hand, Suyin proposed a toast:

'To my wonderful 'usband, a man I'm proud to share extraordinary experiences with …' she announced, winking at Leonardo not-so-subtly.

James immediately sucked in his cheeks and dashed an I-told-you-so glance around the group.

'… Happy thirty-fifth birthday!' continued Suyin, as everyone cheered and downed their raised glasses.

It was safe to say tequila and I weren't the best of friends, but then I always promised myself I wouldn't become that boring boss; so, begrudgingly, down it went.

The venue quickly filled out with the suit-wearing pen pushers and beard-wearing too-cool-for-schoolers that seemed to make up the vast majority of Covent Garden's population.

More of Leonardo's friends showed up. I didn't recognise most of the thirty-odd people there for his birthday, the majority of whom were good-looking, ageing Italians and their gorgeous younger wives and girlfriends. Many of the WAGs had been shooting daggers at Siobhan—and quite rightly: she had been doing her best to peel the stallions away from their mares.

'Have you given Leo his present yet, sweetie?' asked James, sipping his own personal bottle of rosé through a double straw he'd connected together.

'*Ohh,* no I haven't yet. Thankshh for reminding me, I nearly forgot. Letshh go and give it to him now,' I said, pulling him away.

I handed Leonardo the perfectly wrapped box containing the silver pocket watch, which we had engraved with *'Happy birthday from your Glamma Pussies'*. He looked over the moon, attaching it to his waistcoat for all to see. It looked like it was made for him. He then proceeded to drunkenly introduce me to the slurry of his lookalike friends, whose otherwise exotic names unfortunately went in one ear and out the other. After that, I just ended up calling them all *Giuseppe*, and quite rightly allowed myself to be corrected.

After chin-wagging and trying to ignore the looming task ahead of me, I allowed myself just one more drink before I would politely excuse myself to go home due to a migraine (which was at least partly true). But between James and Siobhan's pestering, over the course of the next half hour I somehow had another shot of tequila and two more flutes of Prosecco. My headache had abated and I'd even forgotten about Travis. I mingled with anyone and everyone, telling jokes and being the life and soul of the party, noting with satisfaction how witty and funny I could be, even at a time of such extreme stress.

After a while, I began to feel rather light-headed, so decided to sit down and chat with Jackie and Camilla. My waiter, Marco, approached me.

'Madame, jew are a lovely lady and so I 'ave brought you dis one on de house,' he said, placing down a saucer of oil, olives, and a basket of bread.

'*Oh*, Mario! Thanksss you so, sooo much, that's so, so kind.' I immediately started piling it in, demolishing the lot before anyone else could get their greedy little mitts on it.

Feeling slightly better, I saw James in the process of

buying another round of shots, so I took that as my cue to leave. I quickly made my excuses and fought off any resistance with the old migraine chestnut, explaining that I wouldn't be much fun if I carried on.

I went to the bar and paid off both my tab and the supposed Glamma-Puss tab, as well as leaving Marco a £20 tip.

'Are jew sure, Madame? It's very generous of jew.'

'Keep the change,' I said, petting him like a cat. 'Mario, you are a good, kind young man. You will make a woman proud some day.'

'Eh, thank jew, Madame. I wish my wife thought the same as jew. Jew are a very nice lady as well. And, ehh, just so jew know, my name is Marco,' he said with another wink.

'Oh, sooo sorry! I leaned forward to pat him on the shoulder again, but misjudged and missed completely, ending up comfortingly tapping the wall behind him.

'Be safe, huh?' he called after me as I determinedly made my way to the door.

My mingling with the crowd downstairs had boosted my confidence, and I felt newly invigorated to give Travis a piece of my mind. He'd regret the day he ever crossed Tara Ryan!

I pulled on my jacket and precariously headed towards the exit before spilling out onto the street. I was surprised to see that it was getting dark already. The cold night air hit me hard, and I suddenly felt rather off balance as I fumbled around, trying to put my leather gloves on.

Drawing myself up to my full height, I turned towards the road. The effect of determined-woman-about-to-fight-her-corner was only partly spoiled by my somewhat ungraceful staggering on the uneven pavement.

'Feckin' cobblestones,' I muttered. 'Taxi!'

Within seconds, I'd launched myself into the back of a black cab.

I looked at my watch—*8.45. Am I late? What time did he say to meet?*

Ahh, feck it either way. The fecker can wait!

'Take me to ... *oh, shit.* Umm, it's a really fancy hotel—the *Long* ... the *Lung* ... the *Langham!* Take me to the Langham Hotel, please Mr Taxi Driver!' I said, doing my utmost to sound as sober as possible. (I'd had my share of being refused by taxi drivers; mainly when out with Siobhan).

'Whoa!' I squealed. I was barely in my seat when he put his foot to the floor. 'Excuuuuse me, Mr Taxi Man. I haven't even put my belt-seat on yet! Safety first, pleeeease!'

As I scrabbled to find the end of the belt, I looked up and caught him rolling his eyes in the rear view mirror. It was then that I spotted a familiar face out of the corner of my eye and completely forgot about strapping myself in. On the inside of the taxi was an advertisement for a West End show about Henry VIII, showing a portrait of him.

Heyyy, I remember you ... you helped me sleep in my History classes at school!

You, sir, were quite the womaniser—probably even worse than Travis! In fact, seeing as how Travis and Henry were level pegging in the league of Biggest Bastards of All Time, I decided I'd get some target practice on ol' Henners before I laid into Travis later.

'Firrrstly, Henry, you had like eight or was it nine wives? That's just plain greedy. It's no wonder you became sooo round after so many wedding cakes. Just look at those jowls! Your head looks like a butternut squash with private-part hairs glued on. And someone could've most certainlyyy done with a bit more time on the treadmill—'

'Lady ... are you talking to me?' the driver asked.

'No. Nooo. I'm just shootin' the breeze with old Henry here.

'Anyway, Henners ... your poor deluded wives. Poor show. Reeeaaally poor show, Henry. I happen to think you were a *brute* of a man. A total *brute* in fact.'

I furrowed my brows, looking more accusingly at him. 'It wasn't a good look, Henry, was it? I mean, if I'm honest, you didn't exactly do yourself any favours, did you? Those poor women having to endure sexy-times with you prancing around in stuff like that, and there you were thinking you were giving it 'large' with a paper tutu round your neck, swamped in all that crushed velvet mal ... mal ... arkey.'

I blinked rapidly, assessing him further.

'... And those poncey, brightly coloured, ill-matched tights,' I huffed, screwing my face up. 'What on earth was that all about, Henry?!'

'You know, you're lucky you saw any action at all,' I concluded loudly, poking his picture with an accusing finger. 'All the thanks your poor wives ever got was heartache or their heads chopped off!'

That'll show him, I thought. I'll remember the bit about the butternut squash. I felt the veins in my neck constrict and an ominous burning sensation began to build deep inside. I clutched my chest as the vat of alcohol I'd consumed sloshed up, then down, then backwards and then forwards.

Anyway, I felt like I'd got a load off my chest already, but there was plenty more where that came from. I needed to keep talking, so decided to ask the driver about his life story. I moved forwards and knelt on the floor in front of the exchange hole.

Poking my mouth through the Perspex hole, I said, 'Mr Taxi Man, what's your real name?'

'What? What are you doing? Lady you need to sit down and put your belt on!'

'*Whoa,* excuuushe me, Mister Taxi Man, for trying to be friendly,' I said, scrambling to my seat.

'… Where is the sheat-belt, I mean … *ahh,* there you are!' I wrenched the strap across, but it jammed halfway down. So I yanked down harder, but it snapped back, smartly reeling itself back into its fixture. Grumbling, I tried again and managed to pull it all the way across, but I couldn't get it to clip in, despite jamming it into every socket it would reach.

I will not be beaten by a belt-seat. I mean, seat-belt.

'Hey, Mister Taxi Man! [Hiccup] this's … this's *broken*—look! I can't get it in … [hiccup].'

'Lady, the belt is not broken. You're just drunk.'

'I am not drunk! How very [hiccup] dare you!'

'Lady, I see drunk people like you all day. You need to put your belt on or I'll have to pull over and ask you to get out.'

'*Gahh!* I. Am. Trying! Hang on …'

This guy had better not mess with me, I'm ready to

fight anyone or anything—especially this feckin' belt-seat!

ARGH, SEAT-BELT.

Suddenly, the diver turned a sharp left, the momentum throwing me to the right, causing me to land on my side.

'*Oww.*'

Then I saw some imbecile running out into the road. The driver slammed on the breaks, causing me to shunt forward onto the floor.

'*Owwwww.*'

'Christ,' I whimpered, flat on my back with my legs flung out wildly. 'Take it easy, Mr Taxi Man! That was *so* uncalled for.'

'Lady, lady,' the taxi driver barked, 'you must sit on the seats provided and please put your belt on. Or I *will* pull this cab over right here.'

'*Oh no—please*, don't do that,' I mumbled sarcastically, 'I'm having *sooo* much fun being your crash-test dummy here.'

By then, I was glad I'd had a couple of drinks; I'd heard you don't break as many bones if you're drunk.

I pulled down one of those foldable seats opposite and heaved myself up, but my hand slipped off and the chair flipped back up and the frame smashed me straight in the temple.

'Lady ... wake up. Wake up! We are here at your posh hotel,' said the driver, knocking on the Perspex.

'*Owww* ... my head [hiccup].'

'That will be £20,' he said, flicking on the interior light.

I clambered up onto the back seat and tried to

steady myself. I felt like I'd been out for hours. My migraine had returned, now twice as intense and joined by a new lump on the side of my head. *Great.* I popped two more painkillers from Leonardo, hoping they'd straighten me out before I saw Travis.

'Here's a twenty, keep the change!'

I gave what I hoped was my best winning smile but was immediately distracted by a very dapper doorman who leapt forward and swung open the cab door sporting a black top hat, grey long-tailed tux and a charming, welcoming smile.

'Good evening, Madame. Welcome to the Langham Hotel,' he said in a prim, deep voice. 'Do you have any luggage I can take for you?'

'Umm, yes please—*no*, sorry, I'm ... not staying, actually,' I said, fumbling around for my handbag.

The doorman tipped his hat and offered me his hand, which was clothed in pristine white bellman gloves. Clinging on to him for dear life, I clambered out on shaky legs.

I looked up at the majestic, sand-coloured Victorian hotel in front of me, with its enormous entrance. *So, this is the Langham.* I'd forgotten how wealthy Travis was to be able to afford to stay in such places. I couldn't fight off a flashback of the time he and I stayed at Castle Contarf in Dublin, and how amazing the experience was.

Stop! You can't just go around reminiscing about the good times! You're here for one reason, and one reason only!

I felt the doorman shift uncomfortably and realised I was clinging on tightly to his arm. I eased mine away and drew myself up. 'I'll take it from here; thank you, Mister Doorman. Good job,' I said, petting him in thanks.

I took a sobering breath of cool evening air and steadied myself. Then I smoothed down my hair, brushed the actual grit off my shoulder and adjusted my black leather gloves. At the back of my mind I had a plan to keep my gloves on until a suitable moment, before whipping them off to reveal Lewis's gargantuan rock on my finger.

I took a tentative step forward, staggered left, then precariously shuffled more to the right. Feeling weak-kneed, I pressed on, bumbling up the grand marble-columned steps towards the foyer. It felt as if I was climbing a mountain.

When I reached the summit, I immediately had the next challenge to contend with: revolving doors. Just push and walk, Tara, I muttered to myself. Push and walk. So, determined was I to get this right that I pushed and walked and walked, managing to do two entire circuits of the doors before emerging, breathless, into the grand foyer. I suppose I was lucky I didn't end up back outside.

I emerged from the door flustered, but more determined than ever.

I couldn't help but gaze in awe at the glimmering white marble pillars, the elegant staircases and the enormous vases of pale pink roses.

Very fancy-pants indeed. It's a shame I'm not here on more romantic terms; Lewis would love this place. Instead, here I am rendezvousing with my ex because … oh, I don't even know anymore!

The thought that at any minute I would see the

infamous bastard Travis Coleman sent my confidence back into hiding. My heart was pounding in my chest, my brain darting back and forth into a million different locations and scenarios, the combination of which caused serious gridlock in my already pickled synapses.

What now? What will I do when I actually see him? Should I just abandon ship?

Then I remembered that I had *in fact planned* for this. Sort of. I pulled out my diary to the page with my MISSION CLOSURE plan. I gave it a quick scan and familiarised myself. *Well done, Tara. You're smarter than you look.*

The astute receptionist directed me to Palm Court, the hotel's famous tearoom, where Travis said he'd be waiting. I looked at my watch—*9.25. He had better still be there after all I've gone through …*

For a moment, I stopped outside the hand-cast, jewel-encrusted iron doors leading into Palm Court—the lid of Pandora's box, the entrance to the dragon's lair.

You can still walk away—just turn around and go back the way you came. You can do this another time when you've got a watertight strategy. Meet him in the daytime in McDonald's or something?

Return to your new, better life, and no one—least of all Lewis—will be any the wiser.

But the other part of me fought back. I looked down at my gloved hands and realised that now was not the time for games; this was about the truth. I gracefully peeled the gloves off and marched forward, head held high.

It's now or never. You've got to get your closure, or you'll never get out of the land of limbo. You'll never be free.

Chapter 8

I closed my eyes and walked forward three steps. Then I opened them.

I immediately spotted him. It was impossible not to. There he was, all six foot plus of him. Still polished, still muscle-bound, still God damn beautiful. My mind seized just at the sight of him; then my legs seized seconds after that.

I REFUSE TO MELT, GOD DAMN IT!!!

I will not melt!

I'm melting …

I melted.

I raised my chin, gulping, as I began to assess every inch of him, top to delicious bottom, at a thousand miles per hour. He hadn't changed much: his broad shoulders perfectly set off the lines of his tapered navy-blue suit jacket and blue suede shoes, and you could still chisel granite with that jaw. But in the year and a half since I'd last seen him, there were some subtle differences. His dark brown hair was longer. His skin had a fresh sun-kissed glow, like he'd just come back from somewhere exotic. And he looked like he'd aged slightly —but, infuriatingly, the extra laughter lines actually made him more attractive. Laughter lines indeed! Wanker!

Typical. He was sitting at a table, texting on his phone; probably leading five other poor women astray.

I must've stared for too long, because the waiter near Travis began looking at me with creased eyebrows. The waiter then nodded in my direction, and Travis turned to face me.

Definitely too late to back out now.

His chocolate eyes twinkled, locking onto me and freezing me to the spot. For a moment that felt like an hour, we stared at one another, not saying a word. If my heart hadn't already sunk I'm sure it would have stopped right there.

'Well ... hello, you.' Travis's deep, gravelly voice cut straight through me as he rose to his feet. 'You look better than ever.'

I smiled courteously as he leaned in to kiss me on the cheek.

Smack. I slapped him with a clean left hand. It was automatic; I don't know what came over me. The room's ambience collapsed into shocked silence. Though my hand stung from the impact, I felt the most incredible sense of satisfaction, like I'd scratched an itch that'd been driving me crazy for the last year and a half. My inner cheerleader did an excited happy clap. [+10 points for 'making a scene'.]

Travis took a deep, nostril-flaring breath, his

expression lying somewhere between shocked and amused. Emboldened by adrenaline, I fixed him with an icy deadpan stare—even if I was secretly readying myself to leg it at any moment.

Thankfully, his eyes dropped away from our gaze and he clutched his face.

'I guess I deserve that,' he said, breaking the silence and, quite literally, taking it on the chin (which was probably heavily insured anyway).

Waving off the concerned-looking staff, he addressed our audience in his rugby coach voice. 'It's okay everyone, just a lover's tiff is all—'

'You are *not* my lover!' I scolded, loud enough for our audience to hear. 'He's just a tosspot I *used* to know!'

Red-faced, he crumpled his lips and conceded to my violent demonstration with a nod.

'Feel better now?' he asked, caressing the red handprint on his face and giving me a look of *what did you do that for?* 'You really caught me with that ring of yours,' he said, pointing out my sparkly engagement ring. 'I'll assume that's not just for show.'

'You assume corrrect … I'm engaged,' I said, waving my ringed hand with a flourish so he could see it clear as day.

I watched him shrink as he absorbed the information, enjoying seeing his Adam's apple quiver as he tried to swallow.

Recovering quickly, he forced a smile. 'Congratulations.'

I gave a curt nod, but the adrenaline was causing me to shake.

'Please ... let's sit and talk for a while and if you feel like whacking me again, we can take it upstairs.'

I ignored his childishness and obliged, unsteadily wobbling over to the other chair at his table.

Sit down before you fall down, Tara.

Sitting down, I misjudged how low the chair was and the bloody thing nearly swallowed me whole.

Ignoring Travis's smirk, I eventually shifted to the edge of the chair, positioning myself as if I could just up and leave at any moment (which I absolutely would, if I got any more cheek out of him).

'For a while there I wasn't sure you were going to turn up,' he said, smiling and stroking his cheek. 'Even though you've already clattered me, I'm glad you came. But I do think we need to work on your accuracy.'

I ignored his attempt at a joke with a vacant expression, resting-bitch-face fixed firmly in place, trying my utmost to look through him and not at his handsome physique.

'Have you had dinner?' he asked.

'Yes.' *(If a couple of slices of bread counts.)*

'Okay, well, I have too. What do you want to drink?'

'Nothing.'

'So ... how have you been?'

'I ...' I had to stop myself. I needed to stay sharp and not engage him on that level. *Get in and get out, Tara.* 'I'm not here for pleasannntries, Travis; I'm just stopping by as a courtesy call. You can say your piece and I can say mine, and then I'm outta here. So say what you have to say and get on with it.'

Boom! James would've been proud.

'Okay, fine,' he said. 'So, I've asked you to come because—'

'Actually, you know what? I'm gonna say *my* bit first.'

'*Errr* … but don't you want to know what I have to say?'

'*No*. Not yet. I'm going to go fist, err … I mean first, because, well, I've got a lot to get off my chest and don't wanna fall asleep hearing your … feckin' *boring* excuses.'

He looked stunned.

'Tara, are you all ri—'

'*No*. I'm not all right. I'm sick of all your shit. You need to shut the feck-up for one minute and just bloody listen!'

'Okay, okay. I'm listening.'

But now I'd built it up so much, I actually didn't know where to start. But then I remembered.

'First, you—you—you invade my heart, then you invade my bottom—*without* asking first.'

'*Hmm*. I like to call it *earthy sex*,' he said with a smile, 'I knew you would like it.'

'No, actually, I didn't!' I said, blushing, unable to look him in the eye.

'I think you did. You didn't complain at the time …'

No, I didn't complain at the time, but that isn't the point!

'Look, I didn't come here to discuss my—'

'—Anal preferences?'

The audacity!

'*Right*. That is it. I am *leaving!*' I said, standing up but wobbling off balance.

'No, please wait. I'm sorry. I was only joking. I'm just trying to break the ice is all—it's my nerves. Please, sit down. I'll be good.'

I bore down on him, giving him my best ice-queen glare, raising a threatening finger at him to let him know I meant business.

He put his hands up in submission, so I slowly sat back down and lowered the finger. He really was pushing his luck.

'No more games. If I hear one more bit of cheek, I'm gone,' I said. Then, in an attempt to provoke him, I lunged forward, grabbed his glass of water and downed the whole thing in a show of defiance.

'Eughh …' I coughed and spluttered on what tasted like paint stripper. 'This isn't water!'

He poorly attempted to hold back a laugh. 'No, it *was* a triple grappa on the rocks. I needed some Dutch courage because I was nervous about meeting you again … I don't know whether I'm impressed or concerned.'

Travis handed me a napkin and waved down a waiter.

'Can we get some water for the lady, one coffee and another grappa?'

'Certainly, Mr Coleman. I'll be right back.'

I continued my rant. 'You—you just think you're God's gift to women, don't you? No, you know what? It's worse than that. You think you *are* God, playing with people's lives like they're toys. And when you get bored, you just toss them away like a … an insignificant piece of worthless fluff!'

'[Tutting] Tara, I would never, ever treat you like an

insignificant piece of worthless fluff.'

'Yeah, well, you *did*. And the worsssht … the worst thing is that I—*I let you!*' I shook my head at my own stupidity, raising my hands in disbelief.

'Well, I'm sorry that you feel like that, but if you'd just let me explain—'

'You've just got no idea. No idea how much devastation you caused.'

'I think you're getting a bit over-emotional here. You're blowing things out of proportion.'

My jaw jutted forward mechanically in rage.

'Am I? *Really?* I haven't even started yet! I'm not gonna sugar-coat this for you, so shut the feck up and jussht, just bloody listen for a minnnute!'

'Okay … the stage is yours,' he said, shifting back in his chair and taking a sip of his drink, 'I'm all ears.'

Hold it together, Tara. My mouth started to do that thing where it foams at the corners. *Looking like you have rabies is most unattractive.*

Foaming or not foaming, I had stuff I needed to say.

'Like I said, I refussse to sugar-goat this for you. Look, I was, albeit out of my mind, so committed to you, I was sooo in love with you, and you couldn't give a shit! You didn't even have the decensssshy to message me back most of the time. I waited for weeks on end to hear back from you—I didn't even know if you were dead or alive.

'You used and abused me—you only contacted me when you wanted to have your wicked way, and then you'd leave, with barely a goodbye.

'And then you told me you loved me, just so you could string me along some more. You knew ecksactly how I felt about you. And then, after everything, you just tell me, "We're over, never ever contact me again." What the fuck issh wrong with you?!'

'Please, keep your voice down. Look, you don't know the whole story, that's why I asked you here to explain—'

'Ahh, look, I don't even care anymore about your shhtupid sshtory,' I said, turning my nose up at him and slumping back in the chair, waving my hands around to demonstrate.

'I can't believe I spent three grand on a fur coat to trying to impress you. I even went to Dublin to win you back, practically naked, wearing odd shoes. Yep, odd shoes! Then it turned out that I was actually on the same flight as that teeenager you knocked up—'

'I told you already – the baby isn't mine. Anyway, she was hardly a teenager; she's twenty-four.'

'Huh! So you say. I lost my mind, seeing you two walking away together. I cut up that fur coat—my mum thought I'd feckin' murdered a cat when she found the sleeve off of it.'

The waitress returned with our drinks. Before she'd even put down the tray, I grabbed the bottle of water and noisily glugged it down. Giving me a strange glance, the waitress put down my coffee and Travis's grappa, then turned on her heel.

Once the waitress was out of earshot, I restarted my rant. 'You played God with my life, my heart and soul, then tossed me away. You had absolutely no care in the world for how I felt or what I was going through.'

My heart hammered at the injustice. I had to take a deep breath to pace myself and I was beginning to feel more than a bit woozy. Giving Travis the lecture of his life didn't help.

'Tara, that's not true. If you would just listen—'

'Shh-shh-shh-shh-shh,' I hushed him, holding my index finger to my mouth and shaking my head.

His eyes widened and his eyebrows rose up like drawbridges. 'I've never seen you like this before ... how much have you drunk? Are you on drugs?'

Ignoring him, I continued: 'I nearly lost *everything* because of you. I lost my mind, my business nearly collapsed—I was so depressed that I went into hiding. I lost friends because everyone thought I'd lossht the plot. You know what? I was so fucked up—I actually got addicted to sshleeping tablets—they were just so good at letting me forget about you and your sshtupid, stoopid face. Then, one day, I decided I didn't want to wake up any more and I overdosed. I nearly died!'

For the first time, he actually looked disturbed, sitting there with his fist on his mouth, his eyes flickering around me, taking everything in. Clearly, he didn't know what to say, so I continued.

'And now after all this time you just waltz in asking for forgiveness so that you can go and ruin everything all over again, now that I'm happy with my life? This time—this time, it's you who's lost hish mind.'

Words failed me as my throat clogged up and my eyes brimmed with tears.

He looked down at the floor, frowning. The creases in his forehead finally showed now that his eyebrows had contracted. He looked like he was in pain. 'Tara, I ... I'm sorry.'

'Pardon?' I asked, plunging my fist across the table,

mimicking holding a microphone. 'Can you repeat that please? Just for the record.'

'I'm sorry I treated you the way I did.'

I didn't know what to say to that, as I was far too busy trying to catch my breath and wiping the foam away from the corners of my mouth.

His apology had extinguished the fire I was using to grill him. But then, I decided that there was more than one way he could be sorry. I decided there was more than one way to hurt him and get my revenge.

'Well ... good. You should be shorry. You should be ashlamed of yourshelf. Do you know what? I think that might be the first time in your life you've ever apologised for anything, so I think this calls for a celebration, don't you?'

'Erm, I guess so ...'

I picked up the menu and scanned for the most expensive item. *A £1,000 bottle of champagne ... that's outrageous!* I flagged down our waitress.

'Yes, Madame, what can I get you?'

'Hold on one minute ... Excushe me, *excuse me ...*' I said, getting the attention of the couple on the table to our left and the three men in suits to our right. '*Soooo* sorry to interrupt. We're celebrating a new milestone, so Mr Coleman here would like to offer you both a bottle of the, *err,* Louis Roedererer-er Brutt Vintage 1928.'

'Well, congratulations to you both. That's very generous of you, thank you kindly,' said the lady from the couple.

'Yes, bloody good show ol' chap, well done. Married life isn't all bad, is it?' said one of the tuxedoed men.

'You're welcome,' said Travis to our neighbours, shooting me a playful eye. 'Here's to love and romance, may it never die.'

Bastard. Feckin'. Bastard! I felt like pouring our bottle over his head and then ramming the bottle up his arse. James and Siobhan would've loved it. But I'd never like to be accused of being violent; it definitely wasn't my style. (Apart from the slap I'd given him earlier; okay, and pulling my sister's hair when we were younger.) Anyway, forgetting about that, I decided to go in even harder.

'And of courshe, darling, we should have a bottle too,' I added, turning back to the waitress and seeing Travis pick up the menu, hopefully scanning for the price.

'No problem at all,' said the waitress. 'Can I get you anything else?'

I could feel a belch on its way and capitalised on the opportunity.

'Lady burp coming—*brrrrb. Ooft,* deary me, excuse–a–*me!*' I said, flapping away the smell of olives and bread from my only meal of that day. 'Actualllly, yes,' I said deviously, picking up the menu again. 'I'm rather peckish, hmm ... I'll have the Royal Belgian Caviar. In fact, lassht time I had it,' (lie – I'd never had it), 'it didn't quite fill me up, so please make that two.' (At £290 per portion, I'd certainly hope it was filling.)

'Certainly, Madame,' she said, '—Mr Coleman, will that be all?'

'Yep. That's everything. Thanks.'

I desperately looked for a reaction on Travis's face.

But he didn't seem to care at all, he just looked right back at me with that offensively charming smile of his.

Some people just have too much money. Frustrated that nothing I said or did seemed to be doing him any damage, I shook my head, tossed the menu back to the table, and turned my face away.

'I know what you're trying to do. You're trying to get even, and it's understandable. I'd probably do the same thing in your shoes. I just want you to give me a chance to explain, then if you still feel the same way, you can be as mean to me all you want.'

'A chance to explain what? Were you suffering a major zipper problem or something?'

The waitress reappeared, placing down an ice bucket and two champagne flutes. We remained silent while she expertly filled both glasses before smiling and leaving us alone once again. I immediately picked up my glass and knocked it straight back before snatching the ludicrously expensive bottle and keeping it next to me, continued topping myself up.

'Fine,' I continued, 'I'm giving you a chance, aren't I? I'm right here. I'm listening ...' I said deliberately trying to look bored.

'Okay, fine. Well, as you know, I was being quite ... *distant* towards the end of our relationship.'

'*Relationship?* If you call that a relationship, I dare to think how you treat your mother.'

'Actually ... Mum passed away last year.'

JESUS. Give me a break here, for feck's sake! Now I'm the bad guy.

'Oh ... I'm sorry to hear about that,' I said begrudgingly, even though I meant it.

'That's okay. It was cancer. It came quickly and she didn't suffer much.'

I nodded silently, seething inside at my own stupidity.

'Like I was saying … towards the end I *was* distant; and then, you're right, I did end things without explaining. I'm not denying that it must've been hard for you, but you also don't realise what was going on with me. Do you remember that Christmas we first met in Dublin we were at Dougie's house and I told you my life was problematic?'

I grunted in recognition.

'Well, I'd just come out of a relationship with Anne—the one you saw at the airport that time …'

Anne … so, the brown-jumpered, up-the-duff girl had a name.

'… We'd been together for six months and I just wasn't into her, so I broke things off. This was about two weeks before I met you.'

Manwhore.

'… Please, don't get me wrong; I really, really liked you. You were a ray of sunshine in my life. I knew from the first moment I saw you that you were special; you're beautiful, intelligent and, frankly, amazing in the sack.'

Well, he's not wrong there.

'Tara, I was head over heels for you, but I hadn't seen you in a month and I was lonely, and work had really been stressing me out and then one night Anne turned up in Dublin out of the blue and it just kinda happened … I'm sorry—I made a stupid, stupid, one-time mistake. I can't tell you how much I regret it.'

None of this surprised me at all; but getting it straight from the horse's mouth actually really stung.

'... That's why I was so devastated when Anne told me she was pregnant. Trust me when I say I didn't want her to be the mother of my child – despite her appearance, she's a complete and utter psycho bitch. It was you I wanted to start a family with—I mean, I still do ...'

His words were bittersweet.

I flashed back to when I deliberately tried to conceive with Travis, then to the pain of receiving that phone call, informing me I would never be able to have a child. It still haunts me to this day.

I decided there and then not to tell him that I thought I was pregnant when he broke things off; it would be too painful for both of us, and I certainly didn't want to talk about how it had turned out to be a phantom pregnancy anyway. And I certainly wouldn't be fessing up about my extremely rare case of early onset menopause, but I still wondered every day about what I would be like as a mother. For years, I took my fertility for granted; but now, with Lewis, I felt like I could cope with life not being a mother.

'Tara, let's face it, neither of us are getting any younger—I wanted to have kids before I got too old to enjoy them. Even though the mother was wrong, I was still over the moon that *I* was going to be a father. The thing is, Anne insisted that we get back together for the baby's sake. I thought about it for a while, but things between you and me were going well, so I told her that I couldn't. She completely flipped out and started going crazy, threatening that she would get an abortion ...

I'm sorry, but I just couldn't let that happen.

'So in the end I had to come to a compromise for the sake of the baby. I told her we could try it—but really, I was just waiting for the birth, then I would break things off with her and try to claim custody.

'I'm sorry,' he said, looking right at me, 'this was all going on while you and I were together. I felt so guilty, but I had no choice but to go quiet on you. Then I came to see you that one time at your salon, and somehow she found out about it. She told me that if I didn't immediately stop all communications with you, she would flee the country and I would never see the baby—'

The blackmail ... it makes sense now.

His story frazzled my brain entirely. I began to feel nauseous. Then the room began to spin and I could see three Travises. (Three, I tell you. One was bad enough!)

'I was there the whole way through the birth—I even cut the cord ... but, she wasn't my baby. I didn't even need to see a DNA test: she had brown skin and dark curly hair, right from birth. I couldn't believe it.'

That makes two of us ... wow.

I knew it was the truth—I could see it in his eyes. Usually he was so assertive and confident; now he seemed defeated, his bulky frame looked almost deflated. I couldn't help but pity him. How could I not? I also wanted kids and had had that taken away from me.

All this time I had hated the man with every cell in my being, and yet I was oblivious to what was really going on.

Tension hung heavy in the air, then he looked up at

me. 'I'm sorry I finished things the way I did, but I've been really fucked up too. I was cheated on, lied to, blackmailed ... and after all that, I'd lost you as well. I knew you would still be hurt by what I did, so I tried to break you in gently by sending you those messages.'

I finally found my voice again: 'Yeah, I got the messages all right. But if you loved me ssso much, why'd you leave it another year before trying to get in contact again?'

'Well, you did text me back telling me to never speak to you again. I thought I'd blown it. I wanted to respect your wishes, and so I tried to move on with my life and start again. For a year, I tried everything: I tried getting a girlfriend, I tried numbing the pain with drink, I tried antidepressants ... but none of it worked; hell, I even tried to get a Tara brain lobotomy ...'

What the feck is a brain lobotomy?

'Eventually I realised that I couldn't go on without you—I had to do *something*.'

His words could've been my own. (Apart from the lobotomy thingy).

'And so that's when you decided to turn up at the salon?' I asked.

'Exactly. I would've phoned but I think you'd blocked my number. I found your new salon's address online and tracked you down that way. I was hoping that I could make things up to you and we could pick things up where we left off. Tara, I've loved you since I very first laid eyes on you. Please, just give me a chance to win your heart again.'

My heart sank. I could feel the demon inside Pandora's box beginning to ensnare me. My tower of resolve began to wobble – much like my body, which wouldn't stop swaying side to side in the chair.

Time seemed to stop and I found myself at the fork in the road I'd been dreading. My two potential futures panned out before of my eyes. I could see my future with Lewis, clear as day, sitting in Lewara, nursing each other into old age. Then I looked in the other direction for a future with Travis. I could see glamour, excitement and lust; but I couldn't see myself ever fully trusting him. I could easily see him trading me in for a younger model again—especially now he had admitted how adamant he was about having children. I knew in my heart: Lewis was the one for me. Even though Travis offered a very attractive package, there really was no comparison. Even if I could trust Travis again, he paled in comparison to the unconditional love that Lewis and I shared.

'... Hello? Tara, are you listening?' Travis asked, clicking his fingers. 'What do you say, can you give me one more shot?'

'Well ... no, I can't. I'm happy now. I'm engaged—his face is Lew—I mean, his *name* is Lewis.'

Travis took in a deep breath and looked down at the floor.

'What does he have that I don't?'

'Well, for starters he's never cheated on me or lied to me before. He's actually a vet,' I said proudly, 'and, he actually cares about things and people and animals.' *[+5 points: Rub my happiness with Lewis in his face.]*

'A vet? They're the worst kinds of people—they kill innocent animals for a living,' he said with a wry smile. 'If you ever get sick you'll have to be careful he doesn't put you to "sleep".'

'Don't you dare take the pissh. He's a good man.'

'Tara, babe ... let's not be silly here. This is your last chance for you to get the life you always wanted. You know what kind of future we could have together. We could go out for dinner like this every night, mingle with the stars, jet-set across the world ... you could have all the latest designer gear that you love. You'd never have to work another day in your life. And not to mention the incredible sex on tap all the time.'

'Ha—I don't need all that shiny stuff anymore. And I can make my own way with my amazing, shuper-successhful business, thanks very much! I don't have to deal with being with someone untrushtworthy in order to get these things. I'm not some trophy you can just win and then shove in the cabinet for years. I'm in it for love; the real, meaningful love, and to be honest, I could never love you in that way. There's absolutely no hope of us ever getting back together.'

Well done, Tara, it may've been slightly slurred, but you're getting the message across.

'*Hmmm.* I think you'd be making a huge mistake. You'll never find someone else like me. And I know I won't find someone else like you ... you're breaking my heart here.'

All this time I thought I was stepping into the dragon's lair, when really *I* was the dragon.

I am Deborah Meaden: decision maker, heartbreaker.

'I'm sorry, Travis, but I'm out.'

I was just about to stand up and leave, when Travis began shielding his eyes with his hand, his elbow resting on his knee. I could see his torso shuddering as he tried to catch his breath.

O.M.G., is he crying? [+50 points: 'Make him cry'!]

'Sorry,' he said softly, 'guess I'm just licking my wounds.'

Sighing, I dragged my chair closer and put my hand on top of his.

He looked up at me with a defeated smile, subtly nodding his head. 'This is pretty embarrassing,' he said, taking a deep breath, 'blubbering to you in full view of everyone—'

'It's okay, I understand.'

'… So, let's finish this conversation somewhere more private,' he said, reaching into his pocket and presenting his room card to me, before waving it in the direction of the exit.

Confused, I looked up and saw that all traces of his apparent devastation had vanished, replaced with that mega-watt smile and a pair of suggestive eyebrows.

'… Are you saying what I think you're saying?'

'Well, technically you're still a single woman, so you're free to do whatever—and *who*ever—you like. Don't you want to be 100% sure about what you're missing out on?'

It took a moment for my brain to engage.

Is he … is he feckin' serious?!

'*What?!* D'you think you can jussht cry me into bed, like some kind of perverted snake charmer? Do I look that stooopid to you?'

'No, I don't think you're stupid. A little drunk, yes, but certainly not stupid.'

'Well … *good*. Because I'm not stupid, and I won't

play the fool for you again. *Ever!* You haven't changed at all—you're a-a-a womanising bastard, and you always have been! You're principle ... less. I mean—you have no principles!'

'Look, Tara, I just want a chance—'

'A chance? *Hah!* You're nothing but an egotistical, block of, of ... I won't let you chop off my head.'

'What?'

'I mean ... I won't let you ... *take me to bed.* I won't fall for your weak attempts to charm me. You had your chance and you blew it!'

'Tara, just calm down for a minute. I thought you were supposed to be a Catholic—aren't you lot all about forgiveness? I mean, doesn't everyone deserve a second chance?'

'You know what? I *hate* that saying. No, they don't ... Did Hitler deserve a second chance?'

'*Errr ...*'

'*Exactly!*'

I had no idea where all this confidence had come from. I had never spoken to anyone like that before (except maybe my sisters).

'Look,' Travis said, sighing and putting his hand on my arm. 'You must still have feelings for me, or you wouldn't have come.'

'*No.* Well, yes, actually, I do have feelings for you. Regret. Shame. Pity. But mostly you just make me feel a bit sick. Quite literally, actually.'

Suddenly I had begun to view him in a different light. I had been set free, released from his prison; like a spell had finally been broken. The feeling was so pure and so intense; like I'd been healed.

I knew I no longer loved him. In fact, he actually started to look uglier with each moment. Looking at him, I wondered what I'd ever seen in him in the first place, and why I'd ever let myself get into such a state over such a pathetic excuse for a man. For the first time, I was seeing him for what he truly was: selfish, shallow and narcissistic—*worse*: a self-absorbed, oversized child – like King Henry.

'You—your head … it looks like a *butternut squash*. With pubes on it!'

Take that, you swine!

'*Ohh* come on now, there's no need for *that*.'

I geared up to send another volley of insults, but quickly decided he wasn't worth spending my genius on. I'd had my moment.

Just say your polite farewells and go.

'Goodbye, trashy Travissh. Have a nice life. And do not contact me again—I mean it this time.'

'Tara, please, don't leave like this … I love you—'

'No! You don't. You only love yourshelf. I've heard what you've had to shay. I can forgive you, but I can never forget. Fool me once, shame on you. Fool me twice, shame on … me.'

Is that the saying? Ahh who cares—it's an excellent turn of phrase!

Standing up on wobbly legs, I readied myself to leave. The sudden movement made me feel dizzy, and I had to steady myself against the table.

'Tara, you can't leave now after all this money I've just spent.'

I picked up two champagne flutes from the table. 'Oh, don't worry—it's buy one …' I poured a glass into his lap, then promptly chucked the other in his face, '... get one free! I'd say that's money well spent, *wouldn't you*?' I patted him on his wet shoulder and made for the exit, head held high.

Operation Closure: mission complete.

Chapter 9

I woke with a start, falling out of a black hole into a roasting, sweaty reality.

Had someone been slamming my head in a drawer repeatedly?

A searing pain ripped through my head, like someone had pushed a red-hot poker into my skull. I screwed my eyes tight shut, not daring to open them in case my brain spilled out of my eye sockets. *Migraine.* This was definitely a very, very bad migraine. I tried to lift my head a fraction but the searing pain wouldn't allow it.

The sound of Lewis's breathing was my only comfort.

'Baby, I don't feel very well …' I groaned, putting my hand on his back to wake him and shielding my eyes from the morning light. 'Can you get me some – some water? And painkillers? They're in my handbag …'

'Okay,' he said, instantly getting up and shuffling across the room.

'... Tramadol?' he asked sounding croaky. 'Jesus, these are pretty heavy duty—'

... *eh?*

My eyes flew open to reveal Travis—butt naked—standing over me.

'WHAT THE FUCK!?' I lashed out, kicking and screaming, knocking the glass out of Travis's hand, launching myself to the other side of the bed.

'*Whoa-whoa-whoa!* Easy now, tiger,' said Travis, backing off.

'Travis!?'

'*What?* What's up?!'

No, no, no ... this can't be happening!

The room seemed to collapse in on me. All I could hear was my own heavy breathing.

'Jesus, you nearly frightened the life out of me,' said Travis, picking up the glass.

Recoiling, I wrenched the duvet around my naked body. Broken flashbacks glitched through my mind. Bar21 ... Marco the waiter ... Leonardo's birthday party ... King Henry ... seeing Travis ... slapping Travis ... the accidental grappa ... then, nothing.

The memory-lapse sent me off balance, and I tumbled off the bed, landing directly on one of my boots; which of course I immediately weaponised, hurling it straight at Travis's head.

'Whoa—*whoa!* Take it easy,' he said, raising his arms submissively.

I shuffled backwards, dragging the duvet to hide my modesty, and collapsed into the armchair behind me.

'Tell me this isn't real ... how the FUCK has this happened?!'

'Tara—Tara, just calm down. You came with me last night, after your fall. Don't you remember?'

'I ... no! Oh God ... I remember leaving the hotel, then ... *shit!*'

'Are you serious? ... You would have drunk any rugby player under the table. It was quite impressive,' he said, casually sitting back down on the bed.

'*Shut. The. Feck. Up!* Did—did anything happen between us last night?' I asked, bracing myself.

'Well, yeah – a lot of things happened. Once you'd admitted that you'd forgiven me, you were game for anything and *everything*.'

'No—no, it's not true,' I blurted hysterically. 'I wouldn't cheat on Lewis! LIAR!'

'Well, it *is* true, because you *did*. Tara, don't play dumb – you know exactly what happened. I think you just feel guilty now in the morning light.'

'Fuck, *fuck* ... what have I done?!' I shot up out of the chair in outrage and violently knuckled my skull. 'It's not possible ... I love Lewis—I'm engaged to be married!'

'Well, you certainly weren't behaving like a woman about to be married,' he said, shrugging off my hysteria and examining the packet of Tramadol. 'Christ—these are two hundred milligrams each. How many did you take?'

'I ... I don't know. Like four or five ... or seven. I don't feckin' know!' I began frantically pacing around the room, searching for my belongings.

'You're kidding me, right? Tara, you imbecile—these

tablets are lethal. I wouldn't give more than two of these to one of my rugby lads over the course of a whole day. And you were drinking as well? You could have died! I'm not surprised you fell down the stairs.

'What?'

'Yeah – you tripped down the stairs on the way out of the lobby, just as you were supposedly leaving. Next thing I know, a concierge is dragging me over and you're in a pile on the floor. It was kinda embarrassing to be honest.'

I felt around and found a lump on the right side of my head. *That explains the pain.*

'... After that, you kept complaining about your head, and how you wanted to lie down in my room. I offered to get you a cab home but you said *no*. You told me you were sorry for pouring champagne over me, and that you forgave me—'

'LIAR!'

'Look, if you don't believe me you can ask the concierge, he was there the whole time. You wouldn't shut up about it.'

'After fifteen minutes or so you came back from the dead and just went ... *wild*. You practically mounted me in the lift, and then you dragged me in here and started stripping off. I must say, I'd forgotten how great your body is—'

'Shut up! Don't you dare say another word!'

He smirked at my discomfort. 'Tara, don't pretend you haven't been thinking about meeting up like this. You knew this would happen the second you decided to come to meet me at this hotel.'

He was right – I'd let this happen. The evidence was

all around me. *I'm a whore—and a stupid one at that.*

'Lewis will never forgive me ...' I wailed.

'Why do you even care? You told me you still loved me and that you'd never got over me ... I thought this was the start of our new relationship. I can't believe you're even thinking of going back to him,' he said, folding his arms.

'I don't know why I said that. I don't love you anymore—I don't want anything to do with you, ever again!'

'Oh, for God's sake, Tara, you can't just go around changing your mind like this all the time. You've already ruined your relationship with that chump. It's over.'

'No—it's not over! I still love him! I've just made a stupid, stupid mistake.'

'But, Tara, I love you ...'

'No! No, you don't – you only love yourself. You don't love me; you cheated on me with that brown-jumpered tramp-asaurus. You're a cheater and always will be!'

'Well, it takes one to know one.'

'Bastard!'

I scuttled across the floor, still wrapped in the duvet, frantically pulling on my clothes.

'Where are my knickers?' Kicking his clothes to one side, I picked up his jacket and shook it.

'Oh, just come back to bed,' he said, patting the sheet beside him, 'you don't need knickers here.'

Grabbing the bundle of sheets at the base of the bed, I began flapping them up and down in the hope my knickers would fly out. Then, kneeling down, I fished around under the bed, but they weren't there either.

I appealed to Travis for him to help, but then caught a glimpse of my hand and panicked. 'Oh my God—where's my ring? My engagement ring ... where is it?!'

'Look, just calm down,' Travis cut in, his voice sharp as a blade. 'It's over there on the dressing table. You were the one who took it off before we, *uhh*—'

'—No, don't say it! Please, just don't say anything else. You've done enough damage.'

Darting over to the dressing table, I found my ring twinkling at me ironically with its innocent beauty, before slipping it onto my trembling finger.

The lump on my head throbbed with pain as Lewis's devastated face flashed before my eyes. I felt physically disgusted by myself. Drunk or high on whatever, there was no excuse for what I'd done. Travis's fault, my fault; it didn't matter anymore; the damage was done.

I had to put as much ground between Travis and me as quickly as possible. Pacing over to the bed with hands on hips, I demanded, 'Where are my knickers?! I know you've hidden them! Give them to me!'

'I don't know where your bloody knickers are. You're the one who took them off last night, not me.'

'Oh, fuck it then. And fuck you too! Travis, let me make this crystal clear: I never, ever, EVER want to see you again. Ever!'

A flicker of pain rippled across his face as he spread his arms in protest of his innocence.

'Tara, you're overreacting. Everyone cheats at some point – it's perfectly normal to go back to an old flame.'

'No. That's not me! And if you even think about telling *anyone* about this ... I swear on the Holy Bible, you and your precious reputation will be in tatters. I promise you that,' I said, jabbing a finger in his direction.

'Come on, stop playing games. You know you want me and your actions last night prove it.'

'No they don't! I made a stupid mistake and you took advantage of me, like you always did. You, Travis Coleman, need to go and find the biggest bath of morals and ... and ...' I swallowed my choking voice back, 'drown yourself in it!'

'Call me when you and your supposed "fiancé" have broken things off.'

I screamed in temper and slammed the door behind me, setting off down the corridor like a woman possessed, chin jutted in determination as I approached the lifts.

'I am a hussy. I am a whore,' I repeated to myself as I hammered the lift's call button with my finger.

I know he's stolen my knickers, like some sort of perverted trophy. He's probably got a drawer full of them from his other victims.

Operation Closure: Failed. The enemy had captured me. I may have now escaped, but the enemy had won the battle ... I'd ruined mine and Lewis's future.

Where the feck is this lift? I glanced nervously back at the door of Travis's room, hoping he wouldn't pursue me. In a blind panic, I decided to take the stairs. I didn't even know how high up we were.

'Sick–bloody–knicker–thief,' I cursed, one for each step down. 'Slimeball–smart-arse–flicky–haired–moron ... [clutching chest and panting] slob–pig–gobshite ...'

After dozens of flights and thousands of curses later,

I collapsed against the doorway leading to the lobby. Looking down, I saw something brightly coloured out of the corner of my eye. The knickers. Hanging down from the ankle of my jeans.

Hardly a consolation prize, is it, Tara?

Chapter 10

Three gruelling months passed by. The guilt from the night at the Langham grew like a dark shadow looming over me constantly. I did everything I could to try and distract myself, like making plans for the wedding, and tried to keep myself as busy as possible at the salon. I'd also made a pact with myself and to the Big Man Upstairs that I'd never make such a stupid mistake again; that, and I'd be extra nice and loving to Lewis to make up for it. That way I wouldn't have to tell another living soul.

However, the stomach-churning misery of it all exacerbated my stress levels no end. Several times Travis sent flowers anonymously to the salon and I had to stand there sweating and red-faced and blatantly lie to the staff that they were from Lewis. There wasn't a lot else I could do. I couldn't exactly stop him sending things via Interflora. And of course, this added even more stress, sending my hormones and me a little crazy.

The outcome? I was munching my way through two tubs of Kalms a day and my doctor had to increase my HRT dosage.

Between the crippling guilt and hormonal hurricanes, I began comfort eating myself out of house and home. Somewhere among the depths of my despair, I developed an unhealthy relationship with ... of all things, canned whipped cream. I'd squirt mouthfuls of the stuff morning, noon and night. It was like I was trying to extinguish the burning shame of my infidelity with the calorie-laden foam. Cruelly, I found out that one can't actually overdose on Anchor's real dairy whipped cream (turns out excessive consumption just leads to obesity).

My doctor said it was quite normal to crave high-sugar foods when adapting to hormonal imbalances. He said things would eventually balance out, providing I ate sensibly and exercised. But I didn't. So, I was now the not-so-proud owner of an extra three quarters of a stone. I even went to the gym. But just once. I came out all puffy and red and realised that, sadly for my waistline, I must still be allergic.

* * *

My hen-do soon approached; a welcome distraction from the guilt corroding me from the inside out. My hen party consisted of my closest circle: Laura, Katie, Camilla, Siobhan and, of course, James.

In the end, I reluctantly chose my older and allegedly more responsible sister, Laura, to be Mother Hen. (I don't understand how she ever got this title of 'the responsible one' – she was the devil when she'd been on the sauce, which had become an alarmingly frequent occurrence since ... forever, actually.) She could switch from nerdy know-it-all into wild party animal at the flick of a switch. And by switch, I mean half a bottle of gin.

My younger sister, Katie, had been clean from all narcotics for over two years now. Before her stint in rehab, my poor naïve mum would be phoning me at all hours, ranting away about Katie's 'odd' behaviour.

'Tara, your sister's after findin' herself a new friend, so she has. The girl sounds nice enough – Katie goes on and on about how much better things are with this Mandy around. I think she's even joined Katie's band – she says their jammin' sessions have reached another level altogether with Mandy givin' everyone a right ol' boost.'

'Aww, that's great,' I said, nodding in approval that Katie's career in music was finally getting off the ground.

Mum's voice then dropped to a whisper, 'But I do have to say now, she also seems to be spendin' a lot of time in her room, wrapped in her duvet, starin' all bug-eyed at that ol' lava lamp she got from the charity shop ... very strange. Honestly, I don't know how the child looks at the thing so close, wit' her nose right up so it's touchin' the glass. Will I be bringin' her to Specsavers?'

Alarm bells ...

'Mum ... have you actually met this Mandy?'

'*Emm* ... well, no, to be honest with you now, I haven't. But I'm forever tellin' Katie to invite her round for tea, but Mandy never seems to be around when I'm at home.'

'Oh, *Jesus,* Mum. Mandy is the street name for *ecstasy*. The drug!'

I immediately got on the phone to Laura, 'Katie's been pulling the wool over Mum's eyes, I'm sure of it!' I grassed. 'Get your backside round there, sharpish.'

Laura marched straight around to Mum's, checking every nook and cranny of the house and found a four-foot, 'extremely bushy' cannabis plant—in the lounge, of all places. It even had an innocent little floral watering can by its side. Poor mum – she'd been inadvertently and lovingly tending the plant for months on Katie's behalf. She'd even named it Paddy, after her beloved Saint Patrick.

'Will I be givin' you the Miracle-grow that I had been feedin' it with?' asked Mum as Laura swiftly removed it and gave Katie the lecture of her life.

Not long after this, a local priest had found Katie sobbing and out of her face, wandering the streets with no shoes on. Turns out she'd been laughed out of the local Garda station after she'd handed herself in and confessed that she'd accidentally murdered Mum's budgie, Moses.

Next stop: rehab.

None of us knew how or why she'd gone off the rails so badly. My money was on the fact she never had a father figure around. On the other hand, in Laura's professional opinion (which, may I add, counts for approximately diddly squat, seeing how this was all going on under her nose the whole time) was that Katie was simply doing it all for attention. Poor Mum simply blamed herself for not being a good enough mother and for missing Mass the week before it all started kicking off. However, rather uninterestingly, and much to our surprise, there was no big reveal. Katie said that she simply liked the way drugs made her feel, and that being normal was kinda boring. "You guys should try it—life is so much better when you can take acid with Elvis."

Hence, I tried to explain to Mum that bringing Katie to Ibiza would be the equivalent of imprisoning a recovering alcoholic in a pub for a few days.

'She's clean as a whistle!' insisted Mum, sounding almost offended. 'You need to give that poor child a chance to prove herself.'

There was war over it, but ultimately Mum and Laura convinced me that everybody would be essentially babysitting Katie, ensuring she didn't get into any trouble. (Was I the only one who really knew that tearaway sister of mine? Surely, this was a recipe for a disaster.)

Putting that worry to one side, I was looking forward to spending some quality time with Camilla, who I'd never actually seen drunk. But if she had the same tendencies as Lewis (which she seemed to have with just about everything else), then we were definitely in for a laugh. Lewis would become outrageously silly after a tipple, playing pranks and causing mischief. Camilla had recently got engaged to her partner, a charming car salesman named Alex, so this getaway could be a little celebration for her too.

I did also ask Mum if she wanted to come, but only in the way that you ask someone if they want your last cookie.

'Are you joking?' roared Mum. 'I'd only slow you's

down. Go have a lovely time and make sure you look after Katie.'

So, six neon-clothed, over-aged and seemingly mentally challenged adults set off towards the biggest party destination on the planet in August, peak season.

We had a minibus booked to take us from the airport to our rented apartment. At first, the driver looked pleased to see us, as he held the sign that read 'Team Tara', but I think the feeling was short-lived. I suppose ten miles of us murdering Girls Aloud and Amy Winehouse songs acapella would drive anyone to insanity; and it may've been the last straw when James insisted he wore a plastic diamante tiara.

Either way, the journey was fast, even by European standards.

After picking up our keys from reception, we began the uphill climb towards our apartment block. One by one, we gasped as we reached the top – partly due to the hike, partly due to the stunning building before us; with a boxy, ultra-modern design, whitewashed walls and a sweeping balcony overlooking the sea.

And as Laura turned the key in the door, I was immediately trampled by a free-for-all stampede of hens, everyone presumably fighting for the best room. Katie had made it through first but immediately fell over her case. My ears erupted to the sound of a sharp whistle blast from Laura, our Mother Hen. Everyone froze, even me. We turned around and stared at her expectantly.

'Okay, everyone, listen up,' she said as she led everyone through the hallway, which opened up into a spacious open-plan kitchen/dining/living area.

Everyone stood stock-still and you could've heard a pin drop as our jaws dropped in unison at the splendour of our accommodation. Faces gawped at the huge kitchen/dining area, which housed white gloss units, black granite worktops equipped with all mod cons, and cool white floor tiles. In the middle of the kitchen area was a very large glass-topped table surrounded by six black leather dining chairs. The living area was complete with three beautiful white leather sofas, which surrounded a marble coffee table. And to complete the picture, a large flat-screen TV hung from the wall.

'As you can see, this is a large, luxury apartment.' Laura continued once our attention was back. 'There is plenty of room for everyone. This is Tara's hen-do, and therefore *she* gets to choose her room first. And seeing as how I'm Mother Hen, I'm entitled to share with her. The rest of you wait here and we'll let you know when we've chosen.' Laura grabbed my hand and dragged me back into the hallway, towards each of the three bedrooms.

Each room had an en-suite bathroom, a mini fridge and two double beds. Of course, we chose the flagship room we'd seen on the website, the one with double doors leading out onto our own private terrace, which was only a few short steps to the pool, with the plumpest luxurious sun-loungers I'd ever seen. *And* it had the best view towards the sea. I felt as though I had landed smack bang in the middle of heaven.

'Okay,' I shouted into the hallway, 'you lot can come and choose your rooms now—'

Thunderous banging and yelps came as everyone

clattered along the hallway.

I closed our bedroom door and let the pandemonium commence outside.

Having worked out that the TV had surround-sound and an iPod connection, James connected his iPod and selected his especially put together 'Tara's Hen-Do' playlist, which began with ... The Pussycat Dolls' 'Don't Cha' on full blast. We all happily sang along while unpacking and decided that we would catch the last few rays of afternoon sun by the pool. I, for one, couldn't wait to plonk myself on those amazing sun-loungers.

'Come on, you lot,' Katie shouted from the hallway, 'we've only got a few days here – let's get out to that pool, ASAP!'

'Ready,' I said, pulling open our door, already kitted out in my Beach Bunny bikini with matching sarong, oversized Chanel sunglasses and diamante Havaianas flip-flops.

Katie sauntered out of her room in what I could only describe as a patch the size of a Dorito covering her lady-garden, and two patches the size of Laughing Cow cheese covering her nipples.

'Ready!' said James, waltzing out of his room with hands on hips. I instantly covered my eyes with my hands because at first sight he appeared to be naked, but upon looking through the gaps in my fingers I saw he was actually wearing a gold thong, leaving very little to the imagination.

'Jesus ...' said Camilla, joining us in the hallway in her panelled orange and yellow swimsuit and her blonde hair now tied back. 'Is that legal?'

'Well, you'll be jealous,' said James. 'You wait until I get poolside – I'll be beating men off with a stick—'

Siobhan crashed through the front door, having returned from the off-licence; bottle of tequila in one hand, and an inflated Barry Junior in the other. (Barry Junior was a sex doll who she brought almost everywhere. Barry *Senior*, God rest his soul, had met his end in an unfortunate waxing incident.)

'*Wooo-hooo!* Is it pool time?' she exclaimed, slamming the bottles onto the glass dining table. Rushing to her bedroom, she returned ready for the pool wearing a navy-blue and white striped bikini and clutching boxes under each arm. 'Before we go out to the pool,' she said, 'I'm givin' each of you a present.'

'*Ooo,* I love presents!' squealed James as Siobhan plonked a box on the floor and began opening it up.

'They're holiday accessories that you'll need to be bringin' everywhere you go ... James, I'd like to introduce you to Ben: Barry Junior's gay cousin.'

'Obviously, he'll need a bit of a blow every now 'n' then, if you're up to it. I'm sure you are, I believe in you.'

Laura, wearing a two-piece black and gold bikini, had joined us in the living area after hearing the raucous laughter.

Then Siobhan handed out bags to the rest of us in turn. Both Laura and Katie were also given inflatable relatives of Barry Junior: Laura got Bert, and Katie, inexplicably, got Barbara, who had enormous, pert bosoms and a gaping hole for a mouth; and Camilla got an inflatable dolphin.

Everyone except me had received theirs, amid

laughing hysterically and trying to inflate their 'buddies'. Siobhan finally handed me a small brown box and I tore it open to reveal ... an enormous inflatable penis.

Everyone hit the deck with laughter, letting the air out of their inflatables.

'Tara,' Siobhan blurted, 'the rule is: you can't be seen without Big Ben here, or you'll have to be doin' a forfeit.' Before I could protest, Laura opened the bottle of tequila, filled up five shot glasses and (a Coke for Katie – that's a glass of Coke – not a line of coke) then handed them around to us all. 'Let's have a toast ... To Tara on finding her knight in shining armour and soon to become Mrs Lewis Copeland.' Raising their glasses, they all held their glasses towards me before chinking with each other and knocking back the fiery liquid.

Here we go!

Six people, four inflatable dolls, a dolphin and a giant penis all proceeded towards the extremely inviting pool area. James and Katie charged ahead, holding their life-size buddies in front of them and launched themselves straight into the pool. Laura, Camilla and I found a sunny spot close to the pool bar, which was playing soft Latino music. Slumping down on the sumptuous sun-loungers, we all took a deep lung-filling breath. '*Ahhh* ... finally.'

Having flung Barry Junior into the pool to join the others, Siobhan was first up to the bar, ordering cocktails for each of us, and ceremoniously presented me with a Sex On The Beach. 'Get suppin', Tara, you're on your hollibobs now, woman, this is your last chance to paint the town red before settlin' into Domestos

City.' And with that she was gone, legs and arms flailing towards the pool, belly flopping straight onto Barry Junior.

Katie, Siobhan and James attempted to use their blow-up buddies as a lilos, and splashed around the pool like twelve-year-olds, while Laura (who had shoved Bert firmly under her lounger), Camilla and I enveloped ourselves in the luxury padded sun-loungers, settling into Level One: flat on our backs for maximum sun exposure.

As we watched the sun set over the top of the apartment block, I picked up my phone and scrolled through my photos of Lewis.

Am I really allowed to be this happy? I mean me—Tara Ryan—actually, blissfully happy?

'I can't believe I'm getting married,' I said, moving the armrests of the lounger to Level Two, AKA reading position.

Tears suddenly began snaking down my cheeks. Every time I thought about the wedding and how lucky I was, I got emotional to the point of tears.

'Tara, what's wrong?' asked Laura, looking concerned.

'Oh [sniffing], it's nothing … I just … never knew this kind of happiness existed. In less than a month, I'll be a Missus.'

'Well, we've got somewhere to take you before all that happens,' said Camilla, looking shifty.

'So … where *are* we actually going tonight?' I asked, suddenly feeling very apprehensive.

'It's a surprise,' said Laura, tapping her nose. 'And you're gonna love it.'

* * *

As the sun finally disappeared behind the top of the apartment block, we decided to make our way back to the apartment and ready ourselves for the night ahead. James immediately approached his iPod and selected 'I Gotta Feeling' by The Black Eyed Peas, and everyone danced off to their rooms to shower and change.

As Laura and I were applying the finishing touches to our makeup, James appeared in our doorway. 'Get you, gurl-friends!' he said, snapping his fingers above his head and spinning us both around.

I was speechless. James was wearing a black leather equivalent of the hot pants he wore on the flight over, complete with black suspender braces over his shoulders, a choker around his neck and a black clear-panel vest, which might as well have not been there.

'This is what I call a capsule wardrobe,' he said, shaking the large number of chains, braces and cuffs now adorning his otherwise naked torso.

He turned on his heel, shook his booty, and then, as we followed him to the living area, he poured both Laura and me another shot.

Katie then popped her head out—I swear that girl has a nose that could smell alcohol at a hundred paces.

She had finally taken down her rainbow-braided hair from its messy high bun, draping her long dreadlocks over her shoulders. Each clump was wrapped with brightly coloured bits of wool, and I couldn't help wonder when she had last washed it (these tree-hugging, free-spirited people, they could be housing an army of nits in their hair and they'd never know it). Katie completed the bohemian look with denim cut-off shorts, a colourful Aztec ruched-at-the-front bandeau, and a pair of tatty Converse trainers.

Laura salvaged some family pride and wore a leopard-print bodycon dress with high-heeled black pumps and a gold-chained black leather cross-body bag.

Siobhan sported frayed white denim shorts, cowboy boots and a white gypsy smock top, finishing the look with a straw Panama hat (which you could almost guarantee would not be accompanying her back to the apartment tonight).

Camilla kept it simple with an emerald-green shift mini-dress, a pair of gold-heeled sandals, a jewelled bindi and a gold clutch bag.

I was dressed in a burlesque-style corset mini-dress that had raggedy, feathered edges; a white top hat with plumes of netting; and (of course) white skyscraper heels.

After another half an hour of nattering, teasing and shots of tequila, we all managed to finally get out of the apartment and found a perfect beachside restaurant boasting a small wooden jetty that overhung the seafront.

We sat down and ordered three one-litre jugs of sangria, watched a band playing invigorating Spanish acoustic tunes, and ordered our food. By this point, my HRT-induced food cravings had peaked and I ordered a second portion of paella. (Well, it was probably more like thirds if you took into account me clearing everyone else's plates—I was a seafood junkie.) I justified it to myself by saying that I needed soakage to get me through the night with the copious amounts of alcohol I'd be consuming. Rice, seafood and vegetables—it's all healthy stuff after all. Plus, we were on holiday; I could live a little.

When Laura generously announced that she was picking up the bill, dessert became mandatory. *(I am nobody's fool.)*

I'll start the diet the minute I get back.

I felt exhausted from all the travelling, sunbathing and eating—I could've very well curled up and slept after that, but I needed to push through. We had a big night ahead of us – although quite how big, I still had no idea.

Chapter 11

The parade of neon lights, thumping sound systems and half-naked clubbers whizzed past as we rode in the back of a minibus through Ibiza Old Town. The bars and restaurants all seemed packed to capacity, overflowing with a vibrant mix of noise and colour. I felt breathless just watching it all. Meanwhile, scores of promoters did their best to pull the passing punters into their bars and clubs.

Heading towards the shore, the taxi took a sharp turn left and onto an open plateau, following the hundreds of people walking towards an area lit up in the distance. I still had no idea where we were going; it had been kept as a surprise for me. My hens had been whispering about it in corners for weeks now. I feared the worst – I didn't like surprises at the best of times.

'We're nearly there!' shouted Camilla, pointing out a huge, white billboard with the word *HEDONISM* in bold red writing.

Everyone whooped and cheered—except me. I was shaking in my boots.

Laura, mouth open, looked at me with an expectant face, like I was supposed to be over the moon. 'Tara, please tell me you've heard about this place?' she asked, cocking her head to one side.

No, of course I hadn't!

Before I could open my mouth, Katie shouted over the din of excited, screaming pedestrians and the raucous noise of our party, 'I knew she wouldn't have heard of it, but then again this is Tara we're talkin' about here. Anyways, Hedonism used to be a gay sex club and, I guess it still kind of is in some parts. The ground floor is like a kinky super-club, and then there's a whole floor below that's dedicated to ... well, I've heard it's basically like a kind of a S&M sex dungeon.'

I looked at Laura and Katie as if they had grown another head.

'And that's just in the basement!' said Katie, wide-eyed. 'It opens its doors on Friday morn and doesn't close until Monday afternoon, so right now the party has been goin' for ... like, thirty-six hours already! Can you believe that! Folks have been known to stay there the entire weekend, takin' naps in the hammocks outside and then goin' back in to party all over again!'

'I heard it's ridiculously massive inside!' Camilla said excitedly. 'Some friends of mine went a couple of years ago and said you could find new stairways and rooms even after spending a couple of days there. The whole place is supposed to be purpose-built so it doesn't have any dead ends—even in the bathrooms—so people can just walk around endlessly for days. The bathrooms don't even have any mirrors so people don't have to look at themselves and face the indignity of seeing their faces after an epic partying session.'

No mirrors?! I couldn't believe what I was hearing, let alone the fact I was about to actually enter this place.

James then put his hand on my leg reassuringly. 'It's just what you need before you get locked down with that ball and chain. I can't believe I finally get to go there! I've been dreaming about this place all my life!'

My head swivelled back and forth between my hens, in horror. I just wanted to get a massage and hit the sauna, not be trapped in some kind of freaky sex dungeon.

It took at least thirty seconds for me to find my voice.

'For the love of God,' I moaned, 'please don't tell me we're going there. The queue must be at least five miles long. Half of the people look like they're twelve years old and the other half look like something out of a horror movie.'

'*[Tut]*—you're only as old as the man you feel,' said James, neatly pirouetting out of the minibus.

'Okay everyone,' said Laura, paying the driver. 'Let's go do it!'

We had been dropped off to the sounds of squealing, laughing, whooping, LED whistles blowing, shouting and clapping. The raucous noise was backed up with the low-end, rhythmic beating of the club's sound system, which could even be heard over the commotion outside. The monolithic nightclub looked grimy, and yet artful in an industrial kind of way. The front of the building had a huge video of the Roman Colosseum projected onto it, towards which streams of people were heading.

The prospect of being packed like a sardine into a sweatbox with thousands of sweaty, drug-taking adolescents and non-stop techno did not tickle my pickle whatsoever.

'Can't we go somewhere a bit more ... normal?' I asked as we trundled through the crowds, looking back at each other to make sure we hadn't lost anyone.

'But, I've arranged this especially,' said Laura. 'Just give it a try—I know it sounds crazy, but I wouldn't let you come to a place that was out of control, would I?'

Sober Laura, wouldn't have. Half-cut Laura was a different story.

'I always wanted to see a bit of fetish,' said Camilla as she looked up and down the queue. 'I'm sure this'll be right up your street,' turning to James and pointing to a sign that said GAY FETISH.

But James was clearly distracted by a stag party slightly further ahead. 'I'm ... just going to make a quick call,' he said, 'be right back!'

'I'm comin' with you James, cos I'm not havin' sloppy seconds!' laughed Siobhan, cutting through the queue to join him.

As the queue moved up, I saw James draped over one of the stags, and Siobhan tearing around the place with a traffic cone on her head. Then I looked at Katie. Hmm ... Her eyes were wide as saucers, and not a in a good way. Personally, I thought this was the worst environment ever, even if Laura had insisted she'd look after her. And Laura herself couldn't be trusted in such scenarios, so I decided to take matters into my own hands.

I pulled Katie to one side. 'Kathryn Ryan,' I said, narrowing my eyes, 'promise me you won't do anything stupid, and if anyone *dares* to offer you drugs—'

'Yes, yes, I know,' she said, rolling her eyes, 'I'll make sure I shop around first before buyin' anythin' from the first dealer I see.' She laughed.

I lunged forward in a vain attempt to clip her round the ear, but she deftly avoided my swing. 'That's not funny, missy,' I said. 'If Mum could see you now she'd have a fit, as well you know. You've got to prove yourself a responsible adult and show that you can be taken to a ... well, a weird place like this. It'll only be yourself you'll be letting down.'

'Yes, I know ... I've had enough lectures, thanks very much. It's only a joke. God, Tara, I think you need to lighten up a bit.'

'Yes, well, I'll be inspecting those nostrils of yours,' I said, poking the end of her hooter. 'I've got my eye on you, make no mistake.'

I wished I'd stuck to my guns and gone to a relaxing, peaceful spa somewhere where I'd be listening to whale music with cucumbers over my eyes; not standing in a mile-long queue feeling like a spare part at my own bloody hen-do.

I turned to Laura and gave a nervous laugh. 'Do you think you could be having a midlife crisis or something; you know, wanting to come to a place like this?'

'Tara, you may be ready to join the elasticated beige trouser brigade,' she said, looking me up and down, 'but I am not!'

'I'm just not sure this type of scene ... is my thing,' I said, gulping hard, 'and after all, it is supposed to be about me—'

'B'Jesus—don't be such a wuss!' snapped Katie, stabbing her hands into her pockets. 'Don't be tellin' me you'd rather be at some shitty karaoke bar, singin' like a strangled cat to Madonna or somethin' shite like that?'

Before I could answer Katie that, *yes*, in fact that would be my preference, she began firing at me like a machine gun. 'You're old before your time! Where's your sense of adventure? 'You're a *Ryan*, for God's sake! Mammy has more get up and go than you do these days!'

Both my sisters shook their heads at me, as did one guy standing in the queue in front of us.

'Hey—no need to pick on me! I'm here, aren't I? I'm just saying ...'

But I knew I was fighting yet another losing battle. Sighing and clearly outnumbered, I decided I had no other choice but to go with the flow. (Once married, I wouldn't have to stand up to this kind of peer pressure any more.) And anyway, I thought deviously, if I really, really hated the place (which I knew I would), I'd have a quick drink, a two-minute dance and then pull a sickie or something.

'Feck it!' I announced, desperately trying to save face, 'Come on, let's see what this is all about.'

I mean how bad could it possibly be?

The muffled, punching bass-line resounded over the queue like a dancing monster beckoning people into its lair, stirring nervous excitement amongst the revellers.

My hope of the DJ playing smooth jazz or at least something from the Top 40 eroded by the minute.

As the excited groups shuffled along towards the door in the sweaty night time heat, a high-pitched, overly long scream startled me.

'OH MY GOD ... Sam!' Katie screamed.

Swivelling around to see what the commotion was, we witnessed a man pick Katie up and swing her around like a swizzle stick. A Jason Statham lookalike, Sam was at least six foot three, with an inflated, muscular body and sleeve tattoos on both arms.

'Katie, baybe, 'ow the 'ell are ya?' Sam asked in a thick cockney accent.

'I'm grand ... much better now,' she said, beaming with delight, 'and what the hell are you doin' here?'

'Ahh, you know ... a bit o' *this*, bit o' *that*. Tonight I'm helping out on the door for my mate who runs this place,' said Sam, greatly impressing the weak-kneed women who happened to be listening. 'You 'ere with your mates?'

'Don't be silly – they're my sister's mates—we're here for her hen-do. We just arrived today and heard that this was the place to be.'

Hmm. As good looking as Sam was, there was something about him I didn't like. Charming, good looking—*yes*, but something about his vibe rubbed me up the wrong way. Call it a sister's intuition.

'Well, how'd you lot fancy jumping the queue and coming into VIP? I can sort ya some free drinks an' that as well.'

Cue squealing, hugging and prancing from all the hens. VIP sounded a lot nicer to me than the sweat-pit.

Maybe this won't be so bad after all.

'Sorry, darlings,' James announced to his stag-group friends, blowing a farewell kiss while grabbing Siobhan's arm, 'one can't associate with peasants all the time, but do come and find me when you get in. Toodles!'

I looked back and caught thunderous stares from the other queuing punters burning into our backs as Sam led us up to the club's main door. And even if I wasn't sure about Sam, not having to pay the extortionate €80 entry fee for what was clearly going to be a night of torture made me like him, well, slightly more.

We followed Sam closely, moving through the stream of clubbers at the entrance as we entered a dark passage, dimly lit by overhanging retro-filament light bulbs. Flashing lights and deep, incessant booming seeped through the doors at the end of the hallway, which seemed to be like the gates of hell. I feared this was the point of no return. Even the revellers had fallen silent in their anticipation of what was about to come. With each step, the tendrils of the bass would kick harder, vibrating inside my chest and resonating through my body. I put my hand over my hammering heart, which seemed to be synchronising with the beat of the pulsating techno. With each forward step, the muffled bass became clearer and more refined. My mouth dried up as I felt the adrenaline rising; I imagined being thrown into the Colosseum and having to fight for my life within the next few moments. I linked James's arm out of pure fear as he hopped from foot to foot in excitement.

'You go first, Tara!' said Camilla as we arrived at the door.

I shook my head hard but James pushed through and dragged me into the unknown.

Finally, the lid had been lifted and the vibrations had escalated into a full-blown wall of sound. A spinning, flashing cacophony of multi-coloured lights danced around in time with the music like beacons, illuminating the writhing sea of a thousand glistening ravers peppered with strobe-like artificial lightning strikes. The crowd had their hands in the air, pumping with the pulsating beats, experiencing a chemical madness. A pungent mix of sweat, dry ice and spilled drinks assaulted my already shocked senses. I'd never experienced anything like it.

A dozen prison-bar cages on platforms were dotted around the arena, containing sweat-soaked, scantily clad dancers adorned in bondage accessories. The figures gyrated wildly, gripping the cage bars with faces consumed by a mix of agony and ecstasy. Some dancers hung from high ceiling swings, performing acrobatics high above the crowd; then out of nowhere I came face-to-face – well, actually face-to-arse – with a large, almost naked lady, hanging upside down on a pole, her legs wide apart, with a tiny G-string disappearing into her butt crack. *How was that position even possible without causing serious long-term damage? I think I would need a hip replacement.*

I turned to my hen group, whose expression mirrored my own – gaping mouths and *all* eyes nearly popping out of their sockets. James held his cheeks, mouthing the letters *O–M–G*. I could tell he envied the dancers and wanted to get himself locked into one of those cages and then have to dance his little ass off to get out of it.

Taking my hand, he walked me straight into the firing line of a bright green laser and I had to jerk my head to avoid having my eyeballs burnt out. As this happened, my precious top hat fell off my head—but then I realised it had actually been lifted by some thieving swine that slipped away into the crowd.

'*Oi! Bastard!* Give that back!' I shouted, helplessly watching my hat float away on a sea of outstretched hands.

Bastards! That hat cost me a bloody fortune.

None of my hens even noticed the crime. And even if they had, I'm sure they wouldn't have given a cluck about it.

Sam, clearly an experienced navigator of these shores, had got ahead of us. He effortlessly scooped Katie up into his arms like some kind of damsel in distress, whisking her through the club and whispering in her ear. I'm sure she gave a simpering titter, like something out of a Jane Austen novel, the strumpet!

Sulking and stamping my feet in temper, I followed show-off Sam to the VIP section, clanging up the grated metal stairs and plotting the death of the person who'd stolen my hat, should I ever find them.

The only person who hadn't joined us yet was James. I wondered where he'd minced off to. Then I remembered the 'male only' fetish floor, and couldn't help but assume the worst.

The VIP area didn't fail to impress. Despite the rest of the club being concrete and industrial steel, the VIP area boasted gleaming black granite tiles with sparkling mirror flecks, plush royal-red booths and a back-lit bar with every liquor imaginable. A glass-fronted balcony overlooked the dance floor, thankfully holding back some of the deafening noise, and if I'm honest, it was nothing short of a relief to be led into the safety of the booths.

'Right,' said Sam, gently planting Katie back on her feet. 'I'll send 'ova a few bottles of the good shtuff, 'anyfin else you'll 'ave to order yourselves from the bar. I'd love to stay 'n' chat but I've got some business to sort out. Have fun, 'n' I'll see *you* later,' he added, kissing Katie on the hand and giving her a wink.

YUCK. What a cheeseball!

Laura huddled me over towards Katie. 'Katie ...' she said, eyeing her suspiciously—'

'Yep, I know. I'm not gonna have any alcohol, don't worry. I don't need it to have a good time. I've learned that I can get high just from the experience, the lights, the sound, the music, the people ... I'm just gonna order a Diet Coke,' she said, with surprising maturity.

'Okay, good for you,' said Laura, rubbing her arm, 'you've just got to be careful—it's easy to crumble under the pressure, especially when the drinks are free.'

Katie smiled primly and then scuttled off into the distance towards the bar.

Just then, I heard James squeal from behind me: 'Right – Tara, darling, I've got your hen-do prezzie, but please don't turn around just yet.'

It must've been something truly amazing, as all the girls gripped each other and were stood stock-still, hands firmly clamped over their open mouths.

I felt something nip the back of my leg, but doing as I was told, I stayed strong and didn't turn around. But then I felt something wet on my foot and I couldn't help myself.

... What the FUCK?!

It was a human head, licking my ankle. The masked face then looked up at me with its tongue hanging out.

I jumped onto my chair screaming, then screamed some more. The Thing, which I believed to be a man on all fours, was dressed head-to-toe in black latex, his mask just about leaving room for his eyes and a small hole for his mouth. Around his neck was a collar, attached to a lead, attached to ... *James*.

'James—get him away!' I yelped, screaming hysterically. 'You know I'm scared of dogs [lie] and *things* in latex!' [Not a lie.]

'Darling don't be scared—he's your hen-do prezzie. I got him especially for you. He's called *Brutus*. I wanted to get you something completely unique and something you'd actually use, so instead of a stripper I got you a man-slave.'

Horror crept over my face and the hairs on the back of my neck bristled as the thing began growling, then actually barked at me. Frozen to the spot, I couldn't help but look over towards Siobhan, Camilla and Laura, who seemed to be finding the whole thing hilarious.

'James, get that thing away from me—*now!*'

'Darling, just stay calm—he can smell your fear,' said James, pulling Brutus away from me, having heeded my *do-not-fuck-with-me* tone. 'God, there's no pleasing some people, he tutted, 'you know, it wouldn't hurt you to show a little gratitude once in a while. Who wouldn't want their own personal gimp slave for the evening?'

Brutus continued barking, so James produced a leather-studded paddle and spanked him, at which the gimp then squealed like a dying donkey.

Everyone was howling with laughter. Except me.

'Aww, he only wants you to spank him a little,' said James, rubbing Brutus's back. 'Now—sit!'

Brutus shook his head.

'Some instructions for you, darling, he'll only respond if you discipline him,' he said, spanking the freaky man once again. 'Brutus—sit!'

With another disturbing groan, Brutus obeyed, sitting back on his haunches to the applause from the hens. James then patted Brutus's head and slipped one end of the leash under the table leg to prevent Brutus from getting away. Everyone came around to pat him, as though the scene that had just played out wasn't one of the weirdest things ever.

Moments later a waitress came over with two bottles of champagne, a huge bottle of 'house' vodka and two trays of shots. 'Can we get Brutus a doggie bowl, please? I think he's thirsty,' James asked.

'Of course,' said the waitress, 'I'll be right back.'

'I think we might just have to keep him if no one claims him,' said James, turning back to us all, 'I reckon he's probably quite cute under all that latex.'

What the feck is going on?

Gingerly, I sank down into a sitting position, carefully avoiding putting my feet on Brutus, who had now curled up on the floor beneath me, and then I spotted Katie returning from the bar, drink in hand. She nearly spilled it down herself when she caught sight of Brutus. But before she could question our new group member, Laura reached out, took her drink away and smelt the contents. This distracted Katie and she glared at Laura in frustration before being handed back the drink whilst Laura nodded in approval.

'So, tell me about this Sam guy then,' I said, turning to Katie, 'how do you know him?'

'Oh, we go way back. Isn't he *gooorrrgeous?*'

I gave a tentative nod. 'He's not unattractive, no. But how well do you actually know him?'

'I know where you're goin' with this, but don't you be worryin'. He's a really cool guy. Now, enjoy your free booze 'n' let's party.'

Normally I'd persist, but she was right. This was my hen-do after all.

Laura knocked back a shot, the second of which missed its target and made its way onto her leopard-print dress; which she didn't seem to notice.

Some bloody Mother Hen. Look at the state of her. That one should have a 'Do not feed after midnight' sign stamped on her forehead!

'Okay, everyone—listen up! I'd like to propose a toast,' Laura said. 'Firstly, I'd like to toast to Katie, for being a good girl and staying sober and clean. But most importantly, Tara—you're the best sister in the world and I'm so happy for you to have finally found the right man who's crazy enough to marry you. May you and Lewis live happily ever after. And here's to free booze and VIP!'

Everyone cheered and raised their glasses and

knocked back their drinks, including me.

Siobhan insisted we play a drinking game, like a gang of unruly university students. The game was called Arrogance, and the details are a little fuzzy; all I know is that there were no winners because everyone had to drink, a lot. In fact, the champagne and half the vodka had been guzzled within twenty minutes.

'Come on,' said Camilla, pulling me up. 'I didn't come all the way to Ibiza to spend it not dancing my ass off. Let's go.'

She was right. Since playing the drinking game, my initial feelings about this world being too busy, loud and weird had completely fallen by the wayside. I couldn't wait to dance, even if it was to abstract, repetitive techno music with no lyrics. I even felt okay with the idea of being squeezed into the sweatbox.

Everything seemed to matter less now. Want to take my hat? Fine. Elbow me in the face accidentally? I'll just knee you right back!

I suddenly felt a nervous excitement running through my veins, like I could take on the world.

This place is amazing!

Chapter 12

The crowd whooped, cheered and clapped as the DJ mixed track after track. I recognised absolutely none of the songs, but it didn't seem to matter, which was strangely out of character for me.

I started to wonder what had gotten into me—how could I think this wouldn't be fun or amazing?

James, Siobhan, Camilla, Katie, Laura and I danced for what could've been an hour. As time went on, each of us stepped up the momentum and danced harder than the next.

'Just feel that vibe,' said Katie, twirling her hands in the air, eyes closed.

Usually, I would've brushed off such a hippie-dippy statement; but indeed, I actually could feel the vibe. I'd heard that atmosphere can make you feel lifted, but this was another level altogether.

I found myself feeling a warm, loving affection towards my hens, touching and brushing them on their arms and faces, to which they responded with hugs of affection. I even began stroking Brutus's tummy as he rolled over onto his back.

I got goose bumps as people brushed past me, like a thousand orgasms running through me all at once. God, everyone just looked so incredibly beautiful.

The music had turned more primal now and we moved with the beat like we were part of some celebrating tribe.

I turned to see a sparkle in Camilla's eye, her dilated pupils twinkling as she took in the light show around us. She reminded me so much of Lewis that I actually leant in towards her with my lips pursed, but then I felt Brutus humping my leg and was snapped out of my weird fantasy into the even weirder reality of a grown man humping my leg. I smacked him off, then gazed back at Camilla; it almost hurt at that moment that Lewis wasn't there for me to hold.

A strange nervous excitement flowed through my body, the tingling sensation trickling from inside my scalp and cascading through my organs down to my toes. I was powerless except to dance, compelled by the urge to bop in time with the bass. Grinning like a Cheshire cat, I raised my hands in the air during the crescendos and closed my eyes to fully feel the vibrations. The rushing waves of euphoria built up like the lapping waves of a tide gradually making its way inland.

I turned to see my hens clumped together among the throng, all of them dancing and flowing together with the rest of the crowd.

'James—I feel a bit strange …' I said, leaning close

and talking into his ear, 'like I may be on ... drugs, or something. Do you think someone could've spiked my drink?'

'*Ummm* ... no, I don't think so. The drinks came straight from the bar upstairs. But if you have been taking drugs, I'm very disappointed you didn't invite me along to the party,' he said with a rich laugh. 'I wouldn't worry, darling, you're probably just tipsy from the alcohol and atmosphere.'

'Yeah, maybe. I guess. It's just, I feel really, *really* good. It feels way different from how I usually feel after a few drinks.'

'Oh, I wouldn't worry about it, sweetie. So long as you're having a good time, you should just go with it,' he said, rubbing my arm tenderly, then stroking my cheek. 'Oh, Tara, you're so beautiful, do you know that? I just love you so much ... you're like the mother I never resented,' and he dragged me in for a bear hug.

'I love you too, my little princess,' I said, stroking the back of his sweaty head.

Our embrace seemed to enhance my euphoric feelings, as we held each other for what would normally have been considered a 'weird' amount of time. Then I turned to see Camilla wiping her cheek and holding Siobhan at arm's length, giving her a strange look. Laura seemed to be intervening.

'What's up?' I asked Camilla.

'Nothing, Siobhan just ... *licked* my cheek – the nutter,' she said with a weirded-out smile.

Siobhan leaned in, 'Sorry, sorry, sorry ... I don't know what the hell happened there. I thought you were an ice cream.'

We all looked at her in utter confusion.

'Are you okay?' asked James.

'Yeah! Everyone's just lookin' so tasty tonight,' said Siobhan. 'Are you guys okay?'

We all exchanged puzzled looks, but Camilla was the first to break the tension with her laughter.

Laura then dragged everyone to the nearest bar for another round of shots and I was soon presented with a 'bride-to-be' shooter. I apprehensively necked the golden liquid, which seemed to be made up of tequila, aniseed and God knows what else. The burning liquid didn't go down well, mixing with the adrenaline that seemed to be pooling inside my stomach, churning and gargling in protest.

Within moments, I began to get that all-too-familiar pukey feeling, rising up.

Cupping my mouth, I indicated towards the toilets across the way and, whilst Brutus was looking in the other direction, I darted off. Only when I crossed the threshold did I see that they were those trendy bloody unisex toilets, but I didn't have time to be picky. Fleeing to the nearest open cubicle, I slammed the door behind me.

I dropped to my knees, feeling a stabbing pain in my tummy. I hovered above the toilet bowl and, thinking I might choke, banged on my chest. Then I felt something caught in my throat and coughed—*plop!* I'd regurgitated a whole prawn into the toilet bowl.

Gasping for air, I looked down at the offending shellfish, sinking to the bottom of the toilet bowl. Clearly, I needed to chew my food more. But as I went to flush the chain, something incredible happened. The prawn started twitching, then it grew legs … and a head … and then it started swimming around the bowl and winking at me.

'… Oh my—I'm soooo sorry for eating you,' I said to the prawn, my hand clutched to my heart with complete sincerity, 'I didn't know you were a magical prawn.'

'Tis okay!' responded the prawn in a Spanish accent. 'From 'ere I can get back 'ome to the ocean to see my familia—muchas gracias, Tara!'

The magical prawn swam away through the drain, and I felt a tear of happiness sprout in my eye.

Whoa, wait a second … that's really weird—how did he know my name?

I guessed the universe had mysterious ways. All I knew was that I felt remarkably better. After pulling off a stream of sandpapery loo roll, I carefully lined the toilet seat and sat down. I felt hypersensitive to my surroundings—I could hear the muffled sound of the bass line, some people weeing, and some evidently snorting drugs. Then I heard a bang on the partition between me and the cubicle next door, followed by distinct heavy breathing. A male voice grunted and panted, and a woman gasped in pleasure.

Normally I was too prudish to be remotely near a couple sexing inches from me, but I was mid-flow and couldn't stop, so I just yelled, 'Hello?! People are trying to pee here.'

'Andare più forte,' said the woman.

'*What?*' asked the man.

'Fucky me 'arder!' cried the woman, with what sounded like an Italian accent.

Her lover evidently obliged, as the banging became more forceful, accompanied by wailing from the woman.

These bastards are going hell for leather and I haven't even finished peeing yet!

'Excuse me,' I bellowed, rapping on the cubicle door, 'I'm *still* trying to pee in here!'

Again I was outright ignored: the banging increased in intensity. I feared the partition might cave in at any moment as the girl's gasps reached a clear crescendo with an orgasm of nuclear proportions; but the banging continued unabated.

The female was clearly happy to continue racking-up her orgasms, and as for the bloke, he showed no sign of slacking off at all.

As disgusted as I was, I was also secretly impressed: these noisy bastards had stamina. Then, just as I was preparing myself to make a sharp exit, a walkie-talkie clattered to the floor, landing just on my side of the partition.

I was just about to kick the walkie-talkie back under when it crackled into life: 'Henson, are you there? Over.'

A large hand reached down and grabbed the handset, and he answered in a cockney accent, 'Yeah, I'm 'ere,' said the man, still panting, 'just dealing with an urgent matter. What's up? Over.'

I unlocked my door to leave, when my brain clicked into gear. *I know that voice … the doorman – **Sam.*** Oh my God. Katie's Sam. The dirty dog! I suppose I should've been glad it wasn't Katie being banged up against the cubicle wall—but still, it didn't seem right.

He'd made all the signs that he was after her tonight and she was clearly besotted with him.

I left the toilets and saw Camilla waiting outside, with Brutus sitting on his knees. Brutus had something in his mouth ... *my hat!* Delighted, I went to take it, but he gripped tighter with his teeth and began growling.

It took a moment for me to register what I needed to do. Leaning down, I spanked him hard on the backside. He yelped, then let go, allowing me to wipe the slobber from my beloved top hat.

'There's a good boy,' I said, smiling at Camilla. 'Where's everybody else gone?'

'I have no idea.' She shrugged her shoulders. 'I think everyone's starting to lose the plot.'

Without saying a word, Brutus gestured towards downstairs with his head.

'Oh no. You mean the fetish floor?' Camilla asked, pulling a scared face.

Brutus nodded his head and backside excitedly.

'Looks like we're in for one tonight,' said Camilla, putting Brutus's leash in my hand.

Pulling on his leash impatiently, Brutus led us to an exposed brick archway illuminated by a red neon sign, which simply said: *FETISH*. The idea of going down there frightened the life out of me, but at the same time, it also intrigued me. Holding on for dear life, I prepared myself for ... *the unknown.*

As we descended the dimly lit spiral staircase, I could hear ominous echoes of laughter and music reverberating up from below. Upon reaching the bottom, I stopped dead in my tracks. I'd never seen anything like it. Hordes of naked flesh, lightly adorned in latex, paraded around the atrium. I felt like I'd walked into an exhibition for freaks, gimps, pimps, dominatrices, transvestites (some more convincing than others), slaves, several French maids, angels, devils and, of course, dozens of *Playboy* bunnies. Let's not forget the more traditional uniform fetishes: firemen in fishnets, policewomen in PVC, and nurses in knee-high boots—the place was littered with every kind of fantasy role-playing costume you could think of. (And then some: one guy was even dressed in a red latex Santa outfit – I kid you not!)

I immediately realised that I fitted in rather well down here, in my burlesque-style bridal mini-dress. Not to mention the human dog I was walking around with in hot pursuit of my hens.

Brutus marched forward, tugging on the leash with his throat.

I'm unsure whether it was the out-of-body experience I seemed to be having, or the shock of what I saw, but for some reason I didn't feel afraid. Normal, prudish Tara would have blushed and run straight back upstairs to the relatively normal world above. But I found the scene before my eyes ... *fascinating*.

Music and flashes of light seeped from the back of the atrium, which I assumed to be the main dance floor for this level. On either side seemed to be rooms where the odd fetishist came and went. Signs on various walls, written in English and Spanish, said:

HOUSE RULES:

- Safe word: 'RED'.
- 'No' is not a safe word – neither is begging.

- Wipe down equipment after use.
- Newbies – don't be shy!
- We have eyes and ears everywhere, please treat each other with respect ... and have fun!

... And it went on.

My eyes darted across the madness in search of my hens. 'Camilla, can you see any of them?'

'Nope. I can't take my eyes off that sexy Santa.'

Pausing, I took a deep breath and pulled Camilla away from him before entering the first dungeon-style door on the right. A small crowd of people in masquerade, fishnets and studded chokers stood around watching some kind of show. Brutus and I crossed paths with another gimp 'owner'—a pale, petite girl, with lots of facial piercings and gothic tattoos. Her thigh-high stiletto boots were made from what looked like steel, covered with silver-studded spikes. She wore a one-piece corset bustier, which finished just below her boobs, although, in her defence, she did have the modesty to be wearing nipple tassels. The dominatrix smiled at me before abruptly whipping her gimp for trying to hump Brutus.

'Sorry, ee is alweys doing dees,' she said before dragging her pet away.

Trying the next room, Brutus and I watched a woman chained to an inverted dentist's chair, moaning and then laughing with every spank of a leather-studded paddle, administered by what appeared to be this room's house dominatrix.

We walked past a transvestite wearing a tight leather pencil skirt and an unconvincing black wig. His makeup made him look like a caricature and his hairy chest made him resemble something like a bear.

'Nice hat,' said the bear-like transvestite. 'And I love your dress.'

'Thanks,' I said, delighted by the compliment. 'Nice … chest hair?'

The bear smiled warmly and continued walking.

I felt a strange sense of togetherness and love. I guess these people weren't as scary as they looked. They were actually really quite friendly, considering all the torture and violence they seemed to enjoy. The idea of what was going on around me should've freaked me out, but I realised the dressing up and role-playing was just a game. A bit different to playing hopscotch in the playground, but a game nonetheless.

As we re-entered the main hallway, Brutus pointed out a plump, mostly-naked larger lady, who must have been in her fifties. Moving closer, I saw the woman was passionately snogging a much smaller man, with blonde hair and dressed in black leather hot pants. For a moment, I thought it was James, but he wasn't wearing a pink feather boa coming in. I tried to pull Brutus away, but he stayed put and bit the man on the back of the leg.

The man turned round and patted Brutus on the head, then clocked me.

It was James. Oh my Lord!

I never thought I'd live to see the day *James would kiss a woman!*

He looked like he was having the time of his life, not seeming to care that I'd seen him with … a *she-devil*.

That's definitely a woman he's been snogging, isn't it?

'Taaarrrra!' shouted James, giving me a bear hug. 'This place is like, so mental. Everything is so sexable.' He then proceeded to stroke my hair, which actually felt really nice.

Things became very hazy after that.

I remember going into a room and staring in utter shock and disbelief at the sight of Laura standing over a large man with a ball gag in his mouth, strapped to what looked rather like a Black and Decker workbench. She was striking him with a whip, shouting, 'Tell me why you deserve to be released!'

I couldn't believe my eyes. But at the same time, I didn't dare stop Laura from 'doing her thing', so we all waited and watched as the man on the receiving end enjoyed himself more and more, if you know what I mean. I personally couldn't have imagined anything worse; my innocence and prudishness was being stolen from me the longer I walked around this *Fifty Shades of Grey* getup, but during my drunken state, I could thankfully only see the hilarity of it all.

I also distinctly remember stumbling into a room with an assortment of abstract torture installations. On one fixture, a gimp was swinging from a large swing, being spanked each time he came backwards, when he'd be hosed down with ice-cold buckets of water.

One woman was chained up from all directions, looking like a fly caught in a spider's web. Apparently, groping and other weird business was encouraged. We decided to leave when I saw a man sitting underneath her for what can only be assumed would be a 'golden shower'.

I thought I had seen it all, but I was wrong.

On the stripper walkway, a woman sat on the edge, legs wide, casually stuffing ping-pong balls into her lady-garden.

Ouch, how is that even possible? I thought, wincing.

She then proceeded to somehow squeeze with so much force that a ball literally pinged—with a suction sound-effect—onto the table below and over to a man armed with two ping-pong paddles, trying to return the 'serve' into a bucket bin next to the stage. A sign next to the bucket said 'SINK THE PINK, WIN A DILDO'. *How lovely.* Like some twisted kind of fairground ride. We watched from the back, hypnotised, disgusted, but also secretly fascinated.

The man returning the serve had evidently ran out of balls and the host was recruiting for the next contestant. I could see Siobhan from a mile away gearing up for her turn to return the serve.

Pop. Click. She'd missed. The crowd sighed.

Second serve …

Pop. Click. The ball soared through the air … *clock.* She'd done it! The crowd went wild as she turned to hug the man next to her.

'I've never won a feckin' thing in me whole life!' cheered Siobhan, bounding over for a group hug with her shiny new prize.

The next thing I remember was being in a room that played abstract tribal music accompanied by strobe lights, and more PVC than you could shake a stick at. A crowd of a few hundred danced away in a trance-like state.

As quickly as we'd found the hens, they were all gone again but by chance, Camilla spotted James up on a platform next to the dance floor ... in a cage. I knew he'd be gagging to get into one of those. James teased his audience with a combination of oriental hand movements; bum shimmying and pelvic thrusting, before coming over theatrically shy. He only noticed us after ten minutes, when he realised he needed to pee and couldn't work out how to get out of the cage.

The next thing I knew, Laura began pole-dancing in front of an audience of gaping mouths. I arrived on the scene just in time to see her emptying a bottle of champagne over her hair, face and chest and provocatively rubbing it in to her body. With a surprisingly deft move, she tossed the empty bottle to a bouncer while simultaneously twisting her body acrobatically around the pole. Somehow she managed to hook her legs seductively around it, ending in a position almost horizontal to the bar, and then moved on and came to a halt, vertical once more, back against the pole, with arms up over her head. She was clutching the pole with both hands, using her arse-crack as a guide. She then slid down it into perfect side splits to rapturous applause from the audience. Her head was tilted back against the pole and the smile on her face said it all: she was loving every minute of it.

Fair play to her, I thought, nodding at her in admiration.

Siobhan then decided she also wanted to have a go at being in the limelight. She joined Laura on the stage and together they worked as a double act, doing their best to tantalise their audience of freaks and fetish-loving fiends. However, the act was spoiled by an overly energetic attempt at bumping hips from

Siobhan, sending Laura flying off the stage. (Siobhan barely noticed.)

Siobhan then began what could only be described as a robot stripper in desperate need of a software update. Then, grabbing the pole with one hand and leaning her body out, she began using her other leg in a scooter motion to propel herself in circles around the pole. Faster and faster she went. Round and round. It didn't take long until she was spinning out of control, then lost her grip and hurtled into the crowd, landing smack bang on an unsuspecting vicar.

The whole crowd gasped as they cleared the way to see the pile of bodies, but Siobhan had already pinned down the poor man of the cloth (well, man of the PVC) and was greedily snogging the face off of him.

'Red ... RED!' screamed the vicar, as Siobhan finally came up for air.

'Red? I'd feckin' love to go in the RED room with you!' said Siobhan, who clearly hadn't read the house rules. 'Now come here ... you naughty little priest.'

In seconds, the nightmare-inducing scene was cut short, as bouncers surrounded Siobhan. She was lifted up and marched away whilst the Vicar, who looked rather worse for wear, tried to recover himself. At first Siobhan looked confused, but once she realised they were heading for the exit she began kicking and screaming. 'Oi! Put me down! That man was about to give up his celibacy for me!'

Then she noticed the rest of us looking on in shock. 'Tara! Chickies! Don't leave me!'

We all hung our heads and followed the bouncers as they led her off the premises, after what was most definitely the weirdest night of my life. Surprisingly, Brutus was still following in tow, and had somehow managed to round up the AWOL Katie. (It's true what they say about dogs being loyal.)

'Well, that was *some* performance, Siobhan.' I said, not the least bit surprised our night had ended that way.

'Yeah, and where are your shoes, Siobhan?' asked Camilla, while pulling cocktail bits and bobs out of her hair.

'Some bloke asked if he could try them on, so I let him.' She shrugged.

The last thing I remember is being outside the club, Laura squatting down, knickers around her ankles, peeing, the other three convulsing in laughter, and Brutus ambling off to smell Laura's pee. I'm sure Brutus removed his mask at one point to reveal a rather handsome face, but I couldn't be 100% sure with the all the madness that had occurred.

'I … I just love you guys so, so much,' said Camilla, before pulling us all in together for a group hug.

Aww. This is what a hen-do is all about, I thought. Bonding.

Chapter 13

Six a.m., and the Snore Wars were in full swing and had been for two hours and seventeen minutes.

I couldn't quite find a way to describe the sounds gusting out of Laura.

Wildebeest? No, that doesn't cut the mustard. More like something between a hellish tuba symphony and a dozen Harley Davidsons harmonising with each other.

It was almost impressive. With each pause between Laura's inhale and exhale I held onto the hope: *Please, God, let this be the final one.* But, no: I lay there, grimacing, my blood pressure increasing with each rasping blast.

Ordinarily I would search the grounds high and low for *anywhere* else to sleep; anywhere would be better than here. But James had been 'occupied' in the living room until the early hours and, from the stories he told of his affairs, I certainly wasn't going to venture out there until I knew for sure that the coast was clear.

Our room had two double beds; Laura slept on the right bed, and I not-slept on the left. The culprit lay flat on her back, visibly dribbling; somehow, someway oblivious to the ground-shaking sounds she emitted, merely inches from her own ears. Surely, you'd have to be dead to not hear such a noise, but the noise itself was proof that she *was* alive. It was madness. She must've lost her hearing in the club the previous night—it's the only plausible explanation for her not waking up.

After hurling a flip-flop, a rolled up towel, a kebab box, a bottle of sun lotion and anything else I could lay my hands on, I'd now unfortunately run out of missiles to lob her way. But there she lay, not a care in the world, flat on her back, head turned up to the skies, surrounded by a slightly surreal pile of white feathers from the pillow I had walloped her with an hour before. It had no effect whatsoever, other than filling the room with hundreds of choking little feathers. Okay, admittedly, I had walloped her a few times, but what sort of shoddy cheapo pillows burst on the third whack anyway?

I turned over heavily and wrapped my own pillow more tightly around my ears, knuckles of my left hand in my mouth, waiting for the next crescendo. They came in rhythmical, almost musical waves: three shorter ones and then one long-drawn-out honk. But then something miraculous happened …

I waited,

and waited …

… Nothing.

It was over. *Finally!* I closed my heavy eyelids and smiled weakly at the blissful silence.

But just as I began to drift into an exhausted slumber, paranoia kicked in. I flew up into a sitting position and stared wildly across the bedroom. She was definitely not breathing. Panic began to rise in the pit of my stomach; holding my breath, I began to listen for signs of life.

Nothing.

'For the love of God, Laura, are you dead?'

She didn't stir.

Catapulting myself out of bed, I flew across the bedroom.

'Laura! Laura?' I shouted shaking her shoulder. 'Come on, this isn't funny!'

Still, nothing.

With panic rising and gut, instinct taking over I firmly bitch-slapped her right across the face.

[Pppaaarrrfff-ssshhhhh]—she unleashed a creaking, hissing sound from her backside, and without stirring, smacked her lips and resumed her snoring symphony (only this time the tune had changed to *Wounded Rhinoceros Being Dragged to Slaughter, in B Minor*.)

Lord forgive me, but at the time I wasn't quite sure how glad I was that she'd begun breathing again.

Eventually I must've finally dozed off as I awoke to the midday sun bursting through the shutters. Geriatric style, I carefully lifted my weak body out of the bed and swung the balcony doors open to reveal a bright Ibiza afternoon.

Hanging over the iron railing, I breathed in the warm sea air and admired the scenery overlooking the valley. The chorus of Mediterranean birds and grasshoppers sung their signature lullaby, as I watched the waves gently breaking against the shoreline in the distance.

As serene as the view was, my mind was fixated on trying to piece together just what the bloody hell happened last night. After several attempts at mentally retracing our steps, I gave up and dragged my poached brain off the balcony and back into the bedroom.

Laura still lay there, sleeping, but no longer snoring. *Typical.*

And that's when I saw the bearded man sleeping on the other side of my bed. Screeching, I stumbled and fell back out onto the balcony.

No. No, no, no. Not again! What the hell is wrong with me? How has this happened … again?

I got up and walked through the white sheet curtain, determined to kick the bastard out of my bed as quickly as possible.

Oh. It was Barry. Blow-up Barry Junior.

I almost began to cry in relief. I don't know what I would've done if I'd repeated *that* same mistake again.

Laura still didn't stir, so I decided to venture into the lounge, dreading what lay ahead of me.

I opened the door and gasped; *we must've been burgled!*

But then among the carnage I spotted James's body lying face down on the couch, wearing nothing but a bra. Relief instantly swept over me—he would've been a deterrent for any sensible burglar.

The lounge had a nauseating stench of stale alcohol, cigarette fumes and sweat. Clothes and flip-flops carpeted the otherwise white marble tiles. Playing cards were scattered around like bomb fragments amongst bottles, cans, angel wings, a puddle of spilled sangria and ... glitter. A metric shit-tonne, of glitter.

I considered cleaning up for a moment, but decided against it, remembering I didn't make *any* of the mess and it was *my* bloody hen-do and I'd be doing nothing of the sort.

Speaking of dastardly hens, why wasn't anyone else up yet?

They should be gently waking me with a glass of freshly squeezed juice and delicate continental preserves. Beautiful and serene, I should've been leaning back on my soft white Egyptian cotton sheets, surrounded by my doting hens discussing the relaxing and wonderful spa treatments we'd be having today.

But I'm not fussy – just a cup of feckin' tea would've been nice!

Dodging the fragments of the night before, I made my way over to Siobhan and James's room. The door opened only a small bit before a thud stopped it.

'*Oww-how-hooowww,*' someone yelped.

Then, *of all things*, an actual feckin' *chicken* bolted out of the door and ran past me, causing me and the person behind the door to scream at the top of our voices.

'No—Fabiana! Who let the chicken out? Ye feckin' eejit!' It was Siobhan, of course.

The chicken scuttled around the room, bounding over furniture, fluttering everywhere.

'What—why in Gods name is there a chicken—*ARRGGHHH!*' I screamed as it came near me before darting off again. 'PLEASE tell me why there's a chicken in here!'

James stirred, then looked over before squealing twice as loud as I did; he then vaulted off the sofa, knocking over a bottle of sangria while trying to cover his man-plums.

Siobhan then burst out of her bedroom. 'FABIANA! You little tinker, get back in here!' Siobhan darted past us with a wicker laundry basket in hand. Hurtling forward, she nearly had Fabiana cornered but slipped on a pile of playing cards, falling and skidding into the patio door with a painful thud.

Within seconds, Laura, Katie and Camilla had bolted out of their rooms to see what the commotion was about; everyone stood open-mouthed as they observed the scene.

'Argghh … I think—I think I may've broken me feckin' neck,' murmured Siobhan, cheek to the floor, talking into the puddle of wine. 'Ooh, this sangria is still all right, actually,' she said, laughing to herself.

That started us all off, and I swear I nearly blacked out from laughing. James threw a sheet over himself and rolled around, barely able to catch his breath.

Ten minutes later, we'd managed to calm down but occasionally one of us would crack and start everyone laughing again. We made a half-hearted attempt to clean up, but really, the place was too far gone.

'Well, I thought, seeing as how it's a hen-do I'd, like, get us a mascot,' said Siobhan after she and Laura had tactically recaptured the poor animal.

'It's a lovely gesture, Siobhan, but I think I'll be turning vegetarian after the fright Fabiana gave me,' I said picking up a discarded thong off a table lamp.

'Oh no, what happened to your willy?' Camilla

asked me, pointing at the deflated skin-coloured pile of rubber in the corner. 'Looks a bit flaccid.'

'Think our honorary hen was hungry for the cock last night,' said Katie, pointing out the chicken feathers surrounding the inflatable.

'Wait—what's this on my neck?!' squealed James from the bathroom.

He galloped into the lounge revealing a huge hickey on his neck.

'James, how can you not remember? You were snogging that old biddy for like an hour last night,' I said, putting him straight. 'We thought you'd come over to the hetero side.'

'No ... *nooo* ... I ...' he said, looking utterly beside himself and creasing up in disbelief. 'It was definitely a man. Not my finest catch, I'll give you that, but—'

Katie shoved her phone in front of his face, managing to hold the handset still while containing her laugh just long enough to show him the evidence.

James wailed dramatically. I would've consoled him if I were able to get off the floor from laughing.

'This is bloody outrageous! *Bitches* – the lot of you – why didn't you stop me?'

More laughter.

'Well, I tried – honest to God I did,' said Katie. 'But you weren't havin' any of it, you told me to leave you and Betty alone.'

James looked utterly mortified.

'No, this cannot be true ...' he said. 'But then, I did see someone making a hasty exit at 7 a.m.. *Ohh,* I'm disgusted with myself ...'

'Don't worry, darling,' I said, going over to comfort

him, 'It wasn't Betty who came home with us.'

'Oh, thank God!'

'It was Brutus.' I eyed him knowingly.

'Oh! Yes, now I remember. Well, that's certainly better than Betty,' he said, sighing with relief, 'at least Brutus was a man; even if he was a mere slave.'

'One of the only things I remember is back at the apartment Tara wanted to go for a swim and tried climbing inside a water bottle. One of the funniest things I've ever witnessed!' said Camilla, shortly followed by a chorus of 'Oh my God – I remember that' and 'you nutter'.

I had zero recollection, but despite my protests, there was the photo evidence of a rather haggard-looking Tara, in inverted prayer position, trying to dive into a large bottle of water. The blurry photo reel continued, with much of the incriminating evidence being news to us.

One photo revealed James trying to put jeans on his head, thinking it was a top. And then there was a very interesting video where Siobhan thought she could walk through walls. There was at least one shameful act committed by every one of us.

Whilst looking at her phone, Camilla's head shot up and she looked at us with wide eyes. 'Oh my God ... I've just had a flashback – I think I may've called Alex and broken up with him!' she screeched. 'Shit-shit-shit – I need to call him, like now.'

Siobhan and Laura laughed uncontrollably.

'What is wrong with you guys? Why are you laughing, this is serious!'

Just about managing to speak, Laura said, 'No ...

you didn't break up with Alex. Well, you did, but you didn't tell him that in as many words. Katie, Katie – show her the video!'

Katie crawled over and showed everyone a two-minute video of Camilla talking into a TV remote, telling Alex that she'd entered into a lesbian relationship with Siobhan and was moving out to Ibiza.

'I'm not being funny, but I don't remember drinking so much that I would've ... I can't say it,' said James.

'Played tonsil-tennis with a *lady*?' scoffed Camilla.

'No! Don't! Please. I've mouthwashed several times now and still can't forget the taste. I'm riddled with lurgies now, I'm sure you'll all be delighted to know. Please don't tell anyone, I have a reputation to uphold—'

'Well, it doesn't matter, does it, I mean, we all had loads of fun, didn't we?' said Katie.

'I have no idea if I had a good time, I can't remember anything whatsoever,' said Laura looking baffled.

Everyone shook their heads.

'I was absolutely, 100% trippin' balls,' said Siobhan, 'Fook me, I was seeing feckin' unicorns and all kinds of magical shite! At one point I saw Fabiana breathin' fire, and I was like, I'm not gonna just walk past and *not* pick up a fire-breathin' chicken now, am I? I'm not thick, like. That would've been stupid. Although, to be honest with you now, I was quite disappointed to wake up earlier and find out she doesn't actually breathe fire. Thought she might have even laid us some fresh eggs for breakfast. But she's still cool, like,' she said, shrugging and feeding Fabiana the remainder of a can of Pringles.

'How on earth did you come up with the name Fabiana?' asked James, cracking a smile.

'I didn't come up with the name; Fabiana told me herself—at the time. I mean, I'm not *that* mental. I was having a proper Doctor Doolittle moment, she was tellin' me how she loved livin' in Ibiza and that she's at all the parties on the weekends. We just clicked, you know, and I had to take her with me,' said Siobhan, laughing at herself in realisation of how ridiculous she sounded.

More raucous laughter.

'Yeah, well, I'm sorry, Siobhan, but we're going to have to release Fabiana back into the wild at some point,' said Laura, resuming her Mother Hen role after the craziness of last night.

Camilla smacked her tongue around in her mouth, trying to generate saliva. 'My mouth's as dry as the bottom of a birdcage. Do you think someone could've spiked our drinks?

'Maybe the "house" vodka they brought over included some extra special ingredients. Who knows?' Katie chimed in all of a sudden. 'Look, I know things got a little crazy at points, but that's kinda the idea of a hen-do, right? I mean, everyone had a ball, and no one got hurt or anythin', so it doesn't really matter, does it?'

* * *

Desperate to mong out on the beach for the afternoon, we made moves to get ourselves ready. Firstly checking my reflection in the bathroom mirror, I realised I looked worse than I actually felt, which wasn't saying much, as I felt like shite. I looked like the petals of a wilting flower holding onto the last rays of life before finally croaking and falling off.

But after showering, and putting factor 50 on every single mole, then putting on my new Agent Provocateur bikini, I looked myself up and down in the large mirror and gave myself a half smile. Not too bad, not too bad at all! I'd allow myself fifteen minutes of natural vitamin D, then later I'd lather myself in the full block as I didn't want my skin to burn. I certainly didn't feel 100%, but the recuperative effects of a new outfit can't be under-estimated. And what an outfit it was. It was an extravagant purchase, but who could resist a zesty combination of lime-green, shocking-pink and yellow? No one would look at my blotchy old legs once they copped a load of this little number.

Best not to leave too much to chance though, I thought, reaching for my large pink lace sarong and knotting it around my waist. The sarong was another mid-to-major dent in the credit card, but well worth it. At least, it should've been, if I could work out the best way to wear the bloody thing. With another sigh, I undid the knot from around my middle – it looked too much like I was expecting twins. Frowning, I pushed it down so it hung loosely over my hips. *No, definitely not there.* I untied it once more and stood staring at my reflection, the two ends of the sarong clasped in either hand. I looked like Jesus preaching to the disciples. *Hmm.* Not the sexy, ethereal look I was after. I tried a more alternative approach, wrapping it round my neck and then around my torso. *Nope.* Now I looked like a

Twister ice-lolly. With the longest, most breathy sigh I could muster, I returned to the original style. *This is the best of a bad bunch*, I mused, sucking my tummy in hard as I could.

I didn't even bother with my hair – my skin was so fair, I would most definitely be wearing my large, wavy black straw sun hat. The photo of the model online wore the hat and it made her look like Audrey Hepburn, but of course, it looked nothing like that on me.

After I had located and packed my beach bag with euros and my mobile, I slipped on a huge pair of Prada dark-rimmed sunglasses, then waited at the pool for the others.

We stepped out purposefully, a fearsome group, onto the sun-drenched pavements, leaving the bombsite (AKA "apartment") for the bustling streets. There was a chaotic soundtrack of dozens of scooter horns, traders yelling and tourists laughing and calling out to one another. And of course, house music pouring from every shop front.

First point of call was to get as much greasy, crap food into ourselves as soon as possible, so we headed for the nearest pizzeria.

I was the only one able to finish their greasy, supersize pizza, with everyone else only managing half. Feeling a carb coma coming on, we made a sluggish move to do a bit of shopping. We were hit with a vibrant mix of colour, both from what people were wearing and in the stalls. The locals were selling an infinite range of goodies, from Ibiza paraphernalia, to clothing, hippy knick-knacks, ashtrays, mosaics, jewellery and leather goods.

Taking a deep breath, we plunged into the melee, going from stall to stall, laughing at the patter from the market traders who clearly knew every trick in the book to charm a group of curious tourists. I managed to bat a few away, but before long I caved in and started loading up with presents. I bought a black leather studded belt for Lewis – it would look so sexy on his low-slung jeans – a lovely coloured-glass pendant for Mum, and a tie-dye pashmina for Suyin, plus other small trinkets for the rest of the staff.

With the shopping done, we linked each other's arms and frog-marched ourselves towards the beach. My eyes greedily scanned the horizon, taking in the golden sands and the azure water, studded with boats and jet skis rip-roaring back and forth. Keeping my eyes on the prize, I ran past the looky-looky sellers and made a beeline for the rows of empty sun-loungers.

But I was horrified at what I saw. Rows and rows of empty, standard, rubbish sun-loungers. And right at the front, every single, beautiful, luxury padded sun-lounger had been taken. Not one left! I turned to see the girls catching up, plonking their stuff down on the nearest available crap white, plastic sun-lounger without a care in the world.

'What are you guys doing?!' I asked, hands on hips.

'What are you talking about, darling?' asked James, 'we're just lying down on the—'

'No! This is not what I was promised,' I grumbled. 'These are abysmal. It's not acceptable. You guys told me that we would have luxury sun-loungers. Please, let's just go and—'

'Tara, everyone's too knackered to find any fookin' fancy chairs and we're all in shreds. As long as we're close enough to the bar for me to have an intravenous line attached for some gin and tonic to cure this hangover,' huffed Siobhan, 'I don't care where we sit.'

'I agree with Siobhan,' Katie muttered, stretching herself out, 'I feel like shit beaten up in a bucket.'

'Sorry, Tara, I promise we'll get some tomorrow,' muttered Laura, not looking the least bit sorry at all.

The hens continued to lay out their towels and apply sunscreen.

Tears began to form in my eyes. I'd waited all this time, paid all this money ... for what?

'You traitorous bastards!' I shouted, feeling the foulest mood ever descend on me. 'I should've known you lot would lie to me so that you guys could just go and get pissed on *my* hen-do!' Without saying another word, I kicked a flurry of sand in their general direction, then whipped off my sun hat and proceeded to stamp on it in protest. I'd get my luxury sun-lounger with or without them, I thought, storming off.

My pale skin burned without any lotion *and* the poor soles of feet were almost burnt off me with the molten-hot sand. But I didn't give a shit! I was a martyr, risking my life for my beliefs. I wasn't stopping for anyone, and that was the end of it!

I stomped up and down the beach for what felt like hours. Not one luxury sun-lounger was to be found. Not one; but of course there were hundreds, possibly even thousands of the shit loungers.

People were obviously copping on to the sun-lounger revolution. I looked out at the rows of luxury loungers, giving the death stare to as many people as I could, trying to intimidate them out of them—but to no avail. These people would fight for them, as would I, in their shoes. I instantly calmed down a bit, realising we were the same. Just good, upstanding people who work hard during the year and didn't tolerate low-standard loungers.

I was about to give up and head back to the luxury sun-loungers at the apartment when I heard a wolf whistle. *Really,* I thought, straightening myself up, it can't be for me surely – but it was!

The tall, hunky twenty-something-year-old bronzed Adonis was staring right at me. Staring? No –smouldering. Oh, hello. You've still got it, Tara Ryan! I couldn't believe I was about to give up on the whole beach day and waste an outfit like this if it could draw the attention from guys like this!

I smiled and blushed, but gave him a dismissive wave, pointed at my ring and shook my head. *I mean, I know I'm taken, but there's no harm in a little ego boost is there?*

Then a few more whistles came, but that's when my heart sank and I saw *her* ... 'Miss Latina Beyoncé Booty' walked lazily along the beach alongside me, looking sexy as hell. Her tasselled ensemble flapped around her peachy arse, her taut skin was perfectly bronzed, and she had that tangled, salty-sea hair that would take me hours to achieve in the salon.

It should be illegal to be that beautiful! I thought, nearly collapsing with the heat and flopping down on the burning-hot sand.

I sighed heavily, staring at the tsunami of young

tanned males who surged forward together, forming an impenetrable wall of admirers, each vying for just a smile from this goddess. There was absolutely no doubt about it, when the Big Man Upstairs was making decisions about who was getting what, she was at the front of the queue and got feckin' everything!

It's a weird sensation. One minute you're young, with light years ahead of you, just like Miss Pocahontas over there. Then, before you know it, you're heading fast towards the social banishment of middle age. It's like that feeling when you walk into Top Shop or Miss Selfridge, and you know that you don't belong in there anymore. You're no longer in the gang. Then, horror of horrors, you'll catch those fresh young size twos straight out of modelling school, with their huge natural bushy eyebrows, gawping at you like you're something from outer space. The look on their faces is one of pure pity. They never consider it will happen to them one day. But it does.

I scanned down the beach. It was like my eyes had just been opened. I'm no longer one of you, I thought miserably, watching a group of confident girls stretched out on the sand. I looked on longingly – some of their legs were so long they could've tied themselves in a knot. *Twice*. They were topless, not that it would've made much difference if they were wearing anything, because there were hardly any breasts to cover up. Their ankles and wrists were ringed in beaded and brightly covered bands, and their skimpy triangle bikini bottoms barely covered there no doubt neatly tended lady-gardens.

It's strange how fashions change, I mused as I self-consciously glanced down at my large 'once-sticky-up' boobs that were now most definitely showing signs of loss of elasticity. It didn't matter either way. Flatter chests were most definitely in, and implants were out.

Life can be so cruel.

Geriatric style, I got up, threw my towel over my shoulder and headed back to the shoreline. My spirits were instantly lifted as I spotted a perfect, harmonious scene: a young family were building a sandcastle together; it was actually a relief to see some kind of normality amongst the hung-over teens. Plonking myself back down and looking on, I momentarily felt that familiar pain in my heart of never being able to have a child of my own—and to add to my despair the mother was also showing signs of baby number two growing safely inside her. *Some people just have it all.* She called to her little boy to put his sun hat on but he was far too excited as his dad popped a triumphant mini-flag in their huge sandcastle.

'Oh, wow,' I said, shuffling over to the cute little boy, unable to help myself, 'what an amazing sandcastle you've built.'

I bent down further to admire it when all of a sudden the same stabbing and sickie pains that I'd experienced last night were back, only this time it was different, it was a hundred times worse.

Out of nowhere, I let out a most unladylike booty-bomb. I immediately straightened up, praying to God that that no one had heard it.

'Gavin!' shouted the little boy's mother at the top of her voice, 'if I've told you once, I've told you a thousand times: manners! Say excuse me!'

'But I didn't do anything, Mummy!'

'What on earth have you been eating, son?' his dad broke in, fanning the air around him.

My face flamed but I didn't speak up. Instead, clenching my butt cheeks together, I backed away, waving my goodbyes. I know it was wrong to let him take the blame, and I considered going back suggesting it could've been the dog that had just padded by or something, but I could already feel my insides beginning to creak, growl and gurgle.

For feck's sake, this was just not happening! I spun around on the burning-hot sand, trying to work on my plan of escape. I was overwhelmed with a feeling of dizziness, as another, even hotter, gas explosion was being prepared deep inside me and being shuffled into firing range.

Which way do I run? I went through my options at a million miles per hour. The sea? Back to the restaurant we ate in last night? Dig a hole in the sand? Use the moat of the giant sandcastle?

Gut instinct must've taken over. I found myself scooping up my bag, dismissing my towel, then running, awkwardly, knock-kneed with one hand cupped over my explosive backside, zigzagging and weaving over the sand, hopping over bodies, beach bags and towels. A mini sandstorm followed in my wake, causing a few sunbathers to curse and swear at my rapidly retreating figure.

'Please, God,' I begged as the restaurant toilet door hovered into sight and I hurled plastic tables and chairs out of my way, 'let me make it!'

My stomach had taken on a life of its own. It seemed to be performing a Mexican wave and the ferocious gas bubbles that had been escaping intermittently were now one long rumbling groan …

Just metres away now and looking straight ahead I spied a sign on the door:

TOILETS OUT OF ORDER.

I'd just got my hand to the toilet door and slipped inside when, *oh—FUCK*, the colonic dam that I'd worked so hard to keep up gave way. The world fell out of my arse, leaking gloriously between my fingers before I'd even managed to pull down my prized Agent Provocateur bikini bottoms. Crying to myself, I slumped onto the loo, trembling and shaking, looking down at my once beautiful French-polished toenails, glistering in slimy neon-green poop.

I know I wanted to lose weight, I sobbed into my trembling hands … but *really*, REALLY?!

Once the surge showed signs of subsiding, I rested my head against the cool tiles on the wall. I really didn't care if they were clean or not. Bad move. This new position gave me a perfect reflection of myself cowering on the loo. My face was puce and glistening in sweat.

'What the f …' My ears had blown up to the size of cauliflowers, and … oh my God… my face was now growing before my very eyes and was fast heading towards size of a puffer fish! *Sweet holy Mary Mother of God.* I looked like someone had stuck a bicycle pump up my backside and had pumped and pumped …

I barely had time to consider this rather disconcerting new symptom when it was joined by another, equally unpleasant one. My skin was itching everywhere. It was covered in lumps and bumps. My legs felt like jelly. I wasn't sure I could stand up, and even if I could, I didn't feel strong enough to negotiate my way around the mess I had left on the floor.

Shakily, I glanced around for some toilet paper, but there wasn't any. Remembering that I also hadn't packed any in my beach bag, I released a long whiney pitiful yelp.

'Hey! Señorita? These toilets are out of order!' The statement, in a deep, booming male voice, was accompanied by a determined banging on the door.

'Señor,' I howled, somewhat relieved and yet humiliated,' please, Señor, can you get me some toilet paper?'

Silence.

'Señor? Señor? You have non paper! Señor?? I NEED TOILET PAPER! HELP!'

I heard footsteps retreating and a door slam closed in the distance.

'Bastard! It was probably your poxy food that caused this anyway!' I shouted after him. 'Oh, God ...' I winced as a super-long and ferocious booty-bomb fired out, reverberating around the cubicle, loud enough for the whole world to hear.

Fighting the faint and dizzy feelings that pounded at my head, I got shakily to my feet and began rinsing my hands and face. Gingerly, I turned slowly around to flush the loo. It wasn't working. Sod it. That wasn't my problem.

Still dreading another bout, I fumbled around for my bag. It was sitting unhygienically at the side of the toilet bowl.

'My new beach bag,' I sobbed as the tiny cubicle began spinning once again.

At that moment, my stomach gave another ominous rumble and I spun round and collapsed back on the loo. *Here we go again!*

For the love of God! Why … why … why were my intestines flying out of my ass, on *my* hen-do?

With no choice but to stay put on the loo, I delved deep into my beach bag and dug around for my mobile. Luckily, I found it straight away. In between spasms, I punched Laura's number. Buckling over, I put the phone to my ear. It rang out. I groaned and tried the next number on my list: Katie. Again nothing. Okay, James's turn.

Mercifully, he picked up.

'Tara! Where are you? You've got to come and try this amazing new cocktail—'

'In … restaurant from last night—'

'Now, now! [Tutting] … there's no use in putting yourself into another carb coma. You are, after all, a bride-to-be, remember?'

'I'm not well … stuck in … toiiilet … and, and, and … nooo toiiilettt paaaper!'

My voice sounded strange and slurred.

'Oh, you do have a habit of getting yourself into these situations! I'm on my way.'

I must've passed out because almost instantly I could hear the unmistakable sound of my hens. The cavalry had arrived. I looked up to see Laura, Katie, Camilla and Siobhan peering over the top of the cubicle looking shocked and horrified. Then the heads disappeared and there was a lot of shuffling and mutters of 'oh, you can't do that'. Suddenly, with an ear-splitting crack, the door burst open to reveal James standing there looking rather pleased with himself. The others crowded in behind him and took a collective deep breath at the state I was in.

Laura was the first to break the silence. Stepping forward and holding her nose, she helped me to my feet.

'It's all right, we're here now.'

'She's not well,' said Laura, turning to the others.

'Tara, you fool, weren't you wearin' any lotion?' asked Katie, lifting up her sunglasses and staring at me wide-eyed. 'You look like you're wearin' a Minnie Mouse dress.'

I looked down at my body and was horrified – on top of everything else, I'd become lobsterfied – my skin was now a blistering bright red and was punctuated with dozens of white polka dots where I'd only factor 50'd my moles.

'Jeez,' said Katie, reaching forward to touch my forehead in an attempt to test my temperature. 'You're burnin' up. And Christ, you look like one of those ol' spooky Cabbage Patch dolls. You're not gonna peg it on your own hen-do are you?'

'Stop being so puerile!' Laura snapped at Katie, doing her best to hold me up.

'Tell me what that means and I'll try,' said Katie, quickly handing over her towel to cover me.

I wanted to knock their heads together; I mean, it was quite possible I was dying here.

'She's really not well,' repeated Laura, just as I lost my balance again and slumped backwards. 'The quicker we get her back to the apartment the better. We'll need to get a doctor out.'

I felt the entire packed-out restaurant move their beady eyes up and down every inch of me as my hens escorted me out of the place. The silence was unbearable. I wanted to run, but most of all I wanted to accuse *him* and his bloody restaurant of giving me food poisoning. But I was so weak, all I could manage were crippling baby steps, causing the humiliating moment to last just that little bit longer.

I raised my trembling hand to give the restaurant owner the finger, but even that sagged on me. Instead, I clung to Laura and Siobhan, resting my sweat-soaked head on Siobhan's shoulder as they carefully steered me away from the restaurant and onto the main strip.

Stumbling along at a snail's pace, I became vaguely aware of the hands rubbing my back and a towel wiping my feverish face.

'Stop, stoppp! I need the loo again ...' I cried out, doubling over in pain, getting weaker by the second.

'Katie, Camilla—go and flag down a doctor or something!' barked Laura, her voice full of worry.

'Tadaaah! Me to the rescue!' said James, placing an orange champagne ice bucket underneath me.

'A Veuve Clicquot potty—ingenious!' Laura said, lowering me down onto it.

Perched on my makeshift toilet, liquid now once again flowing freely out of my backside, I could feel myself slipping in and out of consciousness. The next thing I knew, I'd fallen over sideways, collapsed in a puddle on the ground with the whole of Ibiza staring at me.

'The doctor fella's comin'!' yelled Katie. 'She needs smellin' salts or somethin' to bring her back to life.'

'*Ahh*, I've got just the trick,' said James, fumbling through his bum bag and producing a brown vial of liquid, before promptly shoving it up my nose.

The pungent odour enflamed my throat and with flailing arms, I whacked the bottle away.

'Poppers?!' screeched Laura, batting James away. 'Are you mad? That'll make her worse!'

My head began to spin and I felt like I was floating away, beginning my ascent into heaven. I could see a bright white light, so I knew my time here was over. I knew I had to go towards it. I wanted to be beautiful in death, if not in life, so I closed my eyes and pouted my lips in the hope I'd look half decent when I reached the pearly gates.

Goodbye, my dear, dear friends.

Chapter 14

I lay in bed, surrounded by green curtains hanging from a frame on the ceiling. Kind of like the ones you get in *hospital* ... Then I remembered where I was, and that I had to stay in overnight. I lay there squinting and dozing, trying to get my brain back up to speed as everything gradually came back into focus.

The green curtain was swept aside and a man in a white lab coat approached me.

The doctor picked up a clipboard from the end of the bed and began scribbling notes. He finally looked up. 'Good morning. It's nice to have you back with us again,' he said in a posh English accent that sounded almost familiar. I blinked in confusion.

Am I already back in England? Have I missed my hen-do? Am I about to have surgery?

Then, in a barely perceptible way, he cocked his head to one side and grinned at me which made me sure I knew who he was. I peered at his name badge, willing my eyes to fully focus. When they finally did so, I reeled back in the bed in shock.

'I—I know you – you're ... You're Brutus!' I pointed harshly, and then winced as my intravenous line tugged on my hand.

'I'm not quite sure what you're talking about, Miss Ryan. I'm not sure I know you,' he said with a suspiciously warm smile. 'Do call me Rupert, and yes, I am a doctor, and yes, before you ask, I am a real one.

'Your test results are in from last night,' he continued with an air of nonchalance. 'From what we can see, there are a few separate issues going on here. Firstly, its quite evident that you went into shock; you've also got a nasty case of sunstroke and food poisoning.'

None of this came as a great surprise – but Brutus, who just a day before was my man-slave, dressed up in latex, on all fours and wanting to be spanked ... a doctor? Now that *was* a big surprise.

'Secondly, we found a large amount of the hallucinogenic designer drug, commonly known as 2CB, in your system.'

'What!? I've never done a drug in my life!'

'It's been doing the rounds here on the island, and it would've probably been the icing on the cake, so to speak.'

OMG, I'll kill that Katie! She must've put that drug in our drinks at the club. I bet that dirty dog, Sam, gave them to her! I knew it all seemed too surreal for me to have actually enjoyed all that S&M stuff.

'Third, your blood results came back in and were rather peculiar. Your iron levels are up, your potassium is down, your blood volume is up and so is your blood pressure. This all seemed quite abnormal so I ordered a deeper dive into the results and, well, the results from your blood sample shows high levels of a hormone called human Chorionic Gonadotrophin, or *h*CG. I presume from your drug taking, you didn't know you were pregnant?'

The words hung in the air for a moment, not quite absorbing into my brain.

What the feck is this guy on?

'No, I didn't do drugs—and I'm certainly not pregnant!' I said shaking my head and rolling my eyes. 'No ... the doctors in England said I've been going through an early menopause. I've been prescribed HRT patches. It must be that – I haven't had a period in ... like, over two years, so it's impossible, there must be some kind of mix-up.'

He looked at me thoughtfully. 'Though it's very rare, it is possible for a woman to ovulate during early perimenopausal stages. And sometimes these periods can go unnoticed, or are discredited by the woman as a bleed from something else, such as an infection, or, after, say ... particularly energetic intercourse?'

Well, sure. Lewis and I were always having rough and ready sex, and I did remember that one amazing time in the kitchen where I spotted blood afterwards, but I assumed it was just from us going at it so hard.

'The hCG hormone is virtually exclusively released when an egg is fertilised and attaches itself to the wall of the uterus.'

Even though Rupert was clearly a doctor, he was still Brutus to me (a part-time Saint Bernard/gimp no less), just in a different outfit.

'Look, I don't know where you did *your* medical training,' I argued again, 'but you have definitely got the wrong notes. I can't have children.'

'You are pregnant, Tara.'

'No, I'm not ...'

'Yes, you are.'

The fecker was looking for more role-play here—and it appeared to be at my expense! If I could've got myself out of this bed, I would've kicked his doctory arse from here to Timbuktu!

He said no more, and before I knew it, I was being sent over to the maternity ward for a scan.

To save bitter disappointment, I asked if my hens could wait outside.

After a tense few minutes of preparation and having the cold gel put on my admittedly inflated tummy, the nurse muttered something in Spanish to the doctor and pointed to the screen in front of us. I didn't need to understand what she meant. Peering at the screen, there, as clear as day, was a baby—*my baby!*

Immediately I cupped hold of my lady-garden, petrified that he or she would fall out.

'Is the baby going to be okay?' I asked, dissolving into panic and then unfathomable ecstasy because I was actually pregnant after all.

'You and the baby will be just fine,' said the doctor smugly. 'Congratulations. You'll be looking at a due date around 17th February.'

Well, that explains the squirty cream addiction ...

I put my hand on my tummy, feeling the warmth from within. I couldn't understand it – inside *there* was a little, teeny, tiny person. A tiny little version of Lewis and me. This was it. I felt a rush of pure joy. My dream – no – *all* of my dreams, had come true. Lewis and I would be *that* perfect family. People would enviously watch *us* on the beach, building castles in the sand. Counting the months backwards on my fingers, I tried to work out when I would've I conceived. Hmmm, that was around the time Lewis went away for his stag ...

I sat bolt upright ...

Oh my God—Travis!

My world crumbled, then slipped off its axis.

'Brutus ... Rupert ... I mean, Doctor,' I gasped, tugging at his white coat, 'you need tell me the exact date of conception – to the exact hour, the exact minute—'

And whose feckin' bed I was in?!

A frown flitted across his face.

'You will have conceived three months ago, mid-May,' he said. 'But I'm afraid there's no accurate way to say which hour.'

He picked up his clipboard and began scribbling notes down again.

The week of Lewis's stag-do! My heart sank to my toes.

My beautiful baby ... might ... be ... Travis's?!

'Anyway, you're responding well to the antibiotics,' he smiled, interrupting my hysteria. 'Shall I get your sister for you? Laura, isn't it?'

I nodded erratically, gripping the bed sheets in terror.

Moment's later, Laura burst through the curtains. Then she saw my face and her expression contorted into one of concern.

'Laura ... I ... I'm—pregnant!' I wailed, not believing the words that were coming out of my own mouth.

'OH MY GAWD!' She threw her hands in the air and then covered her face. 'How is this even possible? Oh my God, I'm so happy for you!'

Though I was over the moon, I couldn't quite join in with her elation.

'What's the matter, aren't you happy?' she asked, slowly coming to a stand still.

'Yeah, of course I am. I ... I just think I'm just in a bit of ... you know, shock.'

'O-kay ... are you sure? Don't forget, I'm your sister, I know when something's up.'

I gulped hard. 'I'm fine.'

'You do want to keep the baby, don't you?'

'... Yes, yes, of course I do. I've always wanted a baby. It's just—'

'Come on, you need to call Lewis and let him know he's going to be a daddy!'

'Erm ... no, I won't call him just yet, I need a little time to get my own head around it first.'

Laura scanned my face suspiciously. I knew there was no way to hide my secret from her any longer. She was the only person in the world who could tell me the right thing to do. And I knew that if I kept this to myself the guilt would eat me alive, even more than it had already.

'The baby ... I ...' I shrugged my shoulders and watched Laura's eyes widen in anticipation.

'Lewis might not be the father,' I admitted hanging my head in shame.

I braced myself for a verbal attack. I didn't dare look her in the eye.

'Don't tell me ...'

'Travis.'

Admitting it out loud for the first time, I felt as if my life had been turned upside down like the *Titanic*, and the contents of my little head were helplessly sliding into the sea below. If the baby *was* Travis's, my life with Lewis would be over.

Laura took in a deep, audible breath through her nose. The silence compelled me to look at her face and guess what she was thinking.

'What makes you think it could be Travis's?' she asked.

'I ... Well ... He turned up at the salon, completely out of the blue, and basically threatened me into meeting him at a fancy hotel to hear him out. He had an elaborate story about what happened with us, and the only reason I agreed to go was ... well ...because I knew it would help me get closure and I could finally move on.'

Laura didn't say a word, she just sat on the end of my bed, head bowed, listening.

'Only ... I got there and things didn't go to plan ... I don't remember hardly anything from that night. I was out of my head drunk, and on Tramadol painkillers from a migraine. I really didn't mean it to happen. I woke in the morning and I was kind of ... well, in his bed ... It was only a one-time thing,' I added quickly, 'it was just a stupid, stupid mistake and I hate myself for it.'

'Okay, but that doesn't explain how the baby could

be his,' said Laura, moving up the bed and holding my hand, 'especially if it was only a one-night stand.'

'Brutus, Rupert—I mean, the doctor said from the size of the baby that I would've conceived around about the middle of May. I remember because that's when Lewis went on his stag-do and that's when it kind of … happened.'

'Oh, Tara …' Laura sighed. 'How do you know that Travis didn't wear protection?'

'I … I don't know for sure, but he always used to refuse to wear condoms.

The dam of tears burst. Laura slid forward and gently held me, careful not to aggravate the sunburn.

'He's played you like a fiddle. *Again!*' said Laura, glaring, inches away from my face. 'Why on earth didn't you tell me sooner?'

She had every right to be angry; especially after the months of counselling she'd given me. Not to mention that I may've ruined so many lives by doing this – Lewis's, mine, and the baby's.

'What am I going to do?' I asked, sobbing.

She shook her head. 'I … don't know. I'm still trying to process everything you've said.'

'Well, if anyone should know what to do, it's you,' I said, panic rising in my voice. 'You're the one with the degree in psychobabble, *you're* the counsellor here – this is what you do! You fix things. Fix it, please.'

Her face looked pained.

'Tara, I can't tell you what you should or shouldn't do. You have to stand on your own two feet now. All I can do is tell you what *I* would do in your situation, as your sister and not as a therapist.'

'Okay, so what would *you* do?'

'Well, I'd start by looking at things logically,' she said, moving off the bed and over to a chair.

'Option A,' she said, crossing her legs in her professional style, 'is that you tell Lewis when you get back that you slept with Travis and the baby may not be his. It doesn't need to be said that he is *not* going to be happy about this. Within Option A, there are likely to be two outcomes – either he forgives you at some stage and you both wait to find out the paternity of the baby, or, worst-case scenario, he doesn't forgive you and he breaks up with you, even if the baby *is* his.'

Instantly I shook my head. This option didn't sit well with me at all.

'Option B,' Laura continued, 'you don't tell Lewis that you slept with Travis until the baby is born and you get a paternity test to confirm who the father is. The first scenario is that if it *is* Lewis's baby, then you could tell him at a later stage about what happened with Travis – in which case I personally would omit the fact that you thought it could've been Travis's baby, and somehow get him to forgive you as a one-time thing. The other scenario is that if it *is* Travis's baby, then ... well, you should tell Lewis as soon as you get the results of the paternity test. This last scenario would no doubt break his heart, as he'll have gone through the pregnancy supporting you and being excited about having his first child, only to find out he's been stabbed in the back and that his woman had been unfaithful.'

My head was spinning.

'I guess what it comes down to is whether you wait

to tell Lewis about your infidelity before or after the birth.'

'I'm confused ... so what would *you* do in my shoes?' I asked, exhausted from the rollercoaster of emotions going around my head.

'Well, personally I would go for Option B. I feel like you would possibly be doing more damage to yourself and the baby if you told Lewis now. But with this option, if it turns out to be Travis's baby, you will be breaking Lewis's heart. You'd definitely have to cancel or at least postpone the wedding in either case. You could put it down to the pregnancy. I wouldn't allow myself to go through with the wedding without first telling Lewis and giving him the option to forgive you or not. Marrying him on weak foundations means your relationship with him will inevitably crack, sooner or later.'

'I said I wanted you to fix it, not smash us into smithereens. I can't tell Lewis ... it would kill him!'

'In my opinion you'll have to tell him at some point. It wouldn't be fair to drag him along if the baby isn't his. It's the right thing to do.'

'I don't know. I don't know what—'

A knocking on the door interrupted us. Laura walked around to see through the small window in the door.

'It's Katie,' she said. 'Everyone's been waiting to see you for ages.'

'Please don't tell the others about Travis,' I begged. 'I need time to think it all out.'

Despite the trauma of not knowing the father, deep down, the feeling of elation from being pregnant was giving me a sense of hope to cling on to. It was the only thing holding me together, like a divine kind of glue.

The hens piled in through the ward door in their usual riotous manner. Their reaction to the baby news was even more than I expected. A cacophony of squealing, cheering and *oh-my-God*-ing erupted.

'It's got me right there,' rasped Siobhan, thumping her chest and then diving in for a hug – a little too hard for someone with third-degree sunburn and carrying an unborn baby.

'How could you be pregnant?' asked Katie, scratching her head. 'I thought you were supposed to be like ... all dried up and in menopause.'

'How do you think?' asked James, 'Tara and Lewis have been up to no good since the very first date. This is what happens when you straight people get a little crazy – a baby pops out,' he said, rubbing my tummy lovingly.

'I'm going to be an auntie!' said Camilla, bouncing around like a pogo stick.

'Me too!' said James, and so did Katie, Laura and Siobhan too, before I was enveloped in a group hug.

'Well, at least now we don't have to buy a baby on eBay for you,' sobbed James.

I smiled. *I* was pregnant. *Me!* I was having a baby. Sure, things were complicated, but I couldn't help but feel happy. I felt like my soul was dancing in my body. No matter what happened with Lewis, I had a baby growing inside me and I would care for him or her no matter what.

'Oh, and by the way, Laura, you need to have a word with Katie about a certain drug that was found in my system,' I added, sending Katie daggers.

All heads, with eyebrows raised in surprise, turned to Katie, who sheepishly hung her head. Ah come on now,' she said, hands on hips, 'didn't you's all have a hooly?'

Chapter 15

Lewis was over the moon when I told him about the baby, treating me like a fragile china doll and attending to my every waking need. However, Option B grated away at me for the next three months, the guilt tearing away at my soul day by day. At times I thought the guilt was so strong that it might even poison the baby. The worst was when I told Lewis he would make a great father; I knew he would be *great*, but whether he actually *was* father was another issue. There was never any respite; particularly now I was so far gone. The dark secret inside me was growing by the day, ready to proclaim to the world that I had been living a lie. My beautiful life with Lewis was a sham. I had been unfaithful to the man I loved and was quite possibly carrying another man's baby.

Lewis also understood why I wanted to postpone the wedding, due to not wanting to look the size of a bus in the photos (which was only a small lie). If everyone was going to be staring at me, I wanted to be damn sure I looked the part of the blushing bride, however fanciful and far from the truth it was.

My main mantra to pull me out of these whirlpools of guilt was to tell myself that the likelihood of the baby being Travis's was at most 15%. And when that didn't work, I tried to distract myself by shopping. The internet was an amazing encyclopaedia of everything baby—from how to have a baby, bring up the baby, feed the baby and, of course, the best thing ever ... what to buy for the baby before the birth. I had ordered everything from bibs to a rocking horse and furniture for the nursery. As we lived in a pretty remote area near Epsom in the Surrey countryside, our home was hard to find, so it was easier to have all my purchases delivered to the salon. There was always someone there to sign for deliveries. I never failed to get a rush of excitement when I got a call from James or Camilla to say that something was ready for collection. The staff loved crowding around me as I opened each item, and they would 'oooh' and 'aaah' in unison as I opened every parcel.

During those months, things ticked over as usual. The weather got cold. Glamma-Puss carried on taking on new clients. Camilla and Alex had an engagement party. Suyin and Leonardo had been outed as being not-swingers-but-open-to-the-idea-of-an-open-relationship-ists. Katie was sent back to rehab after Laura got a roasting from Mum for not looking after her on the hen-do and so it appeared, for the first time in my life, I was the 'Golden Child'. (Granted, if Mum knew the full facts, and this baby turned out to be

Travis's, I'd no doubt fall to the bottom of the 'favourite' daughter rankings once more.)

At the second ultrasound scan we found out the amazing news—we were expecting a girl. Lewis was thrilled, which of course just worsened my overbearing guilt. We talked about names (a welcome distraction); I had always wanted the name Mercedes, but as that was the name of Lewis's cheating ex-fiancée, it was swiftly taken off the table. Lewis did have a preference: *Indie*. He said it sounded like a confident, free-spirited and adventurous name. I loved it, and so it was decided. As he got the first name, I was allowed to pick the middle name. I chose Rose, which Lewis loved as it reminded him of his mother, Rosemary. Indie Rose Copeland, I loved the sound of it.

Sometimes I'd wake up and forget that I had a baby growing inside me. And each time I was reminded, it was like getting a little present ... until the guilt kicked in, warmly accompanied by sweaty, paralysing fear about who was actually the father of this baby.

The bulging file of wedding paperwork had been gathering dust on a shelf, so, putting on a brave face, I'd taken on the task of mailing everyone who we'd sent a wedding invite to. I received calls about how delighted they were that I was expecting. Of course, some were clearly disappointed to be missing out on the wedding party of the year; *people can be so selfish*. It pained me to cancel the swing band, the caterers, ice sculpture, catering staff and photographer. The once 'had to have' custom-made wedding gown had also arrived at the bridal boutique—but I didn't even have the heart to go and see it. It just didn't mean anything anymore.

Lewis didn't seem to notice the dark shadow haunting my every thought. I'd thrown him off the scent with more fibs about being tired or hormonal (which wasn't completely untrue).

Most mums look forward to their due date. I *did* look forward to it, but the closer I got to giving birth, the closer I got to the overwhelming, heart-breaking thought of having to confess to Lewis what I'd done.

However, I continued buttering Lewis up as much as possible, doing as much as a heavily pregnant woman can do to please her man—planting as many happy seeds as possible. The result was that things between us had never been better. But, internally, this just made me feel worse.

On my day off I received a frantic call from James saying that the stock room was overloaded with parcels and boxes, not for the salon but for me, and that they were having the Christmas stock delivery that day, which would be huge, and there wasn't even enough space to swing a cat. So, I headed to the salon and packed up the Land Rover as tightly as possible.

Once home, I yanked off my heavy winter boots, released my swollen feet and ankles into Lewis's comfy flip-flops, and gradually hauled the packages and boxes up to Indie's room. We were decorating her nursery this weekend – that was if we could actually make our minds up which colour pink to choose. *Who'd have thought there were so many shades of pink?*

Feeling completely exhausted, I sank into the French-style nursing chair in the corner of the room and began going through the contents of each box.

Lastly, there was a large box with the signature

Harrods logo marked along the side, which had me a little puzzled as I'd not bought anything from there in recent months. Having opened the lid and swept aside the masses of tissue paper, I pulled out what could only be described as the most magnificent three-quarter-length white fur coat. Holding the full length of it by the shoulders, I stood gawping for what seemed like an age before wondering where it had come from—*I* certainly hadn't ordered it, that was for sure.

Then the penny dropped: just the other evening Lewis and I had been chatting about the possibility of having a themed winter white wedding at the end of February, when Indie was born. It would've been the polar opposite of the September wedding, which we'd postponed. We had gotten quite carried away with thoughts of a snow-themed winter wonderland wedding, but in the end, and buying more time, I agreed that whilst it was a lovely idea, I would've needed to have lost the baby weight I'd gained, and that it might be late spring before that happened.

But during the excitement of the chat, I'd mentioned that if I *were* to have walked down the aisle in a winter wonderland theme, I would've loved to be wearing a white fur coat.

I was immediately reminded of the last time Lewis surprised me with a present, and he was obviously making up for it …

He had come home from work hiding something behind his back. 'I've got a present for you,' he said in singsong voice.

'Ooh, what is it?'

'You'll have to guess,' he said, teasing.

'Diamond earrings?'

'No, guess again.'

'A pair of Manolo Blahniks?'

'No, it's for somewhere on your body between the two places you've just mentioned.'

'A fur coat?' I asked with a sharp intake of breath.

Lewis was good at surprises. The last one was an exquisite Louis Vuitton overnight bag for my hospital maternity stay, after I'd complained about having no nice luggage.

He pulled out a … ring.

Not a diamond ring, you must understand; no, it was a pink rubber ring, big enough to fit your head through. Like a tiny rubber ring kids use in swimming pools.

'Oh, err, thank you,' I said, slowly cocking my nose up, 'I'm not sure I understand.'

'It's for that beautiful bottom of yours. For your piles—'

'Stop!' I raised my hand, squeezing my eyes tightly shut. 'I really don't want to talk about the vineyard growing out of my backside thank you very much. Besides,' I said, red faced, 'if I sit on my side they don't hurt so bad.'

Coming back to the here and now, I took the new fur coat into our bedroom and tried it on in front of the large ornate mirror which hung just outside my walk-in wardrobe. Pulling the collar around my neck, I shrugged my shoulders up as I rubbed the side of my face against its soft, fluffy magnificence.

Instantly I decided that a huge big thank you was in order. I would seduce Lewis when he got home from work. I would pull out all the stops. Although, I rejected the idea of a striptease – while Lewis had the ability to look at me and make me feel like the most desirable woman in the world, being six months pregnant I just didn't have the confidence in my new boat-sized body. Ruefully, I looked down at my tummy. I hadn't seen my lady-garden for weeks. I hoped she was still there.

Maybe I could blindfold him and wear something that *felt* sensuous; that way he wouldn't have to actually see my body, and I could just place his hands on my best bits. I could use a can of squirty whipped cream and squirt it in places he wouldn't be expecting. That should satisfy our insatiable cravings and of course make the moment that I went down on him even more scintillating.

So what would I wear? Something silky and soft. Ignoring my over-used 'comfort drawer', I began rooting through my 'sexy-times drawer', which was filled with neglected negligees that hadn't seen the light of day—or should I say the light of night—in months. I pulled out my white lace and satin Agent Provocateur baby-doll outfit, with matching teensy-tiny split crotch thong. It was meant to have been for my honeymoon. *No point in letting it go to waste.* Laying it out on the bed, I eyed it cautiously, then sighed.

The baby-doll nightie had looked impossibly small even when I bought it ten months ago; there wasn't a chance of stretching it over my inflated tummy.

So, it was just the split-crotch thong then. I picked it up and looked at it doubtfully. Hooking a finger in each side, I stretched it as far as it would go. *Not a hope. It wouldn't get past my knees, let alone my upper thighs.* Swearing under my breath, I pulled one finger free and watched it ping across the bedroom.

Determined not to give up, I waddled back over to the drawer and, after a little rummaging, I came across a beautiful black silk Empire-line nightie which perfectly cupped my inflated boobs and accentuated my décolletage, the hem of the nightie just hiding my lady-garden and, with its flattering A-line shape, also my enormous tummy. With a sense of increasing excitement, I thought a full-on pampering session would be called for and rushed into the bathroom to run myself a decadent bath.

Reaching out to the shelf, I browsed the stock of potential bubble baths, bath bombs and salts. A White Company bottle caught my eye, *Seychelles Bubble Bath*, 'Combining notes of fresh bergamot, bright orange and rich amber with warming notes of exotic coconut, vanilla and almond.' *YES*. I poured half the contents of the bottle into the flow of water. Now was most certainly not the time to do things by halves.

Now to set the atmosphere. Picking up a box of matches, I carefully lit the small army of candles I had amassed in the bathroom. Hypnotic swirls of smoke curled into the air, releasing an array of sweet scents. I put on my favourite smooth-jazz playlist, which automatically connected to the Bose speaker system (Lewis had set this neat little trick up for me; I wouldn't have had a clue how to perform such sorcery). The sound of the mellow piano and sensual saxophones set the mood off perfectly. For the finishing touch, I lit a row of tea lights on the side. *Perfect.*

I wandered back into the bedroom to undress, kicking the flip-flops into the corner of the room, my clothes following as I flung them off almost stripper-style—next off being my great big maternity knickers (Lord, they were as big as parachutes. In fact, I might donate them to the RAF when all this was over).

Naked, I reached out and picked up a photo of Lewis and me in an ornate white frame from the bedside table. We were holding flutes of champagne, grinning into the camera, carefree and madly in love. It was taken on the day of the engagement in Paris, when we had everything to look forward to. I focused on his handsome face and his ruffled dark blond locks. He had such an upbeat, wild energy about him. *I love him so much*, I thought as I stroked the photograph with trembling fingers.

Pull yourself together, Tara, you've got to stay strong.

Testing the mattress with a little pressure from both hands, I whispered: 'I hope you are feeling strong. You've got a wide load on the way.'

I plumped up the array of scatter cushions at the head of the bed and smoothed down the sheets.

Job done, I picked up my nightie and hung it on the back of the door, headed for the bath, climbed in and sank deep into the mound of tiny bubbles. I let my head fall backwards, resting on the bath pillow. Closing my eyes, I let out a great long satisfying groan.

I had only been there for ten minutes when I heard a door slam in the distance and the familiar sound of feet on the stairs. He was early!

I sat up with a start, bubbles sloshing everywhere as

he peeped his head around the bathroom door like a meerkat. 'Hello, fiancée.'

My God, he was so handsome, and when I looked at his green eyes sparking in amusement and his bronzed, sculpted body leaning nonchalantly in the doorway, I couldn't help but melt.

'You're early,' I said, with a mock pout.

'I couldn't stay away from my two favourite girls.'

I grinned and flicked bubbles at him with my foot, which resulted in a gallon of water spilling over the edge of the bath, covering the bathroom floor in white suds.

'Oops.'

Lewis ignored the mess and gave me one of his smiles, the ones that seemed to hatch a hundred live butterflies in my stomach.

Leaning in, he gave me a long, lingering kiss with those silky, soft lips of his. Passion surged through me as I tugged on his T-shirt, pulling him down to his knees, cupping his face in my hands, and drew him in, nose to nose. He teased some more kisses before his hand slid into the water and moved towards my lady-garden. No – this wasn't the plan, and with a Herculean effort of will, I removed it and gently placed it on the edge of the bath, the foamy water sliding off his knuckles.

'You have to wait. I'm going to slip into something more ... *comfortable*,' I said, eyeing my nightie hanging on the back of the door.

'*Mmm* ... that sounds like fun. But what could be more comfortable than your own skin, naked and dripping wet?' he asked, seductively slipping the tip of his tongue in my mouth.

'No ... you have to wait. Be patient,' I ordered, pushing him away. 'Go be a good boy and wait downstairs and I'll call you when I'm ready.'

'I don't know if I'll be able to wait much longer,' he said with a smile, backing out of the bathroom, barely able to take his eyes off me.

Gripping the handles of the bath, I heaved myself out of the water and onto the now soaked bath mat—I'd clean up the spill later, I had bigger fish to fry. After quickly towelling myself dry, I began to systematically rub my Yves Saint Laurent Body Lotion from head to toe. The moisturiser is supposed to leave extracts of rose on the skin, giving it a velvety touch, like a rose petal.

Tara Ryan will be blossoming tonight.

Body glistening with moisture, I gripped the towel rail to use it as a support so I could limber up – performing acrobatics in the bedroom these days most certainly required such preparation.

I pulled my nightie over my head and arranged my boobs accordingly. Waddling over to the large dressing table and flicking on the lights around the frame, I set to work on my makeup. I decided to go for the more natural look to save time and to ensure that this would be a tactile experience with little visual effect. I worked briskly and efficiently in order to meet my deadline, which was currently panting at the bottom of the stairs.

Staring at myself, I tried to place each hand on my hips in a provocative pose. It was hopeless—my hips were long gone. Working around the room to set the perfect scene, I turned off the main chandelier light and set the bedside lights to the dimmest setting. I selected

Lewis's favourite jazz playlist and pressed the play button on our evening.

Crossing back to the wardrobe, I selected a black silk Chanel scarf that would make a perfect makeshift blindfold. I then decided to slip the beautiful white fur coat on—to give maximum sensory overload.

Realising I'd forgotten the squirty cream, I walked purposefully out of the bedroom and called down to Lewis that I had a surprise for him, but first he was to go get the squirty cream from the fridge, then sit at the bottom of the stairs with his back to me and not look round. He did exactly as he was told.

I wanted this to be all about touch and sensation rather than the visual: the touch of the beautiful fur coat he had bought me; the soft feel of my silk nightie underneath it; and the sensation of my skin under his fingers.

Trying not to falter, I tiptoed down the stairs as lightly as possibly, which was difficult considering the weight I was carrying. Gently teasing the back of his neck with the cuff of my coat, I placed the scarf around his eyes and tied it at the back of his head.

'Thank you, my darling. And now it's time for *your* present,' I teased.

Still standing behind him, I reached for the can of squirty cream and, taking his hand, pulled him onto his feet, guiding him up the stairs and in through the bedroom door.

I nudged him to stand against the edge of the bed and ordered him to strip from the waist down, which he obligingly did. I then pulled his T-shirt carefully over his head so as not to disturb the blindfold, and pushed him backwards until he was lying flat on his back.

My legs straddled his slender hips as I sat just above his manhood. His hands reached out for me but I grabbed them quickly and held them above his head, pinning them to the pillow. I used my free hand and the cuff of my coat to tease down the centre of his bare chest towards his love-muscle, then slowly back up again towards his face.

With the coat open, I leaned over ever so slowly, nudging my bosom into his face while he frantically searched for my erect nipple. Slowly coming back into my sitting position across his hips, I eased his hands away from the pillow and guided them up to my shoulders. Then his hands slipped in, under the coat, and drew it down from my shoulders. I took each of his hands in mine and guided them to my thumping heart, then let his fingers trace the outlines of my breasts.

The tension in the room was electric.

I was in charge here.

He swallowed hard, obviously having trouble controlling his urges. *Good.* Pushing his arms back into the pinned-to-pillow position, I swayed with the rhythm of the jazz, closing my eyes in pleasure as I let myself grind rhythmically against his pelvis. Shocks of pleasure shot up my legs and into my lady-garden, which throbbed so much I quickly decided there needed to be a change of tactics, or this would be over too soon. Ordering him to leave his hands where they were and slipping the fur coat off, I reached for the can of cream, slowly squirting it over his chest and down the middle of his ribcage, inching ever closer to his manhood. Bending over, I slowly licked it all off and moved further down his writhing body until I reached his erect man-muscle, and squirted cream up the length of it. I greedily licked and sucked his throbbing muscle until he wasn't able to take anymore. Then it was time to remove the blindfold.

Looking at me like a present he couldn't wait to unwrap, he lifted my nightie up and took it off, flinging it to the other side of the bedroom.

He sat up, lifting me with him, his hands cupped firmly beneath my bum, and skilfully turned me around, lying me down on the bed beneath him.

'No more,' he panted, 'I'm losing my mind. 'If I don't open my present now, I'm going to explode. You are one damn sexy lady, Tara Ryan!'

Chapter 16

It was late in the evening. Lewis was in a deep slumber, his face a picture of utter contentment. Sleep wouldn't come to me though, even if I *was* exhausted after making love for so long. A combination of overheating and not being able to suppress the anxiety kept me up on so many nights.

I needed some fresh air.

Quietly sliding out of bed, I made for the door, grabbing the fur coat on the way.

I tiptoed downstairs and opened the patio door leading towards the veranda, my usual place of contemplation when I couldn't sleep.

Gripping the rail of the veranda, I closed my eyes, allowing the chilly winds to cool me down. Indie was clearly awake too: impatiently shuffling around inside. She seemed to be as unsettled as I was.

'Tara?'

I swung around to see Lewis walking towards me

barefoot in jogging bottoms and a hoody. I smiled as he came up and hugged and began rocking me form behind. We swayed silently together in the cold November night while Lewis affectionately caressed my bump.

The cold winter wind blew harder. Lewis began shivering, and tucked his hands in my coat pockets. I could feel him ruffling around in there.

'What's this?' he asked, releasing his snuggly grip.

I shrugged, more bothered about him returning to the exact position he was just in.

Turning around, I could see Lewis had backed away and was looking down at a piece of paper.

'What is it?'

He didn't say. He seemed to be reading the paper again, murmuring as he read.

'Is it the receipt?' I asked, playfully stepping towards him.

But as I did so, he raised a sharp hand to stop me. And from nowhere, he looked up, face full of venom.

'Tara ... what the fuck is this?'

My heart dropped. I'd never seen Lewis switch like this before.

He shoved the folded paper into my hand. I looked at him again, confused and alarmed, before reading the handwritten note:

Sorry it's been so long, I've been away on tour.

It was great to meet up last time – shame we couldn't have stayed in bed longer. I still think about you all the time.

I'm staying at the Langham Hotel again this weekend as we've got a game on Sunday. Meet me there Friday at 7 for dinner and fun. I've never been able to get over the thought of you turning up at Dublin airport in nothing but a fur coat, so please wear this coat and, of course, no knickers.
Travis x

Gulping hard, I looked up at Lewis and saw rage in his eyes.

How could I have got this so wrong? Lewis hadn't bought me the fur coat; it had been Travis!

'I'm sorry, Lewis, I can explain …' I said, feeling as though my heart was lodged in my throat.

Lewis raised his hands to his temples and squeezed his fists. 'Is it true?'

The moment I tell him, life will never ever be the same again.

I stole a few more precious seconds; then, swallowing hard, it crossed my mind to lie my way out of this, say it was a coat from yesteryear – when Travis and I were together. Or simply plead ignorance.

But Lewis didn't deserve to be lied to any more.

My eyes widened and blood thumped in my ears. I couldn't look him in the eye; instead, I stared at the ground, noticing his toes were bunched as though he was trying to steady himself. I reached for his hands, but he pulled away sharply.

'Answer the fucking question!' he shouted.

'… Yes,' I admitted, crumbling. I-I did sleep with him, but—'

Lewis turned away.

'Lewis—*Lewis*, I swear it was just a one-time

thing—one stupid, horrible mistake. I only met up with him to tell him to leave me alone.'

Lewis staggered backwards and then forwards. His bloodless face dropped low, before he gripped his whole head in agony. I could hardly bear to watch him. It felt like his reaction was happening in slow motion, with each painful move freeze-framed so I could fully suffer seeing what I'd put him through.

Then, with a sudden movement, he stepped forward, grabbed my forearms and crumbled to his knees. A massive sob escaped his throat. I stroked his head but he shuddered at my touch and quickly stood again, moving far away.

'When?' he asked weakly.

'You'd gone away for your stag. He turned up at the salon, and—'

'Oh! I see,' he said angrily, 'so the minute my back is turned, you think it's a good opportunity to run off and fuck your ex?'

'No, no ... Lewis, It wasn't like that—'

'So how was it then, if it wasn't like that?'

'Please, please – just let me explain ...' My body shook with panic as the words began rolling off my tongue at speed. 'He just turned up at the salon and said he'd keep coming back unless ... unless I agreed to meet him. I made a decision, to go and meet him and tell him to stop harassing me and to never contact me again.'

Lewis stood with his eyes closed, fists clenched, shaking his head.

My breathing was laboured and I could feel my body swaying as I clung to my future with him.

'I went to tell him that I was in love with you and that there was never any chance he could be a part of my life.'

'And you never thought to tell me that he had been harassing you?' he shouted in a pained voice, now pacing furiously up and down the veranda. '*I* would've fucking dealt with him!'

'I was afraid if I did tell you, it could get nasty and … and physical. And you were away; I didn't want to spoil it. I thought I'd do the adult thing and meet him face to face and tell him in no uncertain terms that I was happy for the first time in my life, I was engaged to the man of my dreams, and that he had to stay out of my life …

Lewis stopped pacing; his eyes, now hooded, were drilling into mine.

'It was the night of Leonardo's birthday,' I said, grabbing hold of his hands. 'We'd all gone to Bar21 and I ended up drinking too much beforehand … but what I didn't know was that I'd accidentally taken these pain killers which you're not supposed to drink on. After that, I don't really know what happened, I just remember waking up and I'm in bed next to him at the hotel. I've hated myself ever since.'

Lewis pulled his raging eyes away from me, then turned his back—arms stretched out to the heavens.

'What about *trust*, Tara?' he boomed, swivelling back round. 'Can't I trust you to tell me about important decisions—like meeting with your ex? I would've gone with you for God's sake. What was the point of all this,' he bellowed, indicating the house all around us, 'this dream we had together? It means nothing now!'

I could hear his breathing from metres away as he paced around the terrace.

'I don't know what else to say,' I mumbled in shame, 'I regret it more than anything I've ever done and more than anything I'll ever do again. It's been eating away at me—'

Lewis flipped a chair upside down, sending it flying into the wall with a loud clatter. He stormed right up to me, looking at my bump, then glared.

'My stag-do,' he stammered, tears snaking down his cheeks, 'that was six months ago. Indie ... is she mine?'

I leaned backwards, involuntarily covering up and pulled the coat around me.

Just say it, Tara, just admit that you don't know, argued my conscience— but once those words were out there, I would never be able to pull them back ... *Just say it, just say it ...*

'I ... I don't know.'

'Fuck ... you!'

'But Lewis,' I pleaded, 'I'm almost certain she's yours, there's only a very small chance she's his, I wanted to tell you, it's just—'

Lewis seized a plant pot and launched it, smashing the huge glass patio door into a million pieces. The crashing sound rang through my ears and I quickly backed off the veranda onto a step leading to the garden.

He was like a raging animal. He *was* a raging animal.

'Lewis, please!' I shouted from a safe distance, barely able to breathe through the crying. 'We can get through this – I know we can. She's your baby, Lewis; Indie is your baby. Please, I'm begging you, just calm down.'

'You—*you* have broken us. *You* have broken the trust!' he shouted, storming over to me again and pointing an accusing finger. 'I really hope it was worth it, Tara. We nearly had it all—no, we *did* have it all. And now you've thrown it all away because you couldn't resist screwing your ex.'

'I'm sorry,' I blurted, shaking in shock and shame.

'It was your honesty and innocence I loved,' he whimpered, a sob leaking from his throat. 'How could I have been *so* stupid? This is exactly what happened last time – are all women just cheating whores, or is it just that I attract the ones that are? You know what … this isn't even your fault. I'm the stupid, naïve dickhead here. I should've known not to trust you. What a fool!'

He pierced me with those intense eyes again; it was Lewis, but no longer the same man. He looked at me as though I was the worst person on earth and certainly not the woman he was planning on spending the rest of his life with.

I began wailing, beaten down by his words. 'Please, Lewis. I love you more than you'll ever know.'

I can't lose him, I just can't.

Without saying a word, he turned and trudged through the broken glass, back into the house.

'Where are you going?!'

I heard the bedroom door slam.

Trying to swallow down the choking lump in my throat, I waded through the glass and hesitantly climbed the stairs. But on reaching the bedroom door, it flew open and Lewis stormed out, wearing his biker gear and holding his crash helmet in his hand.

He didn't look upset any more; he looked *possessed*.

'Where are you going? Lewis—Lewis! Please, please don't leave. Let's just talk about this!'

But he said nothing, nearly shoulder-barging me out of the way, and flew down the stairs.

'Please – just tell me where you're going so I know you'll be safe!'

He yanked open the front door and stopped. 'I'm going to find Travis.'

'Lewis, please, let's just—'

He slammed the door before I could reach it. Wrenching it open, I looked but couldn't see him. I ran out onto the gravel and heard the sound of his motorbike starting up around the side of the house. Then his lights came on against the hedge on the driveway. I ran across, determined to block his path.

But it was too late – he'd already gained speed by the time I reached him. I screamed after him, begging him to stop. He looked across at me for a moment. Although I couldn't see his face under his helmet, although he hadn't said it, I knew right in that moment that he would never forgive me.

Helplessly crying, I watched as Lewis powered out of the driveway and into the night.

Running back into the house and into the kitchen, I vomited in the sink. I felt like I was being strangled to death, and Indie was now kicking violently. Eventually, I dragged myself onto the couch in the lounge, lying in a hysterical heap in view of the broken patio door. I heaved the hideous fur coat off my body and let the cold night air attack my skin. I deserved it.

I tried to call Lewis's mobile but his phone just rang and rang. I left multiple blubbering, begging voice messages and texts, trying to explain something I couldn't even explain to myself.

Heaving myself up to the bedroom and picking up my discarded nightie, which Lewis had taken off me with such desire just a few short hours ago, I slowly walked over to the drawers and placed it back inside. I lay on the top of our bed, scrunched up in the foetal position, took the can of squirty cream, and blasted as much in to my mouth as possible.

It dawned on me that here I was, alone *again*, for the second time. Devastation was sweeping through me, with Travis yet *again* being the source of my pain.

I lay on the bed, body shaking and tears streaming.

The ring of my mobile woke me. I must have cried myself to sleep. Disorientated and confused, I looked at the caller ID. It was Lewis.

'Lewis?!'

'Is this Tara Ryan?' said a man's voice.

'Ye—yes ... Who is this?'

'Tara, my name is Freddie and I'm a paramedic. I'm here with a man who has been involved in a serious motorbike collision.'

Chapter 17

Thousands of tiny electric shocks surged through my veins and tore at every inch of my skin. I was paralysed with fear and shock. Everything I knew had given way and collapsed. It was as though my entire being was disintegrating.

I wasn't breathing – holding it all in on the knife-edge of his words.

'Hello? Tara, are you there?' said the paramedic on the phone.

I couldn't answer. All I could do was stare into space as the heartache flooded through the wall of my chest, shattering my heart into a million sharp little pieces. Pulling on my final reserves of strength, I inched my hand towards the fallen phone.

'I-I'm here ...' I managed.

'Okay, Tara, please try and stay calm. What's his name?'

'... Lewis. Lewis Copeland. He's my fiancé.'

'Okay, thank you. Tara, I need you to listen to me very carefully. Lewis is in a critical state. We're taking him by ambulance to the A&E department at Hillingdon hospital in Middlesex. Are you able to get there?'

'… Yes. I can be there,' I whispered, drawing breath for the first time in what felt like hours.

'Okay. Does he have any medical conditions we should know about? Like heart issues, allergies to medicine, epilepsy or anything like that?'

'Err … no, no, not that I know of.'

'Okay. Is there anyone else you think you should call, like Lewis's family and friends, who could give you support?'

'Umm … yes, Camilla, his sister,' I stammered between breaths. 'I'll … I'll tell her to get down there as soon as possible.'

Lewis and Camilla's parents both died when they were teenagers. Her brother meant the world to her – she would never forgive me for what I'd done. I would never be able to forgive myself. But I needed to call her, it was my duty, even if it would break her heart.

Hanging up the phone, I sat on the bed staring into oblivion. I felt physically nailed down. Unable to move or think, time seemed to be standing still. Then I became aware of the sound of my breathing, which was coming in fast and frantic gasps. With superhuman strength, I heaved myself up, shoved my podgy feet into Lewis's flip-flops, called Camilla, left a voicemail to call me asap, then grabbing the nearest garment to me, I attempted to thread my jelly-legs into a pair of tracksuit bottoms.

Screaming obscenities, I yanked the tracksuit bottoms back off, shook out the flip-flops and started again.

More haste, less speed. More haste, less speed.

Like a headless chicken, I flung open the wardrobe doors in an attempt to find something for my top half.

Don't you dare stop to cry, Tara, you don't have time!

My head wanted to go on, but my body was resisting, wanting to simply collapse to the ground in a hopeless, sobbing mess. I was shaking so much I couldn't think straight.

My heart banged against my chest as I yanked tops, dressing gowns and jumpers roughly to the side. Handfuls of different coloured fabrics slipped into a Technicolor mound on the floor. I spun around in circles helplessly, hurling clothes around the bedroom, getting nowhere.

It doesn't matter what I wear. Just get to him. Just get to him!

I grabbed one of Lewis's white T-shirts from the bedroom chair and snapped it down over my head. As I was weaving my arms through the sleeves, I took a deep breath and inhaled his familiar scent.

Lewis.

'Coat, coat, I need a coat!' Without thinking, I grabbed the fur coat from the end of my bed, but the sight of it made me feel violently sick. In a blind rage, I opened the bedroom window and, without ceremony, chucked it out into the stormy night.

Gale-force winds and torrential rain whipped around me as I battled out into the darkness.

Supporting my enormous tummy with one arm, I propelled myself forward with the other. In a matter of seconds, my clothes were drenched and clinging to my body in clammy, uncomfortable clumps. My hair was plastered to the side of my face one moment, and then a bunch of hair would whip round and slap into me with a stinging blow the next.

My car was in the garage for a service, so I had no choice but to use the Defender.

It took forever to stumble around to the dilapidated old 4x4 parked around the side of the house. Holding the door open against the wind, I squeezed my oversized torso through and slammed the door shut. Taking a deep, recovering breath, I stuck the keys in the ignition and twisted. The dim headlights illuminated the gravel driveway and the wipers instantly began clearing the screen of the torrents of rain with a repetitive and abrasive screech.

The car creaked and groaned but refused to come to life.

'Bitch! Come on, you old cow! Please start ...' I turned the key repeatedly, pausing only to punch the steering wheel in fury. I slammed the accelerator once more, desperate to resuscitate the old beast.

After the fifth time of begging, the engine finally spluttered into life and I slammed my foot down on the accelerator, mercilessly reviving the shit out of it. The gravelly rattle slowly turned into a full-blown roar as I slammed it into drive.

The car jolted and began hurtling in reverse—my wet flip-flop had slipped, wedging itself between the mat and the accelerator.

ShitShitShit—'SHIT!' *BANG*. The car collided into our water feature with a sickening thud, sending chunks of stone and debris flying, stopping the Defender on impact and causing it to stall.

Rubbing my neck, I felt Indie move irritably inside me. 'Shit! I'm sorry. I'm sorry, Indie. Mummy's so sorry.' I cried out in relief, rubbing my tummy as tenderly as I could while trying to still my quivering body.

In a frenzied panic, I gunned the engine again. 'What the fuck ... !' I froze to the spot as something ghostly white slapped itself hard on the windscreen.

I screamed and recoiled, and the thing then splayed itself open, blocking my view entirely. It was the white fur coat. I pushed the wipers to full speed and, almost dancing mockingly, it flew off the windscreen and landed on the drive in front of the car. It lay like a dead body. Revving the engine, I purposefully charged forward and ran over it.

The electric-powered wooden gate opened painfully slowly, clearly struggling against the winds. An image of Lewis in a hospital bed, breathing his last breath, flashed across my mind.

Fuck that! I thought. I slammed the accelerator and rammed the gates, forcing them open and snapping the wing-mirror off in the process.

'Please ... don't take him from me, don't take him from me ...' I prayed to the Big Man Upstairs as I screeched out onto the road and headed towards Hillingdon hospital.

After hounding the poor receptionist at A&E, I was

directed through to a waiting room further up the ward. Once inside, I received a frantic call from Camilla—she was on her way.

At 2.30 a.m. a troubled-looking nurse approached me.

'He's in a critical but stable condition. An eyewitness said a tree fell in the road and Lewis tried to swerve and avoid it …' The lump in my throat was set to burst – I couldn't breathe through the tears. 'What we know so far is that Lewis has sustained multiple injuries, including a broken leg and shattered pelvis. It also appears he has a punctured lung. There's suspected internal bleeding and a head trauma which we don't know the extent of yet.'

Each word felt like a punch. I felt like I'd personally inflicted each injury on him. I swallowed, trying to keep the dam of emotions from bursting, then managed to stutter, 'Is he going to …'

My mouth wouldn't allow me to say it. I knew deep down that if Lewis died, I wouldn't be able to live with myself.

'… We won't know the full extent of the damage for some time, but we are doing all we can. The next few hours will be critical.'

The clammy hands returned as blind panic set in again. 'Can I see him now?'

She shook her head. 'He's still in a critical state and the doctors are assessing whether he needs emergency surgery on his brain. He's being taken through for a scan. The doctors will keep you informed and let you know when you can see him.'

I wanted to protest – I wanted to ignore what she'd

said and find him, just to be there, just to somehow … *I don't know.* But the guilt pinned me to my seat.

I broke down in the chair and cried – huge, almost silent sobs, muffled into a wad of tissue.

'Is there anyone on their way to support you?' asked the nurse.

Looking up at the nurse's face of concern, I managed to say, 'Camilla … Lewis's sister. She's on her way now.'

'Okay. Tara, I'm sorry about your fiancé, but he's in the best possible hands. I have to go now, the doctors will give you updates about his status.'

'Okay,' I whispered between sobs, 'thank you.'

She placed a comforting hand on my shoulder, and left.

I couldn't bear this waiting, I just wanted to see Lewis and tell him … *what exactly?* 'Sorry I cheated on you, broke your heart and caused you to crash your bike'?? 'Sorry I lied to you and let you think that you were definitely the father of this baby'?? 'Sorry that I've ruined everything we've ever worked for'??

I began to analyse the situation and it dawned on me that I was probably getting what I deserved. Travis had cheated and lied to me when I was most vulnerable, and now I'd done the same to Lewis. But at least Travis had had the decency to stop talking to me and call it off. I didn't even have the decency to do that to Lewis, stringing him along, giving him false hope. I was a worse liar and cheat than Travis ever was. I had become what I hated so much.

If Lewis didn't make it through, I'd be a murderer, as well as a cheating, lying whore. I'd never be able to forgive myself. So what kind of a mother would I be?

Especially if it did turn out that Travis was the father, the baby would be born of two of the worst lying, cheating bastards in the history of mankind. There'd be no chance for her.

Camilla would never be able to forgive me once the truth made its way to the surface. The salon would probably crumble through me not being able to work, and Camilla would leave on principle—and who would blame her? I'd have to go on the dole. No other man would want me. Katie would probably get Indie into drugs and I'd end up on the Irish equivalent of Jeremy Kyle.

With a panic attack brewing and not knowing what else to do, I called Laura. Luckily, she answered, and I just about managed to explain the situation. She gently insisted that I focus on my breathing and try to keep myself calm for the sake of the baby.

'What do I do? This is all my fault. This is all my fault. Please tell me what to do ...'

Just then, I saw Camilla opening the double doors at the end of the hallway.

'Laura, Laura, I have to go, Camilla is here. I'll call you back in a bit.'

'Okay, that's fine. Just remember to keep your breathing slow and steady. I'm gonna book myself and Mum on the next flight to London – we'll be with you as soon as possible.'

Camilla jogged over to me, tears spilling from her eyes. Her face was ghostly pale, highlighting her bulging red-raw eyes. Her shaky arms were stretched out ready to envelop me.

'Thank God you're here,' I whispered, breaking down.

'H-have you seen him? Is he gonna be okay?' she asked, shaking from head to toe.

I repeated what the nurse had told me, through heart-breaking pain. Saying it out loud further cemented that this was really happening. I watched Camilla's face crumble as I told her that Lewis might not make it. We wrapped our arms tightly around each other, our bodies jerking in unison as we stood helplessly, whimpering in hope.

'I just don't understand ... Lewis is usually such a careful, sensible rider ... it's so out of character for him to go out riding in weather like this,' said Camilla, blowing her nose.

My heart sank. I considered telling her why he went out. Eventually I would, but right now damage control was firmly in place, so I decided to postpone the truth.

Eventually, we sat down and waited for news. Every minute seemed like an hour. Patients, doctors, nurses and cleaners passed by and we still hadn't heard anything. Twice Camilla hassled the receptionist for an update, but she was firmly asked to sit back down and told they would let us know as soon as an update became available.

After an age of us both impatiently hovering in the doorway, we spotted a doctor wearing blue surgical scrubs emerge and approach the reception desk.

The receptionist pointed over towards Camilla and me. Bracing ourselves, we grabbed one another's hand and squeezed.

'Hi. Lewis is stable but is still unconscious.'

'Thank God!' we both yelped, cheering and hugging each other.

'He's just come out of an MRI scan and there is bruising on the brain; we need to monitor this intensively. The good news is there's no active bleeding on the brain.'

The doctor took a breath as Camilla and I tried desperately to absorb the information. He continued, 'As for his body, he has a punctured lung due to several ribs being broken and piercing the plural wall on his right side. His CT scan also shows a fractured pelvis and his right femur has broken. It's a very strong bone usually, this tells us that his accident was quite severe.'

The image of Lewis lying there in a ditch with his body and bike in pieces made me feel sick.

'I'm afraid Lewis isn't responding to certain reflex tests—the current prognosis is that he's in a coma. This is the body's natural reaction to such trauma. And due to the extent of his injuries, we don't want him to wake up just yet. The best thing is for his body to remain in this recovery-state coma until sufficient healing has occurred. The idea is to keep the brain from swelling, as much as possible. I know this is a lot to take in at this stage. The next twenty-four hours will be crucial, but would one of you like to come and see him now?'

Camilla and I looked at each other, hesitating. I was desperate to see him as soon as possible, but the guilt wouldn't allow me to take the first step.

'You go first, Tara. I'll wait ...'

'I ... Okay,' I gulped, breathing heavily to steady myself.

'Be brave.' Camilla sniffed, squeezing my hand again. 'My brother is a fighter. He's got everything to live for ... a family who loves him, a wonderful fiancée to marry, and a daughter on the way. He knows that,' she said, stroking my tummy with a trembling hand.

I felt an insurmountable fear rise within me as we approached the door. Here the surgeon stopped.

'I'm afraid that Lewis won't quite look like his normal self. It was a severe accident, and we're doing everything we can. But you may have to prepare yourself.

My stomach turned inside out. I already knew this wouldn't be easy. But I knew that no matter how he looked, I would be there by his side, whatever the outcome.

I took a deep breath to brace myself, and went in.

Chapter 18

I reached out for the wall behind me to stop myself falling over, and my hand flew to my mouth to shield my cries of horror.

He didn't look like my Lewis. He didn't even look human. He was a mess of bandages, spaghetti wires and tubing. A mask over his mouth connected to a machine seemed to be helping him breathe. The loud, disconcerting hissing of the ventilator and beeping heart-rate monitor was ominous. He was completely helpless and at the mercy of fate.

This was my fault. And I was heartbroken.

I watched his chest rise and fall whilst I searched frantically for an area of his skin that wasn't tubed, black, blue, bandaged or wired. Reaching forward, I carefully held his warm yet lifeless hand and leant down to kiss it. Just touching him made everything feel so real. And with it, so, so destitute.

I searched his face as the blood drained from mine.

'I'm sorry,' I whispered hoarsely. 'I'm so, so sorry. My poor, beautiful Lewis.'

I burst into tears. There wasn't a chance in hell he would be able to respond. Maybe not ever. I pulled his bed sheets to my face and wept loudly in them.

Indie began kicking violently inside me, no doubt stirred by the surge of deep emotion. My tummy hardened in an automatic reflex and I winced in pain.

Holding my face in my hands, I sobbed and sobbed, allowing the barrage of emotions to engulf me. Guilt. Sadness. Anger. Regret. Shame. Hopelessness. The list was endless.

Unable to look at him a minute longer, I kissed his cheek and, like a coward, left his room, sinking down against the wall outside, my legs like rubber bands, unable to keep me upright.

Camilla came bounding over.

'What's going on?' she pleaded, grabbing me by the arm and hauling me back up. 'Please tell me he's okay ... please?'

'He's not good,' I whispered, unable to look her in the eye. 'He, he, he's all bandaged up ... I couldn't take it, Camilla, I'm so sorry,' I said, shaking my head, 'It's all my fault ...'

'No, Tara, please ... none of this is your fault.'

I looked at her innocent expression, the belief in her face that I was nothing but good, that I would never hurt her brother. How little she knew.

'I'm sorry,' I croaked, pushing her aside and setting off down the corridor as fast as my legs would carry me.

Breathless after traipsing up and down around the

corridors, I splayed myself against a wall to recover. Feeling utterly defeated, I sank slowly to the floor and promptly broke down again. I was drowning in an ocean of misery – I had deceived everyone, even my best friends. I wanted to run, to hide; I wanted to find a Number 10 bus and throw myself in front of it!

Except, it wasn't just about me anymore. I was carrying another life, one that wasn't tainted like my own. And that meant there was no way out, unlike before. I couldn't just go and drown myself in alcohol, or sleep indefinitely. I was hosting a precious life, one that needed nurturing.

I couldn't believe how selfish I'd been. Lewis could be taking his last breath right now and I wasn't even by his side. But I just couldn't face it.

I bowed my head in misery and shame, and squeezed my eyes tight. I just wanted to curl up and die. I'd been in this place before. The emotional merry-go-round of hell. It all felt so unbearably familiar: the tightness of my chest; the skin-crawling anxiety. The despair.

I felt a hand gently touch my shoulder.

'Please,' I stammered, flicking it away angrily, 'please, just leave me alone!'

Undeterred, the wiry-looking elderly man crouched down in front of me, holding an old, battered bible. He had wonky, gold-rimmed glasses and his pale-blue magnified eyes were smiling behind them.

He gestured at me, reached forward, and helped pull me to my feet. It felt like I was wearing a lead suit as my body unfolded into a semi-upright position. Linking my arm in his, he walked me slowly down a corridor. We exchanged names, but my brain was so clogged I instantly forgot his and had to ask again.

'Father Damien,' he repeated in a soft Irish accent, guiding me towards the chapel doors. I felt a strange sensation of peace flood through me as I stepped over the threshold.

He walked me over to a set of tatty brown leather chairs in a corner and eased me down. Quite out of breath himself, Father Damien took a seat opposite me.

'I'm caught in the eye of a huge storm,' I sobbed. 'I have to stay away ... it's for the best.'

Father Damien pulled out a mini-notebook and pen from his jacket pocket and wrote down Lewis's full name. I noticed he had dandruff. It sat like glistening snowflakes on his ill-fitting black jacket. They all seem to have dandruff, men of the cloth. I guess they have far more important things to be taking care of than worrying about their scalps; like comforting people who have monumentally fucked up their lives.

'How do you take your tea, Tara?'

'No tea for me, Father. Thank you.'

'Ahh, now, now. No need to be so polite,' he said in a light, jocular tone. 'I think you and your little one would be appreciatin' a strong, sugary cuppa tea, no?'

I let out a half smile and nodded.

'I'll be right back there now,' he said, dashing off and calling over his shoulder, 'just give me a minute.'

I stared ahead of me, my gaze transfixed by the hauntingly beautiful wooden crucifix. It was made of a pale-coloured wood, and it dominated the chapel.

Without thinking about it, I lifted myself up, walked over to the wooden pews, and blessed myself, just like I did as a child.

Bowing my head before the Big Man himself, I placed a dark green velvet hassock on the floor, dropped to my knees and placed my trembling hands together tightly.

'Dear God ... I know we don't talk very often—and when we do, it's because I'm asking for meaningless, pathetic things like not to puke whilst on the back of a motorbike, or worse, handbags, or even worse than that, the latest pair of Jimmy Choos—but this is different. I've done something terrible to a man who didn't deserve it. I know I deserve to go to hell for what I've done to one of your angels and I'm so, so sorry. Even if Lewis wakes up and never forgives me, I don't care. All I want is for him to survive and be okay—whether that's with me or without me.

'I know I've already been blessed with one of your miracles— she's growing inside me now. But please, please, I'm begging for just one more and I'll never ask for anything ever again, I promise.'

I don't know how long I'd been praying when the creaking of the chapel door startled me.

'Don't you be worryin', your fella is still stable,' assured Father Damien, setting down a tray of tea and broken biscuits.

The relief to hear that Lewis was still fighting washed over me in waves.

'There's a woman with blonde hair by his bedside – I'm assumin' you know her?'

'That's Lewis's sister, Camilla,' I said, eyeing the tea suspiciously.

'It's the hospital's finest,' he chuckled. 'Don't knock it. I'm told it has improved. With plenty of sugar in, you'll only taste the sweetness.'

I smiled in thanks and took a tentative sip. It was extraordinarily sweet and my teeth and tongue were instantly coated in a sticky layer of sugar.

'What are you doing up so late?' I asked, noticing how exhausted he looked.

'Well, you see now, I find my best clients tend to lurk in the hallways of the hospital at night,' he said taking a bite of the biscuit. 'That, and I can't sleep for toffee in me ol' age.'

I couldn't help but smile. His presence had a very calming effect on me, despite the crisis.

I looked beyond the priest and over to the only small window in the chapel. First light was just breaking through, but it was still grey and drizzling.

Even the heavens were crying.

I felt so desperately drained. Everything felt numb. My knees had gone well past the pins-and-needles stage. My back was aching and stiff, begging for respite. I put my tea down and nestled together some more hassocks, and lay beside Father Damien on the hard narrow bench. I stare up at the ceiling, unable to keep my burning eyes open a minute longer.

* * *

Father Damien shook my shoulder gently.

'Good morning, Tara.'

'What? What time is it?!'

'It's 10.20 in the mornin'. You've been asleep for a few good hours there, and though I'm a priest, I know better than to be wakin' a pregnant woman who's already sleep-deprived.'

'Oh, God … *Lewis!'* I cried, jolting upright.

'Don't worry—don't worry, I've checked with the doctors, he's still stable and there's been no change in his condition. His sister is still there with him now, so she is.'

'Oh … okay,' I stammered, 'S-sorry for blaspheming, Father.'

'Ahh don't you be worryin' about it child, I'm sure he doesn't mind much about that stuff anyhow. Here, I've got you a sandwich; you're to be keepin' that strength up if you're goin' through troubled times *and* havin' a little one.'

I nodded gratefully and took a small bite but it wouldn't go down; it was like swallowing cardboard.

'The sun's up and the rain has stopped. I pray God will have mercy on you, Lewis and your little one. Oh, wait there now, before I go off and do me rounds – a young man had asked about your whereabouts. But I told him you were sleepin' and you weren't to be disturbed unless in an emergency. I think he's still waitin' outside now. Said his name was … Tommy, I think?'

It must've been James.

'Was he tall with blonde hair and quite … effeminate?' I asked.

'That was one of them, indeed. But the man outside now is a big fella: dark hair, large build. I could've sworn I recognised him from the telly or somewhere. Anyways – I told him that I'd send you out to him when you're ready.'

Alarm bells resounded in my head. *It can't be …*

'... Father, was his name Travis?'

'*Umm*—Yes! Yes it was. I remember now, he said he needs to be discussin' a delicate issue with you.'

I knew it! I could smell that man's bullshit through walls, even sacred ones. I felt quite positively unstable. Not as in nervous breakdown unstable, more I'm-going-to-kill-Travis unstable.

'Okay, thank you, Father. I'll see you shortly.' With steely determination, I rose to my feet.

'Our doors are always open. Peace be with you,' said Father Damien to my disappearing back.

I smiled through gritted teeth; peace wasn't exactly what I had in mind. Turning back, I nodded at the crucifix and pre-emptively asked for forgiveness for what was about to occur. Then I walked towards the chapel door, trying to look as calm as possible while I eyed up my weapons. *Water or foam? Foam, of course!* I picked up the fire extinguisher and peeked around the door—Travis ... it *was* him! The gobshite was there, sitting in a chair facing away from me, so I waited for a nurse to walk past before quietly opening the door and ...

'BASTARD!' I screamed, and as he turned around in surprise, I sprayed the extinguisher right in his face. He squealed as the expanding foam engulfed him and he slid onto the floor.

'It's all your feckin' fault!' Having unloaded the foam over the rest of his body, I dropped the extinguisher and scrambled for a new weapon. 'Sorry about this,' I said to the heavens above as I yanked off the plastic *CHAPEL* sign from the wall and went to town with it:

'YOU [whack, yelp]—HAVE [whack, yelp]—RUINED [whack, yelp]—EVERYTHING!' [whack, whack, whack – yelp].

'Tara—stop!—you lunatic!' Travis managed to deflect the last blow and grabbed hold of my arm.

'Let go of me you bastard, or so help me—'

'Please, Tara, calm down, just hear me out,' he said through the foam.

'Hah! Listen to you? *Listen* to you? Are you out of your tiny mind? That's why I'm in this feckin' mess in the first place!' I managed to yank my arm free and hit him again with the sign.

'[Yelp] *Stop!* Tara, listen, we didn't sleep together – you bloody maniac!'

I paused the assault for a second and blinked.

Then a voice came from behind me, 'Tara, babes, I think he might be telling the truth.' I turned around to see James standing there casually, watching the assault with coffee in hand and Father Damien hiding behind him.

'... James, what are you doing here?!'

'Laura called and told me about what happened to Lewis, and about the hotel incident with Travis. I was about to leave the salon to come see you here, when, by some divine stroke of bad luck, I bumped into *this* swine outside Glamma-Puss, looking for you. We nearly strung him up for everything he'd done, so I dragged him here to, well ... oh, *fuck it.* Look—the sooner you stop attacking this pathetic excuse of man, the sooner he can explain himself and we can get him out of your life for good.'

Travis pulled himself up on the seat and wiped his

eyes, looking like he'd just dug himself out of a blizzard.

'It's good to see you again … looks like you've put on a few since I last saw you—*aghh!*' said Travis after I whacked him again. 'Please, no – stop for one second! Look, I only agreed to come here in order to set the record straight in case any wrongful allegations came my way—not to be assaulted. Just put down the sign so we can talk.'

I abated for a moment, mainly to catch my breath, as opposed to me giving mercy.

'Tara, the baby can't be mine – we didn't sleep together—'

'No more lies! *Please*,' I begged, feeling utterly exhausted by the drama surrounding this man. 'I woke up in your bed, both of us naked …'

'Yes – that part is true, but nothing actually happened. You passed out after hitting your head, after falling down the steps into the lobby. I didn't touch you and you didn't touch me. I wanted to, but I couldn't go through with it – you were so out of your head.'

'But … how do I know you're not lying, *again?*'

Travis huffed, 'Listen – I wanted you more than anything. Tara, I'm a sportsman, and I was losing you. I've been called a lot of things, but I'm definitely not a rapist, for fuck's sake … I'm not!' he said, looking to Father Damien for back up.

'I can't believe you! All of *this* was for nothing?!' I said, foaming at the mouth in fury.

'Tara, please stay calm,' pleaded Father Damien. 'Think about the baby.'

'Lewis—the love of my life, the reason I have to

live—is in a critical condition because of all this. The guilt I've felt all these months has been eating me alive, and for what? What did you get out of this?'

He said nothing, simply looking at the ground and shrugging like a naughty schoolboy.

'You're nothing but a monster,' I huffed.

'I'm not a monster – I'm here, trying to tell you the truth and right my wrongs, aren't I?' he said, turning again to Father Damien.

'So ... my baby ... she's Lewis's baby – and definitely 100% not yours?'

Travis seemed to come back into his own with this question as he adjusted his stance and shrugged again. 'Well, how should I know? I don't know how many other guys you jumped into bed wi—'

I came down on him with the sign again. 'You p ... p ... pig!'

The only thought that kept me going in that moment was the knowledge that Indie was truly Lewis's baby.

Something shifted inside of me. The anger turned to ... release. The guilt I'd been feeling all this time, the pain, the worry about Indie – everything began to lift.

I was overcome with a release from the regret. But my elation was short lived – no confession in the world would be able to help Lewis right now. With this knowledge, though, I'd have the strength to stay by his side, the real father of my child, my husband-to-be, and just pray he'd come back to me. I was no longer ashamed to sit with him. I desperately needed Lewis to wake up so I could tell him that I hadn't been totally unfaithful. In fact, I hadn't been unfaithful at all. I had to show him that I *was* the woman he fell in love with.

The woman he thought I was. The woman *I* thought I was.

Suddenly, the pathetic, foamy mess of a man before me was no longer an issue. I was done with him. I almost felt sorry for him. I hoped Travis wouldn't press charges for my violence, but given the information I had at the time, he deserved it ... *Your Honour*. I'm sure that wouldn't stand up in court, but whatever.

'So we're cool, right? This has all been just a mix-up that got out of hand. I really am sorry about Lewis ...'

'Just go!' I shouted, shaking my head. 'I swear to you, the day I see you again will be your last. Now go.'

Travis turned on his heel, gave me a sideward look, and then spat on the floor. I would've been more offended if he didn't look like a wet sheep, still covered in foam.

I got a single round of applause from James and a relieved hand on my shoulder from Father Damien.

'But, James, how can I explain to everyone why Lewis crashed? Everyone will hate me, even now we know the truth.'

'No, darling, don't you worry about any of that. She can't be mad at you—well, not forever, anyway. You've done nothing except tell a little lie, which, in the grand scheme of things is more than forgivable. You only told a lie because you were lied to yourself; everyone knows that when you lie about a lie, it cancels itself out. In fact, I'm going to speak to Camilla right now to explain this whole mess. The only person really at fault here is that turd who you just beat fifty shades out of.'

In his own little way, I knew he was partly right, but that didn't stop the guilt. Drying my eyes, I apologised to Father Damien about my violent outburst, and replaced the now-cracked chapel sign back onto the wall, before making my way with James back to Lewis's room. On the way, James and I agreed that he would explain everything to Camilla without me being there, and I would hide like a coward until we had a reaction from her, one way or the other. So, out of sight, I nervously paced up and down the corridor nearby Lewis's room, terrified of the outcome of their conversation. Camilla might still have wanted to tear my head off, even if she did know the truth.

After what seemed like an age, James appeared with a muted smile on his face. 'Don't worry – everything will be okay. She's not angry, she just wants to be with Lewis.'

Sighing in relief and sending thanks to the Big Man Upstairs, I turned the corner to see Camilla waiting by Lewis's door, looking through the window. Nervously, I walked over, and without looking at me, she said, 'I understand this isn't your fault, but this isn't about you right now. There's no use in pointing fingers; we've just got to get him through this.'

She was right. And though she obviously wasn't my biggest fan, in time I would try to bring her around.

Camilla pushed open the door and held it open for me as we walked in.

Seeing Lewis in his state shocked me to the core all over again. Despite this, I heard myself saying, 'He is going to get through this, I just know it.' Maybe I was being overly optimistic; but that's what you're supposed to do in a situation like that, isn't it? *Think positive.* So, I concentrated on the best-case scenario.

Best case: Lewis would make a full recovery. Maybe he would come out with some scars, but I could live with that – scars are sexy. Ideally, he wouldn't have any on his face. Scarring on arms and legs is fine, though—perhaps even preferable?

Then a cloud of doubt loomed. 'He *will* get better, won't he?'

'I don't know,' said Camilla, brimming with tears.

'So … what do we do now?' I sniffed.

'We wait.'

Chapter 19

Life had become a blur of doctors, nurses, physiotherapists and visitors. I was now eight and a half months pregnant, and Lewis had been lost in his own world for over two months. Not a sign, nor a squeezed hand, nor a hopeful flutter of eyelashes. Nothing. He had stayed in the Intensive Care Unit at Hillingdon Hospital all that time, so it had become like a second home to me. I even had my antenatal appointments moved there; I needed to be near him as often as I could.

A week after the accident, the doctors allowed Lewis to start breathing on his own. Then I watched the cuts and bruises eventually fade from his body, leaving only the scars on his abdomen and leg where they operated. Then, as he stabilised, much of the life support machinery was removed, save for a few bits monitoring his vital signs and giving him nutrients. He still had to wear a bowel management system and a catheter for waste, as well as needing daily massages to keep his muscles from atrophying. But importantly, the neurologist said that there was very little identifiable damage to his brain, so theoretically he was still hanging in there.

At first, I used to fantasise about an idyllic, Hollywood-esque wake up scene. I'd be there, the pregnant, glowing fiancée, beautiful in my grief, yet holding strong with glamorous fortitude. He would slowly open his eyes and be in perfect condition, and after a bit of joyous crying and elation about his waking, I'd tell him the whole truth about what happened, and he'd say that he'd heard everything and knew the truth the whole time he'd been comatose. Then we'd hold each other and cry in happiness for half an hour or so.

But he still hadn't come back.

For the first five days, I had camped beside Lewis, as I simply couldn't be apart from him. But before long, the friends, family, medical staff and even Father Damien insisted that both the baby and me 'would be more comfortable at home'. I knew they were right, but it broke my heart to leave Lewis's side. I couldn't bear staying in our house alone, so was delighted when Camilla and I buried the hatchet and she offered for me to live at hers with her partner, Alex. Being around Camilla was a double-edged sword: lovely because she looked after me and I for her; but also extremely painful, as she reminded me so much of Lewis (at one point, their similarities got so much that I considered moving in with James, but just the idea of having to move everything again exhausted me).

The doctors told me that *if* Lewis did come out of his coma, then it would be a gradual process and not a sudden awakening. They said it could take weeks, months or even years – there was no way of knowing. And even if he did wake up, due to the severity of the accident there may well be complications, including: amnesia, hormone imbalances, irrational anger, depression, post-traumatic stress, fatigue, reduced sex drive, loss of motor-reflexes, inability to control his inhibitions, reduced spatial awareness and overall mobility. His cognitive abilities may have also been impacted: reasoning, memory recall, empathy, speech, and understanding of language. Not being able to see, hear, smell, taste or touch in the same way. Even day-to-day tasks like making a cup of tea or driving a car could be impossible. He might never have been able to hold Indie.

The only thing I knew was that no matter how long it took, no matter what the damage done, even if Lewis was no longer the Lewis I once knew, I would be there. We didn't need to be married for 'until death do you part' to apply. Like a dog refusing to part from his sick owner, I would be there, no matter what.

I hadn't felt like doing anything, hadn't felt like breathing, but my body did it anyway. As day turned into night and night turned into day, life went on, whether I wanted it to, or not.

Every day I'd explain to Lewis how Indie was definitely his baby, and what really happened when I went to meet Travis. It became a daily mantra I'd perform when no one else was in the room fussing over machines or drips.

'Indie *is* your baby ... Please, please wake up. I need you. *She* needs you,' I would beg and cry as I bent over and cuddled into him for hours on end. It almost came to the point where my body had forgotten how to stand straight – but then, how could it, when the weight of the world was upon my shoulders and the only response was absolute painful silence?

It frustrated me so much to sit by his side and have absolutely no idea what was going on in that head of his ...

... Maybe he could hear everything I told him, and he was desperate to call out, saying, 'Tara, I'm so bored of you telling me that you didn't cheat – you tell me every day. I know this. I just wish I could tell you to shut up!'

... Maybe my worst fear had come true—that he could only remember the events leading up to the accident, replaying a the moment he thought I had betrayed him, over and over twenty-four hours a day. No escape from the infinite nightmares. No chance of him getting closure. If this was the case, the agony would have been too much to bear – no wonder his mind had battened down the hatches and refused to come out.

... Maybe he had amnesia and still thought his ex, Mercedes, was his fiancée and that he still loved her deeply. He might not have had a clue who I was.

... Maybe he would have woken up to be a completely different person – angry, unloving and abusive.

... Or maybe his mind was simply no more, with just his body ticking away with no hope of ever becoming conscious again.

I was full to the brim with regret and remorse that there lay this beautiful man—the epitome of all that was good, with not a bad bone in his body—and was the one who had reduced him to a state of lifelessness. There was nothing I could do except hope that one day he would find his way back to us, back to me, back to our baby.

Camilla came into the hospital most mornings and often broke down as she clasped at her brother's hand. It was painful to watch. I'd hug and kiss her, but she would be in a world of her own grief. I understood that feeling and would sometimes leave the room so she could be alone with her beloved brother.

Mum, Laura and Katie (who had been allowed temporarily out of rehab) stayed for a while to console Camilla and me. Apparently, Katie had painted and decorated Indie's nursery back at our house, but I still couldn't bear to go there. Mum thankfully stayed in the UK with me – quite honestly, I'd never needed her more. Katie went back to rehab as promised, and Laura went back to work in Dublin.

The doctors said that speaking to patients in Lewis's condition in a specific way could not only be heard, it could also help to awaken the unconscious brain and speed recovery. So, I would play Lewis's favourite music and listen with him, ranging through Led Zeppelin, David Bowie, Kings of Leon and even The Chemical Brothers. People express themselves through what they listen to, and so I felt closer to him having heard his favourite tracks. In a way, I felt like we were communicating.

Sometimes Camilla would sit there with photo

albums, reflecting on their childhood together, using as much description as possible. She said that despite the fact she would always get Lewis into trouble for things that *she* had actually done, plus all the frequent bickering, Lewis had always made her feel safe. He'd always looked out for her, like the time he decked a boy who had pushed her over in the school playground. And the time her first boyfriend dumped her, Lewis was there to mop up her tears. One photo showed them visiting Caswell Bay in Wales. Camilla described a sandy beach, her wild hair blowing in the gale. Before long, a crashing wave hit the shoreline and swallowed up the sandcastle they'd spent hours building. She cried hysterically and Lewis had comforted her, saying that the one they had been building was only a prototype – and that they would build a bigger, better one away from the shoreline, one that would last forever. It was still there the next morning when they all left to go home.

I tried so hard to push aside the painful reality so I could remember the happier times. There was the very first time we clapped eyes on each other. (Well, perhaps not the very first time, when the Big Man Upstairs had tried to push our paths together in Ann Summers). I'd been obsessing over Travis at the time, in what Laura liked to call my 'super insecure phase'. I'd got stuck in that bastardly imprisoning catsuit, in a poor plan to win Travis over. Lewis happened to be in the queue, buying underwear for Mercedes). In the more sanitised version of our first sighting, Lewis had driven Camilla in for her interview at Glamma-Puss. I remembered how shy I'd felt in his company, and how disappointed

I was when James had labelled Lewis 'A bum hole engineer—absolutely, 100% gay,' (which nearly ended up in things not taking off between me and Lewis). Then there was our engagement in Paris. Nights out with friends. Dinner parties. The time he took me to London Zoo. Our first anniversary.

Each time I tried to clear my throat and relay our memories to Lewis, I struggled to keep my voice steady. An overwhelming mix of heartache, loss and sadness would overpower me and I simply couldn't continue. So, instead of talking, most days I would just squish myself into the bed next to him for a cuddle. Space was limited, so I'd lie on my side, my head on his chest and baby bump close against him. I'd lift up his warm yet lifeless hand and place it on my tummy, holding his other hand in my palm, hoping that somehow, through the energy of my touch and thoughts, my love would penetrate through his deepest sleep and somehow rouse him into waking.

I pushed back his overgrown, straw-coloured floppy hair from his face and gently traced his perfect cheekbones with my fingertips. Usually Lewis would have stubble on his chin, and I'd shave him a couple of times a month to keep him from going full beardo; but I decided, and in keeping with the fashion, that he kind of suited wearing his beard a bit longer.

'Please don't fly too close to heaven, my darling,' I whispered. 'Once you're there, you can't get back. Just make your way back to me – back to us.

He always looked so peaceful; yet, I know he was lost, adrift even, in that awful place of limbo where I couldn't reach him.

'Please, open your eyes and look into mine,' I begged, aching with emptiness at his deafening silence. I watched his chest rise and fall and wondered if he was dreaming. I hoped I was in them; and if I was, I wanted it to be the Tara from the old days. The happier days.

Picking up his iPod next to the bed, I placed one earphone in my ear and the other in his and flicked through the tracks listlessly, looking for something to reflect how I felt. Sometimes it's scary how the shuffle mode can so perfectly select a track that matches your mood, like it somehow just *knows*. 'Chasing Cars' by Snow Patrol: The utter sadness and hope in the lyrics got to me, leaving a lump in my throat.

If I lay here ... if I just lay here ... would you lie with me and just forget the world?

The energy of the song flowed through our bodies. I scanned his face in hope of a reaction, brushing the golden hairs backwards and forwards on Lewis's forearm. Nothing; still his impassive self. The hope within me, while it was still there, had dulled.

I placed my head on his chest and it rose and fell beneath my cheek. I wiped the puddle of tears from his gown and stared up at his pale, blank, beautiful face. At his bedside were 3D images of our daughter's scan. Again I described in detail what Indie looked like, painting a picture of her tiny hands and feet, all curled up and tucked in safely inside me. I begged and pleaded for him to open his eyes so he could see for himself.

But he didn't.

I miss him, and his love, so much.

I'd begun telling him that if he really loved me, he would wake up. I'd begged time and again for him to just open an eye. I'd been praying. I'd been doing everything the doctors asked. So why wasn't he responding?

In my desperation for him to wake, I began refusing to go back to Camilla's house. Indie needed her daddy to wake up, and I needed him more than ever.

At one point I even pulled his eyelids open to try and get him to see me. But there was nothing. Another time I became so desperate that I actually smacked him, first on the arm, then around the face. When he didn't respond, a wave of shame, guilt and despair came flooding over me. I begged him to forgive me, crying and holding him tight.

No matter what I did, he remained in God's waiting room.

* * *

My body ached and creaked as I rolled backwards and forwards, then finally heaved myself off Lewis's bed. My back felt broken.

'How're you holdin' up, pet?' came Mum's familiar voice as she walked over to the bed, placing her hand on my shoulder.

I shrugged and shook my head as fresh tears pricked my eyes.

'Why, Mum? Why won't he wake up?' I sobbed, burying my hands in my face. 'He has a baby on the way and he doesn't even know that he's the father. He still thinks I cheated on him. What if I never get the chance to tell him the truth? How am I supposed to live with that?'

'He *can* hear you, Tara. I just know it. Even the doctors say he can probably hear what people are sayin'. You can hear us, can't you, Lewis?' she asked, then began to fix his bed sheets with the same efficiently as the nurses did.

I took a shaky breath and placed my hand on my aching lower back, looking over at Lewis in wonder.

'God works in mysterious ways,' added Mum with an assertive nod of her head, as though this was the most normal situation ever.

'If Lewis could hear us, then he wouldn't keep putting us all through this, would he?' I said. 'I just … don't understand.'

'Miracles won't happen if you don't believe in them. Sure, aren't you experiencin' a miracle right now – growin' inside of you, right this moment?'

'Yes … but, I'm not strong enough, Mum,' I said breathlessly, feeling like I was about to fold down like a deckchair. 'How can this little life inside me keep going when my life … my life has fallen apart?'

'You're a Ryan,' Mum cut in matter-of-factly, pulling me into her and hugging me hard. After a moment, she pulled back a little, cupped my face in her hands and locked her eyes directly onto mine. 'Your dad gave up—he was a broken man. There was nothin' any of us could've done. And at the minute, the only thing we can do for Lewis is be here in the hope that he will wake up to see your beautiful face.'

I couldn't help but roll my eyes. The guilt of my father's death always hung over me, and now the same guilt with Lewis was bubbling up. But I wouldn't make the same mistakes this time. I swept up the memory of

Dad and told it to join the queue in my already crippled heart.

Of course, Mum knew about waiting in vain better than anyone. She'd spent years trying to pull my dad out of the place where his demons haunted him. My dad was always physically present, but mentally he was unreachable. I shivered at how disturbingly similar it was to my situation with Lewis.

'He's still here, look at him there, still fightin'. God love him,' said Mum, bringing us both back to the here and now. Mum sat down, reached into her bag and pulled out the little booties she was knitting for Indie and frowned, holding up the oddly shaped thread of uneven stitches. 'I can't remember how to be castin' off me knittin'. I'm gettin' old. I've left instructions of how I want to, you know, *go*. As you well know—'

'Mum! Please, not this again. This is not the right time to be talking about you dying when Lewis could be lying on his deathbed.'

She'd been on and on about her funeral and her cremation, and I'd started having nightmares about it. I'd already lost one parent; the last thing I wanted right now was to think about losing another. I really wasn't strong enough to discuss the logistics of how to get her ashes scattered in the Irish Sea so she could do some sort of macabre world tour 'around Spain, Malta, and then on to South Africa'. All I could visualise was her remains being gobbled up by some great big stupid fish. Odds are, some trawler would then catch the fish, and she'd end up in someone's Saturday takeaway with chips. Or, worse, in fish fingers: smothered in tomato ketchup and gobbled up by some spotty teenager.

'Mum, you could clear a room in seconds, you know that?' I said, shaking my head.

She looked at me with kind and knowing eyes.

'I do, yes,' she nodded sagely. 'Why don't you be gettin' home for a few hours, give yourself a break and have a nice hot bath? Maybe you could pop into the salon and get your hair done? I've spoken to James and he'll be ready in a heartbeat to come pick you up ...'

I shook my head as I stroked Lewis's face.

'What if he wakes up and I'm not here?' I asked in a shaky voice.

Behind me, Mum gently gripped my shoulder and eased me round to face her.

'Tara, you've a phone; the first signs of anythin' happenin' I'll be lettin' you know immediately.'

I shook my head as the guilt swam around my thoughts. I just had a feeling in my bones that something was going to happen today; but then again, I did most days.

'Listen here to me, we're all wild with worry, pet, but both you and the baby could do with a break from the hospital, could you not? It's not good for either of you, and to be honest if he woke now, you'd give the poor fella a fright and scare him back to sleep, lookin', well ... like that.'

As insulted as I first felt, I knew deep down she was right. My excited thoughts of Lewis waking up and me trying to look the sexy fiancée were long gone. Instead, I resembled what I actually was – a heartbroken, frightened eight-and-a-half-month-pregnant woman.

'So you'll be gettin' yourself out of here for a bit then?' asked Mum, physically peeling me away from

Lewis and promptly shoving me out the door.

Shortly afterwards I was forcibly squashed into James's bright red Porsche Boxster and speeding back to Lewara, surrounded by the sounds of Whitney Houston's 'I Wanna Dance With Somebody' on at full volume. James pretended to squeeze his man-plums when an attempting to match Witney's unsurpassable vocals—and he was losing. I know he was only trying to cheer me up, but the one thing on my mind was for him to turn the car around and get me back to Lewis.

Preferably wearing earplugs.

Chapter 20

I thought my heart was going to explode in my chest as we arrived at the gates of Lewara. It felt like a lifetime ago that I'd bombed out of there, adrenaline pumping, to get to Lewis.

My trembling fingers pressed hard into my face in a fruitless bid to stem the steady stream of tears.

The bare trees stood swaying in the February cold. The place had a bleak, almost morbid vibe. I shivered as my waterlogged eyes travelled across to our junior Trevi fountain, which I had accidently demolished on that fateful night. Now a dry, crumbled, pathetic mess of broken lights and rubble, the fountain personified how I felt about my and Lewis's lives. I then caught a glimpse of the Defender; missing the left wing mirror, a huge scrape down the left side and the rear completely crushed. I winced at the scars of my reckless driving on Lewis's pride and joy.

I recoiled as I relived the agonising scene when I

confessed to Lewis that I'd slept with Travis and that Indie might not be his baby. The flashback brought waves of grief and I began to weep wildly and uncontrollably once again. I would've given anything – *anything* – to rewrite that life-altering mistake of going to meet Travis that night at the hotel.

'It's all going to be okay,' announced James, bringing the car to a halt and deftly hopping out. He bounded round to the passenger door and opened it for me, offering me his hand. Heaving me up with uncharacteristic strength, he hugged me close before leading me arm in arm to the front door.

I didn't feel ready for this – it was bad enough being outside, let alone facing the painful memories inside.

Time slowed down as I turned the key in the lock. I felt as though I was watching someone else go in. Unsteadily I stepped in, and in that instant, the smell began the rapid ferris wheel of memories, cycling around my head. The house seemed as cold inside as it was outside. Our footsteps echoed around the lifeless hallway. This didn't feel like home – it felt more like I had stepped into a haunted house.

'I'll turn on the heating and pop the kettle on,' said James, walking ahead of me.

Nodding and taking a deep breath, I began to mechanically climb the stairs, willing my muscles to keep moving.

I stopped, mid-climb, and viewed a trio of photographs of Lewis and me in Paris. We looked so *happy*, grinning like schoolchildren. His thick, unruly hair and dazzling smile lit up the picture. I rested the tip of my finger on his face through the dusty frame, almost trying to absorb the warmth of the moment back through to the present day. That happiness seemed a million miles away, as if it had happened to someone else.

As I walked up and across the landing, I noticed a note on the door of Indie's bedroom:

> *To my wonderful future niece, sorry for drugging you before you were even born.*
> *I'll make it up to you when you come out to play.*
> *Love, your Auntie Katie xxx*

The note made me well up with pride. I'd forgotten all about Katie decorating the nursery. My heart warmed in excitement as I pushed down the handle and opened the door.

Wow. The room was covered in the colours of all things girly; a marshmallowy wonderland of puff-powdery pinks and soft whites. Whitewashed wooden floors surrounded a huge pink fluffy rug. The windows were framed with elaborate bowed pink and white curtains with matching tiebacks and light shade. The large, distressed-pink wardrobe was obscured only slightly by the cutest lemon baby-tutu, which sat on a pink padded satin hanger.

The room was full to the brim with wooden toys, fairy dolls and teddies. Where there was space, Katie had positioned a couple of giant, fluffy Mongolian beanbags; I ran my fingers along their fluffy surface, nodding in approval. Katie had truly redeemed herself and painted a feature wall with a beautiful mural of a fairy-tale castle set against a pale-blue sky. And sat underneath—well, wonders will never cease—she'd also managed to assemble Indie's cot! To top the nursery off, individual pink and white ribbons hung from carved wooden letters painted in white, spelling out Indie's name.

Something sat in the corner of the nursery, mysteriously covered with a white sheet. Curious, I pulled it off, and jumped at the sight of the pink pram. Gulping hard, I gripped the handlebars. Even the inanimate pram seemed to have lost the fond brightness about it.

The battle Lewis and I had had over the two prams seemed so irrelevant and meaningless now.

'There's no way on this earth I'm pushing around a pink— *pink!* —pram,' Lewis had said after seeing my first choice in John Lewis.

'Well that's fine, because it's *fondant*—not pink, so you won't have to,' I argued, hands on my long-lost hips.

Bemused, he scanned the brochure. '... Plus, Tara, the thing weighs thirty-seven kilos. Thirty. Seven. Kilos. That's, like, more than half of what *you* weigh—'

The look on my face said *tread carefully, boy*.

'... and even if you *could* lift the bloody thing, it wouldn't actually fit in the car – it doesn't even fold down. It's bigger than your Fiat altogether.'

Surely this is a minor detail?

The pram I had chosen was, in my opinion (and according to the brochure), the Rolls Royce of baby transport – i.e. the *only* pram to have. Whether it fitted in the car or not was irrelevant.

'"The Silver Cross *Balmoral Vintage* coach-built

pram is the definition of luxury …"' I pointed out, reading from the shiny brochure. '"Its British-engineered design exudes quality and craftsmanship, from the polished chrome chassis to the hand-stitched fabrics and the hallmark hand-painted fine line detail … A sumptuous cotton pram liner and mattress ensures that your baby is transported in the greatest comfort, and with the classic Balmoral suspension, peaceful strolling is guaranteed for your newborn …"'

Clearly, Lewis didn't understand the importance of having such a magnificent vehicle to carry our first child. He looked very thoughtful, first running his hands through his hair, then through the stubble on his jaw. He then looked slowly back at the Balmoral and I was sure he was just about to cave in when suddenly he spotted the funky Silver Cross 'Surf' in the distance.

'Look at that one,' he pointed, his face lighting up. Without waiting for my response, he began to make his way over to it.

I knew what it was without even looking at it. It was exactly up his street. The Silver Cross Surf: my sworn enemy.

Simply put: he was not allowed it. I'd be getting my way here; I just had to break it to him gently.

'But all the celebrities have these ones,' I pleaded to his disappearing back. 'And look,' I wailed, holding up the Balmoral's baby bag mid-air, 'it even has a matching fondant baby bag with loads of different compartments!'

I held on to my Vintage Balmoral pram for dear life and, for good measure, lifted the strap of the baby-bag across my body. *Let's see someone try to wrestle this off me*, I thought, folding my arms in protest and point blank refusing to budge or even *look* at Lewis's choice.

'Please, just take a look at this one,' he asked, effortlessly lifting the pram down off the display shelf.

I'd already chosen. However, I didn't want to be accused of not being reasonable (even if I wasn't actually allowing myself to be reasoned with). So, in the spirit of fairness, I walked over, took one obligatory glance and, with a show of indifference, turned my back on the Surf.

'It says, "the Surf delivers exceptional handling over any terrain thanks to its large, rugged wheels".' Lewis read the label while strategically ignoring my protests. 'Puncture-free tyres ... it's even got air-spring suspension for when I go off-roading with her in the mountains,' he said, deliberately trying to wind me up. With the dexterity of a racing driver, he manoeuvred the pram around me, running it down the aisle then back up at speed.

'This one is better, the wheels actually steer on this one,' Lewis said excitedly, inspecting the pram like it was a second-hand car. 'It's much more practical.'

Practical!? That word ought to be removed from the dictionary! I *hate* that word; I hate it with a passion. I mean, what does it actually say, other than boring, unexciting, or just plain ugly? I tell you what practical means—not getting what you really, really want!

Yes, it was probably going to be easier to lift; and granted, it would possibly (okay, definitely) fit in the boot; but ... that meant nothing. Even if it ticked all the boxes, my *–our* – baby would not be rolling around in a ticked box on wheels.

The situation required tough action. Jutting my chin forward in determination, I wheeled my Balmoral over to block Lewis's path. Hugging the baby-bag to my chest, I squeezed my eyes tight till they were burning, and tried to force out crocodile tears.

They were normally right on cue – but when I needed them the most, did they come?

Did they feck!

When her back is against the wall, tears are the bullets a woman needs to get what she wants. And I was fresh out of ammo. Pretending to sneeze, I leaned down and prodded myself in the eye. Twice. This classic move is almost guaranteed to get the tears in motion. Then I finished off the effect with a quivering bottom lip, sprinkling in a few sniffles and an unsubtle whimper.

Lewis's face showed signs of cracking.

Masterful, Tara, truly masterful.

'*Ohh*, Tara ... please don't look at me with those eyes ... please. This pink one, it's just not practical.'

I stopped my routine in its tracks, changing my demeanour from whimpering schoolgirl to towering dominatrix.

'Yes, Lewis, I know the one *you* want is *practical* ... But do you know what my definition of the word "practical" actually is, Lewis Copeland? I define *practical* as a woman (your woman) no longer wanting to have sex with her man (that's you, Lewis) for the *remainder of her pregnancy*, because she's already pregnant and that just wouldn't be *practical!*'

The fondant (pink) Balmoral pram and matching baby-bag were both swiftly ordered.

A faint smile broke through as I imagined our baby smiling back at me from within the gorgeous pram. I knew that if Lewis, God forbid, didn't make it, he would be smiling at me from heaven, saying, 'Ha! I didn't have to push around that pink pram in the end – *nur nurr.*' The thought made me sad and laugh at the same time.

Forcing myself to focus on the present, I thought about how much support I was getting from everyone. James, now back at my side, handed me a cup of tea while Indie was kicking away safely inside me, and I was safe in the knowledge Mum had things in hand at the hospital. But, despite all this, I'd never felt so alone in my life.

'Thanks,' I said, taking the tea and holding the cup with two hands to warm me up.

'Come on, I'll run you a bath,' said James, ushering me out towards the landing.

Closing the door behind me, I padded out towards the master bedroom. As I stepped through the doorway, my heart quickened and my hand flew up to my mouth. The memory of the phone call about the accident still hung in the air – the atmosphere in the bedroom made me feel like I couldn't breathe. Dashing to the window, I forced it open and stood panting as the sheer curtains billowed in the fresh breeze. I pressed hard on my temples as I glanced around. I couldn't stop myself from opening the wardrobe and taking a great armful of his clothes and sinking my face into them.

'Tara, your bath is now totally overflowing with bubbles, just how you like it ... *Oh my*, darling, it's okay,' he said, coming over to hug me awkwardly.

James may have been a far shot from a typical man, but he was still a man nonetheless, so dealing with a pregnant, emotional wreck of a woman in tears was not one of his strong points.

'Lewis doesn't smell like Lewis at the hospital. But here ... his living smell is still here,' I said, wiping away the snot and tears. 'I miss him so much. I need him here. I can't do this without him,' I cried, flopping myself on the bed with one of his shirts covering my face.

'No—yes, you can, Tara Ryan,' he said, gently but firmly pulling me upright and holding my shoulders straight. The gutters of his eyes were wet. 'And you *will* do this without him. If you have to. There's still a few weeks left before your due date, so there's every chance that he might wake up before then. And if he doesn't, then we're all here to help you both get through this.'

'He was an angel,' I cried, 'and I came along and clipped off his wings.'

'There there.' James pulled me closer and rubbed my back. I shuddered and clung onto him, releasing the flow of pent-up sorrow and despair.

'This place ... this place,' I howled, waving at everything around me, 'this place is Lewara. It's Lewis *and* Tara. Half of its soul is missing. Without him, it's nothing. What is this place if he never wakes up? Who even am I if he never wakes up? What would I do?'

James sat in silence, holding me. After five minutes of us both sobbing, he took my mobile phone, broke away and led me into the bathroom. Gently, he undressed me for my bath, like my grief had rendered me disabled.

'I'll go and make you another tea,' he said with a forced smile, wiping his eyes.

The water was the perfect temperature. The smell of the frankincense Lush bath bomb with its violet bubbles overflowing from the Victorian-style tub looked inviting. Slowly I immersed myself and my bump into the water, allowing the blissful water to caress my senses.

Within moments, I felt the pains in my back subside slightly. The anxiety began to pass. I was drifting in and out of complete and utter exhaustion. But the thoughts of Lewis lying in that hospital bed completely alone wouldn't leave my head.

I sank back and submerged my head completely under the water. The lack of oxygen from holding my breath was a welcome distraction from the pain, both mental and physical.

Maybe, just maybe I can disappear for a minute ...

I could see Lewis's face.

'Tara ...' he said, smiling at me as if to say everything was okay. As if it wasn't my fault.

'Lewis ...'

'Tara!'

Suddenly my fantasy disappeared as I felt someone pulling my arm up and my head penetrated the surface. I gasped for air as I held onto the handle of the bath.

'... You're worrying me,' said James, picking up a flannel and wiping the bubbles from my face. Avoiding eye contact, I pulled my knees up and rested my chin upon them.

'I'm sorry. It's just ... my back is really aching and I wanted to lie flat. I'm okay. Just give me a few more minutes and I'll get out. You are keeping an eye on my phone, aren't you?'

He whipped my phone from his back pocket like a cowboy-style fast draw.

James shook his head. 'I've laid out some fresh clothes for you and there's a fresh cup of tea on your bedside table.'

Having resurfaced, the great, sharp, stabbing pains in my back returned, impossible to ignore. My stomach turned somersaults as I became ever more worried about Lewis.

My all-consuming thought was always: would today be the day he wakes up?

With a great deal of effort, I hauled my huge, inflated body up, stepped out of the bath and began to towel myself dry. I tutted in annoyance as I didn't seem able to stop the light flow of water from trickling in-between my legs. It just kept on dripping ... and dripping.

Indie's pressing on my bladder, I thought as the flow showed little sign of abating. I perched on the loo and the dribble thankfully stopped—that was until I stood up and had a full-on hosepipe gush.

... Oh.

... Oh my God. OH MY GOD.

I stood there hovering as perspiration trickled down my neck and a sharp draggy pain shot across my lower back—and everything went out of focus. My waters had just broken. I was in labour.

Labour!

'No ... no, not now. This has to stop!' I shouted, weeping into my hands. 'Indie ... please. I want you more than ever, but this is *really* bad timing. Go back to sleep – or kick Mummy – give her heartburn – but please wait for Daddy, don't come out yet!'

I could hear James clattering across the landing.

'Everything okay in there?' he knocked rapidly.

'*Ummm … errr …* no! James I've gone into—'

I hadn't heard such high-pitched screaming since the school playground days.

'I fucking *knew* this was going to happen on my watch. I didn't sign up for this!' said James, standing there in horror.

'Jaaaames … we have to get to the hospital—right now. We have to stop her from coming out … it's too early and-and-Lewis-will-miss-the-birth!'

Screaming, I held onto the bathroom sink as another agonising pain darted across my back. James appeared to be speechless – something I'd never seen before. His ghostly pale face seemed to overpower even his fake tan.

'I can't have this baby now – we have to try and stop it!'

James whipped over to my chest of drawers, throwing the contents out before moving to the next drawer.

'What are you doing?!' I asked, doubled over in pain.

Within seconds, he was holding up a pair of tights, testing the strength of the gusset.

'What the bloody hell am I meant to do with those?'

'Put them on – it might stop the baby from coming out, or at least keep it contained until we can get to someone who isn't vagina-phobic!'

I gave him a look only the devil could muster.

'We need to go … now … in your car … to the hospital … James, do you understand?'

He looked me in the eye and tilted his head forward in what could have been either a nod or an involuntary twitch.

'Uhh—*umm* … how far apart are your contractions?'

James pulled out his phone and started fiddling with it to find the stopwatch.

'I don't know … I didn't even think I was having contractions! The pain is all in my back – I've been like this all week,' I gulped.

James seemingly did the impossible for a man and managed to have two phone conversations simultaneously, with my mum on my phone, Siobhan on his.

'Your mum is saying … err, okay … apparently you're having a back labour, or something.' He spun me around and lifted up my towel. 'But, Missus Ryan, there's nothing coming out of her back!'

'Tell Mum we're coming back to the hospital now and won't be long,' I shouted, gulping for air.

'O–M–G, I'm falling apart like a cheap watch here!' James said as he ran around in circles, juggling hair clamps, tights and two mobile phones.

'What!? Siobhan is suggesting you Superglue your lady-flaps together … really, Siobhan, I don't think that would work.' James dropped to his knees, lifted up my towel and peered between my legs. 'Ugh … way too much foliage for that, Siobhan. It'd take an industrial strimmer to get through *that*. No offence, Tara,' he said, blinking rapidly.

'No—sorry, Missus Ryan … no, I wouldn't dare put glue in your daughter's vagina.'

Clinging on to my towel, I made my way across the bedroom. I did have a labour bag all ready and set up – it just happened to be at Camilla's. I waddled over to the wardrobe, pulled out Lewis's rucksack, and began systematically filling it with things.

When the bag was full, I just needed to decide what I would actually wear to the hospital.

'I can't have this baby now. I can't!' I said, sobbing intermittently, with James battling to get my humongous, roaming breasts into my maternity bra.

'Yes, you can!' wailed James, snapping a totally impractical dress over my head.

'What the hell is this?' I screamed. 'I'm not off to a feckin' cocktail party!' It was a full-length, sheer, tight white dress with a vicious floor-to-hip slit. It was too tight even when I bought it pre-pregnancy.

'Nonsense,' said James as he continued to yank the dress into position around my ballooned humps and bumps.

I looked myself up and down in the mirror and turned to James with horrified disbelief.

'You're right,' said James, tapping his fingers on his chin. 'The dress is fabulous, but something's not quite right … Blusher! We need blusher.' I batted him away with my flailing arms. 'Just some shoes to finish off—'

'Get me to the hospital – now!' I slipped on Lewis's flip-flops and made for the door.

'No need to be nasty,' said James, pouting, 'I'm coping with this situation the best way a gay man knows how to, and that is to make sure you look just as good as me when we arrive at the hospital. By the way, we're not strolling down a Dubai beach so there is no excuse for those monstrosities on your feet.'

'They're Lewis's,' I cried, 'and they're the only things that fit me since I grew cankles.'

'Oh, sorry, darling,' James meekly replied, ushering me towards the stairs. 'Hopefully no one will notice them, now let's get going!'

I hobbled out to James's Boxter as he ran out ahead of me and fumbled around in the car's boot. Ignoring him, I opened the door for myself and attempted a three-point turn to get in.

'No—Tara, what are you doing? You are not getting in my car in your vaginal state! I just had *him* valeted and you're not about to get fanny batter all over it.'

'I'll kill you! I said, as he produced a Waitrose Bag for Life from the boot.

'Please, just, like, wrap this around yourself.'

Gripped by another wave of immense pain, and not having the strength to argue back, I chose the path of least resistance.

James crouched down and held open the bag, saying, 'One leg at a time ... there's a good girl,' as I threaded my fat legs through the handles and somehow ruffled the bag up to my hips, effectively turning it into a plastic nappy.

I didn't have strength to protest the humiliating situation, as James lowered my trembling body into the car. Before setting off, he leaned over and punctured the bottom of the bag with his fingernail.

'What are you doing?!' I swotted his hand away.

'Well, babies need to breathe, don't they? It's so if it falls out mid-journey it's got a hole so it can breathe. See, I would totally make a great mid-husband ... if I didn't find vaginas so terrifying.'

I started crying as James sped out of the gravel driveway, laughing to himself.

'What's so funny?' I asked, using the length of my white dress as a tissue.

'I bet the people at Waitrose never thought their Bag for Life would be used in such a literal sense.'

Looking down at myself, I wondered if things could actually get any worse.

Chapter 21

Bracing myself for the next contraction, I reached over and grabbed hold of James's thigh, digging my nails in hard. 'Sorry-sorry-sorryyyyy!'

The pair of us shrieked like alley cats as the car swerved abruptly. This was the third time this had happened on our journey to the hospital.

'That contraction was different. It's like someone is shoving more hot pokers up there with each one,' I said, shaking my head and releasing my grip from his poor thigh. I slapped my hand against my chest and tried to catch my breath.

'I'll shove a hot poker up there if you keep on slicing into my leg like that!'

'James,' I winced folding over in agony, 'remember – I need to remember everything. Every single detail of this birth. No matter what I say, DO NOT, I repeat, DO NOT let me have drugs.'

'What?' he shot me a sideways glance. 'Isn't that the

best bit? That would be like giving away an organ and not expecting to be paid.'

'No matter what I say,' I emphasised again, cutting my hand through the air. 'I told Lewis that I wasn't having drugs. It's the least I can do.'

'You're out of your mind.'

Before I could react, another excruciating contraction took hold and rendered me ridged.

Maybe I've been a little too hasty with my decision about not having any drugs?

We arrived in the hospital car park in record time, and with one swift turn of the wheel, James swung the Porsche into a Disabled parking space.

'You can't–pa-*haha*-ark–heeere ...'

'Pregnancy is a severe mental and physical disability – I don't care what you straight people say,' he said before checking his hair, patting down one stray wisp and jumping out.

'And what's crazy, you hetero's actually *choose* to do this to yourselves. It's madness,' he said after pulling open the passenger door. Leaning in, he put his hands under my armpits and lifted me up and out. He then poked his head in the car, to presumably check for any residual mess. The handles of the Waitrose nappy were starting to cut off the circulation in my swollen legs.

'Help me get this bloody thing off—wait, where are you going?!'

James had scuttled off towards the main entrance without me. Once again, I had been deserted by the only male in my life that I thought cared.

'Bastard!' I burst out crying. 'I hate men. All of them! I should be in my baby-doll birthing outfit now, with Lewis sitting beside my bed, wiping my brow with scented water.'

Then, out of nowhere, James was skipping towards me with a ... *wheelchair*.

Breathing a huge sigh of relief, I eyed up the rickety old chair suspiciously. One of the front wheels appeared to have a mind of its own, judging by how hard James seemed to be finding it to control.

'Ta-dah! Your carriage awaits!'

'Take me straight to Lewis's ward,' I shouted, lowering my soggy backside into the chair, 'We have to get him to wake up before Indie comes out!'

To begin with, the wheelchair seemed determined to do its own thing and would only turn in small circles, but after a swift kick to the brake, we were off. We both huffed and puffed as James frantically rolled me through the doors and headed off into the maze of corridors towards the Intensive Care Unit.

James didn't bother to slow down for double doors, and why would he when he could simply use my legs to bulldoze his way through? Patients and visitors scattered left and right as we cut a determined path down the centre of the corridor. Suddenly, we crashed headlong into a wall. James insisted he'd been trying to dodge a gaggle of geriatric wheelchair users, but it was a strange coincidence that we also happened to be passing a group of male junior doctors at that exact moment.

'Concentrate!' I shouted. 'And why are you slowing down now?'

'Oh my actual God ... the *cow!*' said James, looking at a brunette with her arm in a sling who was hurrying off in the opposite direction.

'What?!'

'That woman—Jenny, or Jessie or whatever her name is—she told me she was moving to Spain months ago and couldn't be my client any more – the lying bitch! I hope that arm never heals. She had terrible nails anyway; her cuticles were a horror show.'

'James!'

He set off again, muttering under his breath and huffing all the way towards the lifts. Then something very, very extraordinary began to happen to my body. I clutched my pounding chest. *Am I having a heart attack? A stroke? Or worse – BOTH?*

I raised my hand like a traffic cop and James's skidded behind me as the wheelchair screeched to a holt.

'Oh … no. *Owh*. Holy-Mary-Mother-of-God. Feck [pant] … feck [pant] … *ooowwhhh* … [panting] she's … [panting] feck-feck-feckkk … Indie'sss comiiing!'

'What—right now?'

I nodded hard, unable to speak again, gripping the arms of the wheelchair.

'You've been holding her in there for eight and half months already, can't you just hold on for a bit longer, like you're holding in a wee? Use your pelvic floor—'

'It doesn't work like that! *Owwwhowhoww!* She's coming, she's coming!'

'Tara, I'm sorry but Lewis is gonna have to wait. We're gonna have to get you to the labour ward – I can't have you popping out a baby in a lift!'

Within a split second and both of us screaming obscenities, James had executed a handbrake turn and we were hurtling in the opposite direction, back out through doors through which we had already crashed – skidding around bends, taking corners on one wheel and flying down corridors even faster than we had before.

After the rollercoaster ride, we finally arrived at the labour ward.

'Please help me!' James screamed, tears of terror smearing mascara down his face as we hurtled straight past the reception desk. I realised to my horror, James had let go of the wheelchair altogether and completely forgotten to put the brake on as I merrily free-rolled into the corridor, smashing into a set of swinging doors with a thud.

Powered by fierce rage and the fear of death itself, I propelled myself up and out of the wheelchair and fumbled over to the desk.

'I'm the one who's going to die from this pain—*ahhhhh*—[panting] please—please get a crash team as soon as possible, I don't want me and my baby to dieee—'

The all-consuming pain and palpitations intensified as I gripped the desk and took deep gulps of air. The thought of dying before ever meeting my baby girl made me even more hysterical.

'Her waters have broken and her baby is trying to come out,' said James to the nurse, rummaging in my handbag and handing over my birthing plan, categorically pointing out (would I ever learn to keep my mouth shut?) that I wasn't under any circumstances to have any pain relief.

'I'm having a heaaart attack and a stroke and [panting] my baby is two weeks early and my fiancé is in a coma in the Intensive Care Unit. You need to stop the baby from coming out until he's awake!'

'Ms Ryan, I need you to calm down and take some deep breaths,' the nurse said, putting her hand on my shoulders. 'Everything is going to be fine.'

The nurse called over a heavy-set, Afro-haired midwife.

'Okay, Tara, my name is Geraldine and I'm going to be your midwife todee. We're going get you through to a delivery room and teek a look at you. Is this your ... husband?'

'Of course not!' James said, 'Does she look the right gender to you?'

'Ignore him,' I spat, 'James is my surrogate birthing partner, aren't you?'

'No I certainly am not! My contract was to be a chauffeur only – my poor leg's already in tatters thanks to this woman's unfiled nails—'

'James, don't you *dare* leave my side. If I'm going to die from all this pain, you're going to watch. And call Mum while you're at it!'

James fell into step behind us, squealing in protest as a smiling, happy-go-lucky Geraldine led us down a corridor.

'Where's the crash team?' I asked as I collapsed onto the bed, tearing off the Waitrose bag whist wailing in horrific pain.

Within moments, Geraldine had quickly and efficiently checked my blood pressure and heart rate. 'I 'tink you may be having a panic attack, Tara. Take some nice deep breaths for me.'

'*Noooo,* I'm definitely [panting] dying here!'

Donning a plastic apron and gloves, Geraldine proceeded to spread my legs akimbo, then dropped out of eyeshot to examine me.

'Okay, dear, ya quite far gone – just over seven centimetres dilated,' she added, smiling back up at me from in between my legs. 'Ya doing really well. Keep it up.'

I didn't believe her. I knew my body. I was definitely dying.

Then alarm bells went off in my head.

'C–can we not stop her from coming out?'

'I'm afraid not, my love,' she said, smiling.

'No, no, you don't understand, my fiancé is in a coma – he needs to be here, and I'm not ready for this, she's not due for a couple of weeks!'

'Tara, *you* may not be ready, but your baby certainly is. You're going to have to accept that your baby is coming out and there's nuttin' we can do to stop it.'

I let out a half sob, half wail. 'I need a prescription for a broken heart! No wait, I need to wee—oh God, *no-hooo!*'

'It's okay, dear, don't get upset, ya waters are still coming out,' said Geraldine matter-of-factly.

'Oh, so I didn't wee myself?' I asked, dignity levels slightly restored.

'No, dear, ya definitely peed yaself,' she said, smiling as she placed a fresh protective sheet underneath me, 'But don't worry, I'm used to it.'

It was official; my dignity had died before I had.

'I'm gonna be sick ...' I said, shaking my head and thrashing around like a fish as another contraction hit me like a thunderbolt. Writhing in pain, I promptly batted away the cardboard dish Geraldine had offered to me to puke into.

I shot a panic-stricken glance over at James; he was collapsed into the visitor's chair, one hand covering his eyes, the other fanning himself.

'James, for God's sake … get over here, this isn't about you today. Man up and grow a pair!'

'Don't worry about him, most men turn to mice when it comes to childbirth,' chuckled Geraldine, checking my notes.

'I feel sick and I can't breathe and I'm having a baby all at once,' I shouted between wails. 'I can't deal with this pain!!! Is it too late for a C-Section? I'll pay, how much? James, get your wallet out!'

Geraldine shook her head.

'I'm dying … Just save the baby,' I said, giving in to the inevitable end as any mother-to-be would.

'Jus' try to relax,' Geraldine soothed. 'You need to control ya breadin' or you'll stress out de baby.'

But the mental pain was quickly replaced by the physical, as I twisted and screamed in agony. A compulsion took over my whole being.

'Please – I can't take it. I want gas and air. Anything and everything you've got. Drugs, gimme drugs!'

Geraldine nodded and handed me a plastic respirator, which I mercifully snatched from her.

'NO!' shouted James, swiping my lifeline away from my open mouth, leaving me gawping like a goldfish. He looked at me accusingly with the respirator in one hand, the other on his hip.

Shaking his head, he turned to Geraldine and said, 'Under no circumstances are you to give her any drugs of any description. It says so on the birthing plan, right here. You even signed it.'

Up until now there had been only a few times in my life when I had been really angry with James. But right then, I wished death upon the man. I glowered at him, trying to kill him with my eyes.

'It's a drug!' he said defensively. 'You said to not let you have any drugs under any circumstances.'

'It's not a drug—it's gas and air!'

'What do you think the gas actually—'

'*Ahhh!* [Panting] Listen, if you still want a job by the end of this—*ah … ha ahh … owww …* JUST GIVE IT BACK!' I flailed my arms like an attacking windmill, trying to grab the dispenser back and smack him simultaneously.

'She—*oww!* Now now, there's no need for violence. And what happened to you having a natural birth and all that?'

'Well, it's not a feckin' natural situation is it?!'

'Geraldine, *she* told me "under no circumstances" was she allowed any drugs of any kind,' he said, swatting my arms away.

'Give it back you massive bastard! Liar! THIEEEF!' I screeched in agony as Geraldine jumped in to separate us.

'It's de mother's prerogative to cheenge her mind if she wants to,' said Geraldine, prising the dispenser off James and handing it back to me. 'Okay, Tara, you're doin' really well. Take deep, long breaths. The gas and air will take de edge off de pain.'

I took a deep breath and sucked on the tube like my life depended on it. Within moments my toes, which were previously clenched in pain, began to relax and a warm, fuzzy feeling spread through my brain, easing the agony and numbing my nerves. Then I thought about Lewis not being present, and proceeded to fall apart again.

'Give me drugs ... God damn it! Lots and lots of drugs! Every drug you've got, give it to me now. Extra doses ...'

'If she is getting drugs, then I should too,' said James. 'Especially as I can't get hold of your mum for back up, Tara.'

I drowned my sorrows by taking another huge breath of gas and air. It was the only way to cope with the enormity of what was happening.

'It's not wor-king ... it's not work—I'm dyyy-ing. I'm dyiiing I tell you!'

'The gas'll only work if you keep it in your mouth and keep breathing it in, Tara,' said Geraldine, giving me a smile. 'Okay, love, you're doing really well.'

I was a little delirious now, thanks to repeated huge drags on the wonderful gas and air. In fact, I felt like I was on a cloud. Not quite cloud nine, maybe like cloud four, but a cloud nonetheless.

'It's ... it's working! This is good shit, man! No wonder Katie needed to go to rehab for this shit – it's well *good!*'

I waved the tube in the air triumphantly with a grin before gobbling down on it again for another hit. I had the oddest sensation that I couldn't make out where everybody was. Everything was slipping in and out of focus. I lunged across the bed and found myself dangling over the side. I was dribbling and nearly fell off the bed before Geraldine hoisted me back up.

'Hellooo, Geraldiiine, I'm so, so, very sorry I peed myself earlier. Forgive me. It's never happened before, I promise.'

'Actually, darling, it happened in Ibiza on your hen-do, remember?' said James.

'Aha! Yes – yes, it did. That was hilarious! Geraldine, I shat absolutely everywhere!'

Geraldine dived down to take another glance at my lady-garden, which I was now more than happy to show off.

'Geraldine, Geraldine, I think you're sooo great. Nurses are sooo great, you guys are so brave.'

But suddenly another, even more brutal contraction came, like my body was playing a game of tug-of-war, sending me into a whole new league of pain.

'No—no woman in the world could ... go through with this and ... come out alive!' I screamed as the pain reached a crescendo of crippling agony. 'Please, gimme drugs ... more, more ... this gas shit isn't working!'

'Okay, okay. I can give you a shot of Pethidine—'

'Yes! I don't know what the feck that is, but please give it to me now!'

Babbling away, Geraldine turned me over. I felt a sharp stab of pain as she injected something into my bum.

'Ahhh. Awwwwuh.'

'You're doing well,' she said, helping me back into position, 'just over eight centimetres dilated now; just remember each contraction is one less to endure.'

'Still only eight!? Oh God nooo. So what the feck has my body been doing, giving me all that pain and not getting anywhere!'

My outburst was brought to an abrupt halt by another toe-curling contraction. With each torturous wave, the pain radiated and my lower back would seize up and everything pulled tight. Like the muscles inside were slowly twisting harder and harder until it became almost unbearable, and then it would slowly subside. I screwed my eyes shut until the pain dissipated. When I opened them again, James was peering into my lady-garden.

'Excuse me?' I said, indignantly.

'You want to get a designer vagina job booked in,' he said in an authoritative voice. 'After this head comes out, your lady-garden will have a pair of hammocks flapping around. You'll be like a human parachute!'

'Fuck off, James!'

Geraldine tutted loudly and advanced on James, who scuttled back to his chair.

'Do ya breathing and pant.'

'Yeah, pant,' said James, puffing out his cheeks, 'you don't want to tear.'

'I need Lewis,' I sobbed, shaking my head back and forth and gripping the sheets. 'Indieeee has no daddyyy ... Go and tell Lewis his baby is coming, James, please. I need him to wake up. I can't do this without him, I just can't!'

If Lewis really could hear things in his coma, then surely he'd wake up once he knew Indie was on her way?

James nodded, got up to go, but then I had another flash of panic.

'Don't you dare think about abandoning me!' I screamed like a banshee.

'Okay, okay … Honestly, you are making a bit of a fuss. I'm sure if you calmed down you would've given birth by now.'

I lobbed a pillow at him and closed my eyes to shut out the pain, willing myself to float off on a cloud of gas and Pethidine-fuelled numbness. The pain hummed constantly in the background as I tried to focus on the strange yet comforting sounds of Indie's heartbeat vibrating all around me from the heart monitor.

'Oh my God, thank God you're here!' said James.

'Sweet Jesus, you'd wake the dead woman with all that howlin',' said Siobhan, waltzing in and planting a kiss on my forehead.

I was delighted to have another woman in the room, but realised that Siobhan was about as much of a woman as James was a man.

'How's your fanny doin'?' Siobhan popped her head down to have a gander. '… Jesus Christ, are you sure this is worth it? Will it ever go back to lookin' normal again?'

Geraldine was about to answer when Siobhan launched into one her stories. Strangely, I welcomed the distraction.

'You won't feckin' *believe* what happened, right. I was at the train station, goin' up the

es-que-lator and when I gets to the top and start walkin' away – I noticed me feckin' skirt was caught in the little mechanical teeth thingamagigies! Next thing I know, the teeth had gobbled half it and me skirts ridin' down me ankles. The es-que-lator gets jammed, but I'm like stuck there, tryin' to pull me fookin' skirt back up. Then everyone starts walkin' up and past me with me knickers on show. Not one of the feckers stopped to help me – they must've thought I was a mental case. I had to tear the fooker to get it loose. Look at the state of it,' she said, hitching the hem up for all to see.

Both James and Geraldine laughed, and even in my drugged up, pain-saturated state, a giggle managed to find its way to the surface.

'Anyways, I got a dummy for the baba.' Siobhan said proudly, pulling one out of a carrier bag with a picture on it. 'See, it's got *VOLUME CONTROL* on it. Get it?'

I moaned in pain as she tried to show it to me.

'Look, stop all the moanin' or I'll be shovin' it in *your* gob,' she said, laughing away.

'De baby's head is crowning. Not long now,' announced Geraldine.

I watched as James and Siobhan clung onto one another other, phone in hand, daring the other to look.

Drugged up to my eyeballs, I indicated that I needed both my best friends to come up this end and to hold each of my hands as I began to brace myself.

'Oh-my-god, I've just seen her devil's door bell,' said James, turning his head away. 'Siobhan, take over the videoing. This is way too much sharing for me.'

Videoing!? My vagina! It would be all over Facebook! And what if I poo everywhere again?!

Siobhan grabbed the iPhone.

'... And here we are, with Tara's hairy Mary,' she added in nature-documentary stylee. The baba's head is ... sweet Jesus ... it's like comin' out, enlargin' the fangita to four times its normal size.'

I could feel myself nearly levitating off the bed in horror, and launched myself at the pair of them.

'Mammy Ryan, get over here quick,' squealed James, hiding behind Siobhan, finally getting through to her phone. 'Bring some holy water, I'm terribly afraid to report that you're daughter has turned into the Antichrist, her head is spinning and everything!'

'I wanna pussshhh ... I wanna to pussshhh ...' I moaned as my whole body began bearing down. 'I want my mum, I want my mum.'

'It's all right, it's time to push now,' said Geraldine informing me I was ten centimetres dilated.

'Lewis ... Lewis,' I shouted, shaking my head from side to side.

As each contraction ended, I'd get a split second relief before the next one started; then it became one long continuous contraction.

Mum's face hovered into view. I immediately wrapped my arms around her neck as she stooped to give me a supportive cuddle.

'Lewis?' I asked.

'It's all right pet,' said Mum, wiping my brow. 'Sure, Father Damien is with him. He's givin' him a runnin' commentary. Not that any man would have a clue what us women go through. Still, his heart is most definitely in the right place.'

'James!' Siobhan snarled pushing him towards me, 'For one moment, stop bein' a manwhore. Tara needs to be bitin' down hard on somethin'! Give her *your* hand, why don't you?'

'Why mine?' asked James, looking petrified and instantly shoving his hands behind his back. 'These hands are my fortune. They are like the Michael Flatly legs of hands.'

'God bless us and save us ... Take my hand, Tara.' Gratefully I gripped her frail hand. 'Actually,' she said, quickly releasing it and stepping back, 'at my age, and with me osteoporosis and all that, it may break.'

So I grabbed two hands either side of me, unsure of whose they were, and tensing every muscle in my body I began pushing with everything I had.

'Stop de pushing.' Geraldine's head shot up from in between my trembling legs, 'Do your breathing and pant.'

'Pant,' said James. He puffed his cheeks out, then held his breath with me. Three sets of eyes, Mum's, James's and Siobhan's were gawping at me as they panted frantically.

'Now, push on de *next* contraction,' said Geraldine.

'It's nearly over,' said Mum. All three of them were by my side, holding on to me or running up and down to my lady-garden to spur me on.

'Good girl, it's nearly over,' said Geraldine.

'I ... caaan't do it. It's ... it's like p-p-pushing out a-a-a three-piece suiiite! A c-c-corner one!'

'Is that really the best you've got?' asked James, flapping his arms in frustration. 'Come on, push and hurry up. I want to teach Indie how to be a diva!'

'... And flirt,' added Siobhan.

It felt like my vagina had fallen out, but I kept pushing anyway.

Sounds were fading in and out, then magnified as I heard Mum muttering about whether Father Damien would Christen my baby.

My jaw tightened, and with clenched teeth I pushed with everything I had. Lewis's name left my lips and I could hear myself screaming out for him as I felt my baby finally release herself from my body.

Siobhan screamed. Mum was crying. James was retching. And finally, my baby girl was crying too, as her lungs kicked in.

'Congratulations!' Geraldine said, planting her in my arms, swaddled in a cotton blanket.

Her big navy-blue eyes were expanding and seemed to be looking straight into my soul.

'Hello, Indie,' I sobbed, 'I'm so, so happy to meet you.'

Chapter 22

I woke in the early morning light to the shuffling, murmuring sounds of the maternity ward. Rubbing my tummy, it took me a few moments to collect my thoughts. That was when I turned over and nearly fell off the bed at the shock of seeing a teeny-tiny person lying soundly asleep in a cot next to me.

A deep, uncontrollable wave of excitement surged through me as I pushed up and peered in at her.

She was the most beautiful thing I had ever seen. Swaddled in a pink cotton blanket, eyes closed behind puffy eyelids, well-rounded cheeks, skin glowing a rosy pink, tiny button nose; Indie was a vision of wonder.

'I can't believe I made you,' I whispered, nervously picking up my bundle of joy, then beginning to try and breastfeed her, just as the midwife had shown me. 'We're going to go and meet your daddy today,' I said, catching with a bib the little dribbles of milk that cascaded down her tiny chin. 'He's very lazy and has been sleeping a lot lately,' I whimpered, trying to hide my tears from her. 'It's okay though, my darling, because we have each other, you and me. And until Daddy wakes up, you've got wonderful aunts, two of whom are flying over from Dublin, one uncle who thinks he's your aunt, and the best Nana in the whole wide world, who is at home waiting for us.'

I tenderly kissed her warm, pillowy cheek, before laying her down gently and threading her teeny-tiny arms and legs through the pink velour baby-grow that Camilla had brought in as a gift the night before. Getting her dressed was trickier than I thought, and she became evidently irritated as I struggled with the poppers.

'I know your daddy would think you are the most beautiful baby ever, if he could actually see you,' I said, picking her up and rocking her in my arms.

As for me, I felt like a saggy, partially deflated balloon, and wanted to cover as much of me as possible. I had a case of the 'feck it's, and went against everything I vowed I wouldn't do as a mum: shamelessly rocking out the obligatory towelling dressing gown, leggings and Lewis's flip-flops.

Leaving the maternity ward and making my way over to the Extended Care Unit, I caught a glimpse of a TV screen in a waiting room. A reporter was standing by a bridge, with the overlay caption 'Paris "love locks" removed from bridges'. I walked up closer to the TV so I could hear what was being said. '... City officials have begun removing padlocks that have been symbolically fastened to one of the French capital's main bridges by loved-up couples. Securing a "love lock" to the Pont des Arts before throwing the key into the River Seine beneath has become a tourist tradition in recent years. Unfortunately, part of the bridge's railings collapsed under the sheer weight of the estimated one million locks—weighing around forty-five tonnes—some are due to be cut off over the next few days ...'

The picture of the scene filled me with utter despair as I made my way to Lewis, thinking back to the day when I'd made my wish with him on that bridge.

Drawing a quivering breath, I hesitated for a moment outside his door. I'd entered Lewis's hospital room hundreds of times, but today was different. Today I was about to introduce Indie to her father. It was a scene a million miles away from the picturesque scene where Lewis would have been there to cut the umbilical cord, but I made an effort to bring myself back to reality and try and appreciate the moment anyway.

But before I could take another step, Lewis's neurologist, Doctor Monaghan, abruptly walked out from his room. He looked disturbed, which instantly turned my stomach upside down.

'Ahh—Tara, I need to speak with you ... please, take a seat,' he said, indicating the row of chairs against the wall.

Gripping Indie even tighter in my arms, I eased myself onto the plastic seat.

'We've just had the results back from Lewis's latest MRI,' he said, sitting awkwardly beside me, 'and, well, I'm afraid it's not the best news.'

My eyes locked with his and I shook my head.

'What do you mean?' I cried out, so frightened I could barely breathe.

'Lewis's brain activity has degraded significantly since the last scan. Both myself and Doctor Shanouk have concluded that the likelihood of Lewis making any kind of significant recovery is, at this point, extremely unlikely. I'm so sorry to say, that in all likelihood, Lewis will deteriorate into brain death within the next few months,' he said, with his head bowed. 'Again, I'm ... so sorry that it's turned out like this, especially with your newborn.'

I nearly jack-knifed as his words landed. The joy I'd felt just hours before at the birth of my daughter instantly evaporated, sharply replaced with desolation. I stared into space, absentmindedly rocking Indie in my arms.

My worst fear had come true.

I looked down at Indie, staring back at me with her big navy-blue eyes. How simple the world was in her head. Little did she know of how painful life could be.

What do I do?

Where do I go?

How can I live without him?

'... Tara, there's never a good time for this, but I have to ask you a difficult question: were you aware that Lewis is registered as an organ donor?'

I knew he was. We both were; we registered together after seeing a program about it.

'I–I know he is, but I can't accept that he's ... gone. He hasn't even met his newborn baby yet.'

Doctor Monaghan placed a sympathetic hand on my shoulder, 'I understand. There's no immediate rush, but we generally find that it's easier for everyone involved to make a decision quickly about these things in order for the healing process to begin. By doing this, he'd be saving people's lives – something I'm sure you'd all be proud of.'

I couldn't even contemplate what he was saying. Right then, I didn't care about saving other people's lives; I wanted Lewis to live. I simply nodded at the doctor, raised myself up and made for Lewis's door.

Even though I'd seen Lewis like this a thousand times before, it felt different this time. Cautiously approaching his bedside, I leant down and I kissed his dry, motionless lips.

'I think Daddy would like a cuddle from you,' I whispered, fighting back the torrent of tears. Indie, serene and oblivious, made a little gargling sound as I unravelled her from her blanket. With my free hand, I pulled his bed sheet back and gently laid Indie face down on his chest. I held my breath, half expecting her to cry out. But she didn't seem to mind, simply snuggling down into the foetal position, as though she was right where she belonged, enjoying the rhythmical rising and falling of her father's chest.

'Lewis, this is Indie ... your daughter.'

Indie's head bobbed slightly as she adjusted to his body, smelling him with her minuscule nose as she slept.

I placed Lewis's warm yet lifeless hand on Indie's back. The two most important people in my life lay there, asleep together. I decided I would join them in our first activity as a family together – our choices were rather limited after all. I clambered onto the bed and laid my head on his chest, my hand gently resting on his. The sound of her shallow, peaceful breathing and his rhythmic, deep breaths was heaven. It wasn't exactly how I'd planned things, but here we were, the three of us, together at last. I drifted away, forgetting everything except this precious moment.

Then we were in Lewara, all lying there on a bright Sunday morning. I could hear Indie's morning routine: her starting to whimper, before graduating to a full-on cry.

'Mmm ...' I murmured, 'It's your turn to feed her, mister.'

'Hmmmm ... I was having such nice dreams,' Lewis said, yawning, stretching, and kissing me on the arm.

I looked up to see Lewis holding Indie, looking straight at me, with a smile on his unshaven face. He lifted the duvet off me, and I felt a cold rush of air on my legs ...

I jolted awake and was back in the hospital room. Indie was crying loudly, moving around uncomfortably on Lewis's chest. I sat upright and lifted her into my arms. And that's when I became aware of the urgent blipping of the heart-rate monitor. Then something caught my eye.

Lewis's foot was twitching. In plain sight. I immediately ripped the bed sheets back.

'Lewis?!' Holding Indie tightly, I jumped down from the bed and stared at him. He was frowning and seemed to become increasingly distressed with each of Indie's wails. Suddenly, his eyelids began flickering – then his emerald-green eyes burst open.

'Lewis? Lewis!' I screamed, nearly jumping out of

my skin as I watched them, like lead weights, close again.

Hitting the CALL alarm beside the bed, I began to shake him by the shoulder, calling out to him, desperately trying to claw back the moment of consciousness.

Where the hell is everyone?!

Flinging the door open, I stuck my head out of the room and frantically scanned the corridor for assistance. Not a soul. *Feckin' cutbacks!!!*

Making a split-second decision to leave the room, pausing only to inform Lewis to not go anywhere, I dashed off with a wailing baby in my arms as quickly as my freshly stitched lady-garden would allow.

'Hello? Hello?!' I yelled into the empty corridor. 'Please, send someone quickly – he's waking up, he's waking up!'

As I skidded around a corner, I nearly took out a nurse coming the other way.

'Wha—did you call the alarm? What's wrong?'

'Lewis is waking up, come quickly!' I shouted, seizing her arm and dragging her in the direction of his room.

Breathless, I followed her and flung myself back through Lewis's doorway. I was shocked by what I saw. The heart-rate monitor beeped away with no signs of movement what so ever from Lewis, his facial expression now showing that blank look he always wore. It was as if nothing had happened at all.

'... His foot—his foot was moving, he opened his eyes and ... he looked at me,' I said, bursting into floods of tears.

'Did he say anything? Or look like he was trying to communicate?' asked the nurse.

'N-no. But I ... he *is* trying to wake up, I know he is—'

'Lewis? Lewis, can you hear me?' she asked loudly.

I bounced Indie gently in my arms and held my breath, praying he would respond.

The nurse began the tests I'd seen them do so many times. She applied pressure to his index fingernail with a pen. Normally he would involuntarily recoil at this, and I would feel some hope when he did. But this time he didn't move at all.

Then she tried pinching his shoulder. Then she tried applying pressure to the top of his eye socket. He didn't move an inch.

'Tara, I'm sorry—'

'But he ... he moved – his face changed when I put Indie on his chest and she started crying ...'

'Okay. Well, I've tried getting a reflex and he's not responding now ... him moving when the baby cried might have been a chance reflex, like a glitch in a computer.' She put a hand on my shoulder, with a look of pity. 'Sometimes we want things so bad that our minds exaggerate, or even imagine things.'

'But ... I saw him! His foot was moving—he opened his eyes!' I said between sobs. 'I had a dream that he was waking up in our bed at home, then I woke up because I could feel him moving ...'

'I'm really sorry, but if you were dreaming about him waking up, then maybe you were still dreaming?'

The nurse gave my shoulder another squeeze and slipped out of the room to give me some time.

I hung my head and nuzzled my wet cheek on the top of Indie's warm head.

'I know Daddy was trying to say hello to you, my darling, I just know it,' I whispered as Indie and I began a joint crying match.

For the next hour, I anxiously hovered around Lewis's bed, praying for another sign. I even placed Indie back on his chest and recreated the entire scene from before. But nothing happened.

Eventually, I looked at the time and realised Siobhan, who had offered to pick us up, was due any moment. The thought of leaving him there made me feel sick, but in my heart I knew Lewis would agree this was no place for our newborn baby.

'I'll be back to visit you soon and I love you more than you'll ever know,' I told him repeatedly as I tearfully kissed him goodbye.

I decided it was best I didn't mention to anyone else that I thought Lewis had tried to wake. The pain was too much to bear, and, quite honestly, I'd begun doubting myself whether it actually even happened.

And I certainly wasn't ready to tell Camilla about what Doctor Monaghan had said about Lewis not being likely to recover just yet. I needed to get today out of the way first, clear my head and think about how to best break the news that her brother would most likely never leave this hospital alive.

Geraldine helped me collect my things from the maternity ward, then escorted me over towards the exit as we said our goodbyes.

Of course, Siobhan was nowhere to be seen as I waited anxiously, pulling the blanket closely around

Indie in the fresh February morning. I watched with envy as a proud father greeted one of the other mothers from my ward, and soon grandparents from both sides joined them, carrying balloons and flowers.

Then I heard Siobhan's voice well before I saw her.

'Look,' she said, addressing the two security guards stalking behind her, 'it'll be out of your way in no time at all. It's not my feckin' fault you've got nowhere for me to park! Surely to God you wouldn't be wantin' to deprive a lift to a poor woman with a newborn while her fiancé's in a coma? You're disgraces, the lot of ya, you should be ashamed of yourselves!'

The guards looked stunned.

Siobhan spotted me and made a mad dash over, carrying the car seat Lewis and I bought together, casually rolling her eyes at the heated situation.

'You'd think I'd just landed a feckin' jumbo jet the way that lot are all carryin' on. Hello, babe,' she said with a huge smile, sticking her two fingers up at the security guards behind her. Luckily, they had already turned their backs and wandered off, shaking their heads.

'Howerya?'

'I'm ...' I tried to put on a brave face.

'Look, you don't need to say it, the look of you says it all. Hmm ... Ahh, well *hello there,* little princess ... Well, you are just gorgeous, aren't ya? I think I might just eat you up for lunch – I haven't eaten anythin' all day.'

Indie looked impossibly serene, as she stayed fast asleep, safe and warm in her little pink wool hat that her nana had knitted.

'She's so good. All she's done is eat and sleep. Barely cried at all, compared to a lot of the other babies on the maternity ward.'

'C'mon, let's get us out of here before these eejits try and clamp me.'

Siobhan whipped Indie out of my arms, secured her in the baby-seat, grabbed my belongings and scarpered ahead, singing, '*There was an old woman who swallowed a fly* ...'

I did my best to keep up. But as we headed towards the car park, Siobhan's encounter with the security guards started to make perfect sense.

Oh-my-feckin-god-almighty ... A huge yellow concrete-mixing lorry sat on double red lines, lights flashing, the rotating drum churning away, with a group of men standing beside it, gesturing wildly at Siobhan.

'You're kidding me, right?' I asked, standing there, mouth flapping open, pointing at the churning cement.

'I know how it looks,' said Siobhan nonchalantly, 'but I promise you it's not nicked. Larry from the pub owed me a favour and I told him I needed a vehicle pronto. The imbecile never mentioned it was a feckin' JCB, but I figured it would be fun and probably safer than James's little fookin' toy car. So there you go.

'He did say I'm not supposed to switch off the spinnin' thing, or the concrete will be useless. And I left the lights on because they're fookin' ace. We're the queens of the road now, baby!'

'But ... I wasn't worried about it being stolen—I ...'

'... I'm gonna have to make some serious bedroom noise for borrowin' this, I can tell you that. Only the best for my little Princess Indie. Her first ever ride in a vehicle gets to be in a massive lorry, how excitin'! I'm teachin' her a valuable life lesson: size really does matter!'

I should've been leaving the hospital with Lewis in a hired Bentley or Rolls-Royce, or at least something that didn't have eight wheels and flashing feckin' lights! Instead, I'm leaving Lewis behind and taking our baby daughter home in a cement-blender, or whatever the feck it was.

In a miserable daze, I went with the flow and passed Indie in her car seat up to Siobhan, who hoisted her up into the cab. Ignoring the security guards' stares, I gingerly heaved myself up into the lorry, checking Indie was strapped in tight.

'Siobhan, there's no airbag on the passenger side, right? It's against the law—'

'No, there's no airbags in here whatsoever, but no worries, I've got you covered.'

I was both pleased and unnerved after hearing that.

'Tara, just relax, babe. I wouldn't be havin' Indie break the law—would I? Me li'l *aaangel?* That'd just be wrong, wouldn't it? How could your mammy think I'd do such a thing? No, not until you're at least a year old, and you can make your own decisions,' she said, pushing buttons and pulling levers randomly.

'Do … d'you even have a licence for this thing?'

'Yes, of course. I've a licence for everythin', she laughed mischievously. 'All you need is a decent printer, and away you go!'

I couldn't be bothered to question whether she meant that or not.

'Come on, lighten up. I've even got you some nice whale music,' she said, fiddling with different knobs.

Siobhan gunned the engine and bullied our way out of the hospital car park, hissing at other drivers, telling them to 'fook off' and to not to wake the baby in a manger. But Indie slept on in blissful ignorance.

Siobhan continued gabbling on, but unable to help myself zoning out all I could think of was what the doctor had said.

I couldn't tell anyone yet; it felt like if I said the words out loud, then somehow it would make it real. Lewis was going to die. I just couldn't say it.

'So, how's the ol' fangita holdin' up?' Siobhan asked as we bounced up and down along the road. 'Did they manage to put it *all* back inside?'

I was brought back to the present by that question. 'I don't know. I daren't look.'

'I'm just grateful the flashbacks of witnessin' the horror show of you poppin' out this little one are gettin' less by the hour, thanks-be-to-God.'

I don't think I was with it enough to be offended at that point.

'Don't worry, I'm sure it'll be pingin' itself back to normal size in a couple of months or so. Or will it be years? I don't know,' shrugged Siobhan, but it'll be grand ... so long as you keep that ol' bush of yours as long as it is now, Lewis'll never see it properly anyways. Mother Nature isn't always kind,' she added, but sometimes she throws in the odd little miracle.'

I couldn't help but chuckle inadvertently. Siobhan was reliably witty, even in the grimmest situations.

'Oh, I'm so excited about this, she's like a real little

person!' she said. 'Now, I'm not supposed to be tellin' you yet, but I can't wait, so: James sent me over the birthin' video of our little Indie here, so I sent it to Daz … and he's gonna edit it and make you and Lewis a DVD!'

'Wait … what? Who the hell is Daz!?'

'Daz. You know *Daz*. Everyone knows Daz, ' Siobhan said whilst the JCB chugged into third gear.

'No, I don't know *Daz!'*

'Oh. I thought you knew him. Well, I'd say by now Daz knows *you* and your *fangita* very well!'

I cupped my face in shame.

'Don't worry though,' she said in a reassuring voice, 'he's gonna put some music on it to drown out the insane racket you were makin'. And he's gonna edit out the bit when you shite yourself, so it's all fine.'

I tried to pretend I wasn't really there. Caressing Indie's warm, docile face, I felt overcome by exhaustion, weighed down by today's news from the doctor, and rather jealous of Indie's serenity.

* * *

I woke to the sound of screeching tyres and horns beeping aggressively all around us. Indie was bawling her eyes out. I looked around—we were sideways, blocking the road from both directions.

'TARA!' Siobhan yelled as she wrestled with the huge steering wheel, huffing and puffing. 'Jesus, woman, would you ever feckin' wake up?'

'What?! And please stop swearing in front of—'

'Oh just shut the feck up and listen … Camilla just phoned—'

I felt sick. A doctor at the hospital must have told her.

'We're goin' back to the hospital – they think Lewis is wakin' up!'

Chapter 23

My head swivelled round to Siobhan.

'What? ... What are you talking about?'

'What does it sound like, woman? Indie's daddy, your fiancé, Lew-is. The nurse said he's startin' to respond to stimulus, or somethin'.'

'How ... A–Are you sure?' I asked, holding my breath. 'Tell me *exactly* what she said.'

'She said somethin' about him openin' his eyes and respondin' to verbal commands. She said it was a feckin' miracle!'

My body juddered as I gave a series of nonsensical shrieks, which set Indie off.

Abandoning her twelve-point turn halfway through, Siobhan let go of the wheel and hugged me, ignoring the furious queues of commuters around us.

'Daddy has woken up, little baby! Daddy is coming home!' I shouted, leaning down and nearly drowning

Indie in soggy kisses.

Siobhan drove like a demon all the way back to the hospital and back into the highly illegal space she'd parked in before. I flew out of the cab like a greyhound out of its trap, carrying a sleeping Indie in her car seat. I'd let Siobhan deal with the irate parking warden.

Skidding knock-kneed through the corridors, I made it to Lewis's room in no time at all.

'Hello, Tara,' a portly nurse said, whisking me to one side. 'Lewis seems to have made rapid progress within the last hour. One of the other nurses came in shortly after you left, and during that time he had his eyes open and seemed to be making sense of what was being said to him.'

'He was waking up to meet his baby,' I said, staring down at Indie proudly.

As to be expected, he seems to be confused about where he is and what has happened to him, but the signs are positive. It's still early days to pass any solid comment, but Doctor Monaghan said he'd only ever seen or heard of a couple of cases of such rapid recovery before.'

'I'm so desperate to see him, can I go in now?' I pleaded, my hand already on the handle of his door.

'Yes, of course, but he's only able to respond in phrases or single words at the moment, so take it easy. If his recovery continues, the doctors are hopeful that he may recover without severe disability, but only time will tell. A doctor will be around shortly to explain in more detail than I can. Good luck,' she said with a smile, and walked away.

Elated, I took a deep breath and made a mental note

to be extremely careful not to overwhelm him – the last thing he needed was to have me, and Indie bawling our eyes out in front of him.

This was finally it. The moment we'd all been waiting for.

In what seemed like slow motion, I pushed open the door. There he was, his green eyes lighting up the room. My heart stopped.

It was really *him*. He really was awake.

His sleepy eyes followed me as I edged towards the side of his bed. I placed Indie, in her car seat, down on the floor gently, just out of his view, suppressing the overwhelming urge to do a full-on dive and snog the face off him.

'Hi,' I said, my voice cracking with emotion as I watched him scan my face. 'Lewis, do you ... do you remember who I am?'

He locked eyes with mine and stared at me intently.

The corner of his mouth tweaked into a half smile. Then I heard one of his classic affirmative man grunts as he nodded and blinked.

A huge watery-eyed grin spread across my face.

'Oh, thank God,' I said, turning away, then discreetly wiped my tears with my sleeve. 'How – how are you feeling?'

He took in a deep breath and grunted again, shuffling his shoulders slightly.

'I've ... I've missed you, so much,' I said, slowly getting closer and gently placing my hand on his.

'S-sorry,' he whispered. His smile widened and his emerald eyes glimmered from underneath his sleepy eyelids.

Indie began to stir and whimper from her car seat below.

'Wh-wh-what's that?' he asked.

'Ahh, well, while you've been sleeping, things have been a bit hectic,' I said, trying not to give the game away, 'but I managed to find some time to get you a little welcome back present.'

If this was *The Lion King*, then I was Rafiki holding up and presenting Simba to the animal world. I could even hear 'Circle Of Life' playing in my head as I unclipped Indie from her seat, I lifted her out and held her out to Lewis.

'In-In-die?' he asked.

With tears snaking down my cheeks, I nodded and placed her in his open arms. He had a look of awe on his face. 'You're a daddy now. Here's your beautiful daughter,' I said, joy bubbling within me.

Tears sprang from his eyes and his heart-rate monitor increased as she lay there, swaddled in her blanket, gargling away in her father's arms.

And that was the moment I knew everything was going to be all right.

* * *

A lot happened after Lewis's awakening. In just over seven weeks, he was deemed well enough to be discharged from primary care at the hospital and was finally going to be allowed home.

The doctors described his recovery as 'nothing short of miraculous'.

By the ninth day of waking, his speech had all but

returned to normal, except the occasional stutter.

By the time Lewis had woken, his pelvis had already healed and he was allowed to begin active physiotherapy on a daily basis to rebuild his strength; particularly on his leg, which was still weak from the accident. The doctors said he would probably always walk with a limp (he said he'd gladly take it over being dead).

He underwent occupational therapy to ensure he was able to carry out daily tasks, as well as to do his job as a veterinary surgeon when he eventually went back to work.

Lewis's cognitive and intellectual abilities had come a long way – he started reading again, and within a couple of weeks, he was even walking.

He did, however, have problems regulating his emotions at times, but I was told that this was a normal reaction and, with time and support, it should improve.

In theory, Lewis's memory could have sustained no damage at all, meaning he'd be capable of recalling everything that happened until the accident and even some things he heard during his coma. And it seemed that this was the case. However, the one thing he seemed to have no memory of was the argument around my *false* confession just before his accident.

I knew, of course, there would come a time when Lewis would need to know the circumstances surrounding his accident, but I was thankful that, this time, I could do it properly. As soon as he was emotionally and mentally strong enough to deal with it, I would tell him everything: the truth, the whole truth, and nothing but the truth. I had nothing to hide.

As for Indie, she'd puked, pooped, slept and cried for England. She was the light of my life—not quite the little angel she'd had us believe in the beginning—but lovely nonetheless. She'd sprouted a few more curly, soft strawberry blonde hairs, and her dark blue eyes had turned sky-blue, like mine. In fact, the Irish genes were strong, except she had her father's nose and ears, which quite frankly, I was delighted about.

Mum had stayed with me at Lewara to help out, with Camilla visiting every other day while she managed the salon full time. Without those two, I don't know where I would've been.

* * *

It was hard to believe the day had finally arrived for Indie and me to pick Lewis up from the hospital and start our new lives together as one happy, lucky family. Everything was ready. The house was a mass of brightly coloured flowers, helium balloons and Welcome Home banners.

The Defender had been fixed, and our mini Trevi fountain had been returned to its former, wonderfully lit, glory. Mum had been given strict instructions to make herself scarce later in the evening so we (Lewis, Indie and I) could spend some much needed quality time together.

I decided to wear something cool and casual rather than something obviously sexy for his homecoming, shoe-horning myself into a pair of stretch black skinny jeans and a black rock-chick T-shirt – and from a distance, if I squinted my eyes, I didn't look too bad at all.

A now chubby Indie wore her lemon tutu, matching flower headband and tiny baby shoes, and once we arrived at the Glamma-Puss salon for a makeover, she became an instant celebrity, fussed over by staff and clients alike.

Camilla had to confiscate Indie from James when he looked like he might be trying to paint her nails. Still, it gave me some free time and I had the full works done: roots bleached, nails done and, of course, waxed to within an inch of my life (you could've clothed a sheep with the amount of hair that came off me).

'You look bloody fabulous, darling. Couldn't have scrubbed up cleaner myself, dare I say. Go get your man, girl!' said James, clicking his fingers like a diva.

As I said my goodbyes, I called Lewis to let him know we were on our way.

'I can't wait to see you both,' he said, 'I feel like a child at Christmas.'

'We can't wait either, my darling. Don't forget to thank all the doctors and nurses for looking after you, sweetheart.'

God, I am so thoughtful. It's all about setting examples for the little one.

As I approached the hospital entrance in the newly fixed Defender, Lewis stood outside in the drizzly rain. *Oh, still my beating heart …*

'There's Daddy!' I squealed to a fast asleep Indie in the back of the car, looking like a mass of yellow candy floss. Although he looked pale and tired in his loungewear, Lewis still took my breath away. *I have to remember not to smother him*, I thought, immediately wanting to rip the clothes off him and have my wicked way right there and then, in the grounds of the hospital car park.

After an excited yet careful drive home, I felt a huge sense of relief as we pulled onto the driveway at Lewara. I just knew that the moment I got him over the threshold of the house, everything would be okay. It was the finish line in my mind. The end of the tragedy that had enveloped us over the last few months was finally in sight.

Helium balloons and *It's a girl!* cards lined the hallway tables. Mum was stood in the doorway with marigolds on and an apron, applauding Lewis's return.

'Hello, pet, welcome home,' she said with a beaming smile, hugging him and then greeting the baby. 'Now, I've got boiled bacon, potatoes and cabbage on the go for us all, that okay?'

'That'd be lovely, thanks,' said Lewis, lifting Indie through the hallway, battling through the balloons and into the lounge.

I gave Mum a deep hug, even though I'd only left hours ago. She knew how much this moment meant to me.

'How well do you remember the house now it's been renovated, darling?' I asked.

'Umm ... it's still a bit hazy,' Lewis said, looking around him.

'Baby, you go and take a look around the place and re-familiarise yourself with our wonderful home. I'll go and put the kettle on.'

'Sure,' said Lewis, gazing out of the window into the garden.

After a quick chinwag with Mum in the kitchen, I

came out to the lounge to see Lewis outside on the veranda. Seeing the rain still pelting down, I grabbed my coat, then pulled the sliding doors across, to go join him.

'Ooh, darling, it's cold and wet out here. Do you want a jacket?' I asked, shivering, then pulling the hood of my coat up.

He didn't seem hear me, so I walked up beside him, watching him look out onto the garden. He seemed to be watching the rain.

'I've got your tea,' I said, holding the mug out to him. 'Lewis—what have you done?!' I shouted, noticing his hand was dripping with blood.

Slamming the tea down on the garden table, I pulled his hand towards me as fresh blood oozed from his palm. He was squeezing a shard of glass.

'Found this glass on the decking,' said Lewis, indicating the patio doors, 'it's triggered ...' His expression darkened as he analysed the veranda space around him. 'Do you have something you'd like to share with me Tara, like ... an affair with Travis?'

There it was.

I knew this would come sooner or later. But I wanted to tell him myself, in my own way, in my own time. I never thought for one moment he'd just suddenly remember.

'No, I didn't. I—'

'But I remember ... I remember you told me about it – it was out *here*. You told me that you'd cheated—you said Indie might not be mine!'

'It's ... difficult to explain, but please just listen to me. I didn't have an affair and I didn't cheat. Indie is

100% your baby—'

'So, what? I just imagined this memory? I smashed the patio – that's where this glass came from—you cheated!'

'No, please, Lewis, listen! I know this sounds crazy, but I thought I'd cheated when I actually hadn't. It's complicated, and I was planning on telling you everything, but only when you got better.'

'Well, I'm better now, so why haven't you told me already?'

'Because ... because you weren't mentally and emotionally fully recovered yet. I just wanted to get you home, make you safe first—'

'Tara, you tell me right now what happened, or so help me ...'

'O-okay. Please, just sit down and hear me out. Stay calm until you've heard everything.'

'I don't want to sit, for fuck's sake! I want you to tell me what the hell happened, now!'

So, that's what I did. I told him everything that happened, word by word ...

'... Lewis, it was such a mess and I'm so sorry, but I promise, nothing happened.'

He took a deep breath and stared me down again. I was scared, but I knew that what I'd said was true and logical; it would only be a matter of time before he realised that I hadn't really done anything wrong.

'So ... all that time, all those months, you'd been lying to me? You deceived me for all that time, making me think the baby was definitely mine, when you thought she could've been his?'

'No, Lewis, I ...'

I checked myself and realised – he was right. I had lied. I had deceived him.

'Yes, it's true. I did withhold the truth. But it wasn't even the truth in the end!' I added, nearly choking.

'I … I'm confused. I don't know what to say,' he said, shaking his head.

'I know it's really confusing, and that's why I didn't want to put this on you yet, you've only just come out of the hospital—'

'No, I'm not confused about what happened. I understand what happened all right. And what's happened is that I made a bad decision to get engaged to someone who would willingly lie to my face to protect her own skin—'

'No, Lewis, please—'

'You *knew* how badly I'd been cheated on and lied to. My best friend since childhood – my best fucking friend slept with my fiancée and they both denied it. And now you go and do *this*?'

I burst into tears. 'Lewis, I promise you: nothing happened with Travis and me. I swear on our baby's life – nothing happened!'

'I've been having flashbacks of what happened again and again. I kept trying to push them out of my mind, I kept thinking the wiring had gone wrong in my head, and you know what, I thought—I *thought* I was being ridiculous. I thought: I love Tara and I trust her to the ends of the earth. She'd never do such a thing to me. She would've told me by now. So, I didn't give in to those thoughts. But you did. You betrayed me.'

'Lewis, please,' I begged, reaching out to him, 'we can get through this …'

'Get off me!' he snapped, 'I know nothing happened between you and Travis and I know that Indie is my child. I believe you. But what you did … you lied to me and I nearly died on the bike because of it!'

'Lewis, please calm down … the doctors said that it would be difficult to adjust – that you might feel overly angry or sad about things—'

'You're right – I am angry, but this has nothing to do with my accident … I built this house—*this house*—so we could live in it together. I thought our relationship was built on absolute trust.'

There was an unbearable silence that went on forever. I was about to stage an Oscar-winning performance by dropping to my knees and begging, when I heard Lewis say something I never thought he'd say.

'We are done, Tara.'

'Please don't do this, Lewis, please, you're ingrained in me, I'm nothing without you. Please I'm begging you … don't do this …'

'I appreciate you being there for me, I do. And I can forgive you for what you did. But I can't forget. And that means I could never trust you again.'

'What are you talking about?' I stuttered, desperately trying to recover the situation. 'We're meant to be together. You and I … we've been through so much …'

I stopped and studied Lewis's body language. He was behaving like I was a complete stranger.

My palms sweated as we stared at each other, our breathing heavy. Lewis looked away and I could see he was totally disgusted by me.

'Tara, it's over between us,' he said flatly. 'I can't do this. This has nothing to do with the accident. I'm going to sell the house. And we're going to have to split our time with Indie.'

I felt as though a bomb had just gone off in my head. With no clue of what I was doing, or where I was going or what I was going to do, I mechanically began to walk away, back into the house and towards the front door. I didn't want to look back at him. I couldn't bear to see the hatred and disappointment in his eyes a minute longer. I'd done that to him. Me. All by myself.

'There's breast milk in the fridge, look after Indie,' I called over to Mum as I picked up my handbag from where I had left it by the door.

'But what about the bacon—'

I heard Lewis's voice echoing behind me and I turned back to glance at him. He was holding Indie in his arms, using one of his hands to protect her face from the rain. I had no intention of going back. I couldn't bear to hear again how I single-handedly broke us and condemned this little family to live a life divided.

Chapter 24

There was only one thing on my mind, and that was to get away from the house as fast as possible. So, blistering with sadness, I drove. And drove.

I don't remember much about the journey, except for seeing the signs for *Brighton*. My father always said there were answers in the sea. (Then again, he was pissed most of the time, so he may've been talking shite, but I rolled with it nonetheless.)

My little Fiat's windscreen wipers struggled to clear the sheets of pelting rain.

It appeared that God was doing all my crying for me.

I parked up in the only free space next to the seafront, despite the fact that the sea might gobble up my little car at any given moment. Cold, hard, whipping winds pulled at me as I battled to open the car door. Shining through the storm, the lights from Brighton Pier seemed to be calling out to me, so I trundled towards them through the horizontal rain.

Finally, I reached the end of the desolate, long pier and looked out onto the water. The sea was an endless black cloth, violently clawing at the land – terrifying and yet beautiful at the same time. It seemed about as troubled as I was.

Turning inwards, the shock and denial had by now worn off, and I had to face the reality of my situation head on.

My Happily Ever After had finally come crumbling down. It was over. I'd wanted to have a child more than anything else in the world, and now I had one. I also wanted Lewis to wake up, and he had. But I had never expected *this*. I thought that if, and when he woke, everything would go back to how it was supposed to be. How could I not have anticipated this? Why did I have to lie to him for so long?

I now knew how selfish my thinking had been. If I thought *I* had been through hell, then look at Lewis. First, his ex-fiancée cheats on him with his best friend. Then he finally gets over it, finds the new love of his life, only to find that she's deceived him about a baby that might not have even been his. Oh, and then he's nearly killed in an accident that throws him into a coma.

What made things worse was that it wasn't like *I* didn't know what it was like to be lied to: Travis virtually did the same thing to me, and that drove me to overdose and near suicide. Now I had virtually done the same to Lewis. *I am a hypocrite; no wonder he doesn't want me*. I didn't deserve him, and he certainly didn't deserve someone like me. In fact, I felt like I didn't deserve a life at all.

And how could I possibly be a good mother to Indie

when I was such a bad person? I would just be dragging her up in a broken home with a broken mother; she'd end up just like me: a selfish, deceitful waste of space. She didn't deserve that.

I gripped the rusty iron railings with numb white knuckles and caught a glimpse of my engagement ring. I once wore it with absolute pride and joy; now it seemed meaningless, mocking me with its brilliance.

The tears finally sprouted, momentarily warming my face in the freezing cold.

It's over. Tara Ryan is over.

The familiar despair I'd felt during my nervous breakdown two years previous seeped back into the crevices of my mind, gaining on me once again. I felt the inevitable doom, like being sucked down a plughole.

I welcomed it. It was all I was worth.

So, with weak limbs, I lifted myself over the railing and hung off the other side. I closed my eyes and remembered how my life had plummeted into darkness after Travis broke my heart. And here I was again, wanting out of life; wanting the waves to rise up and drag me into the black oblivion below.

Suddenly, I couldn't feel the railings anymore. The noise of the crashing waves had stopped, leaving nothing but dead silence in its wake.

Hello Darkness my old friend,
I've come to talk with you again …

My dad was obsessed with Simon and Garfunkel's 'The Sound of Silence'. I never really understood the lyrics, until now.

Lost in the darkness once again, I was faced with a choice. I could end it all now and I wouldn't have to suffer anymore; or I could fight through the pain in the hope that one day, things would get better.

A faint, glimmering light of all that was good in my life began to emerge from out of the abyss. Indie. My family and friends. My future. And then I could hear Laura's voice breaking through:

'No storm lasts forever … Hold on and be brave …
You are strong enough to survive on your own.'

She'd said this to me just a few times before: after our dad died, when Travis broke my heart, and again when I thought Lewis was sure to die.

Clearly, I still hadn't learnt from my past. When Dad died, I couldn't live with the guilt that I couldn't save him. Then I became obsessively dependent on Travis's affection to feel wanted and valued. And now I was relying on Lewis's love in order to carry on living.

Did I really need someone else in order to feel complete? Did I need a man to validate me and to make me feel worthy?

I mean, Laura always said that the only person responsible for my happiness was me …

… Time to break the habit of a lifetime.

… Time to find my own Happily Ever After – even if it was just me and Indie.

… Time to be the role model she deserves; I owe her that much.

Something had shifted – I didn't want the universe to swallow me up anymore. At long last, something Laura said had actually kicked in … *I do believe I'm having an epiphany!*

What the hell was I even thinking? I couldn't believe I'd even *thought* about abandoning my baby … I brought her into this world and now I wanted out because I couldn't bear to be alone again?

'Get a grip on yourself, Tara, for once in your poxy life!' I heard myself say. 'You can't just throw in the towel every time something goes wrong!'

Besides, I'd tried to end it all once before, and was clearly shite at it. Aside from being horrifically cliché, throwing myself off Brighton pier wouldn't go the way I wanted it to anyway. I'd probably end up breaking a leg, failing to drown due to abnormally buoyant milk-and-silicone-filled boobs, then pathetically washing up on shore, only to be rescued by a lycra-wearing dog walker called Terry.

No, things were going to be different from here on in. I had loving friends and family who would support me through this – not to mention a gorgeous baby girl who needed me and said buoyant milk dispensers.

Now, I just wanted to be a mum – but not any old mum, one that could show her daughter how to be happy, no matter what life threw at her.

The new me was going to have a fresh start. I knew I had to accept there was no way Lewis could forgive me; he never forgave his ex or his best friend, and nor did I ever expect him to forgive me. Now the trust had gone, there was no going back. No, my Happily Ever After wouldn't need Lewis to be in it, despite how much I still loved him. Of course, I'd still make sure he got to see Indie as often as possible. And I could move back into my old house I rented out after moving into Lewara. Maybe I could sell the business to focus on being a full-time mum.

The sea does have answers, I guess. A smile spread across my face, and I sent a private thank you to my dad.

Opening my eyes, I felt suddenly cold, wet, and … in mortal danger. It then dawned on me that I was—*oh, shit*—still very much hanging off the edge of the pier.

Suddenly petrified, I practically vaulted myself over the railing and back to dry(ish) land. The storm seemed to be worsening, so, battling the winds to stay upright, I made a mad dash back to my car. Soaked through to the bone, I hauled myself into the safety of the Fiat, and immediately gunned the engine, blasting the heaters in the hope I'd dry out on the drive home.

My second course of action was to call Mum to check on Indie, but I found my phone had died. And I didn't have a charger in the car. *Bollocks.* (Though, it might have been a good thing – Lewis and Indie needed some alone time together, anyway.)

The storm lashed against my poor little car from all angles, now throwing in thunder and lightning just to scare the shite out of me even more. With the likelihood of my car being swept away, I made the adult decision not to drive home just yet. Instead, I closed my eyes and listened to the rain, which after a while sounded less terrifying and more …

* * *

Knock, knock, knock.

Startled, I awoke to the sight of a parking warden rapping on my window and peering inside my car.

I looked at the clock—*five a.m. … shit!*

Waving off the warden (and being grateful for not getting a ticket), I rubbed my face and remembered the epiphany I'd had, and the promise I'd made to myself that I would be strong, even if Lewis had already packed my stuff and was ready to kick me out. Whatever would come would come. Feeling motivated by the idea of my new start, I then began my journey back to Lewara.

Within an hour and a half, I pulled onto the gravel driveway and saw both James and Camilla's cars parked up next to … a police car.

Oh my God. OH MY GOD. Indie!? Lewis!?

I raced up the drive, scrabbling around for my keys before booting the front door open. 'LEWIS?!'

'Jesus wept!' cried Mum, running out of the lounge with tears in her eyes.

'Mum—what's happened?!'

Whack—she had clipped me around the ear, and suddenly I was eight again.

'You selfish little article! Where HAVE you been?! We've had the world out lookin' for you!'

What the …

'She's here, she's here!' announced Mum, frog-marching me into the lounge, where, thankfully, I could hear Indie crying. I bounded straight over and whipped her up out of her pram, kissing and rocking her intensely. 'I'm so sorry, baby, I'm so sorry … Mummy will never do that again, I promise.'

Indie quietened down straightaway.

'Ohh, thank God! She's not stopped whinin' all night. I was lookin' for an *OFF* button,' said Siobhan, pulling me into a bear hug.

'Tara!?' Lewis skidded out of the kitchen, followed by James, Camilla and two female police officers. 'Where have you been?! You've been missing for twelve hours!'

'Sorry, my ... my phone – it ran out of battery,' I stammered, taken aback by how much Lewis seemed to care. 'I-I just went out ... I needed some air and I ended up falling asleep in my car ... I'm sorry.'

'Tara,' said James, running over for a hug while Mum took Indie from me, 'we all thought ...'

I knew exactly what they all thought. And they were right to have been worried. But thankfully, my moment of madness had come and gone with no casualties.

'Okay, looks like things are sorted here then, mister Copeland; we'll call off the search,' said one of the officers, before talking into her radio.

Siobhan, James and Camilla enveloped me in a group bear hug and scolded me on my Houdini disappearing act.

I wasn't expecting this ... still, if they all want to make a fuss about me, who am I to stop them?

Once the emotional gaggle had died down, I turned my attention to Lewis, who had been keeping his distance.

'Don't *ever* do that again,' he said, approaching me. 'We all thought ... Oh God, thank God you're safe.' Teary-eyed, he lunged over and cupped my face, before kissing me hard.

What the … ?!?!

'Tara, I … I'm sorry I acted like that last night. When you'd gone, I realised I just couldn't imagine my life without you in it.'

'No, Lewis, don't be sorry. *I'm* the one who's sorry … for everything. I don't deserve you. I understand that you can't love me anymore—'

'No, you've got it wrong. I never stopped loving you, Tara Ryan. And I don't think I ever will.'

He kissed me so passionately I nearly fainted. Our audience clapped and whooped.

'Just one thing,' he said, coming up for air, 'this doesn't mean I'm pushing around the pink pram.'

I managed a choked laugh.

'It's *fondant*, not pink,' I said, squeezing him tight.

'Ohh, this is bloody *adorable*. Does this mean the wedding's back on?' asked James. 'Because if it is, we need to organise another hen-do … and I've got the perfect idea!'

Also by C. B. Martin

Fur Coat No Knickers

The Bestselling Romantic Comedy

Fur Coat No Knickers: Blurb

How the hell am I supposed to give a man the silent treatment when *he's* the one being silent?
My lunatic best friend has started talking to (and sleeping with) an inflatable doll called Barry …
And as for mum – she's only been tending my recently-rehabilitated sister's cannabis bush, thinking it's a tomato plant!

Hurtling through her thirties, Tara is still yet to find her perfect man despite gruelling efforts to transform herself into the perfect woman.

Tara's prayers appear to have been answered when she miraculously falls into the arms of Travis Coleman - the famed, silver-tongued sex demon. It would seem the years of curling, plucking, painting and waxing may have finally paid off …

However, Tara's fairy-tale soon spirals out of control when Travis inexplicably ceases all contact with her.

Distraught and desperately stumbling from one crisis to another, Tara ultimately loses her mind, her dignity and —shamefully—her Knickers.

***Fur Coat No Knickers* is a hilarious, touching and outrageous tale; bound to relate to any woman who has ever feared becoming nothing more than a booty call.**

Printed in Great Britain
by Amazon

86555823R00220

Part of the Fur Coat Series

The #1 Bestselling Romantic Comedy Continues

THERE ARE TWO SIDES TO EVERY STORY...

OMG – Tara Ryan, Hair & Beauty Salon owner and walking calamity, has finally got her shite together; she's **bagged Mr. Right** (AKA Lewis) and is well on her way to Happily Ever After. However, given her track record, **disaster is long overdue**, when a demon from her past re-appears.

The disturbingly addictive **Travis Coleman has returned**, with a **scandalous explanation** behind his brutal dumping of Tara the year previous. Consequently, her new fairy-tale life begins to unravel, exposing **unhealed wounds** and reigniting **toxic temptations.**

Battling to keep the lid on Pandora's box, Tara embarks on a daring mission, putting her potentially **perfect life with Lewis on the line...**

Fur Coat Big Knickers is a hilarious, touching and outrageous tale; featuring cringe-inducing catastrophes, dubious hen-do's and momentous wardrobe malfunctions. Prepare yourself for a rollercoaster ride of Love, Deceit and good old-fashioned Denial.

POOLBEG

Find us on Facebook:
Fur Coat No Knickers - The Book

Also available as an eBook

ISBN 978-1781993187

9 781781 993187

Written by: C. B. Martin   Artwork by: Nicola Robson